RECRUITING
BLUE CHIP
PROSPECTS

RECRUITING BLUE CHIP PROSPECTS

KEN HOGARTY

atmosphere press

Dedicated to students, colleagues, friends, and family (with some names borrowed for characters in *Recruiting Blue Chip Prospects*) that I've been fortunate to know, and especially to three women who continually enrich my life daily: my granddaughter, Melissa; daughter, Erin; and wife, Sally.

1.

LOOKING BACK
TODAY

The past doesn't just birth the present. It colors or darkens it. Nurtures or neglects it. Clarifies or muddles it. Magnifies or diminishes it. Inspires or dulls it. Reflecting upon and coming to terms with my story, set in the past, has colored, nurtured, clarified, magnified, and inspired who I am today, what the events of the 1990–91 school year shaped me to become.

Make no mistake, this is my story even though it gets set into motion and becomes weightier with the recruitment of T.R. Ward, a top collegiate basketball prospect. T.R. remains quite capable of telling his own story.

The 1994 movie *Blue Chips* featured cameos by real hoopsters Shaquille O'Neal, Larry Bird, Penny Hardaway, and Kevin Garnett. Famous college coaches appearing included Jerry Tarkanian, Rick Pitino, Bobby Knight, Jim Boeheim, and Dick Vitale. The Nick Nolte film depicted a world in which the best college recruits, Blue Chip prospects, fell under the sway of unscrupulous parasites. As my tale tells, college athletics had already become big business at the expense of those involved and the sport's promises of equitable play.

The label "Blue Chip" emerged with a nod to blue poker chips, typically the most valuable. Companies and stocks earned Blue Chip designation when recognized as having a history of sound financial performance, weathering market storms and yielding high returns. The equivalent high school basketball recruits promised to make lesser basketball programs significant and perpetuate more renowned ones. If an open market existed to procure their talents, they'd have been high-priced commodities.

T.R. Ward, a heavily recruited student-athlete at LaSalle High School in Sacramento, became one of California's first Blue Chip prospects.

Not surprisingly, though not as sophisticated as today's recruitment of athletes, legal and illegal, unsavory manipulation existed throughout the 1980s. Americans during that decade, after all, responded to President Ronald Reagan's business-first attitude that led to economic expansion and booms but also excesses and crises. Deregulation, scandals, and insider trading emerged from that time's Wild West, anything-goes view of reality in money circles and life. By 1990–91, the notion of "following the money" had become explicitly tied to sports at all levels.

1994's *Blue Chips* did a fair job, albeit primarily from a coach's point of view, of capturing a sporting world transitioning to today's norm where our most powerful sporting leagues get sponsored by gambling sites. My story, with the perspective of the intervening years, provides a historical insight into how we got to today's recruiting world. In our time, big-time collegiate prospects play for high school basketball prep schools/programs promising to fast-track participants to college scholarships and benefits and, ultimately, professional basketball careers.

Today's Blue Chip prospects blatantly get financially recruited. They can legally weigh offers of financial incentives, "play for pay," provided by boosters and other entities even beyond the control of academic institutions. The recent approval of NIL (the acronym stands for name, image, likeness) allows compensation paid to N.C.A.A. student-athletes to "promote, partner, or represent brands."

4

The NIL approval by the N.C.A.A., and even the Supreme Court, allows so-called student-athletes to get paid for providing autographs, developing their own merchandise, promoting products or services, and appearing at events, all as a result of their personal celebrity. High school kids can now initiate their own brands, endorse brands, and become their own brands. In a sense, they become like branded cattle, another expensive commodity, even when they think they're controlling everything.

Where did it start?

Was T.R. Ward nothing but a commodity? Did some of the rest of us in this story, even more unwittingly, become commodities also, recruited by various people, in the thrall of various causes and values, without realizing it?

After decades of teaching high school English at LaSalle, I've decided the time's right to tell my unvarnished story. Not just along for the ride during this story's events, I saw hopes, relationships, and values change dramatically. This narrative, told from the third person point-of-view I embraced after discovering New Journalism, discloses the unfolding story of how I, and others, also became Blue Chip prospects, if often unknowingly, along with T.R. Ward.

2.

LATE MAY
JUNIOR YEAR

The LaSalle Lance trumpeted the return of basketball to campus after a two-month absence:

Cagers Prep for Summer League
By: Patrick Kiernan

While most Sacramento youth sweltered under the hundred-degree sun at the American River or Folsom Lake, next year's edition of the LaSalle Lancers basketball team sweated under the watchful eyes of veteran coach Jerry Burke at Brother Arnold Gymnasium.

The Lancers, led by T.R. Ward, a major college Blue Chip prospect, are fresh off of a campaign that saw them finish second regionally. Many pundits predict a berth in next year's state championship game at the Oakland-Alameda County Coliseum Arena.

Burke's arduous end-of-the-school-year workouts prepping for the City Summer League are the first steps toward that goal.

Coach Burke, while downplaying his team's prospects, sees this time as valuable. He noted, "C.I.F. state rules don't allow organized practices after school's out until November. Kids will work out on their own during summer and the first two months of the school year. These last couple practices before summer will focus us on the team concept so that everyone learns his role. Also, players taking the minutes of graduating seniors can get acclimated."

Burke can't coach the independent summer league team but will leave it up to his players to reinforce the concepts and principles they're learning these last few school days while improving individual skills.

An improvement by Ward, who averaged 21.2 points per game while sweeping nine rebounds a game, will make him a potential All-American. Many colleges, judging by his mail, have already placed him on their most wanted lists.

LaSalle loses two seniors, Tim Roan and Wallace Banks. The Lancers, however, should more than compensate with talent up from the champion J.V. squad.

"I feel good about our prospects," said Coach Burke. "Still, we have to pay attention to details, not get affected by hype, and ward off outside influences," he concluded, chuckling at using T.R.'s name in a different context.

The LaSalle Lancers, sporting club jerseys, albeit with the green and white colors of the school run by the Christian Brothers, a Catholic teaching order, shot the ball up court so fast it might have been a pinball. T.R. Ward, the Lancers' awesome center, took the last crisp pass, soared toward the hoop, and jammed the ball as effortlessly as a kid dumping a rolled-up paper into a garbage can. Though no crowd cheered and no scoreboard numbers spun, the players knew they had reached toward the perfection Coach Burke sought.

Burke blew his whistle. The veteran leader understood the value of ending practice on the right note. The quick, pinpoint passes and final rip through the net by the man on whom fortune would rest made this seem like midseason.

Burke glanced at his watch as T.R. strutted alongside at mid-court. "C'mon, Coach. Can't get better. That's a ten."

7

Burke smiled. His troops knew he glanced at his watch for their benefit, but he had a different game in mind. His loud, raspy voice rose from somewhere around the sox on his short, hairy legs. "Okay, Tony. Intended to end ten minutes early, but you haven't even worked up a sweat." T.R., mopping his brow with the bottom of his warmup jersey, stopped abruptly. "What d'ya say, guys?" Burke raised his voice to make sure all heard. "You have as much energy left as the big fella?"

Mock groans echoed throughout the small gym, but T.R. controlled the situation. This was his team. The two seniors were at graduation practice. T.R. needn't worry about overshadowing upperclassmen, though his skills had done so for two years. This was truly his team, even during practice. Burke enjoyed the exchange, which gave notice his once-shy superstar intended to lead, even if his leadership manifested itself by ribbing the coach at the end of a relatively insignificant workout.

"C'mon, Coach, gotta get home to study for finals. We flunk out, we won't be around to make you look smart."

"Sounds like you're the smart guy, Ward," Burke snapped, his grin betraying his tone. "Tell you what," he addressed the youngster who towered a foot above him, "let's bring back an old tradition. You get one free throw. Make it, practice ends. Miss it, we do baselines."

"Baselines," T.R. shrieked. "You're gonna kill us." The two straddled the mid-court line. Other team members, with something at stake personally, gathered around.

"Course, you could have somebody else shoot." Burke's needle was well placed. T.R., 6'8" and 235 pounds, devastated opponents near the basket. Moreover, his jump shot improved all through his junior year so that he stroked the ball well from within twenty feet. He dribbled like a pro, ran like a deer on the break, and willingly passed like a guard. But free throws? T.R. had hit 68% during the year. Respectable for a big man, but not a sure thing.

"Baselines! Not fair." Anybody on the team might have shouted it. The notorious conditioning drill—starting under the basket and sprinting to a line a quarter way down the court, then back, halfway down the court and back, three-quarters of the way down the court and back, and finally full court and back—must have been a drill sergeant's innovation. Baselines after practice were like studying the minute a test ended.

"'Course it's fair," LaSalle's captain refuted as he strode toward the free throw line at the far end of the gym. The other players clammed up. Even Sammie Spear, the feisty little guard who had grown up with T.R. on Sacramento's rough South side, knew better than to open his mouth. Ward played to his teammates: "If Loyola Marymount's Bo Kimble could hit a free throw lefthanded in this year's N.C.A.A. tourney game to honor teammate Hank Gathers, who died on the court a few weeks before, I can nail this one. T.R. in the clutch. Let's do it!"

Burke loved it. T.R. wasn't going to back down. Pressure now would make pressure more easily handled in-season. Make or miss, the team would coalesce behind their captain. Burke sprinted ahead of T.R., like a ref preparing a technical foul shot. "What about Larry or Sammie shooting? Same stakes. They hit about eighty percent."

No answer. T.R. approached the line. Burke bounced him a ball. The rest of the team followed respectfully behind their coach and star as if afraid to get in T.R.'s line of fire.

"I make it, we split, right?"

"One shot. It's on the line."

T.R. cradled the ball in his coffee-colored palms. He bounced the ball a few times. The rat-tat-tat echoed like gun fire through the still gym. "Bet them recruiters love this." T.R. jerked his head in the direction of the other end of the gym.

"Yeah, my man," Burke acknowledged. "You up for it?"

T.R. breathed deeply and sighted the basket. His right toes played with the free throw line. The ball shot toward the basket and nudged a little iron but found mostly net. Thudding to the floor under the basket, it split the silence like a drum starting a parade. T.R.'s shouting teammates practically carried him the short distance to the dressing room. Ward grinned widely as the team jostled past Burke. "Had it all the way, Coach. Gotta believe," he enthused.

"A good bounce, Tony," Burke joked, looking like a loser but feeling like a winner. "Now get showered, all of you. And go hit the books. I got to talk to a few people."

"Helluva way to end practice, Coach," the recruiter approached, hand held out.

"Not bad at all," Burke's enthusiasm bubbled over now that the kids had departed. "We should be pretty fair next season," he downplayed.

"Mike. Mike Webber. Met you at the coaching clinic down the Peninsula. Webber," Like a politician, Webber pumped Burke's hand. "Webber," he repeated. "Webfeet. Oregon Ducks. Oregon Webfeet. Easy to remember." Burke didn't. "The kids seemed pretty happy," Webber waved toward the dressing room from where laughter and loud talk spilled out. "Cripes, that Ward's a stud. Handled pressure well too."

"Hi, Jerry." Carl Schipper, reporter for *The Sacramento Star*, the only daily paper covering prep sports in depth in the area for years, knew he was doing Burke a favor by cutting in on the conversation. "Let's talk. I'm considering a big offseason piece on your team. The *Monarch* and *Trib* are trying to horn in on our turf when they realized the story your team might be."

"Sure, Carl." Burke, who didn't suffer fools or college reps gladly, appreciated the gesture. "Mr. Webber. It was Mr. Webber, right?" Burke needled.

"Yeah, Webber," the nattily dressed young man echoed.

"I'll introduce you to Brother Curt, our Dean of Discipline." Burke ushered the visitor to the entranceway of the gym, engulfed by the presence of a burly, thirtyish African American wearing a flowing back robe set off by a white collar in the shape of Ten Commandment stones. "Brother Curt, meet Mr. Webfoot from the University of Oregon. I think he's looking for some good LaSalle students. Specifically, Ward. He probably heard what a good student he is. That right?" Burke wheeled toward Webber, already pumping the hand of the Christian Brother while correcting his name.

"Yeah, a few minutes," Webber stammered.

"Can you introduce him when T.R. comes out? Give him a few minutes before Tony goes home to study. I have to talk with Carl."

"Gotcha," Brother Curt boomed. "The other kids too. At La-Salle, we do things as a team." Students called Brother Curt "the enforcer" for good reason, not the least being his imposing appearance. He dealt with all discipline matters in the school. Firm but fair, he commanded instant respect and, from some, a bit of intimidation.

"That'd be great." Webber looked beaten. "Thanks, Coach. See you around. During the season."

Burke didn't have his own office in the gym. Despite nineteen seasons and three hundred and forty-seven career wins, he accepted LaSalle's Spartan facilities. He moved to shower and change in the Athletic Director's Office, which during any basketball activity was his, in practice if not in name. "Thanks, Carl. Thought I was stuck with the guy. C'mon in." He turned the key to unlock the door of the tiny office.

"Those guys get to you, don't they?"

"Yeah. Cookie cutter types. Young. Handsome. Wearing big people clothes. Really, like butchers examining sides of beef. Users."

"A job, Jerry," Schipper soothed. "A tough one. You know the pressure on college programs. Produce. Right now. Instant success. Like the world of business and investing. These guys making initial contacts have the toughest job."

"Contact, sure, but recruiting's a plague. Then the big sharks, the coaches with reputations, come in for the kill." Burke kicked his shoes off.

"What better way? Public school coaches, administrators, and alums think you guys and Loyola do the same with elementary school kids, attracting guys like Ward."

"You know we don't recruit illegally, Carl."

"No need. Your reputation recruits for you. Still, with the colleges, schools try to keep it clean, but it's impossible. Kids love the attention. God, some of the kids haven't had it so good."

"Tell me!" Burke jerked his sweatshirt off. "I've walked with these kids for years. We need to keep them away from the wrong people."

Schipper fidgeted. "Looked good today. Sammie was really moving the break." He knew Burke would appreciate the mention of another Lancer besides T.R. Though clearly realizing Ward's talent and potential, Burke had built his reputation molding great teams without superstars.

"Yeah, off the record, a good chance to win it all next year. It's a good class, even beyond the team." Burke also taught Social Studies at LaSalle. "The whole chemistry's right if outside influences don't screw it up. Tony's sensitive. I don't want him hurt. It would hurt us all." Burke stepped gingerly around the corner toward the shower stall. Schipper amused himself by paging through the completed season's *Lancer Press Guide*.

"This guide was impressive," Schipper offered when Burke returned while toweling off.

"Yeah," Burke replied absently while dressing, "good talent there too. Kiernan did most of it with advice from our English/Journalism guy, Wilson. Kiernan's a great kid."

"I know. Hate to tell you, but I'm recruiting too. I want to offer the kid a job."

"Summer job?"

"Yeah. School year too. Sort of an internship, but paid. A great parttime job and a real break for him. Hear from Wilson that the money wouldn't hurt either, with his mom raising him by herself. He told me he thought Patrick would love it. Any objections?"

"You too hustling kids?" Schipper flipped the pages of the suddenly closed guide, feeling like a player Burke was questioning after a bonehead play, though it was just a courtesy running the hire by Burke.

The coach's frown turned to a smile as Schipper looked up. "Just kidding, Carl. Sounds great for Patrick. Wilson has him set up on a special schedule so he can still help us next school year. I think he's getting an independent study besides his regular newspaper class and all his A.P. classes. Sort of assistant S.I.D."

"Didn't know you had a Sports Information Director," Schipper boomed, feeling as if he had just wriggled off a hook.

"Don't. Just a lot of assistants working together. Wilson did a lot this year and will again next year. Even Brother Charles realizes we'll be in the spotlight next season. He's freed Wilson from moderator duties and one class to give him more time to work on publications and public relations. And Kiernan can help a lot, even if he's writing for you after school."

"Sounds great. Patrick can handle it. His writing's impressive. I'll talk to him. Saw him watching out there."

"Probably waiting for Tony," Burke combed his hair. "They're in charge of planning the traditional end-of-the-year dance tomorrow night. A rite of passage for the rest of the student body as the juniors replace graduating seniors as leaders."

Schipper stood up, putting the Guide aside. "They good friends?"

"Yeah. This school usually works well at bringing kids from different backgrounds together. Maybe we're not the brain factory that Loyola is, but ..."

"Except for the coaching staff," Schipper interrupted.

Burke chuckled. "C'mon, Carl. You already got what you came for." Burke tossed his wadded-up towel into a basket as he often had his opponents over the years. "We get smarter kids than fifteen years ago, but that's not the main thing. You see a white kid like Patrick, into writing and literature, and a guy like Tony, Mr. Popularity, the school athlete," he pronounced the word with reverence, "and they get along well and make each other better. I'm proud I've spent my career here."

Schipper pondered offers Burke had supposedly entertained to move to the collegiate level as an assistant after his initial years of coaching. Next year's club would surely bring him back into the limelight if that's what he really wanted. Maybe even a shot at being a collegiate head coach. "Should be quite a year, Coach. Can't wait."

Outside, Burke moved to check on Webber as Schipper spotted Patrick Kiernan, changed out of school attire and sporting a red GAP pocket-T over white gym shorts and his knock-off white Vans. "How ya' doing, Patrick?" Schipper greeted. Though he was in his thirties, Schipper's rumpled look, his unpressed khakis and faded Sacramento Kings sweatshirt, made him look like an old-time newspaperman.

"Hey, Mr. Schipper. Not bad. Good practice, huh?" Patrick stepped away from T.R. and a few of the other players that Brother Curt had arranged to be with Webber.

"It's Carl. Mr. Schipper's my father."

"Sure, Carl," Patrick shrugged. "Here to do an article on us?"

"That's part of it. Also wanted to offer you a job."

"On the paper?"

"Yeah. *The Star.*"

"Doing what?" Patrick's interest flashed in his eyes. "Copy boy? Stringer?"

"No, assigned stories. As a paid intern. Think you could be objective covering prep sports? Even LaSalle games? I don't want those Jesuits at Loyola after my backside."

"God, sure I could, or at least give it a good try," Patrick gushed. "Sounds great."

Carl Schipper extended his hand. "Thought you'd like the idea. You'd start now covering summer league basketball and some summer baseball games. Prep or J.C. football in the fall. By then, you should be ready for the big time, maybe sidebars on LaSalle games. And, game stories when I can't make it."

"Wow. Can't believe it." Patrick finally shook Schipper's hand, which he had been clasping. "I was just going to do some odd gardening jobs this summer. This is great. It's a deal."

"Don't you want to know the pay?" Schipper smiled, basking in the kid's exuberance. "I mean ... ten cents an hour ..." Schipper stopped himself. "Seriously, we'll take care of the paperwork and details—hours, pay, that stuff. For the hours and contract in mind, don't have to worry about a union card. I'll arrange it so you're an independent contractor, but, in my mind, I want it to be a pretty good time commitment, a solid parttime job."

"When do I start?"

"How 'bout today? I have a story in mind."

"Sure. About what?"

Schipper chuckled. He knew he could give the kid a story about the local elementary school's dodgeball team and make him happy. "Well, this guy Webber gave me an idea. Why not something about recruiting from the player's point of view? About T.R. Not too thorough yet. More of a 'puff piece' to start. We'll do something in-depth in-season. For now, just highlight the rules Jerry's set up for the process. He did set something special up, didn't he?" Schipper knew he had but wondered what, if anything, Kiernan knew.

Patrick looked up. "He did. I've talked to T.R., but I'll check again. I'll see him tonight anyway. And I'll interview Coach Burke today before he leaves."

"Good. Try to get me the piece in a couple days."

"Length?"

"Don't worry about that. Inverted pyramid; we can cut it anywhere." Schipper fished into his coat pocket for a scrap of paper. "What's your home phone number?"

Patrick told him, though, in his excitement, he had almost forgotten.

Schipper dashed off while Patrick trotted over to T.R. He couldn't wait to tell him about his new job. They were both going bigtime next school year—together.

3.

LATE MAY
JUNIOR YEAR (THE NEXT DAY)

After the last classes before finals for all but graduated seniors, Patrick helped arrange the gym for the traditional "Take-Over Dance." On the way home to get ready before returning for the evening, Patrick surprised Carl Schipper at *The Star* office, where he dropped off his first story. It read almost exactly as it would in the paper the following Tuesday:

Area Blue Chip Prospect Looks to Recruiting Process
By: Patrick Kiernan

T.R. Ward, LaSalle High School's rising senior basketball phenom, is the prize prospect in what surely will be the Capital City's greatest recruiting sweepstakes in years.

The likeable Ward, a veteran of two varsity campaigns at the Christian Brothers school in the Oak Park neighborhood, lives in South Sacramento. He remains unruffled by the attention but surely has not seen anything near what he'll see before announcing his collegiate choice. That decision should come around April 15th, the day letters of intent can officially get signed.

Ward's mother, June, who works for the Post Office while raising T.R. and his three brothers, seems overwhelmed. "I can't believe all the interest in Tony," she said. A number of recruiters could explain to her.

Ward has personally necessitated extra postal service himself since he's had inquiries from over a hundred colleges. Additionally, college recruiters have flocked to Lancer games in the last two years. During the recently completed season, the six feet, eight inch, two hundred and thirty-five pounder led LaSalle to a second-place regional finish.

Jerry Burke, LaSalle's longtime mentor, has counseled his star in preparation for the recruiting blitz. "Coach Burke and I have discussed procedures," Ward clarified after he and his teammates completed a spring workout. "Neither of us want it to get in the way of team goals. The main priority's my senior season at LaSalle."

Ward's mind remains open concerning his ultimate collegiate destination: "I'm not sure if I want to stay in state or not. I do know I want to play in a bigtime college program."

Basketball experts believe college won't be Ward's final basketball stop. Mike Webber, an assistant from the University of Oregon, sees T.R. as an eventual pro prospect. Ward, popular around school, shrugs off such talk: "Of course I'd like to play in the N.B.A. It's a dream, but success next year's not even a sure thing, let alone something years down the line."

Ward, whose given name is Antony Reginald, has received letters from most Pac-10 schools and other major programs up and down the coast. Other correspondence has come from traditional basketball powers such as Kentucky, Indiana, Georgetown, St. John's, Notre Dame, and most A.C.C. schools.

Coach Burke outlined the selection process for his star: "T.R. will begin visits during the fall before basketball season. Otherwise, he'll not see or respond to recruiters except through me at school. We'll designate time in the fall. We've allowed initial contacts the last few weeks, but will cut that off until the start of the school year."

Burke stressed his rationale: "T.R. is first and foremost a LaSalle student and basketball player. We do, however, appreciate pressure on college programs to sign and admit Blue Chippers like T.R. This way, everything will be honorable and aboveboard."

Burke emphasized Ward's grades (a B- average, taking college prep classes) and future schooling are of the greatest importance. He encouraged recruiters to stress educational advantages and the support they might offer T.R., interested in business education.

Ward summed up the remaining ground rules: "We'll announce a final five around Christmas. Coach Burke thinks that should work to eliminate distractions before league season starts. Still, I'll have options. Now, I'm just going through brochures and catalogs colleges have sent."

Ward confided he's even received letters from places he didn't know existed. "It's a real geography lesson," he deadpanned.

The blaring chords of Van Halen's "Jump," belted out by local band Lightning, rocked LaSalle's gym. "Save those moves for the court," Patrick trumpeted during the last notes before a break.

"Think I'd ever run out of moves?" T.R. retorted, high-fiving Patrick without raising his light blue dress-shirted right arm. "Suzie. Looking fine." Ward drew his last word out. He stole a quick look at his date. "Everybody looks great out of school polos and dress code."

Suzie Andrus, her blond ringlet curls falling almost to the spaghetti-strapped neckline of her floral summer dress, smiled through her just-begun conversation with T.R.'s date, Doris Long, herself striking in a form-fitting olive number with a sweetheart neckline accentuating her mahogany skin tone. "I was telling Doris about Patrick's story about you. I read a draft. Did you?"

"Yeah. Showed me. T.R., the businessman." Ward's broad smile mocked himself impishly. "Loved it. Proud of my man." T.R. engulfed Patrick's shoulder, rocking it back and forth. "*The Star*. Not bad!" Letting go, LaSalle's star swiveled to face Patrick. "What did Schipper say when he read it?"

"Think he liked it," Patrick flushed. Suzie gave Patrick a quick glance, imploring him to bypass his natural humility. "Yeah, he liked it," Patrick conceded. "You and Coach helped. Especially those quotes from you and even from your mom last night. Appreciated that."

"Okay, rook. Set for the summer, huh? Reporter for *The Star*. Or, is that star reporter?"

"It'll cut into my b-ball play with you. I guess I'll have to stop schooling you shooting threes," Patrick teased.

The two couples strolled past admirers to a table near the crepe-papered gym wall. Other students gravitated around them but remained in the background, like subs during a timeout.

"What are you doing this summer?" Patrick, preppy dressed to match his Michael J. Fox looks, turned the conversation toward T.R. after giving Doris, a good writer herself, particulars about his new job. "Besides playing hoops to keep Coach Burke happy?"

"Reading catalogs, according to your story," T.R. responded, looking down at his pal. "This my friend asking, or a *60 Minutes* reporter?"

"Your friend," Patrick intoned solemnly, aware for the first time, though T.R. was kidding, that harmless questions might take on a different significance now.

Suzie broke in, addressing T.R.: "Besides holding open house for every college in America?"

"Watch it," Patrick whispered. "The N.C.A.A. might be listening."

"The what?" Doris asked. Obviously, T.R. didn't just talk basketball recruiting with her.

"They control college sports. Conferences, recruiting, everything. National Collegiate Athletic Association." T.R. turned to

Suzie: "Summer league. Coach wants us playing all the time. I'm also going to camps in Orange County and Berkeley. Scholarships paying the way. Each a week."

"You working?" Suzie wasn't sure if she asked for Patrick or herself.

Doris smirked. "You kidding? A talent like this?" Despite her lack of height, her sarcastic retort made it obvious that Doris walked at the same level as her boyfriend. She rolled phrases like "Tony, the star" off her lips with an inflection meant to keep T.R. somewhat humble.

T.R. hooked his thumbs into the pockets of his vest before turning serious again. "Hope to do what I did last summer, at least the last three or four weeks. Go to Grass Valley and work on Mr. Mullan's ranch. Made me strong last year, pitching hay and stuff. Even Sammie muscled up, and, God be praised, he needs help in that department." T.R. tossed his head in the direction of Sammie Spear, who buzzed around the background, flirting with girls who cozied up near the table as if they were playing a zone defense against LaSalle's big center.

"Hear Mr. Mullan pays LaSalle kids well. Maybe that's what Patrick should have done." Suzie tweaked Patrick's bicep playfully. Solidly built and just a shade below six feet, Patrick belied the stereotype of the bright student as athletically hopeless.

"Yeah, real good. Summer on the farm for LaSalle athletes," T.R. chuckled. "Surprised Loyola hasn't raised a stink to match barn smells up there."

"Or the stink I'll raise when smelling you when you come back," Doris interjected before Patrick pointed out that there was nothing amiss since Mr. Mullan, a booster, paid all LaSalle students who worked for him the same wages. "Still, I get lonely without *my star*," she gleefully noted, nuzzling up to T.R. at the same time.

"At least you know," Patrick picked up the banter, "he's not getting into trouble there. Just him and his animals. Maybe the only six foot, eight inch Black cowboy in the county."

"That's right, pardner," T.R. laughed. "And Percy Forte promised me odd jobs around the neighborhood, too," Ward tossed off as he stood up, looking ready to dance despite the absence of music.

"Thought Coach wanted you to avoid him?" Patrick held up. "The Pied Piper of South Sac."

"He's okay. Coach thinks he's bad news, but he don't live where we do. Percy acts uptown. The flashiness ain't nothin'. You have to know where he's coming from." T.R. practically swept Doris from her chair. "Let's boogie. C'mon, Suze, the band's returning. I'll get 'em to play one you white folks can dance to. It was painful watching Patrick barely get off the ground when 'Jump' got played." Though Patrick smirked, he and Suzie followed as if taking up the challenge.

Before the four got far, a tall, skinny, grey-haired Christian Brother intercepted them. "Mr. Kiernan. Mr. Ward. Miss Andrus. Miss Long," his hallow voice sounded as if he were taking roll in his Chemistry class. "Chet couldn't make it tonight," he began, referring to the class president. "Has a cold. Anyway, here's the check to pay the band."

"Brother Raymond, what's up?" T.R. finally voiced his greeting just as the stern figure thrust the check into Patrick's hand and began edging away.

"Oh, and give that speech you suggested to Chet at the meeting yesterday," Brother Raymond, the class moderator but still a mystery to just about every junior in the school, shot over his shoulder, leaving as fast as overmatched students did daily from his classroom.

T.R. stammered, "Praise God I never been in his class."

"He just didn't want to fumble around for the right handshake when you 'what's upped' him," Patrick joked. "It might have ruined his Bunsen-burner trigger finger. Suzie, excuse me for a minute?"

"Man, I'll go with you," T.R. announced to Patrick and the girls. "Okay, Doris?"

"Sure, Tony. Suzie and I'll talk about Brother Raymond. Decide if he's the school's biggest chauvinist. And fight off the guys who'll probably surround us when they see you two gone."

"Cut me some slack. Just wanted to help Class V.P. here conduct his duties and ..."

"Really, Doris," Patrick butted in, "he thinks I might hand him the mic. You'd think he had a big ego or something." T.R. followed Patrick, protesting all the way, as if the sarcasm had pierced the big ego.

"T.R., gotta talk." Patrick maneuvered Ward alone on the stairway leading to the stage. "Just between us, but I hear Forte's bad news. I overheard Schipper talking to Burke in the A.D.'s office while running off releases."

"About me?"

Patrick lowered his voice: "Schipper said the guy got caught in a hustle a couple years back with that running back from Taft."

"Williams?"

"Yeah, the 'Taft Terrific' who got into big trouble. Lost his baseball eligibility his senior year, and the college flirted with probation. Williams hasn't even played yet," Patrick shook his head.

"I know him, man," T.R. offered soberly, standing below Patrick on the steps so the two looked each other in the eyes. "He had other problems than Percy. And, besides, nobody proved nothing."

"But talk had it Forte paid him off his senior year. Arranged through some big-time alum back there. Burke said the school may be holding off the N.C.A.A. by sacrificing the kid. And they couldn't quite tie that alumni guy directly to the school the way he funneled the money. Be careful."

T.R. trusted Patrick. That trust had been cemented early in the school year when Patrick showed up at his house to give him a ride back to school for a class activity. He knew even well-meaning white guys might have gone out of their way to avoid South Sac. Few would have been as comfortable right away in his house and with his family. "I am careful. Coach, or Schipper, or you don't know life in the streets. You leave here, go home to Carmichael or Rancho or someplace. I leave here, it's different. More like this neighborhood that scares lots of white kids off to Loyola. Percy's like the Mayor on my blocks. Good to the kids. He knew us growing up. Helps us. Sets us right. Gives us something to look toward. He helped send me here. You know that?"

"No."

"Well, he did. Ask Brother Blood about him; he's wise to the streets. Percy's helped a few guys here." T.R. referred to Brother Curt, who had grown up on the streets of central L.A. but found his calling as a student at Cathedral High School, a Christian Brothers' school near Dodger Stadium.

"T.R., I'm not telling you what to do. But, remember, everybody's watching. And everybody's going to want a piece of you. Even if things are right, you can't give 'em stuff to talk about. Too much to lose."

"Yeah, we're gonna kick ass this year," Ward beamed. Patrick smiled. T.R. had a knack for disarming Patrick and others with the ease with which he disarmed basketball opponents, his personality powerful and winning like his game.

Patrick noted Ward's use of "we," making Patrick feel like part of the team. "We better get out there, or Brother Charles is going to kick my ass. Or worse, send Raymond to talk with me again."

The two met the band to hand over a check from the class treasury. T.R. jived around with band members, pretending to convince them he should sit in on drums during the next set. Patrick muffled that talk by suggesting the only practice T.R. had was drumming his desk when bored.

Patrick strode to the mic. "Attention," he confidently affirmed. Though his peers didn't cluster around, he commanded their attention. Well-built and handsome, with reddish-blond hair and a ruddy complexion, Patrick appealed to the girls, his intelligence a bonus. Winning over the boys had been equally easy. He had proven he was more than a bookworm or one-dimensional student. Dressed casually in beige pants and a blue and red striped rugby shirt, Patrick looked the picture of a confident student. Though naturally a bit shy while warming to an audience or subject, Patrick had spoken enough before large groups to be comfortable. "You'd better pay attention," he laughed. "T.R. here has promised NOT to sing if you do."

T.R. jumped into view like a rock guitarist wearing black slacks and his stylish shirt under his leather vest. Still, he remained in Patrick's shadow, as much as a person his size could, while his friend continued.

"Won't keep you long. We, next year's seniors, along with next year's student body, should look forward to the coming school year. Sports, dances, rallies, activities, studies, everything." T.R. adlibbed a pantomime for each item ticked off. "And you're the ones who'll make it happen. Thanks for coming tonight. Our class would also like to thank faculty members and parents chaperoning to make tonight possible." T.R. exhorted crowd applause. "Looks like T.R. wants to be a cheerleader too. Anyway, the Junior Council would like a round of applause for everyone who helped put this night on."

T.R. grabbed the mic. "Now, c'mon, let's dance. We'll shake this gym all season. Let's shake it now too." Ward gyrated onstage as the band returned. "Get it on!"

"Let's go, big fella. They might really make you play or sing."

"Oh, man, no respect," T.R. snapped.

"Better hurry. The girls will start dancing without us."

"Not likely." But they had. Suzie danced with Sammie Spear, while Doris danced with another basketballer, Lance Hall. "Man, this interracial stuff's gotta stop," Ward proclaimed when he moved close enough that the dancers could hear. "Look at that skinny white boy trying to get down," he squealed to Patrick.

Hall, a tall, gawky sophomore, practically tripped himself when he saw and heard T.R.'s presence near him. Clearly, Sammie, who looked like a whirling dervish as he pranced and spun everywhere but into the floor, had put him up to this. Turning to Patrick as if hurting, T.R. asked, "Shall we give a couple other ladies a thrill?"

"Go 'head, T.R. I'll wait for Suzie. Need to make the rounds. My mom's here chaperoning, and I want to thank Mr. Wilson too." Lance Hall gestured to T.R., wondering if he wanted to cut in so he could wriggle away, but Ward pretended to be so wrapped up in his conversation that he didn't notice.

"Patrick, teach that boy to dance. God knows, it's hard enough teaching him basketball." T.R. raised his voice: "C'mon, Lance. You got the prettiest lady on the floor. Show some moves, man. Watch Sammie. At least, follow the blur of his multi-colored flares."

Patrick watched Suzie. A good dancer, she had no problem keeping up with Sammie, the Lancers' point guard. Her curled hair bounced in place as she glided about quickly and gracefully. Though only 5'4" and dressed and made up in an understated way, she looked like a woman rather than a high schooler, an effect heightened by her confidence.

Amazingly, her mature look emerged even during school days while wearing her traditional parochial school plaid skirt and white blouse. Just as surprising, she didn't look like a little girl even when wearing the unisex emerald green school polo shirts the girls tied in back to make them look a bit more form-fittingly feminine.

The song over, Sammie walked Suzie back to Patrick. "Whew! Some foxy lady."

"For sure," Patrick asserted as he hugged Suzie. He loved the feel of her skin as his hand traveled around her neck affectionately. Sammie trotted off. "There goes Doris after T.R. Would you chase me like that?"

"Probably not," Suzie began, "but then you wouldn't expect

me to." A winning smile crossed her face. "Course, I'd scratch the girl's eyes out who tried to take you from me." Suzie squeezed Patrick's hand intimately before nodding across the suddenly filling dance floor. "There's your mom dancing with Mr. Wilson. You wanted to talk to them both, didn't you?"

Patrick hesitated. Earlier, T.R. Ward, upon first spotting his mom across the floor, joked that if it weren't for Doris, Patrick could do worse than fix him up with his mother. Patrick knew T.R. was joking, but it discomforted him. His mother did look young and pretty, dressed almost like some of the more mature teenaged girls. She and Mr. Wilson, Patrick's favorite teacher, weren't missing a beat keeping up with the youngsters with whom they shared the floor.

"You can't just stand here. Let's dance over." They did, eventually switching partners so that Patrick danced with his mother. When the song ended, the four eased off the floor together.

"Where's your wife?" Patrick asked his teacher.

Steve Wilson, a blond, green-eyed English teacher, looked like the surfer he had once been since shaving his scraggly "Walt Whitman" beard. His smooth features and trim frame contributed to an outward manifestation of a characteristic all his students noticed and appreciated, his sensitivity. This even though, before taking over as newspaper moderator, he had been an assistant football coach after playing collegiately, albeit for the Whittier College Poets. "Home with the kids. Had to work late today and was wiped out by the work week. Luckily, Sheila's keeping me busy on the dance floor so I didn't sneak out for a pop with the guys who had the first shift." Wilson turned awkwardly, smiling at Patrick's mother.

"Love the band," Sheila Kiernan added. "Fun to dance. It's been a while. Patrick let you read his article, didn't he, Steve?"

"Yes. Quite impressive."

"Pretty soon, he'll be making more money than both of us." A well-regarded local architectural firm employed Sheila Kiernan as an administrative assistant. "Though, God knows, good teachers should make more than they do." She spoke assuredly, aware of Patrick's unabashed regard for Wilson.

Looking embarrassed, Wilson shifted the conversation: "Suzie, what are you doing this summer. Movies? The stage?"

"No, politics." She turned the offhand remark into a factual statement. "My highlight's going to Girls' State."

"What's that?" Sheila Kiernan asked.

"Student leaders," Wilson quickly responded, "chosen statewide. There's a Boys' State too."

"I thought Patrick was going to attend," Suzie interjected, "but Chet Howard is. They're at different times anyway, and, of course, they keep the sexes separated so we can really get about the serious business of simulating political conventions and debating hot issues." Her tone of voice indicated she thought this separation ridiculous.

"Well, that should ease your mind," Sheila Kiernan joked. "I mean not being separated yourselves for both sessions. And, I guess the fact that you're not there together should ease my mind, too," she smiled. "What kind of hot issues do they debate?"

"Oh, the girls just talk about boys, a big slumber party," Patrick suggested through a smile.

"What an oink! And here I thought your mom and I had liberated you."

"We should all be totally liberated," Wilson blurted as if cutting off a class discussion. He winked at an obviously bemused Sheila Kiernan. "Dancing's liberating. Would you like to lead this time?"

"Sure, Steve. My turn again?" Before she sauntered toward the dance floor, she spun around on her heels to question her son: "Food afterwards? Bring a few friends?"

"Food and beer?" Patrick responded.

"How about food and Coke?" And after a pause for effect: "The kind you drink." The two faced each other easily and comfortably.

"Talk about chauvinistic. I bring the guys over, and you're cool with a brew or two. But, it's not cool when girls come too."

"You know that's only when the guys stay overnight. No coed pajama parties, dear. You coming over?"

"Nah, we'll go to the River," he alluded to LaSalle's favorite post-activity hangout.

"Be careful, Pat," Sheila Kiernan found herself saying almost involuntarily, but Wilson quickly strode back to whisk her onto the dancefloor.

Patrick stared at them as they talked earnestly while dancing. Suzie broke the silence: "He's probably reassuring her not to worry about the River. She, no doubt, sees you in jail or me in trouble. He knows the score. He'll tell her how the Sheriffs will do a walk-through at a suitable time after the dance to clear everybody out, but nobody'll get arrested. Either that, or if there's a big crowd, they'll have Brother Curt put in an appearance first. Tradition. This school is built on it, and most of the Sheriffs graduated from here."

She smiled reassuringly, much the same way that Wilson smiled at Sheila Kiernan out on the dancefloor. Both Kiernans responded in kind. "Besides," Suzie continued, "I couldn't possibly get in trouble. We wouldn't have the time or opportunity. Everybody's going tonight. Even Sammie, T.R., and Doris, who usually don't. T.R. has his new wheels to show off."

4.

LATE MAY
JUNIOR YEAR (LATE THAT EVENING)

Months before, Patrick had written a piece about LaSalle's favorite American River spot for *The Lance*:

My River
By: Patrick Kiernan

Mark Twain's Mississippi lured Huck Finn and Tom Sawyer. Similarly, the American River invites LaSalle youth. Though all of Sacramento's three main rivers are back-lane highways compared to the mighty multi-lane freeway of a river that cuts America in two, the American's appeal speaks to our time and place.

The American offers quick fixes rather than the long, extended drifting that Huck found on the Mississippi. Maybe the Sacramento River, which Pac-Mans the American River before heading to the Bay and Delta, is a bit more like the Mississippi. Our Capital City segment of the river winds around the old, rich mansions of Riverside Drive near Land Park after meandering past downtown. It speaks to old-for-California money. Folks drift on it, fishing for supper. Indeed, one wouldn't be surprised to imagine Huck Finn drifting by in a nineteenth-century raft.

On the American, by contrast, you'll typically see rubber

rafts of avid sun-worshippers, thrill seekers, and beer drinkers. One wonders if the whole economy of the North area is bound up in raft rentals rather than the countless shopping centers, fast food places, and new housing tracts that flare out from the American. Would Huck Finn living today have undertaken the rite of passage known as the American's Sunrise Float or stuck to the Sacramento?

LaSalle students share their River. Loyola students, who go to school near the River in Carmichael, have their own spots, though they'll sometimes fraternize at ours. Even our public-school friends sometimes leave their malls to hit the River. LaSalle's special haven is Paradise Beach.

During the day, the River offers instant relief from the heat with a quick splash or a shady spot under a tree. It rushes past like minutes in our tightly scheduled school day.

The River can also offer solitude. When you need to think about past, present, or future, it's helpful to wander the River. Stopping to skip a rock, you'll feel aware of the River's past, present, and future in the calming sound of flowing water.

A couple parking areas provide spots for those with no desire to mingle except with that special someone. The more social often cluster together on the beach near the clearing. There, the typical LaSalle game or dance reaches its conclusion.

Huck Finn found adventure and freedom, drifting for months. LaSalle students freely make their own adventures instantaneously at our River. The freedom of setting our own rules, with some limits, and being responsible for ourselves and each other, yields a paradise of sorts for Lancers.

Patrick eased his old Toyota Corolla between two newer foreign cars. "Not too intent about parking off by ourselves tonight," Suzie observed as she squeezed Patrick's knee. The lengths Patrick went to park in relative isolation were an ongoing joke.

"Hoping they're gone when we get back," Patrick suggested. "Underclassmen shouldn't stay late." But, clearly, the number of cars seemed to dampen hope of parking lot privacy. Patrick hopped out of the car before circling to meet Suzie.

"Guess helping the band break down ensured we'd be among the last here. The good news is somebody probably scored beers already."

"Stereotypical Irishman," Suzie chided, knowing it wasn't true. "Hey, there's T.R.'s Chevy. They must be down below."

"What a bomb," Patrick chuckled.

"Make you feel better? Doris insinuated at the end of the evening that you asked about it."

"An old beat-up Chevy isn't exactly the way he described it."

"His first car. The way you talk about yours sometimes makes it sound like a Porsche." Suzie leaned on Patrick for support as she stepped across an overgrown tree trunk.

"When you mentioned Doris said he got it working for Percy Forte, I was afraid he'd show up driving a late-model Caddy."

"Upholstered with twenty-dollar bills? Relax, Pat. He isn't dishonest, and he sure isn't stupid."

"I know, but ..."

The serpent inhabited LaSalle's paradise that night: A fight.

The loud voices could have meant nothing else. At first, Patrick thought a few foolish Loyola students had crashed the gathering. Shouts reverberating off trees in the large clearing, however, all came from LaSalle mouths.

Some epithets were obscene. Others racial. None friendly. Patrick rushed toward the cluster of students. "What's going on?" he shouted at nobody in particular. Tammy Dickerson, skirting the edge of the crowd with friends, sprang upon Patrick immediately.

"The football guys. They're hassling Sammie. And T.R. just stepped in. Do something!" she shrieked. Without getting a clear look through the crowd, Patrick knew who she was talking about. The football guys—LaSalle's hard-drinking, fast-playing jocks. Remnants of an older, all-male LaSalle, they gloried in "keeping up the reputation."

Patrick had enjoyed good times with many of them, mostly in male-only social gatherings at the River, but they seemingly took on a different persona when egging one another on in front of girls. Though loyal to the school, if yelling loud at rallies, firing up fellow students, and maligning rival students meant anything, they walked a different line—often into Brother Curt's office.

Other LaSalle students regarded them with a mix of awe, respect, and fear. Awed by pranks the merry band pulled off; respected for the hard work and dedication manifested in sunscorched football practices; feared for their proclivity to go for the throat, with everything from tasteless nicknames to hallway comments, mischief at lunch, and hijinks at the River.

Patrick forced his way to the group's center, as if he were a quarterback entering a huddle late. On one side, Ralph Smith, Franco Togneri, and Sean Foley stood together as they often did when manning LaSalle's offensive line. Behind them, six or seven teammates pushed forward.

Sammie Spear, though restrained by Lance Hall, gesticulated wildly as he faced the footballers.

T.R., like a giant redwood, planted himself between Sammie and his adversaries. Thirty or forty other students milled about. A timid junior reached out to touch Foley's arm to calm him down. Foley shouted, "Don't touch me, fag!" The intimidated junior melted back into the crowd.

Frank Tucci, who played quarterback for the football team and third guard on the basketball team, strode between T.R. and his linemen. "C'mon, guys, knock it off. Just forget about it," he pleaded.

Ignoring him, though blocked a bit by his presence, Foley took a half step forward and pointed over Tucci to Sammie Spear. "I want you, little man. Right now." Sammie struggled against Lance Hall's hold.

"You're going over me to get him," T.R. spoke calmly.

"Not your affair. Him and me."

"And your buddies?" The sweep of Ward's hand as he motioned toward Foley's potential reinforcements reiterated for all his giant wing span.

"They'll stay clear." He, too, had a moment to factor in T.R.'s presence. "Just him and me. Man to man. Then it's over, and everybody can shake hands."

"That's not the end game, Sean. How 'bout you and me. Closer to the same size." Foley grinned nervously, as if he hadn't expected this, but he didn't have a way to back down without losing face. Doris Long knifed through the drawn-together crowd. "Patrick, stop this. Tony, let's go."

T.R. looked at her. "Didn't ask for this, Doris."

Patrick had heard enough to size up the situation. He judged Foley wanted no part of T.R. Though Foley respected T.R.'s athleticism and talent, the two generally spoke grudgingly at school. Foley and, by extension, his football cohorts couldn't understand why the stud tight end that helped them vanquish foes as a ninth-grade J.V. star chose not to play football, though he surely would have been a superstar in that sport too. There had been a sort of a truce at school for two years with the hope T.R. would change his mind and return to the gridiron. "You're right, T.R., you didn't ask for this, and it doesn't concern you. It's the elf there with the big mouth."

"That elf's my bro," T.R. tensed. His patience, noteworthy though he had never gone public about the racial motives of some of these guys even if he had chatted at length with Brother Curt and Patrick about them, was wearing thin.

Patrick stepped in. "He's my friend too, Sean. And I thought you were too. Besides, we're all Lancers. Don't know what caused this, but I can guess. You guys left the dance early and got a head start pounding the brews. Whatever, it's stopping now." Patrick spoke quickly. As he did, Suzie crossed behind him to Doris, obviously agitated by developments. Patrick stretched for a way to diffuse the situation. "Sean, just because you haven't fought anybody for a couple days doesn't mean you have to do it here. Why don't you guys go buy up for us? We need a few more six-packs to cool off." Foley's ability to buy or get beer was legendary.

Wriggling off a hook, Foley tried to sound playful: "Sure, Patrick. You paying?"

"No, think you ought to," Patrick intoned firmly. "You got a lot of people upset." Patrick walked Foley off from the crowd, talking to him by himself just outside the clearing. When he returned, he asked Suzie to stay with Doris while he moved T.R. and Sammie toward a path along the River.

Still fuming, Sammie sputtered, "That guy's a ... a total jerk!"

T.R. spoke deliberately: "He should've had to apologize directly. Gets away with murder. We all know that. Even Brother Blood. He'd can his butt in a minute if it wasn't for his old school ties and old man."

"No doubt," Patrick placated. "What started it?"

"He said I had to—" Sammie began.

"To not dance with everyone's girls," T.R. interrupted. "Honky code. He's ticked off because Sammie was dancing with white girls."

"They wouldn't dance with him anyway," Sammie affirmed.

"You'd think it was the '50s," Patrick shook his head. The River rushed by. The three sat on a tree stump.

"I'm going to get that guy," T.R. proclaimed. "That sweet-talking, jive-ass honky came up to me early at the dance and told me he was on a recruiting mission. Said it was my duty to play football next year. Can you believe it? LaSalle spirit. I can play football with him, but Sammie can't dance with a white girl. I'm gonna get him," he repeated.

"And he said he'd get you," Sammie gasped. "He be messin' with T.R. 'bout the car too. Bad enough, but then talkin' that smack too."

"What'd he say?" Patrick questioned.

"What could he say?" T.R. responded. "Hinting at stuff. The racist punk probably thought my wheels he's speculating some-body else paid for should have been a Cadillac or stretch limo."

Patrick's eyes guiltily found the top of his loafers, but Sam-mie picked up where he left off: "Talkin' nonsense. Sending letters to the league and stuff. He don't know jack, but he be mouthing off 'bout T.R. like he's got a clue. I shoulda kicked his big ass."

"The problem," Patrick bit off. "They are big mouths, with big mouth parents. What did he say about the car?"

"Typical stuff. T.R.'s in Percy's pocket." Sammie turned quick-ly to face T.R. "Good thing he pussed out on you, Tone. That River'd be for washing off Foley blood now." His neck swiveled to look back at Patrick. "He implied Forte's calling the shots for a delivery, and T.R.'s cashing in already."

"Can't see those boys having spies in South Sac," Patrick joked, trying to lighten the moment. All three looked at one another. "It ain't me," Patrick shrugged, evoking tension-cut-ting laughs.

The three returned to the clearing. Though they stayed for almost an hour, and almost everybody else did too for fear of missing something, the footballers didn't return.

The beer did show up, though. Some late-arriving juniors toted it down to everybody. They explained that Foley had told them he and his friends had to go to Nevada to find some real action to relax before finals. The comment elicited the reaction Foley hoped to achieve, at least among a few present.

Patrick remarked to Sammie and T.R., "It's their way of apologizing. Not manly, but what did you expect?"

5.

LATE JULY
SUMMER

The following ran in *The Star* following the tournament game that concluded LaSalle's organized basketball efforts until autumn:

Lancer Players Win Summer Cage Tourney
By: Patrick Kiernan

Tuning up for the coming year's basketball campaign, a team made up of LaSalle Lancers captured the Sacramento City Summer League high school tournament yesterday, bombing a team comprised mostly of Carmichael High hoopsters, 82–67.

T.R. Ward tallied twenty-five points and gathered thirteen boards before being replaced as his team, coached by Ed Link, a friend of Jerry Burke's, coasted to the victory at American River Junior College.

"They're awesome," Bud Daniels, the opposing coach, lauded. "We were playing outstanding ball before but were never in this one. Ward makes a big difference."

Ward, LaSalle's potential high school All-American, didn't play in the previous meeting between the two club teams, in which the mostly Mustangs (which added grads and players from three other schools to its Carmichael nucleus) edged

T.R.'s squad, 68–65. Ward missed all three of his team's losses in pool play before his team waltzed through the ensuing playoffs. During the earlier games, the solidly built center participated in two summer basketball camps in Southern California and Berkeley.

Sharp-shooting guard Del Hayes, from El Rancho, paced the opposition with twenty-three points, mainly from deep.

Sammie Spear orchestrated the offense for the squad carrying the banner for the Lancers, tallying sixteen points and dishing eight assists. The scoring attack also featured a fifteen-point binge by Lance Hall, a reed-like junior-to-be.

"That pleased me most this summer," said Coach Burke in attendance. "The summer league provided experience for guys like Hall and [Frank] Tucci, players LaSalle is going to need big efforts from down the line. Hall gained confidence in the four games Ward missed. We were in them all, even though we dropped three. We're definitely not a one-man team." But, oh, that one man makes a huge difference. Just ask Bud Daniels and his collection of stars.

"Can't believe I'm here." Patrick took in the Oakland Coliseum from the press box. "I'm used to sitting out there." He pointed to the bleachers.

Carl Schipper surveyed the scene: "Usually quite a bit going on out there."

"It gets wild. I'd hate playing leftfield for the visitors here."

"The 'Stick across the Bay has that reputation too. On a cold night, I think the fans stay warm in leftfield by roasting the opposition."

"The problem tonight is I know some of the most merciless fans here. Foley, Togneri, Smith. The football guys. Saw them in the parking lot."

"Could be a down year for LaSalle football."

"They'll win their share."

Schipper focused on closer surroundings: "I thought you'd

like this. The press box, the Yankees, and a short visit to the locker room with Pete after the game." Schipper referred to the paper's beat writer who covered the A's or Giants during homestands.

Patrick couldn't believe his fortune. Different stories—summer league basketball, local baseball in many guises, an amateur golf tourney, and a swim meet—provided good experience and a lot of enjoyment. Impressed, Schipper saw taking Patrick to the A's game as his way of telling Patrick he thought of him as major league.

About the third inning, after a burst of run-scoring excitement by both sides, the good-sized crowd, including many Yankee fans despite the Bronx Bombers' desultory season, settled in for a pitcher's duel between the Yankees' recently acquired Mike Witt and the A's Bob Welch, who had won ten in a row and was having the best season of his career. Carl Schipper began paternally quizzing Patrick about his future: "Hear you're interested in Princeton."

"Besides everything else, their recruiter really impressed me. And my mom's from the East Coast and thinks going there, where she met my dad, would broaden my horizons. So, I'm a legacy, even though my father has virtually disavowed me. Brother Raymond speaks highly of the Ivy League too, but I still think I'd like it."

"And major in being a preppie?"

Patrick laughed. "No. English."

"To write the great American novel? Maybe even about baseball."

"I wish. Malamud and Roth and others have already taken their shots. Besides, Mr. Wilson thinks the greatest of all time's settled. He thinks *Huck Finn*'s the great American novel. But I do love sports. Almost feel guilty taking a check writing about it."

"Never feel guilty getting paid to write. People who earn their living with words never get paid enough."

Patrick looked down at the diamond: "It would be great

to throw a ninety-five-mile-an-hour fastball and be on center stage out there."

"I'd love it too. Probably in the mind of most sportswriters. Still, the fastball goes. Usually, unless you're a lush like that other Princeton guy, F. Scott Fitzgerald, talent with words, which you have, doesn't." Schipper downed his beer with a big gulp. "You want a hot dog?"

"No, not now."

"Anyway," Schipper changed his tone, "I want to make sure you know you have a lot of potential for sports writing. And, you could find worse work. Mr. Wilson tells me, though it's hard to believe, teachers make even less than us."

"For sure. Know anybody near Princeton to contact for me for a parttime job writing sports?"

"Sources in the Bay Area, but not near the Big Apple."

"Well, I'm really looking at Berkeley. Maybe if I went there, Pete would be ready to retire and turn this beat over to me. I could arrange my classes around it."

Patrick laughed, but Schipper responded seriously enough to stir Patrick's dreams: "He's only fifty-six, even if he looks like he covered Babe Ruth. But he's mentioned he'd like to ditch the long commute. We sub-let a cheap apartment during the summer for him. He never did move here. It'd be a helluva workload with studies and everything, but I'd sure like to keep you. You'd find it tough just working for the *Daily Cal*, regardless of its high quality, after this gig. And that's not even considering pay."

Patrick's mind wandered. His neat, orderly world—deciding between Princeton and Berkeley or entertaining other choices—suddenly had a new consideration emerging. He sat quietly.

In the sixth inning, when a two-run uprising by the A's tied the score at three, fans responded. While stomping back and forth on top of the home dugout, a cheerleader exhorted fans.

"Ironic," Patrick remarked. "He gets fans riled up while security does everything to calm the bleacher creatures. With Foley and them out there, no chance."

"Fans here cheer in unison. Your impetuous football boys do whatever strikes them. I'll give Coach Mack his due. He gets them fired up and playing together. Like a cult, and they play over their heads." Schipper alluded to LaSalle's Athletic Director and football coach.

The two swapped LaSalle football and McEntee stories. Patrick told Schipper about some of the self-proclaimed remnants' more audacious pranks. Schipper recalled interviews with McEntee and other dealings at banquets, meetings, and public events.

The A's scored in the bottom of the seventh to take the lead. Simultaneously, a cherry bomb, or something similar, exploded in the concourse under the leftfield stands.

"Up to it again," Patrick harrumphed, forgetting for a minute that the rest of the leftfield stands weren't populated by angels.

The conversation turned to Suzie. "I should've gotten you access for her too, or at least a seat close," Schipper apologized.

"That's okay. She's busy packing for a trip tomorrow. Up to Yreka near the Oregon border for a week to visit her aunt's family. Her cousin Daphne is our age. They're close. Then, they're both going to that Girls' State Convention in Chico I told you about. Two weeks together for them."

"Better give our lonely boy extra assignments. You want to go up to Rocklin with me a few days for the Niners' training camp? We can watch them sweat together."

"The Niners! Super, Carl. Can't tell you how much I love this."

"Actually, Mr. Cynic here loves seeing your excitement. You know, Patrick," Schipper emphasized, "the Ward story can make you a good name. At your age. Stay close to him. Get the scoop you deserve when he nails his choice down to the five schools."

"Deserve?"

"You're friends. Who better? Bigger than our little area. I presume college choices will be in big population centers. Stories about him will get play there and even on that national sports network that's getting more popular. A scoop for Patrick Kiernan of *The Star* would impress when he picks the lucky program. It's important not just to be good at writing stories but also good at getting them. I've spent time cultivating people over the years. This is your backyard. Don't let the story get away. And if something's cooking, let me know. T.R.'s recruitment should play big all year."

"I know," Patrick said solemnly as the crowd cheered a defensive gem. The game ended quickly thereafter, the A's hanging on for a one-run victory which made the quick visit to their clubhouse after the game more enjoyable.

"Fun to attend a game without a task for a change," Schipper confided as he and Patrick wound their way around the outside of the stadium to the parking lot. "And, isn't Pete a good guy?"

The two passed near Sean Foley and friends. Patrick pretended not to see them, but Foley shouted out, "Patrick Kiernan. Ignoring fellow Lancers? Want some suds?"

"No, Sean," Patrick called back. "I'll be right back," he said to Schipper. "I should say hello, but I won't take long."

"Fine. I'll start the car. Meet me there."

"Hey, guys." Patrick addressed the seven or eight Lancers gathered between two pickups. "Good game, huh?"

"Not bad. What we saw." Foley stepped away from the others to confront Patrick in front of the trucks. He spoke loudly, not a drunk loud, but a loudness chosen to ensure his Greek chorus heard the conversation. "That Schipper with you?" Foley snarled after a belch.

"Yeah. You guys raise hell out there?"

"Nah. We were saving ourselves, sort of the way some wusses save themselves for marriage." Foley overemphasized his leering wink. "We might go to the city to 'bag some fags.'" Patrick blanched, thinking of the LaSalle letterman, some wearing block sweaters, rolling around San Francisco, picking out suspected homosexuals to hassle. He nearly suggested they play their games with people near the Coliseum, figuring they'd probably get their lunches handed them.

Though uncomfortable with not confronting Foley's values directly, Patrick chose a different direction: "Better be careful. They might decide they like a stud like you."

Foley looked at Patrick almost soberly. "Kiernan, I like you. You're quick, and you're not a flower. You don't back down like most twerps at school. But don't push your luck."

Ralph Smith shouted, "Why not ditch Schipper, have some fun with us, and we'll get you home?"

Foley, though, picked up where he had left off: "Speaking of pushing your luck, tell the big spade we expect him at our first practice in three weeks. I hear you're playing hoops with him when you're not sucking up in the paper."

"Kiernan," Franco Togneri shouted, "You gonna give US some ink this year with that new job of yours, right?"

"All you deserve, Franco," Patrick stated vaguely. He turned back to Foley, the only one who really mattered. "I hear you're implying stuff about T.R. Who's your source for your alleged dirt?"

"Mr. Newspaperman, indeed. Source," Foley scoffed. "It's that Doris chick. You know I like 'em dark, and she really likes me," Foley cackled. "Nah," he hastily corrected as if the assertion's ridiculousness even went past his bounds of credibility. "It's Coach. He's got his sources. The old goat should after all these years. And he's still really sore Ward isn't out for football. He's stiffed us since freshman year. School spirit. You're into that. You should be on our side with this."

Patrick, realizing McEntee and his charges actually felt snubbed by Ward, thought about reasoning with Foley—the simple truth that it'd be foolish for someone with T.R.'s future to play another sport like football and risk injury. But he knew Foley, or any LaSalle old-school remnant, could care less about Ward's future.

Patrick also considered turning the conversation on end,

telling him he thought Foley would prefer not having another African American on the team and that T.R. was doing him a favor.

But, mindful of the need to meet Carl quickly, he settled for the simplest approach: "You know Burke would never let him play football. He and McEntee have been feuding over athletes for years. No, Sean, it's football or basketball. This isn't like you doing track and field just to stay in shape."

"What about Tucci?" Foley pointed his finger at Patrick's chest as he inched toward him like a baseball manager moving in on an umpire. "Answer me that!" he challenged. Patrick realized he was playing with something dangerous, the truth.

"The feud between the two coaches is real. The exception proves the rule. Tucci doesn't start in basketball. That's the difference. It's not the end of the world if he comes out for hoops late. Even if you boys actually make the playoffs."

"It'd be okay for the spade too. Just tell him that. It'd be in his best interest."

"Or what? You threatening him? With what?"

"He'll see. Three weeks."

"I wouldn't mess with him if I were in your shoes. You ever consider asking him nicely? A helluva recruiter you'd make." Patrick didn't want to hear more. "See you guys."

"No more happy talk?" Foley seemingly lived to get under people's skins.

Worked up, Patrick turned back. "Talk about school spirit, Sean," Patrick's sarcasm bubbled forth. "I don't see you playing two bigtime sports. You'd be a great hatchet man under the basket. What's wrong, Sean? No school spirit? Happy just running track in your offseason?"

Before turning again, Patrick measured Sean, expecting he might see Foley charging at him or giving him his famous one-fingered wave goodbye. What he saw was worse. Foley, looking like *The Thinker*, seemed to be considering the challenge.

Carl Schipper drove to where Patrick had wandered. Patrick crawled into his car. "You okay?" Schipper wondered. "They mess with you?"

"Worse," Patrick confided, slumping into his seat. "I might've given Foley the idea he should go out for basketball."

"Somebody should give him some new ideas," Carl made light, but Patrick stared vacantly out the window during much of the drive home, fearing he might have been an unwitting recruiter.

6.

ALMOST MID-AUGUST
SUMMER

Patrick stayed in contact with Suzie during her absence. Some phone conversations bothered him. That's when he, a willing letter writer, penned this one during Suzie's stay at the Girls' State Chico Convention:

August 10ᵗʰ

Dearest Suzie,

Although it's been ten days, I feel better with you in Chico, a little closer than Yreka. Can't wait until Saturday when I pick you up. Will be good seeing Daphne again too. Sounds as if she's changed and quite happy.

Mom said to say hello.

Work is going great, though a golfer I interviewed did ask me if I was reporting for my school paper. T.R.'s up working at the ranch. Sammie too, and a lot of other guys. Thank God that Foley and his posse worked there earlier. The situation's not good. I'm worried about next year. I met Percy Forte for the first time a few days ago at T.R.'s. The guy's slick but doesn't seem as bad as I heard.

God, I miss you ... and love you. I didn't mean to get upset the other night on the phone. You sounded so excited about that club Daphne's so into. Guess I felt a little left out. I have problems with "born-again" movements. Maybe, it's because my own faith's weak; people who feel strongly put me off. It's as if they're salesmen. Anyway, I wasn't very sensitive—probably doubling down on that right now. Still, I need you to know how I feel.

Daphne's staying with you until the middle of the week, right? You'll have to tell me what the vote ends up on that Middle East resolution at the Convention. Think about me even though you have a million other things to ponder. I can be covering an exciting game, but suddenly, my thoughts turn to you. Miss you.

Love,

Pat

After phoning Suzie that evening, Patrick felt compelled to seek advice elsewhere. There was no question whom he would choose.

"Patrick, come in," Steve Wilson greeted his acolyte at the door of his Craftsman house in East Sac, a favorite city area for Patrick, who lived in Carmichael. Houses like Wilson's were older and typically one with their treelined streets. Wilson's brick-bottomed house was set back from the street behind an iron gate and a well-manicured front lawn.

"You sure this isn't too much trouble this late?" Patrick asked. Wilson's two daughters, Becky and Anne, ran to jump at Patrick, who had babysat them.

"No problem. My wife's taking a management course. She's out late. Just need to check the girls every now and then. Let's go out back to talk."

The two settled into deck chairs, their conversation punctuated at times by interruptions from Wilson's two blond-haired children. The talk started with catching up on summer activities. When Wilson excused himself to ready his protesting girls for bed, Patrick enjoyed the cooling that came with dusk.

The darkness had asserted itself by the time Wilson returned. He drank from a tall glass of Jack Daniel's and water while Patrick sipped an iced tea. "Well, our drinks look the same," Wilson quipped. "What's up? Suzie? You steered the conversation that direction."

"A regular Sherlock Holmes," Patrick remarked as Wilson lit his pipe, enveloping himself in a cloud of smoke before achieving the draw he wanted. The smell of the pipe aroma intertwined with jasmine drifted Patrick into a relaxed state.

"I prefer to see myself as Sigmund Freud. My sister-in-law figures to make sixty-five to seventy bucks an hour. Can you imagine? I tell her that's a lot of money since all psychologists essentially do is convince people to like themselves." Wilson puffed his pipe.

"I do want to talk about Suzie." Patrick leaned forward. "Something's changed her these last couple weeks."

"That's what people do when they're young. Change. You mentioned her cousin and that Christian group. Is that it?"

"They're Catholic by name. But, yes, that's it."

"Tell me about it."

"Not sure. Not a feeling I'm used to. Can't quite nail it down. Maybe nothing."

"Feelings aren't nothing. What do you know?

Not much about women, apparently. That's why I came to you."

"You flatter me. Glad my wife's not here to hear that. She'd wonder what I was saying in class."

"You know," Patrick struggled, "you seem to understand people."

"Even without the sixty-five bucks an hour."

"And I wanted to talk to a man. Not mom."

"So, tell me what you know about this group and Suzie's involvement."

"Yeah." Patrick straightened in his chair. "Her cousin Daphne in Yreka has gotten active in this club called Disciple Fellowship. It's a Catholic group, but they sound like 'born-agains' in everything but name. And seems they're always trying to convert people, even people like me, already Catholic."

"Proselytizing," Wilson offered. "You sure don't use your 'born-again' label very positively."

"I view them somewhat like Moonies you see at the airport, or Mormons or Watchtower people. Suzie describes it as an active faith testimony sort of thing. She says it's getting popular on college campuses. Newman Centers. One at State and another at Davis. And American River J.C. near me. She and Daphne apparently spent time together at the Newman Center at Southern Oregon College in Ashland."

"Whereas, you or I would have spent our time with the Bard, maybe another Catholic, at the Shakespeare Festival."

"So, anyway," Patrick smiled before continuing, "she really got her head turned around. She just didn't seem the type. 'Born-agains' strike me as needy. Religion's been important to her, but now she's like a God Squad salesman. Talking about setting up booths at school when we're back."

"You overstating a bit? Besides, school booths might not be a bad idea for some of the boys. Maybe, at the River too. Foley, Smith, Togneri, Jensen might benefit." Patrick forced a laugh. As he did, Wilson ran into the house, where he had heard some commotion from the girls' room.

Patrick, left to himself for ten minutes, thought about Suzie. Another strained conversation that night had gotten to him. She seemed rushed to get off the phone to go with Daphne to a Chico State Disciple Fellowship meeting. Feeling sorry for himself, Patrick watched Wilson return, carrying another drink. Wilson sat back down across from Patrick and reached for his pipe. After tamping down a new bowlful, he lit up immediately and spoke from the ensuing cloud: "There's nothing wrong with religion or strong faith. A little jealous? Jesus is a tough rival."

Patrick winced. "Yeah, maybe a bit. It's like Daphne and that group swept her off of her feet."

"Give women space. Good women like Suzie will reward you for that. Look at your mom, a real model of a woman for you, and she's very self-directed."

"But she practices her religion quietly. She's not out there telling everybody about it."

"You know, there's another thing to consider. You've had a lot of success with different things while you two have gone steady for the last year."

"So?"

"She might feel a need to assert herself. Something her own. Something she initiates. These years are a time of growth and testing," he remarked, as if including himself instead of solely referencing high schoolers. "Hard to do as an extension of you. Course, I'm speculating, and I'd rather you didn't bring this up with Suzie. At least, not using my name. Just a possibility. How's she been getting on with her mom and sister? Quite a readjustment these last six months."

"Pretty good, I think," Patrick responded. "All three of them still feel the loss of Mr. Andrus a lot. Suzie idolized him."

"What was he like?"

"Quiet but strong. Old-fashioned but not a fossil. Easy to talk with. A man's man. A lot older than his wife. He studied for the priesthood for years."

"No."

"Yeah, came within a few months of taking final vows. Why are you smiling?"

"Oh, amateur psychology. Maybe way off-base. A chauvinistic way of looking at things; still, worth a thought."

Puzzled and intrigued, Patrick blurted, "What?"

"You're not a bad replacement for her father. Almost improbably so for someone your age. And Disciple Fellowship. Almost like following in her father's footsteps. Maybe fulfilling something in a way he didn't, or sacrificed for something else. Honor thy father."

"C'mon, Mr. W. Pretty heavy. He would have hated that Disciple Fellowship thing. Too Protestant. Next, you're going to tell me she's going to be a nun."

"Not necessarily. T.R.'s working on a farm, you said, but I doubt he'll end up being a farmer. I don't mean to trivialize what Suzie's doing. A lot of concerned, committed Christians live successful secular lives. Groups like that are popular for a reason, though. Our times spawn them. When she gets back, talk things out with her. Respect her feelings and ideas. Maybe go with her to a meeting or two and withhold judgment until you can reflect on it. Then, be honest, but respect her decisions."

"But Daphne will be here too. That concerns me."

"Why?"

"It'll be hard to find time to talk alone without Daphne being involved."

"So, involve her. Speak of ideas. You're pretty good at that."

"These people can be beyond reason. Purposefully."

"These people? That's unlike you. Keep an open mind."

The conversation drifted to other things before the two heard a minivan pull into the driveway. Wilson's wife, looking a bit harried, appeared in the backyard.

"Hi, Steve. Patrick." Dropping books on a table, she bent down to give her husband a peck on the cheek. She turned to Patrick. "How ya' doing? Here to remind Steve it's almost time to go back to work?"

"Not exactly."

"You're right. He still needs to patch house cracks and paint the kitchen like he promised in June. I wish he was as handy with that stuff as he is with words." Patrick could care less about Mr. Wilson's skills around the house. He knew this had been a handy conversation.

7.

EARLY SEPTEMBER
SENIOR YEAR

The following rundown of the LaSalle Lancers' football squad appeared within a league summary Patrick wrote prior to the post-Labor Day school resumption:

LaSalle Lancers

"If it hurts, cut it off." So seemed the philosophy of veteran coach Alex McEntee of the LaSalle Lancers during two-a-day practices two weeks before the season's first game at Calistoga High School in Napa County.

McEntee, a former Marine, is legendary for the dedication, camaraderie, and discipline he espouses and inspires. He's also very quotable: "I'm getting these boys ready. End-of-summer sweat trickles down to grow October and November victories. We don't always have the best athletes, but we aim to have the best team in the league. We're not deep, and we don't have that one real stud offensive threat that every team would like, but these boys hang together like bananas on a bunch."

The best of the bunch anchor LaSalle's line. Seniors Sean Foley (6'1", 215), Franco Togneri (6', 210), and Ralph Smith (5'10", 195) return to form a formidable forward wall on offense and defense.

When the Lancers have the ball, the line will attempt to

open holes for returning scatback Wes Solt (5' 8", 170) and to protect senior flinger Frank Tucci (5'10", 180). Tucci, also a guard on the Lancers basketball power, replaces two-year letterman Neal Corkery. Coach Mack called Tucci "not flashy but dependable." The return of the rest of the offensive unit, though McEntee claimed he could use a few more dependable receivers, should ease Tucci's task.

The Lancers' defense is green. "We have to hang in until our young secondary adapts to this level of competition," suggested team captain Sean Foley. The most promising newcomer is Jerry Jensen (5'11", 170), who'll play safety, where he can flash his centerfield skills. Ted Presto (6'2", 210), a promising lineman, should help the defensive rush and take pressure off of the offensive line stalwarts, who often tired in the fourth quarter last season while playing every down.

"Spirit will do it for us," McEntee emphasized, waving his hands wildly. "We'll have to suck it up and play like one. That's what this school and this team are all about. It's guys like Tucci and Foley, who both plan to go out for basketball and probably would sell programs if you asked, that make us successful. I just wish we had a few more bodies out that could help."

Without those few extra bodies, LaSalle still should be interesting and competitive. Figure them for 7–3 overall and 4–2 in league play.

"That gung-ho atmosphere seems phony," Patrick pronounced as he and Suzie, her long hair back to its normal tease that always looked so perfectly coifed, emerged from a Friday night Disciple Fellowship meeting at Sacramento State.

Suzie stopped in her tracks. "You haven't given it a real chance."

"How can you say that?" Patrick turned toward her. "This is the third meeting I've come to. One for all, and all for one. Like LaSalle football practices, except everybody's smiling and there's no swearing."

"What's wrong with that?" Suzie's voice betrayed its usual

calm. "People think you're always smiling around school."

"I'm not on the make, wanting to win people over. Let's tell stories about who we've talked to lately about the Lord, God, Jesus Christ," Patrick poorly mimicked. "It dominates everything."

"It should," Suzie retorted. "We're talking salvation, not some silly football game. The most important thing in the world. The Bible says ..."

"Don't," Patrick interrupted. "These people, you people, get fired up like shooting stars, but there's no room left for other light. For life. For not knowing. For not having answers. I mean," Patrick gathered himself, letting out some of the frustration he had held for three weeks. "What about you and me? Not taking everything seriously? Music? Dances? Having fun? What about ..."

"Sex," Suzie taunted. "Is that what's bothering you?"

"Try love," Patrick almost stammered. "If it was just sex, I could've joined Foley and the boys on their trip to Moonlight Ranch this weekend instead of being here with you. That's unfair, and you know it. I've never pushed you beyond your limits."

"Those guys are disgusting," Suzie flared but then regained her composure. "Besides, the Patrick I know wouldn't want to go to a ... to a house of ill repute. Would a brothel even allow those guys in, even in Nevada, even if they're over eighteen?" Suzie pulled Patrick to her. "I do love you, Pat. I see this as hard for you, but I've committed to Jesus. That doesn't mean I can't be committed to you too. God knows, I don't want to shut you out."

The two hugged, though Patrick resisted, his body tense and mind racing. He considered bringing up things he had talked to Mr. Wilson about but decided against that.

"Daphne told me to expect this," Suzie continued earnestly. "It's hard for people who are close not to feel threatened."

Trying to change the mood, Patrick playfully suggested, "Like St. Paul's horse after it threw him off." Suzie laughed, more out of habit than conviction. "That's what I miss most.

Your laughter. This group is making you too damned serious. My Jesus surely laughed a lot."

"I don't want to change you," Suzie comforted. "I don't need to. You're sensitive and kind and loving. I need you, Pat, but I need other things too. To have a purpose. To do good and help people. You do it naturally. I have to work hard at it."

"Come on, Suzie," Patrick protested. "You've always been loving and giving ..."

"Or you wouldn't have dated me?"

"Sort of," Patrick smiled. "This threatens to change everything, though. Suddenly. Daphne seems so into it, and you do too. I felt overwhelmed. Like you came back a different person."

"I hope I did. A better person. And I hope you'll recognize that soon. It'll work, Pat. Just give it time." The two faced each other in silence beneath a star-twinkled sky and full moon.

A group of Sac State club members came by and greeted Patrick and Suzie as if they hadn't seen them for days. Though simply walking to the parking lot, they looked, Patrick admitted to himself, as if they had found $10 bills every few steps. They smiled, giggled, exchanged small talk, and obviously considered Suzie a prime recruit. Patrick tried to be his usual congenial self, though, curiously, he felt the way he had when he interviewed Coach McEntee. This was someone else's show.

When the group moved on, Patrick wheeled back on Suzie. "Even this weekend is out the window. You have to participate in that session after Mass on Sunday ..."

"Want to, not have to," Suzie corrected.

"Whatever. Labor Day weekend. I thought we'd go up to Kyburz to that cabin on the American River Mom got from Mr. Walters at work."

"We can go. Sunday afternoon and stay until Monday night. Or, instead, maybe watch some TV on the couch at your house. By ourselves," Suzie winked and smiled, practically melting Patrick.

Still overshadowed by a silence that felt like a grudging truce, the couple resumed walking toward Patrick's car. Both knew their relationship was being born again.

8.

EARLY SEPTEMBER
SENIOR YEAR (A WEEK LATER)

Even though essay writing in AP English (LaSalle combined juniors and seniors into a two-year AP program though only the senior class received the designation) would be devoted to weekly literary responses anticipating test essays, Mr. Wilson traditionally began all classes with a prompt designed to ease students back into the school year while promoting interaction among students. The assignment also enabled him to get a sense of the writing of students he hadn't taught.

It also promised a fascinating session when students would read their completed efforts to a small group, with ones chosen to be repeated for the class. Mr. Wilson's instructions began, "Since you were in kindergarten, teachers have asked you to write about what you did during summer. I want you to write about the most interesting thing you didn't do." After providing details about length and format, he added, "One focus rather than listing different things. If I wanted a list, I'd read an ingredients label. And make it appropriate to read in class. No sordid details. I don't want to read how you didn't sleep with some movie star. A modicum of reality would be apt."

Patrick pondered appropriateness, but reality won out. A reaction to school tension? Writing in a different mode than the serious, objective newspaper stories he'd been writing? Venting his frustrations about Suzie's new interest? In any case,

Patrick read the following to the class on the first Friday of the school year:

Does the Common Synonym for Lady of the Evening Start with an "H"?

I didn't conclude summer vacation by going on a field trip with classmates to a famous ranch near Carson City, Nevada.

Field trips are valuable and instructive educational experiences. While a LaSalle student, I have attended plays and concerts, visited the State Assembly and McGeorge Law School, investigated various museums, and participated in programs at Sacramento State University and U.C. Davis. None of those, however, promised the instant excitement, gratification, and enrichment the Labor Day field trip I missed offered. In an educational sense, of course.

It wasn't sponsored by Davis or some local 4-H Club. This excursion was initiated by LaSalle's "remnants," a group that reveres "old ways." Previously this summer, these good old boys worked at Mr. Mullan's Grass Valley Shamrock Ranch. Apparently, they wanted another taste of ranching before summer ended.

The Moonlight, world-renowned and whispered about by just about every schoolboy in the Capital area, is known for its innovative techniques. Supposedly, the workers transform even the most inexperienced youngster into someone who can plant, if not sow. Lessons take place in hothouses where immature saplings receive tender loving care.

Despite this, I chose not to go. It's easy to regret my decision since one hears almost nothing else around school this first week except about the field trip and its participants. My decision was not made in haste since I want to know as much about professional agricultural advancements as the next fellow. No, my decision was purely selfish.

I anticipated Mr. Wilson's first assignment and wanted

something novel to write about. What does LaSalle's new 4-H club stand for? In the outside world, the letters stand for head, heart, hands, and health. I can only hope the latter was well accounted for while the first three were exercised. Otherwise, animal husbandry might be jeopardized.

That afternoon, Patrick found himself sitting in Brother Curt's office by invitation. Brother Curt swept in after conducting detention. "Well, well. Patrick Kiernan, LaSalle's agriculture writer." Brother Curt sprawled behind his desk, his feet up, and loosened his religious collar as if to show he meant business. "Understand you gave quite a performance in A.P."

Patrick squirmed. The network Brother Curt cultivated to know everything in school inspired awe. Patrick feigned ignorance: "What? Junior girls raving about my good looks?"

"No, mortified by your raving, Patrick," Brother Curt snapped while outlining his well-trimmed beard with thumb and forefinger. "Your washing-the-laundry-in-public narrative."

"About agriculture? How's that shocking?" Patrick kept up the act, if only because he and Brother Curt knew each other so well.

"The football players' Nevada trip. Satire's supposed to be subtle. Yours exploded like an atomic bomb, from what I hear."

"Didn't have much time to finesse it. Stories for *The Star* every night."

"That's weak, Patrick. Do you want me to put a stop to that?" Patrick became very serious. "What comes first, *The Star* or LaSalle?" The abruptness, though characteristic of Brother Curt's no-nonsense approach to everything LaSalle, took Patrick, in his guilt, off guard.

"LaSalle."

Brother Curt glowered, as he seldom did in dealings with Patrick. "Then why in the hell did you go public with this? I should be grateful you didn't print it in *The Lance* or *The Star*."

"You know," Patrick protested half-heartedly, "word of their little jaunt was all over school already. Those guys have big mouths and seemed quite proud."

"Still, hearsay for the most part, though, before you and your megaphone made it more public. If underclassmen believed every rumor about these guys, we'd have a combination of James Bond, Superman, and Charles Manson in our midst. But we don't. We have Sean Foley, Franco Togneri, and Ralph Smith, unique characters in themselves but still youngsters. LaSalle kids. With families who care about their reputation, even if you and they don't. You need to show respect. For the school, if not for them. For me."

Patrick nodded.

Brother Curt continued while drumming a pencil on his desk. "You've always been a responsible kid. Actions and consequences mean something to you. That's why this concerns me. To be aboveboard and fair, you'll be sitting in detention with me for a while. I hope you haven't gotten a big head with this job."

"No! You're right; I shouldn't have done it. Things have been bothering me."

Brother Curt leaned forward. Though Dean of Discipline for three years, he loved reverting to his original calling as a personal counselor. This, no doubt, accounted for part of his popularity. "Like what?"

"Personal stuff."

"You can trust me."

"Well, part of it's Suzie."

"Her new Fellowship 'born-again' thing?"

"Yeah."

"Really into it?" Brother Curt didn't wait for the answer. "The first day of school, she approached Sister Joan about forming a club here. What's it called?"

"Disciple Fellowship."

"Poor Joan's just taken over as Assistant Dean, still learning about this school. She says it sounds interesting, that students usually didn't come forward with spiritual suggestions at her past schools, and asks about the club at the local colleges. Meanwhile, Suzie supposedly goes on about an hour, as if trying to convert a heathen."

"Sounds familiar," Patrick harumphed.

"Anyway, Joan spends the whole afternoon asking everyone who this Suzie Andrus is and promoting her Fellowship idea. People thought she was nuts. Fellowship? Suzie? Until Steve let us know Suzie is into this."

"No doubt."

"She made it pretty clear the rest of the week. You involved too?"

"No, I'm the lost sheep. Will she get the club on campus? It's important to her."

"I would think so. It's not the thing a Catholic school would look good stopping. Brother Kevin, who probably thinks having good-looking students on the Campus Ministry Leadership team will help him recruit others, and Mrs. Joyce are interested. They're going to a few meetings with Suzie to check it out. Besides, it's better than starting your 4-H club around here." Patrick laughed. "Now, don't get me wrong; the club's probably a good thing. I grew up near churches like that, not Catholic for sure, but giving people purpose and hope. I'm worried, though, that she's jumped all-in so fast."

"And left me all wet."

"That's between you two. Just don't let whatever's going on impact everything else."

"For sure. Not easy. Foley's in my face about going out with Saint Suzie or the Blessed Virgin Suzie. Those guys go for the jugular."

"Right." Brother Curt stood up to close the door and the blinds so he could light a cigarette. "They attack vulnerability and are damned good at spotting any. Maybe because they're vulnerable themselves despite the bravado. They shed others to protect themselves."

"Wish we could shed them. The school would be better off."

Brother Curt chuckled. "More tranquil, but I'm not sure better. I didn't exactly grow up on River Road. And I don't consider myself a bad person. In fact, a little adversity, including learning to deal with difficult people, can help. The real world isn't populated with all ... real Christians." Brother Curt smiled broadly at Patrick, who grinned in kind.

"That's what I've been telling Suzie, but she's decided she's going to convert them all."

"Anyhow, it helps to learn to face problems like this at school, where there's somebody around to pick you up. Having guys like Foley around's just as important as having Black, Latino, or Asian faces in the student body. You get prepared for a diverse world. And from the school's point of view, we've turned a lot of kids like him around over the years. But, when you make this public with your paper, it forces me to act in the open instead of handling it the way I wanted to with them."

"Sorry."

"Think about it. Maybe not too different from your reaction to Suzie's new interest. The fact that she's so open about it might bother you more than her beliefs."

"Huh?"

"Openness and honesty are fine. That's why I really like guys like you and T.R. and most kids in school. You're straight with me, and I get respect by being straight with everybody. Even Foley and them most of the time. Sometimes, though, truth hurts. You don't have to lie to avoid confrontations, but sometimes it's best to keep your mouth shut. Or your pen down."

"Listening to you makes me feel bad. I'm the one usually turning the heat down, and it's me stirring the pot. Maybe I should apologize to Sean and his boys."

"Apologize? They probably welcomed the publicity. I've told them I want word of this to die. Quickly. More importantly, I'm concerned about things in general. In fact, I left word for T.R. to join us. A week of detention for you, but I want to talk to you and him about the bigger picture, the 'us against them' attitude seeping in around here."

Almost on cue, T.R. strode into Brother Curt's office after a perfunctory knock. He fumbled with Brother Curt for the right handshake, but the Christian Brother didn't respond as playfully as he usually did. "Brother Curt!" T.R. blurted. "What's this summit conference about?"

T.R. waited out the ensuing silence, his mood shifting to match the others present. As if speaking at a funeral, Brother Curt said, "Well, gentlemen, I wanted you together to work out this problem around school. I've never seen the animosity ..."

"The what?" T.R. interrupted.

"The bad vibes. Hassles. Fights. Brooding. Bad feelings." Brother Curt added in a clipped tone as if angry T.R. didn't recognize the word. At the same time, he liked the fact that his protégé wasn't afraid to acknowledge with him when he didn't know something since it showed trust from a young male. "This is LaSalle. First week of school, and we've already had one fight ..."

"Not much of a fight," T.R. responded. "Foley cheap-shotted Sammie after an intramural game. Me and him, one on one, now that would be ..."

Jumping to his feet, Brother Curt demanded the floor: "Quiet, Tony. That's the problem. It's getting so there's only one way to change things around here, and it's not right. Where I grew up, changing things seemed hopeless. That's why I had friends getting recruited by the Crips and Bloods. Doing so offered togetherness but also some hope for change. There's no way I'm putting up with not being able to change things here."

"So, we do what?" Patrick hoped the question might soothe Brother Curt.

"Start with a meeting with Foley and them and you guys to bury the hatchet."

"In him?" T.R.'s remark pushed Brother Curt toward a five-minute rant.

Downshifting, he finally remarked, "Now, gentlemen, you can see this really bothers me. Let's do something positive."

"He's gonna try to get me about recruiting," T.R. murmured. "Even started calling me 'moneybags.'"

"And I hear you've gotten some shots in, too," Brother Curt interjected. "'Scumbag'? Your greeting to him?" T.R.'s face dropped toward his chest.

"What's this 'moneybags' thing?" Patrick asked. "If he's spreading lies and rumors, we can take that away from him."

"He's telling people I'm on the take. From Forte."

"Well?" Brother Curt sounded like a judge.

"He's talkin' trash. Even accusing my mother of getting paid."

"How is the recruiting going? Decisions?" Patrick's interest was more personal than professional, though what he would hear eventually appeared as an unconfirmed rumor at the bottom of a rambling Carl Schipper *Star* column.

"Not really. Pretty much decided on a school near this Coast, the A.C.C., or one near Chicago, D.C., or New York. Nothing definite."

"I remember when you were deciding to come here," Brother Curt mused. "I hope I had something to do with your decision. And that this one will be just as honorable."

"Right on. Me too. Coach is setting up a visitation schedule at school. For a few weeks, we'll just make initial contact with reps, like the end of last semester. Lucky. The C.I.F. just changed rules lessening contact through junior year. Went through a boatload of brochures and pamphlets over the summer. Doris helped. And, of course, there's always the regular college admissions people who visit campus for everybody."

Though this sounded good to Patrick, he registered a dim awareness that T.R. hadn't given the one-word answer that Brother Curt's challenge sought: "'Cept most admissions departments only mail stuff out when students request it, or they have captive audiences here. In your case, every coach in America is making the request for you."

"Yeah. Lots of recruiters and coaches showed up for summer league and camps. Just supposed to watch. No contact."

"Stick to that?" Brother Curt challenged.

"Some didn't at the camps, but I told them to contact Coach Burke."

"Not Forte?" Patrick's budding journalism career guided him to press a point.

"Hey, man. Whose side you on?" Ward screeched.

Patrick backed off, though still realizing he didn't get a straight answer. Brother Curt jotted a note.

Like a basketball player taking off on a fast break, T.R. turned the conversation back: "When you want us to meet with these guys? I'm back East on college visits the next two weekends."

"How about Monday after the first football game? That'll give us about ten days to see if it blows over." Brother Curt looked directly into the eyes of both young men. "And, like I told them, I better be satisfied you're trying. I'll talk with Sammie too. No getting even. No taunts. Already warned him once."

"What if Foley calls me 'nigger'?"

"Ignore him. I can tell you from experience you'll hear worse in your life. Remember that game up north when those rednecks taunted you unmercifully? They hoped to rile you so you'd lose focus or do something to get tossed. And they almost succeeded. You've got to learn that your manhood isn't on the line every time some ignorant ass challenges you. It takes more of a man to keep cool. Got it?"

Patrick felt the necessity to defend his friend: "He's done a good job. Turning the other cheek's not easy. Or always the best practice," he added. "Besides not letting these guys get to him this year, there was an incident at the River at the end of last school year when he had every opportunity to bust Foley up, and he let him off the hook. I don't know if I could've ..."

"Heard about it," Brother Curt concluded. "It's what I expect from you two."

9.

MID-SEPTEMBER
SENIOR YEAR

Patrick filed the following story after LaSalle's football opener:

Lancers Squeak out 14–13 Opener
By: Patrick Kiernan

The LaSalle Lancers traveled to the Wine Country last night, where they bottled up the Calistoga Cowboys to earn a hard-fought 14–13 victory.

The Lancers struck quickly, putting pressure on their North Bay League foe by jumping to a 14–0 halftime lead.

The home team, however, put the Lancers on the ropes, grinding out two fourth-quarter touchdowns, the second coming with just a minute remaining. Calistoga coach Gary Cannon elected to go for the win with a two-point conversion, but the Cowboys' big fullback, Tim Vermeil, failed to make the necessary three yards on a bolt off of left tackle. Led by Sean Foley and Franco Togneri, the stingy, though overworked, Lancer defensive line made the stop. After recovering the ensuing onside kick, LaSalle coaxed the final seconds off of the clock.

The two LaSalle scores resulted from big plays. Wes Solt broke an end run for a 39-yard score before the crowd settled in at the Napa County Fairgrounds. In the second quarter, the LaSalle defense, which gave up yards in the middle of the field but not much deep, came up with a big play. Sean Foley tipped a screen pass, plucked by Ralph Smith before it hit the ground. Smith rumbled for forty yards before being run down at the Calistoga three. Two plays later, Frank Tucci punched it over from the one. Jerry Jensen booted extra points after both TDs, the eventual victory margin.

To the delight of the home crowd, the second half was all Calistoga. Still, the pressured Lancer defense bent but didn't break. The Cowboys outgained the Lancers 348–222 yards. Wes Solt totaled 96 yards rushing, but Frank Tucci completed only three of nine passes for forty-seven yards in his debut as first-team signal-caller. Jim Allen averaged 39 yards on six pressure punts.

Coach Alex McEntee breathed a sigh of relief after the game: "I felt like Custer at Little Big Horn, but we held them off and will take it."

The following Monday's meeting took on epic proportions of a summit conference. Brother Curt began things, though Brother Charles, the long-time principal, and Ed Finley, the Dean of Studies and Assistant Principal, also attended. Patrick, T.R., and Sammie Spear flanked one side of the conference room's table while Foley, Togneri, and Smith sat across. A slouching Coach McEntee and ramrod-straight Coach Burke attended, though not lined up with their respective sides.

Coach Burke spoke frequently and politely, going out of his way to smooth over hard feelings between players on the two teams. Though almost visibly cringing when the subject came up, he said he would welcome Sean Foley on his team if he'd perform well at the tryout he'd set during the football team's bye week, closer to basketball season.

The carrot-topped Foley glanced at Ward triumphantly, as if he were extending an invitation for a future practice skirmish under the basket. He also turned to Patrick and nodded his head as if to thank him for the idea. T.R. started to protest, but Coach Burke cut him off.

T.R. later told Patrick that Coach Burke pulled him aside after to explain he thought things would go better this way. He'd have a say in Foley's behavior in the meantime, and later he could cut him if he proved disruptive. In any case, there'd be no whining about not getting a chance.

Coach McEntee, on the other hand, remained uncharacteristically uncommunicative throughout. He spoke begrudgingly when addressed. He did, however, have one incendiary speech prepared, summing up his players' gripes as if listing bullet points: "Ward should be playing football because the team, and therefore the school, needs athletes to step up. That's why Foley's sacrificing himself to play basketball. Second, the basketballers are courting too much publicity, especially during football season. And third, and I want to be careful wording this, I've been hearing unsavory allegations about certain members of the basketball team that could drive the school's reputation into the mud and blacken the reputation of my players and me, though we're clean as a baby's wiped bottom."

Patrick, noting that T.R. almost bolted from his chair, braced himself when McEntee chose the word "blacken." Nobody else, however, reacted, and the conversation moved on, with McEntee offering no specifics when others tried to pin him down. His players followed suit, remaining taciturn as McEntee parried requests for details. They looked like poker players holding buried winning hands.

Brother Curt, despite sharing his desire to get the situation resolved, ran up against Brother Charles' "happy babble." As if hoping to gloss over anything not right at school, the silver-maned principal repeatedly pontificated about the good character of the LaSalle man in general and all present in particular. To hear him tell it, the school was a cinch to go undefeated in both football and basketball, with each team forming a fan club for the other. He added, "The relationship of these two coaches is one of mutual respect, like a good marriage."

Burke later told Carl Schipper that he would have filed for divorce years ago if that had been the case. McEntee's comments would, no doubt, have been coarser. Even Ed Finley chuckled at that outlandish Brother Charles' statement. The meeting ended with another Pollyannish summation from Charles: "You'll all continue being model LaSalle students and win a lot of games in the bargain."

Brother Curt, obviously frustrated, halfheartedly agreed, though his tone differed markedly: "If anybody instigates anything that extends these ugly feelings and allegations, you'll deal with me. You could expect athletic suspensions or similar remedies."

The fact that the words rang out in the middle of football season, before the hoopsters suited up, didn't escape anybody's notice. Foley muttered to Togneri on the way out, "Better watch it. The spade's showing his true color."

That afternoon Patrick met Schipper to get his assignments: "Thursday and Friday nights, you cover the two football games, Loyola vs. Rancho and LaSalle against Placerville. I'll do the city league teams. Good?"

"Sure. At least I won't have to phone the stories in from a telephone booth on Calistoga's main street. Anything else?"

"Yeah. Give me a few minutes to finish this layout. Then, I'll take you to coffee." Patrick watched as Schipper deftly completed laying out a couple pages. "Okay," he announced, "let's go up the street. You have time, right?"

"Sure."

"Merle, I'm back in an hour. Check the jumps and look the layout over, will you?" Schipper scooped up a well-used attaché case and escorted Patrick out the door.

Schipper doused his coffee with cream and measured out two teaspoons of sugar. Watching this ritual, which had been played out repeatedly, Patrick wondered if blood or voluminous amounts of coffee concoction ran through the newspaperman's veins. Patrick sipped a Coke.

"How's school?"

"Okay. Mr. Wilson got all over me about the article the other day."

"He didn't like it?"

"He liked the article. He teased me about using 'off of'—no such phrase—instead of 'off' twice. And wondered about the *Star*'s proofreaders."

"First ever grammatical error in the history of the *New York Times* West," Schipper joked. "What about that meeting today. You guys get everything cleaned up and ... off of ... the agenda."

Patrick laughed: "No, we didn't get them ... off of ... our backs. It smacked of whitewash, so to speak. Charles was in rare form. He ought to be a politician."

"He is," Schipper stated. "You've been at functions when he's milking alums."

"Well, he looks like a principal. Brother Curt and Mr. Finley really run the school."

"You'd be surprised. Day-to-day operations, probably, but businesses reserve spots for people like Charles. People with juice in the community love the old man. Things done and undone at City Hall. Like Foley's old man who contracts lots of work from the city and state."

Patrick detailed highlights of the meeting. Schipper only seemed surprised that Burke committed himself to letting Foley have a path to making the team. He thought it would be hard to cut the Booster Club President's son if he did come out. The rest of the meeting, he thought, went predictably, even McEntee's silence.

"The old geezer's on to something. He gets that way when he's holding a lead in tight games. You were on the field with him in Calistoga. You notice? He sorta crawls into himself when he thinks he's holding the winning hand. He rants and raves when he doesn't."

"Thinking back, maybe you're right."

"Reading people's important in this profession. Not proof you can use, but it points you in the right direction to get the story, the truth. And speaking of the right direction, did Ward seem upset I leaked that rumor you gave me about him at the end of my weekly column?"

"No. Rumors are his norm. He has been unusually lowkey lately." Patrick sorted the ice at the bottom of his glass with his straw. "He flew east this weekend, and he's going to Chicago next weekend. Probably lots on his mind. He studies all week and is gone over the weekend. And the football guys have been focused on their games. Been cool since Foley cheap-shotted Spear."

Schipper got to his main point: "I want you to do a news/feature about Ward's two recruiting trips. Human interest. Maybe even front of the paper. Where'd you say he's going next weekend?"

"Chicago."

Schipper ordered and doctored another cup of coffee. "Notre Dame? DePaul?"

"Both. He's leaving Friday morning. He'll stay at Notre Dame until Saturday evening. Gets to see the Michigan State football game. That would impress anybody."

"Surprised DePaul's wasting a visit on a one-day stop. What do they show him to outdo that football game, an intramural basketball matchup?"

"Meeting the old coach would probably be impressive. I think T.R.'s eating lunch at his house Sunday before flying back. Besides, T.R. hates the cold. Don't think he'll go back east again. With no direct knowledge, that might tip his ultimate selection. Some like it hot."

"Maybe, too hot," Schipper responded. "I want to show you something." He reached into his bursting attaché case and fiddled in it for a while as Patrick worked on another Coke delivered to the table. Finally fishing out what he sought, Carl said, "Take a look at this."

Patrick glanced at the wire-service copy. "This one?" He pointed to a U.P.I. story marked with an asterisk.

"Yeah. It's about Ward. See there. Quoting a New York paper. Probably planted by a nameless school he visited last weekend. New York or D.C. Their A.D. claims he's leaning in their direction." Patrick skimmed the article as Schipper voiced highlights: "They quote an 'influential family friend' of Ward's as saying he's practically signed, sealed, and delivered."

Patrick looked up, troubled: "Forte?"

"My guess," Schipper replied clinically. "Unless they're completely blowing smoke, trying to keep the rest of the top twenty away. Though, I doubt they'd play with their reputation without somebody they could point a finger at if need be."

"What's this mean then?"

"Maybe nothing. Maybe everything."

"Your best guess?" Patrick dropped the paper as if it were too hot to handle.

"An educated guess. I called a friend at the phone company. Now, realize this is borderline and hearsay, so I'd deny it on the record. Not to mention protecting my friend. I verified Percy Forte completed three calls to D.C. over the weekend. Coincidence?"

Patrick stared in disbelief. He was becoming a character in a novel. The ramifications of the story about Forte warred with Patrick's shock at Schiffer's tactics to get information. Patrick tried to decide what troubled him most. "Really playing hardball, aren't you?"

"We. Big story," Schipper downplayed. "Relax. The phone calls don't prove nothing. Could be a friend. We would never use them. But things like that point me in the right direction to find things I can use or ask about. A timesaver. Be aware that this recruiting stuff is high-powered. Your rookie season might be in the big leagues. Up for that?"

Patrick slumped for a minute before sitting up rigidly. "So, what do you think? What's worst case?"

"Ward's in Forte's pocket. He visits these places so Forte can string them along, and maybe even some others he doesn't visit. But the big names are often bait. They're not where the payoff would come. Reputation's paramount to schools like Notre Dame or DePaul. It's the up-and-comers on the make you often need to watch for. The big dogs just make the payoff worth more. Basketball's the worst with recruiting because a few top prospects can turn a program around immediately or make sure one stays on top."

"Well, good to know you don't think every program's dirty. Thought you'd tell me Santa Claus doesn't exist. What sort of money are we talking about?"

"Off the record, an assistant coach claimed the going price is well above six figures, plus the sweeteners. And, of course, tuition and room and board and summer jobs in basketball camps. I'm just worried about Forte leading Ward down the path for his cut."

"Okay, that's worse case. Try another," Patrick pleaded.

"Well," Schipper considered, "maybe Forte's helping the family, and he's liking the spotlight and just pops off. On the train for a ride, but nothing illegal going on. Or acting on his own. Lots of possibilities. Maybe even keeping the kid's nose clean. I'm going to see him this week. Hush-hush, of course. He runs an office at the Redevelopment Agency, among other things. And, that way, I know he's in town this weekend and not flying separately to Chicago."

"You'd think you worked for the N.C.A.A. Or C.I.A."

"We have to know what's going on before anything pops. Don't want to lose this to the *Monarch* or the *Trib*. McEntee and Foley are tight with Ed Donovan at the *Trib*. I fear they'll run to him if they have anything. The guy has almost as many sources as me."

"Why? What good does it do McEntee?"

"Ask Jerry. Or, on second thought, don't. A little personal jealousy, maybe? He's old school. Maybe, he doesn't want too many Blacks in the school except a few to carry the ball, catch passes, and play on the corners. I think he's scared to death that Brother Curt's going to attract more African Americans. How do you think his coaching style would play then?

"Remind me I'm in high school."

"You're also in the real world, Patrick. Your choice. Do that story about Ward. Set it up this week and do it for next. Last weekend's visits and this one too. Get everything you can, but keep it fun and factual. His highpoints and impressions. Nothing we've discussed. I'll handle that stuff."

"Yeah."

"Okay? Problems?"

"Yes, but not about the assignment, though I'm not sure I knew what I was getting into."

"Hang tough. It's a helluva learning experience, and not just in a book."

"No lie. Think I owe myself a trip to the River."

"The River?" Schipper downed his coffee and squeezed his case closed.

"Yeah. It's where I sort things out." Patrick pointed to Schipper's stuffed case. "When I feel like that."

10.

LATER SEPTEMBER
SENIOR YEAR

Patrick interviewed T.R. two days after Ward's Midwest sojourn. T.R. insisted, somewhat testily, that he limit the article to the just concluded trip. Patrick wondered if this indicated a guilty conscience. Schiffer had informed him that Forte probably had nothing to do with the Chicago trip, though he had been quite evasive talking about the weekend before and his role in Ward's choices. The article ran in *The Star*, only edited slightly from Patrick's copy:

Dream Weekend
By: Patrick Kiernan

Imagine you're a high school senior. On Thursday, the most exciting thing that happens is your lunch-time Frisbee game. You're concerned about homework assignments and understanding the Constitution and Bill of Rights. Still, you can always catch up on the weekend.

On Saturday, however, you're sitting on the forty-yard line in South Bend, Indiana, a guest of the Notre Dame Athletic Department, to witness the Irish football team clash with the Michigan State Spartans. Your only cares center on whether you'll be fresh enough for the excitement planned in your honor the next day back in Chicago at DePaul.

Such was the experience of LaSalle's heavily sought hoopster T.R. Ward, who stepped back onto the confusing but exciting recruiting treadmill in earnest this past weekend, his second weekend visit east in a row.

Ward flew to Chicago directly from Sacramento. Though he had traveled to D.C. and the New York area the week before, Ward confessed he doesn't get a lot done on planes: "I planned to do homework, but I was too amped up and just watched a movie."

Notre Dame coaches met Ward and two other potential recruits at O'Hare Airport to shuttle them to the iconic campus on the other side of the city. Ward gushed, "Obviously, somebody put a lot of thought into details. I think they matched up the three of us purposefully. We got along well."

The first day on campus consisted of sightseeing: "The campus itself is beautiful. The Golden Dome stands out like our State Capitol Building. We also saw the dorms and athletic buildings." Accompanied by current Fighting Irish basketballers and assistants, Ward and his fellow prep roundball standouts attended a spirit-generating bonfire rally on campus. "It was like Rocky. Loud, like a Walkman blasting in my ears. Made me think about what it would be like to play for those fans. Coaches spoke of just that. We had football prospects with us, too, and got to meet some players who played the next day."

With the time change and excitement, Ward should have been exhausted. "I was so pumped, though, I hardly noticed." Saturday dawned crisp, clear, and sunny over Northern Indiana. "The Athletic Department must have arranged the football weather with God." Maybe, God had something to do with the game, too, since the Irish squeaked out a thriller. "We sat on the forty. The crowd was awesome. Even if I don't go to school there, I'll root for their football team ... unless a different school I'm playing for plays them."

That evening Ward returned to Chicago to get delivered

to DePaul. "It was all very friendly," Ward noted. "Even some joking. Since DePaul is called the Blue Demons, the Notre Dame people said they felt bad 'taking me to the Devil.' One of the DePaul people said he felt like James Bond, taking delivery of a person from 'the other side' before the Berlin Wall fell."

The evening stayed relatively lowkey at Ward's request: "I met and ran with some of the basketball players, but they had plans later. They would have included me, but I spent a quiet night resting. Good thing. Sunday was busy after church. Admissions and Athletic Department people accompanied me in a limo on a sightseeing tour of Chicago. They told me about the school and answered questions, selling the city as much as the university. I think they got alums to set things up. I felt like a head of state at the Hancock Building, Horizon Arena, and City Hall.

"The highlight of the day had to be dinner at Coach's house. There's no doubt either of those schools would be a good place to land." So goes the life, or at least the weekend, of a major college basketball Blue Chipper.

"Wired still, I didn't even sleep on the way home," Ward concluded, acknowledging how lucky he was to enjoy all this. "The only bummer of the weekend was finding out when I landed that my LaSalle football brothers dropped their game to Placerville Friday night without me rooting them on."

Patrick's suggestion to T.R., who agreed Brother Curt would appreciate it, prompted the last quote.

"Death of a Salesman," focused Mr. Wilson's class discussion the next day. "Can anybody," Mr. Wilson wondered, "compare the play's theme with another American classic?" After entertaining suggestions, the teacher turned to Patrick. "What about *Huck Finn*, Mr. Kiernan? You loved that one last year. Common themes?"

"What?"

"*Huck Finn* and Miller's play. Common themes. Remembering your fondness for Twain, thought you might impress the juniors with something meaningful."

"Sure." Patrick stalled while getting his mind and soul back from the River where they had drifted. "Mobility is important in both, though different."

"How?" Wilson wouldn't let his prized pupil off the hook.

"Huck finds freedom on his River, but Willy Loman is locked into his territory. It's his son Biff who's looking for the freedom Huck found." Needing more time to think the developing idea through, Patrick threw a curveball: "Course, if my name were Biff or Huckleberry, I'd probably stay on the move too."

The class rocked, but Mr. Wilson didn't like being one-upped on his stage: "Your actual point is interesting. Anything to add?"

Patrick's mind raced: "Another theme connects the two."

"What's that?"

"Selling. The great American profession. Huck was an amateur con artist, you know, always selling himself, the different roles he played."

"I do know, Mr. Kiernan, but half these ladies and gentlemen will be reading Twain next year. Make the point for them and refresh the rest of our memories."

Used to Mr. Wilson getting students to learn collaboratively, Patrick barely missed a beat: "Huck cons people. He recruits people to his side. Willy, on the other hand, is the con. He's not who he thinks he is. Less so than Finn, even when Huck's adopting a persona for the situation." Patrick smiled. "The way you say most teenagers do. And, Huck's not malicious, even with the Duke and the Dauphin, the scallywags he hangs with on the Mississippi."

"Example?"

"When he cons the two men who were going to search the raft and find Jim by making them think the hiding figure is his contagious father. He's a master salesman because he listens to and reads people. And stays good."

"Willy Loman?"

"With him, it's about 'being well-liked.' He's conned his sons.

Biff, at least, sees through him, even as he too becomes a con man when he says he's the Giants' quarterback to hit on a woman in a bar. Maybe America always produces con artists. Willy's selling something for somebody else. Not like his father, who traveled around in a cart selling the flutes he made himself."

Mr. Wilson began to steer the class in a different direction, but backtracked when other hands went up. "And the cart was like Huck's raft," Tammy Dickerson interjected. "Freedom. Mobility." Her excitement mirrored the rest of the class. "But, Willy's left with that old car that the boys polished to death. The one breaking down."

"Super!" Mr. Wilson wheeled to include the rest of the class in the challenge. "Great. Symbols now. The cart. The car. The raft. The flute. Other tie-ins between the two works? Mr. Kerwin?"

"The sneakers."

"Ah, the sneakers." Mr. Wilson savored the word. "What about the University of Virginia sneakers Biff wears? Seems headed there on scholarship. All-city football star. The sneakers symbolize his future glory. And then he burns them. Chucks his Chuck Taylors into the furnace as if he's giving away his life. Why?"

"He catches his father with that woman ... that buyer. You know that scene," Sean Foley, intelligent and well-read, though often hiding that outside of class, thundered, "where he's going to ... where he's just gone to ... the boneyard with her." He flashed a smile of satisfaction for finding what he thought was a suitable euphemism. "The one he gives the stockings to in that hotel room when Biff sees everything his father has taught him as a lie."

"Good point, Mr. Foley, though I might quibble with your phrasing. Can you tie that in with *Huck Finn*?"

"No." Caught up in the excitement of a moment, he didn't mind lateraling the thread of the conversation off. He had advanced the discussion toward the goal line.

Patrick raised his hand, feeling the way he did when he

swam in a muddy part of the River and hit the surface. Light then sight; the world clarified: "Burning his shoes mirrors the burning of Huck's letter, his soul. The famous line—'All right then, I'll go to hell!'—when Huck tears up the letter to Miss Watson telling her about Jim. He thinks he's doing wrong, and he is according to everything he's learned from his society, but he can't send it because 'it's a lie.'"

"Excellent."

"He's willing to burn in hell rather than betray Jim because he listens to his own experience. Biff, though, symbolically tosses the life Willy's taught him into the furnace. His scholarship. His athletic success. Everything."

"Powerful."

"The real world, Mr. Wilson." Patrick immediately dialed it back, realizing he sounded as if he were lecturing his mentor.

After the bell rang, Mr. Wilson kept Patrick for a minute before he left. After praising points his star pupil made and led others to, he intimated, "Almost seemed as if you were speaking personally. Need to talk?"

"Yeah, but later. That was refreshing, abstracted enough, but I still need to chew on things at the River. Maybe Huck will sail by. I'm worried about what's going into the proverbial furnace around here.

11.

LATE SEPTEMBER
SENIOR YEAR

Although Suzie wrote for *The Lance*, she didn't think it appropriate to write the article about LaSalle's Disciple Fellowship. Patrick volunteered, though without attribution. He frequently redrafted, tripping over tone, structure, and wording as he seldom did when writing for *The Star*:

Jesus Wants You!

LaSalle's newest club is unique. It is unlike the Block Club, Rally Club, or even the Games or Stamp Clubs. Like those, however, this club attempts to form a bond among students with like minds and focus, at the same time reaching out to others. The scope of this club, the newly chartered Disciple Fellowship, exists to save souls for Jesus Christ and model Christian behavior, especially through social justice outreach.

Its newly elected president, senior Suzie Andrus, who initiated and organized it at LaSalle, modeled it upon several college chapters that impressed her during the summer. "As far as I know," she stated, "we are one of three or four high school chapters in the state. Sacramento State, U.C. Davis, and American River Junior College have all helped us get off to a good start."

So far, the club, moderated by Brother Kevin and Mrs.

Joyce of the Religion Department, consists of about fifteen Lasallians. "A lot of others have shown interest," Andrus enthused. "We're not a cult. And we're definitely Catholic. We recognize, however, that Catholics today shouldn't be content to sit back and let others control Christ's message. We aim to be 'born again,' but only in the best sense of that phrase."

Andrus described herself as being a "Sunday Catholic" until this summer. "I attended meetings with my cousin Daphne and saw the power and love. I wanted to be part of it and bring the message to this place I love."

Andrus explained that the main "business" on campus will revolve around weekly meetings during which members give personal testimony. Andrus, heretofore most known around school for her drama stardom, pointed out it will be from these individual testimonies that the direction of the club will flow.

The Disciple Fellowship is already working with Father John, the school chaplain, to help orchestrate the school's second student body Mass. Besides testimonies and other campus activities, the club plans a service thrust into the larger community, individually and as a group. That's the component that really fires up Mrs. Joyce.

Some activities, though, might raise eyebrows. On Wednesday, a Marine recruiter will be on campus to talk to those interested in R.O.T.C., the Naval Academy, or post-graduation enlistment. The Career Guidance staff has invited military recruiters to campus along with college admissions reps for years. In response, however, the Disciple Fellowship Club will offer speakers on Thursday who will talk about draft registration counseling and alternatives to the military.

"In no way are we taking a stand against the military," Andrus emphasized. "We are not necessarily against draft registration, nor are we a resistance group, though, obviously, Catholics should have misgivings about war. Several members felt that, as a Catholic school, we should enjoy contrary

viewpoints besides those coming from military recruiters. I realize, especially with both Mather and McClellan Air Bases here, many students come from military families and see such vocations as service to God and country. We just think it's good to consider alternatives that may emphasize other values."

If Thursday's program does nothing else, it will call attention to the new group and its planned Friday activity. Festooned with recruiting signs ("Jesus Wants You!"), a booth in the plaza will be the place for students to "Register for Jesus." Though obviously not binding, or even a sign-up for the new club, the registration is meant to publicly "affirm openness to hearing the word of Christ" and play off male selective service registration.

Andrus wryly added, "Disciple Fellowship has no plans to draft at the present time. We'll be happy recruiting. If you're a human being, we figure God has chosen you already."

That evening Patrick discussed the story with his mother during dinner. "What do you think?"

"About the steak?" she joked. "Good story, Pat. A little long but good. What does Suzie think?"

"Generally liked it, but she found faults. She thinks it's too much about her, too little about the club. I told her she'll sell the club, but she doesn't buy that. Think she's worried about the reaction of fellow Disciple Fellowshippers getting jealous. Can you pass the sour cream?" Patrick scooped heaps on his baked potato.

"Most people would be flattered, even if they might not show it."

"Suzie's not most people these days, if she ever was."

"That doesn't sound encouraging. Nice to have you home more, but I liked it better when you were together, over there or here."

"She's really into this. And, I had *Star* stuff, which made school catchup important."

Sheila Kiernan sipped an iced tea, "Excuses?"

Patrick plowed on: "She thinks I editorialized at the end about the political thing."

"You think? Your bias does creep out."

"It was hard to write," Patrick admitted. "The plans for tomorrow and Friday do strike me as political."

"Obvious from reading your conclusion." Sheila Kiernan patted her stomach. "As obvious as this huge potato will be on my tummy."

"Come off it, Mom. Women your age would kill to look like you."

"Nice to say, but the trouble's that phrase, 'your age.'"

"When you dated that architect and went to the Fair with Suzie and me, Suze said she felt she was on a double date with an older sister."

"Love that girl, but, as you know, the dates have been few and far between. You going to listen to that speaker tomorrow?

"I'll drop by. I actually listened to most of the Marine recruiter's pitch today."

Patrick's mother arched her eyebrows. "Really?"

"Relax. I'd eat glass before I'd sign up." Sheila Kiernan sighed. "Just curious. He was effective. Wouldn't be surprised if he won a few converts today."

"Your football team friends?"

"You got it." Patrick pushed his plate away while his mother finished slowly, as if measuring each calorie. "They sell pride and camaraderie. Different recruiting programs now. Delayed enlistment. Special bonuses. Make it sound pretty attractive for guys not going to college even with worries about all the stuff brewing about Iraq and the Gulf."

"With the Air Force bases here, you'd think the Marines couldn't compete. Learn a job in that service branch, and it might translate to the real world. Not sure that typical Marine jobs translate. What about you? You did just register for the draft on your birthday, didn't you?

"For Jesus and the Disciple Fellowship?" Sheila Kiernan folded her napkin precisely while waiting for her son to become serious, but he persisted: "The N.B.A. draft?"

"Draft registration. Still the law."

"A crock, but, yeah, I took care of it. I do want to hear what's said tomorrow, if nothing else, as a contrast to today. I told Suzie to make sure she gets the right speaker. If she gets some guy who looks like he should be proselytizing in an airport terminal like one of those Moonies or Evangelicals, they might get laughed out of the auditorium." Patrick strode to clear the dishes before returning.

"Suzie's really busy with this, then?"

"Yeah, no time even to run for Homecoming Queen. She'd be a shoo-in. And it's not until the Loyola game later in October. I think she figures it would be too much like a beauty contest where the losers wouldn't feel good. Competitive. Unchristian with her new point of view."

"Stretching it a bit? I assume it wouldn't be like some meat rack Miss Universe."

"Agreed. I think other girls in the club are influencing her. You know how empathetic she is. Some of the others would have as much chance as T.R. or me."

"A little catty there. Shoo-in, you say?"

"Yeah, she's so popular she's probably the only one who could pull off this Disciple Fellowship thing without turning others off. No doubt she'd win. Not exactly a dog, either."

"Pat! That term's cruel."

"I said she wasn't."

"But implied others are. Wash the pots and pans tonight, and I'll dry. Have to keep my paws looking good."

"Funny," Patrick responded, filling the sink with dishes and silverware to rinse for the dishwasher.

"Still a bit rocky between you two?"

"Things will work out. She won't stay this enthused forever, and she's certainly worth waiting for. Not a bad time, really.

I've been busy too, covering games."

"This is high school. With *The Star* and everything, I don't want you to forget that. Plenty of time to be an adult later."

"Think I started early."

Sheila Kiernan gripped her son by the shoulder tenderly, surprising him as he turned from the sink. "I think you started a long time ago after your father left. What about college? Still aiming for Princeton?

"I guess."

"Not as enthusiastic as before."

"Want me on the other coast? All those hot architects you work with?"

"Please. I just thought the experience would be good for you. A whole new world."

"Relax. I'm kidding. Though, I always tell you to accept those invitations you're probably always getting for wild weekends."

"With the girls?" Sheila Kiernan started drying pots and pans and putting them in their cabinet.

"Hardly. Tennessee Williams would think you'd have many 'gentleman callers.'" Patrick's mom blushed like a schoolgirl. "I really like this new job, and I've always liked where we live. I'll still apply to Princeton and other Ivies, but I've really thought about Bezerkeley lately. And I don't know where I'll get accepted. At least at Bezerkeley, you probably wouldn't have to worry about Marine recruiters getting to me. Don't think they've been allowed in the city since Vietnam. When you were a young hippie, no doubt."

"I beg your pardon, young man." Mrs. Kiernan's feigned indignant reply barely camouflaged her joy. They finished up the dishes and put away leftovers. "I'm glad we can talk like this, Pat. Whatever you do ..."

"I know, Mom. The trouble is sometimes I don't know what to do. You should have seen Sean Foley with the Marine recruiter today. He looked like he had found God. I sometimes wish things could be that simple for me."

12.

FIRST OF OCTOBER
SENIOR YEAR (TWO DAYS LATER)

"Put it in writing," Brother Curt told Patrick. "Something I can refer to while cleaning this mess up."

"I'm not an objective source," Patrick protested.

"A close as I've got. Pretend you're reporting on a story and divorce yourself from your loyalties the best you can. You did pretty well in last night's game story after we got pasted by twenty."

"Want it Monday?

No, right now. No story. A list. Yesterday and today. You're not covering a game this afternoon, are you?"

"No. Loyola against St. Mary's in Stockton tonight."

"Good. Write the list for me. I'm going to sort the main participants away in different places to grill separately." Patrick wrote the following:

(Yesterday)

1) The three speakers D.F. lined up began presentations in the auditorium right after school;

2) About fifty people showed to start, with more drifting in while a few others drifted out;

3) The first speaker from State was somebody I met before with Suzie. Andy Hill. Decent guy, and an effective speaker, though a bit intense like a lot of those people. He's handsome, which a lot of the girls noticed;

4) The two older speakers were from the community. A woman lawyer was compelling. The other, a guy, supposedly had been involved in anti-draft stuff for years, even when there wasn't mandatory registration. Soft-spoken and a bit effeminate, maybe not a good choice for LaSalle, at least for "the remnant";

5) Sean Foley came in about halfway through his speech. He listened for a while and then started popping off;

6) At first, he asked questions, some even intelligent, though the floor hadn't been opened for them yet. He gradually became Sean Foley in-your-face obnoxious;

7) Apparently, he was on his way to the gym for a team meeting. Gets intense in football mode;

8) Luckily, the rest of his gang wasn't with him;

9) He bullied his way into dominating the conversation. Questions became statements. He did everything but sing the Marine hymn;

10) Nobody stood up to him until Andy and Brother Kevin asked him to leave. Did you talk to Kevin about it? See him for background;

11) Foley raised a ruckus but finally left. Suzie was crushed. The meeting never returned to normal.

(Today) The roof fell in!

Brother Curt returned to his office to find Patrick staring at the paper. "Finish?"

"For yesterday, but today's too raw." Brother Curt looked over Patrick's paper.

"The roof fell in! I hope that's not factual. I know this isn't easy for you with everybody involved, but I need your help. Suppose you just talk through today. I'll take notes, even try not to interrupt. Backtrack to questions I have when you're done."

Tired and distracted, Patrick tried to relate the day's events. His voice cracked occasionally, and Brother Curt had to ask him to speak up a couple times. His story:

"I came to school early. Without a lot of sleep after finishing my game story. I guess a lot of people came tired and angry today after the game, which probably started people on edge. I helped Suzie set up her booth while club members put up signs to remind students to 'Register for Jesus' and tell them where to find the booth.

"Suzie was still fried about Foley's commandeering the meeting the day before, though the adult speakers told her after it wasn't that uncommon. I reminded her most of the meeting had been good. She mentioned that Andy might come by to help since he could man the booth when she and others were in class. She cleared that with Kevin.

"The signup went well before school. A good crowd gathered. T.R. and Doris and Sammie and Lance Hall and even Frank Tucci darted around like sheepdogs bringing in strays to support Suzie. Amazing that Tucci could even stand up after the beating he took in last night's game.

"That's when Sean and his boys showed up. He said hello to everybody, even T.R. and Sammie. Then he talked to Suzie. He told her he was sorry if she thought there had been a problem yesterday, that he just felt strongly about the Marines, and he felt the last speaker was taking a shot at the military. He babbled about how his father's Air Force experience set him on the path to success. Ironic since he usually puts down his father.

"I thought things were okay as I hovered nearby. He said if he hadn't been so preoccupied by that night's game and getting to the gym, he would have waited to ask his questions. Mrs. Joyce practically fell over herself, trying to believe him.

"He joked about the registration list, even asking if God would change the football team's luck if he was on His team too. When he scrawled his signature, other players paraded to sign too. The first bell rang. I walked away, thinking I had just lived a dream. The nightmare came later.

"As planned, Andy stayed in the booth taking signups between classes and even catching stragglers out in the plaza between or during classes. He didn't have classes himself that morning or bagged them. By the time I met Suzie there at lunchtime, she was ecstatic. They had signed up over fifty percent of the student body. Most probably saw it as a lark.

"The boys came back. Some of the girls were flirting with Andy, quite the attraction. That's when Foley whips out his 'Recruiting for Bacchus' paper. Mocking what Suzie's group was doing, he had come up with this alternative in homage to the mythological god of wine and revelry. At least his loyalty there was honest, homemade sign and all.

"At first, I thought it would be a joke he'd quickly relinquish. Maybe, even funny. He pursued it, though, the way he pursues most things, head down and full speed ahead like a Coach Mack run up the middle.

"If he's really doing a delayed jarhead enlistment, it should be as an officer. He totally manipulates the rest of those guys. Soon, they're headed everywhere on 'recruiting missions for Bacchus.' And, of course, thinking it's funny or because they were intimidated, ninth- and tenth-graders signed in droves.

"Sean stayed just across from Suzie's booth, taking his signups and keeping his presence spotlighted. He spouted off about the 'big initiation' his club would throw at the River.

"We still might have been saved by the bell with the whole thing blowing over, but just before seventh period, Sean saunters over to ask Suzie and everybody to sign his list. I refused, 'pussed out' in his words. I probably should have exerted myself more to step in, but I was trying to live up to what you had told T.R. and me about deescalating things.

"He kept pestering club members, almost to get Suzie's attention. Suzie's near tears.

"I don't think I was afraid to step in. Not physically. Maybe morally. It's hard to stand up for a group I equate with Bible-toting 'born-agains.'"

"She calls it a Catholic Disciple Fellowship," Brother Curt interjected, allowing Patrick to come up for air for a few seconds. Patrick continued his narrative without missing a beat. "Suzie was into it. God, she was it. Regardless, she was upset, and I should have done something.

"Things ratcheted up when Andy, this story's Prince Charming, came over. He made a stand for Suzie and Disciple Fellowship. Foley called him an outsider who didn't belong on campus. He made some remark about turning the other cheek and practically mooned him. People gathered.

"I tried to calm Suzie, to no avail. I don't know what Andy said, but Foley decked him with one punch. Andy fell like a diver doing a back flip. T.R. jumped in. He had a righteous cause. It was suddenly morally right to take his revenge on Foley. He spun Sean around as if spinning a top. The first punch to Foley's midsection doubled him up. Mrs. Joyce, the Service Club, and faculty prefects clustered near, but nobody had the nerve to step in. This wasn't a schoolboy fight judging by the rage on T.R.'s face.

"The next punch, an overhand windmill, landed on the back of Foley's head, driving him toward the ground as if he were a railroad spike. Foley, sprawled out, amazingly gathered himself enough to go for T.R.'s long legs, scissoring them so that the two grappled on the ground. It then became Foley's wrestling match until about ten people waded in to separate them. Foley had bit, scratched, kicked, and flailed the way he probably does beneath a pile on the gridiron.

"A bunch of people finally pulled the combatants off. Foley had gotten rocked, though he pretended not. Sammie rushed up to high-five T.R., but he shook it off. Sean had fooled him, having something left after taking his best shot.

"Suzie tended to Andy. I thought the Disciple Fellowship might have its first martyr. Feeling jealous made me feel guilty. That's when you showed up, breathing fire."

"Yeah, the roof fell in." Brother Curt shook his head. "No

questions for now. No answers either. Remember, you acted the way I told you to act."

"Not much consolation. What are you going to do?"

"Don't know yet, but after making threats, I have to follow through. I'd toss Foley, but I know Charles won't let me. Sort of like your problem. Wanting to do something but being constrained by someone else. Shouldn't be speaking out of school."

"Can I go now? Think I need a nap before Stockton tonight. Or maybe a cry."

"Cry some for me, too. Don't think I'll have time this weekend."

Leaving school, Patrick found Suzie in the nurse's office with black-eyed Andy Hill. Brother Kevin and Mrs. Joyce grouped around as if they could blot out the reality of the day's events. The biggest black eye of the day belonged to the school.

Andy insisted he was fine, though Brother Kevin convinced him to verify that in an emergency room. Suzie appointed herself driver of Andy's car while Brother Kevin indicated he would follow to drive her back.

Walking to the parking lot, Patrick cornered Suzie alone: "Don't let it get to you. The club made a fine showing. Foley just made an ass of himself."

"And paid the consequences," Suzie smirked. "T.R. got him bad after what he did to Andy."

"You sound glad. I would've done something, but was afraid it didn't exactly go along with Disciple Fellowship principles."

"We're 'born again,'" Suzie snapped, "not cowards. Standing up for what's right is part of the deal. I need to go with Andy. I'll talk with you tomorrow." She turned to walk away and then spun back. "I guess you were right. Maybe this week was too political." Being right didn't offer Patrick much solace.

13.

EARLY OCTOBER
SENIOR YEAR (4 DAYS LATER)

Patrick's first draft for *The Star* provided more details, but Carl Schipper thought it ill-advised, though Foley was over eighteen, to provide too much information about a student's suspension. It appeared this way:

Lancer Captain Out Two Weeks
By: Patrick Kiernan

Sean Foley, LaSalle's starting offensive guard and co-captain, will miss the next two games because of a school-imposed suspension.

Brother Curt Davis, F.S.C., the school's vice principal and Dean of Men, announced the penalty.

Brother Curt noted that the suspension will keep Foley out of the Lancers' last non-league game against Sacred Heart Cathedral of San Francisco and the league opener against American. Foley should return, however, in time for the second league game, the traditional contest against archrival Loyola.

That early evening, Patrick visited T.R.'s South Sacramento house, ostensibly to watch a baseball playoff game between the Pirates and Reds. Both quickly grew bored, however, and

T.R. switched to the station which regularly broadcast Kings' games during the season. A program came on previewing and hyping the upcoming NBA campaign, which would start the first week in November.

Following the Kings was not for the faint of heart. They had finished a lackluster seventh in the Pacific Division the past season while just 90 miles away, the exciting Warriors featured the wonderfully captivating Run-TMC show—Tim Hardaway, Mitch Richmond, and Chris Mullin.

T.R.'s NBA stars to emulate included Karl Malone, David Robinson, Hakeem Olajuwon, and the undersized Charles Barkley, all featured in the program with highlights that wowed him. The show, though, dwelled on Michael Jordan's Chicago Bulls. T.R. loved watching MJ footage. He called him "the best." And both T.R. and Patrick relished seeing highlights of nearby Elk Grove's own Bill Cartwright, Chicago's center, as he subtly flashed innumerable skills to help Jordan and his Bulls win.

Ward's mother provided snacks after getting home from work. T.R.'s three younger brothers popped in and out, though they spent most of their time outside on the browned front lawn.

T.R.'s voice came from somewhere deep within the lap of the old brown armchair in which he had sunk: "Good you kept my name out of the article. What do you think about Foley's punishment?"

"Bet Curt would have canned his ass, but Charles wouldn't let him. One last chance. Coming back for the Loyola game's a master touch. Foley's gonna be so fired up he'll probably single-handedly tame those Wildcats," Patrick concluded. "Publicly punish him, but not enough to ruin the season. With your detentions, Charles can think of it as a wrap. Maybe, McEntee's the one who won the point here."

"Nah, think it's Charles. Old man Foley must have that dude on payroll. Maybe a new cafeteria or something courtesy of Foley Construction. Or more flower gardens."

Patrick, sitting in the straight-backed chair he had moved

from the kitchen, laughed. "Probably right. Sometimes I think the whole world's on the take."

A knock, whining of the screen door, and high-pitched squeal announced Percy Forte's presence. "What's hap'ning, Brother?" Forte turned his machine gun talk toward Patrick: "How ya' doin', man?" Gladhanding Patrick like a politician, Forte kept babbling while throwing himself onto the sofa.

Forte and Patrick established they had met before. Patrick was struck again how Forte very much reminded him of the character Jody Starks in Zora Neale Hurston's *Their Eyes Were Watching God*, which Mr. Wilson had taught. In the novel, the protagonist Janie's second husband wants to be the "big voice" in his all-Black town.

Mrs. Ward charged into the room. She fawned over Forte the way recruiters did over her son and Janie did over Jody at first in the novel. T.R., however, had remained fixed on the couch during the elaborate greeting ritual. Finally, he came to life, unfolding himself from his sanctuary. "Percy, got to talk," he implored.

"Fire away, man. Truckin' to a Frisco meeting. The Caddy's horses are fed and wantin' to run." Patrick stole a quick glance out the window at the white Caddy, which had attracted a crowd of youthful admirers beyond T.R.'s three brothers. Forte, decked out in a well-tailored suit with a white shirt and conservative tie, looked like a banker or a broker. "What ya be needin'?"

"In my room. Don't want to distract Patrick from his beloved Kings." Patrick smirked. "By the way, he's the guy I told you 'bout who writes for *The Star*. Remember?"

"Like it is." Forte turned to Patrick as T.R.'s mom retreated to the kitchen. This time his small, dark eyes measured him. Finally, he smiled, a flash of gold visible among his white teeth. "With Carl Schipper, huh?"

"Yeah. Carl's Sports Editor," Patrick squirmed.

"Met him recently." Forte seemed on the verge of offering an opinion but then wheeled to T.R.: "Let's talk. Hoping to hit

Eli's Mile High in Oakland after my meeting to groove on some good blues."

Patrick mindlessly watched television. Loud voices sent shouts through the still, humid air in the tiny box-like house. Though T.R.'s small room, which he shared with Otis, his twelve-year-old brother, was two rooms removed, voices rang out. Patrick considered turning the TV sound down to make out words, but as he started to do so, Mrs. Ward reentered the room. "Hotter than blazes. Be nice to have air conditioning instead of that broke-down fan."

Pretending he had stood to stretch, Patrick reclaimed his seat. "Glad I'm not dressed like Mr. Forte. Pools of sweat would run off me."

"Honey, pools of sweat run off me when I looks at that man," Mrs. Ward boomed earthily. "And he's advising Tony with the college thing. Quite a man!"

"With the recruiting?" Patrick tentatively asked.

"Advising. He thinks he knows everybody and everything, and he's not all that wrong."

Later, after Forte left, amidst hugs from T.R.'s mom, a sulking T.R. and Patrick went outside, where the younger kids had cleared away as fast as the Caddy's driver had whizzed it toward the freeway.

T.R. didn't waste any time: "Told me something's coming down. Worries me."

"What?" Patrick asked.

"An article tying him to me in the *Trib*. That guy Donovan saw him today. All over Percy's back about stuff. You really watching this highlight show or want to shoot some hoops?"

During the two-block walk to the court, the rat-a-tat-tat of the basketball on the hot pavement helped soothe T.R. Upon arrival, he raced straight toward the basket and unleashed a deadly dunk that crashed through the chain "net." His blood-curdling whoop accompanying his slam stirred the air.

14.

EARLY OCTOBER
SENIOR YEAR (THE NEXT DAY)

On his way to school the next morning, Patrick dropped a note off for Carl Schipper:

Carl,

With T.R. last night. Thought you should know something's up. Think Donovan at the Trib's going to print something today tying Forte to T.R.

Forte dropped by T.R.'s house while I was there. After, T.R. told me Forte said Donovan's been all over him for a few days. Donovan showed Forte a draft of a piece he's running, today, I think.

Filtered through T.R., Forte maintains it's short on fact but loaded with rumors, hints, and innuendoes. I'm guessing Percy said it was filled with something else. He did tell Donovan he had no comment. Think maybe you ought to contact Forte after reading the article. Maybe, he'll talk to you. Can't imagine him staying silent without blowback.

I'll come by right after school,
Patrick

When Patrick dropped by, he saw Schiffer bouncing around the newsroom like a Game Boy figure gone wild. "Can't believe they printed that. It's devoid of facts. Even if Forte and Ward are up to their foreheads in dirt, the article is still irresponsible. *National Enquirer* stuff. Typical Donovan," he fumed. "Never checks sources and leaves readers more questions than answers. And he beat us to this. That infuriates me. It's our story."

Patrick winced but said, "You can probably get an exclusive with Forte now. He almost has to talk and won't go through Donovan."

"I have a call in. Where's Ward? How's he taking this?"

"He was in Burke's office when I left. Brother Curt with them."

"Good. Merle, keep trying to get Forte for me," he shouted. "At home or his office. Keep phoning, and if you get him, don't take 'no' for an answer. Patrick, phone LaSalle for me. Better chance of you getting through. Ask for Jerry. I bet he gets Forte to come there, and I want to be there too. At least McEntee won't be in the A.D.'s office. He's got practice. God, I'd like to nail him if he primed the pump for Donovan."

"Ahead of you. Talked to Coach Burke before I left and asked him to phone here around three thirty. He said he would. Even earlier if Forte shows up before. What time is it?"

"Three twenty. Good work. Stay near the phone and be ready to dial immediately at three thirty. Sweet talk your way past whoever answers. Don't want Jerry getting hung up and forgetting us. This is ours. If I had been thinking, I would have had you stay there on top of things. You were at Ward's last night?"

"Stuff's getting to him. They even pulled the phone off of the hook." Patrick pondered correcting his usage but plowed on: "The recruiters were driving them crazy even before this went public. You can't discount that the family needs somebody like Forte, or they'd be overwhelmed."

"He's got Jerry. Is he on the take?"

"T.R.? Can't believe that."

"I meant Forte."

"As far as T.R. says, no. But he did admit Forte has been talking to people. Testing the market, as he says. He doesn't think money's changed hands, though he's been doing odd jobs Forte's arranged since summer at pretty good pay. But he has done the work. I don't want T.R. going down. That's my main concern," Patrick emphasized.

"What about LaSalle's season? The season of glory. Jerry must be livid. My money says he tries to get Forte out of the process entirely. Even if everything's been up-and-up."

"I wish somebody'd get McEntee too."

"The old man's clever. Probably threw mud, but he's sitting back now washing his hands."

"Like Pilate." Just before 3:30, Jerry Burke phoned. Patrick dutifully handed the phone to Schipper.

"Yeah, Jerry, read it. Forte there? Good. He's got to get his side out just right. I'm your man. Keep him there." After a pause: "I'll help you and the school with statements and releases and how best to get them out. And other *Star* writers can do a drumbeat with follow-ups the days after mine appears if I get what I want with Forte. Maybe, get Wilson to help with the releases. And don't talk with other papers. I'll bring Kiernan back with me. This will get play beyond our region."

Patrick marveled at a pro taking charge. Schipper seemed concerned with everybody's interests while not forgetting his own.

The meeting went well. At first, Forte vented about suing the *Trib*, but eventually, Schipper impressed upon him that, though the article suggested improprieties, Donovan worded the piece carefully enough to avoid libel. The best way to respond to the article, Schipper reiterated, especially considering it contained implications rather than charges, was to refute them in a more reasonable forum, a.k.a. *The Star*.

Brother Curt and Jerry Burke demanded an accounting in full from Forte. T.R. sat silently throughout.

Forte emphasized his role remained the same as when he helped steer T.R. to his high school choice. Even then, he stressed, public school coaches screamed when they lost Ward.

He looked to Brother Curt to acknowledge he'd simply acted as an advisor, helping somebody in his neighborhood to inspire many. Financially, he said, his most important role came in convincing the LaSalle Boosters Club to pick up 90% of T.R.'s LaSalle tuition. This, even though the powerful group of alums and parents almost always limited assistance to less than 50% to spread more money among more kids.

Brother Curt explained to Schipper the group made the exception not because T.R. was a star but because Forte convinced them that working for the rest of his tuition wouldn't be viable as easily as for other kids. He would need to contribute money he made working off-season to his family and would be too busy with practices to work during the season at a job with regular hours.

Only because of this arrangement, Forte underscored, could T.R. have attended LaSalle. Besides working summers at the Mullan ranch, T.R. was employed by a contractor friend, Forte admitted, who owed Forte a favor or two. "He does the work," Forte blurted. Looking at Burke, he continued, "Tony files, bills, and stuff like that so that within limits, he can set his own hours, even working some at home. Not during practice, Coach."

Forte claimed he was just handling calls and things for T.R. and his mom. Sure, he'd ask about jobs at the prospective college for spending money and other legal perks, such as availability to tutors and advisors, but nothing underboard. "Basically, I act like the kid's father would if he was in the picture." He drew a look, however, from those present when he quickly added, "A few people from different places may have sent money in his name to South Sac youth funds, but that was their choice to help neighborhood kids."

Despite Forte's protestations, Burke won the day. To avoid any "bad look," T.R. would cut himself off entirely from Forte going forward. Forte agreed only when Brother Curt convinced him it was in T.R.'s best interest, he'd act as a father figure with the family, and Burke would spearhead recruitment to take as much pressure off the family as possible. Forte muttered about the racist efforts to separate African American families from the community leaders that could protect them, but eventually, he agreed.

The statements formulated, from Coach Burke, Percy Forte, and T.R. Ward himself, made the same points: 1) No laws or N.C.A.A. rules were broken; 2) Allegations in the *Sacramento Tribune* story were false; 3) Nevertheless, to avoid further harassment of Ward, his family, Forte, LaSalle or its basketball program, Ward would quit all jobs having anything to do with Percy Forte, directly or indirectly. All, however, pointed out how unfair it was that "irresponsibly published rumors" would rob a family of the counsel of a respected community leader and a young man of money he could earn to help his hard-working mother. Forte started smiling again when realizing the imminent stories might transform his role from villain to victim.

Schipper's initial story, focused on Forte, would play up his community importance and brush off past allegations, for example, concerning his relationship with the "Taft Terrific," Cy Williams. Though tempered by Schipper, Forte's quotes did feature phrases such as "recruiting vultures," "biased newspapermen who probably never set foot in South Sac," "scandal-mongers," "journalistic jerks" and "dirt devils." Forte did express complete faith that Coach Burke would make the best of the situation for T.R. and his family.

The next day's article, focused on Burke, mandated that going forward all college recruiters and reps would only contact Ward through him. All calls to Ward's home would be unanswered, and the family number would be changed. Since this was what Burke had pushed for all along, he figured he secretly owed his adversary McEntee for this imprimatur on "my plan from the start."

The last article, for the third day in the news cycle, was going to be Patrick's T.R. interview. Schipper insisted this should appear last so that T.R. could have the last word. T.R. also had the last word at the meeting. "What about McEntee? He leaked this to the *Trib*." Everybody spun toward him as if he had lighted a cannon fuse.

"Strong accusation," Brother Curt boomed. "You sure?"

Even Coach Burke gulped. Later, Carl Schipper solemnly told Patrick, "That's when I knew we were playing hardball."

T.R. charged ahead as if going for an unmolested dunk: "Donovan phoned last night. With everything happening, I answered. After you left, Patrick. He read me the article and wanted my reaction. I strung him along like a foxy lady at a dance. And then he said it. He'd deny it, but he told me his source—McEntee."

"Good for us to know, Tony, but he's right. He'll deny it, and you can't prove it," Brother Curt said.

"Yeah?" Ward whooped. "I got it on tape." Primitively recorded, Donovan's words would never be admissible in a court of law, but they spoke loudly in the court of public opinion present.

Percy Forte laughed gleefully. "My man, I underestimated you, but not as much as McEntee did. We got his sorry ass now."

15.

ALMOST MID-OCTOBER
SENIOR YEAR

Carl Schipper thought his protégé caught the right tone in his *Star* article spotlighting T.R.'s response:

Blue Chipper T.R. Ward Responds to Allegations
By: Patrick Kiernan

"Basically, it's my decision to pick a ticket [school] right for me. Percy [Forte] was just helping me and my family, new to things like this. He knows the world well, and he knows my family. It was only right he help," explained T.R. Ward, LaSalle High School's heavily recruited and suddenly beleaguered Blue Chip collegiate basketball prospect.

"Giving up Percy as an advisor is a hardship, but I know the score. If I must go it without him, I will, though it's unfair. It'll just be me and my family and Coach Burke, who outlined recruiting procedures that will be followed. We tried this approach before, but it didn't stop recruiters from blitzing my family. This time, we'll make it work. If schools don't cooperate, they'll have whistles blown on them."

Ward's remarks followed published rumors in another metropolitan paper that implied Forte, a South Sac community leader, intended to arrange an illegal deal for Ward at a college recruiting him. Ward categorically denied the insinuations:

"They're groundless." In this, he echoed Percy Forte, interviewed two days ago in The Star.

"The only important basis of fact in that article was that I hold my friendship with Percy Forte highly. The man is a positive driving force in Sacramento's Black community. Some people probably hate to see a successful African American. They take shots.

"He practically singlehandedly collected funds to build our area's Meadowview Community Club a couple years back. The suggestion that he's personally on the take is ridiculous.

"Though my mother works hard to support my three brothers and me, anybody who checked facts or even visited my house would see we are not living in the lap of luxury."

Ward sees Forte as a sacrificial victim: "I will not associate with Percy Forte until I announce a collegiate choice after basketball season." Ward emphasized that he hopes those responsible for the misplaced allegations have second thoughts: "I agree with Coach Burke. We have to do this for the good of the program and my future, but I regret that those whose own lack of scruples are on display can question Percy Forte, a real community asset."

Patrick met T.R. in the hallway at school that morning. "Hey, man," T.R. roared. "Appreciate your article. It's right on."

"Basically, what you said," Patrick downplayed. "Just fiddled with language a little. You hear?" he asked excitedly.

"What?"

"On the sly, but I hear they crucified McEntee. To save face, nothing 'til after the season, but he's on the way out."

"As A.D.?" T.R.'s eyes widened.

"Even football coach. Curt prevailed with Charles. That tape of yours got him. *Adios* after the season. If he doesn't resign completely, he'll just be a regular teacher. We've promised to keep the reasons out of *The Star*, and in turn, he's promised not to go to Donovan to spin his story his way. At the end of the season, McEntee will just announce he's tired of the grind. How'd you get it on tape?"

"I'd been talking to Doris and played her a Luther Vandross cut I had taped. That's why I had the recorder near the phone. Kept him going a long time. He wanted a rebuttal from me bad."

"To claim both sides were heard while hoping you'd say something that would come back to bite you."

"He bit, not me. When he told me McEntee was the source, I had him repeat it. I squinched my ear down with my little tape recorder and taped other things to make sure there was no doubt who was talking. Not bad, huh? Like that Sherlock Holmes dude."

Patrick tried to picture T.R. wearing Sherlock regalia, but the image only made him chuckle. "Now you can play basketball instead of worrying about this garbage."

"It's football season, man. Still gotta play that out. You going to the Homecoming Dance Saturday? Got to make sure Doris and I have a few friends if we go."

"I'll be there. Just hope it's with Suzie."

"Still hanging some with that college dude, Andy?"

"The club, she says. Maybe you should have let Foley waste him more before you stepped in to save his ass."

"Feel 'born again' myself. Hopin' to have a little action over my place after the dance. Can you two come?"

"Sure, and bring Andy?" Patrick elicited a hearty laugh from T.R.

"Yeah, don't think it's the night for us to go to the River. Not sure I ever want to see that place again," T.R. voiced.

16.

PAST MID-OCTOBER
SENIOR YEAR

Patrick considered why LaSalle scheduled its Homecoming Dance the night after the Loyola game. He assumed the tradition began when Lancer gridders typically held the upper hand over their archrivals. As Patrick's *Star* article noted, things had changed drastically:

Wildcats Pounce on Lancers
By: Patrick Kiernan

For the eighth time in the last ten meetings, Loyola defeated the LaSalle Lancers, 20–7, last night at the Wildcats' Carmichael field.

With the win, the Wildcats remain undefeated in league play after two games while pushing their season record to 5–1. The Lancers, who edged American last week in their league opener, fell to 2–4 overall.

LaSalle led 7–6 when the final quarter began, but Wildcat QB Pete Fatooh riddled the Lancer secondary, striking for two scores. He threw five yards to flanker Bob Meadows for one touchdown and hit speedy Ed Hughes for the backbreaker from forty-seven yards away.

The Wildcats scored first in the opening quarter. Todd Ellington recovered a blocked punt and took it the final fifteen yards. The LaSalle front wall, however, led by co-captain

Sean Foley, just returned from a two-game suspension, rushed through to block the conversion attempt.

The inspired Lancers' offense, otherwise contained throughout the balmy evening, took the ensuing kickoff and marched seventy-three yards to score. Wes Solt swept the right side for the final six yards. Jerry Jensen booted the ball through the uprights to provide the lead LaSalle would grudgingly relinquish late.

The Wildcats piled up three hundred and twenty-eight yards of total offense to the Lancers' two hundred and fifty-two. Fatooh completed twelve of twenty-one pass attempts for 197 yards, while his LaSalle counterpart, Frank Tucci, connected on eight of seventeen for 102 yards.

The Wildcats won the game in the trenches. Winning Coach John Murray noted, "We gave Fatooh time to spot receivers. Tucci, on the other hand, hung in gamely, but our rush prevailed when their line tired in the fourth quarter. Their linemen go both ways, and four of our five sacks came late."

Lancers' Coach McEntee did single out Foley, particularly on defense: "Good to have him back. He bottled up everything up the middle, but by the end, he might have needed smelling salts for the rest of his linemen."

The Homecoming Dance mirrored the school's subdued mood. Few football players attended. The local band, falling under the gathering's spell, appeared to be going through the motions. Even its intent to cover an M.C. Hammer number proved inept. Between the second and third sets, Chet Howard took the microphone to introduce the Homecoming Queen, Shirley Harrison. She looked unnerved by the short speech she was to make after the princesses and escorts were announced and assembled onstage. "Her voice sounds shot," Patrick whispered to Suzie just after Shirley exchanged greetings on her way up the steps.

"From leading cheers at the rally and game. She still plans

to say some things to pull people together," Suzie confided.

"Regrets? That could or should be you."

"None. My sister Cristin wanted me to be Queen more than I did. Been pretty busy this week anyway."

"I'll say," Andy Hill interjected. He had come to the dance with Tammy Dickerson. "Your chapter of the Disciple Fellowship is probably the most community-active club around," he enthused. "Even more than area college chapters. We should take a lesson. How many official members?"

"Forty-one," Suzie returned proudly.

"And Shirley Harrison is next." Patrick couldn't stop himself. "The club only seems to get the most attractive girls."

"Hey, man, what's the word," T.R. roared as he, Doris Long, Sammie Spear, and Erica Howard, who clutched Sammie's hand, joined Patrick, Suzie, Andy, and Tammy.

"Dull," Patrick responded. "This atmosphere is like a morgue."

"Coming over to my crib after?" T.R. asked.

"You don't mind if Andy and Tammy come, do you?" Suzie questioned.

"Whatever," T.R. agreed, glancing at Patrick as if wondering what else he could have said. T.R. turned to Andy Hill. "Looking livelier than last time. Thought you was dead."

Andy Hill earnestly thanked T.R. for his intervention. To hear Hill tell the story, Patrick thought, T.R. came across as Emperor Constantine defending and legitimizing Christians. Patrick had spent much of the evening steering himself and Suzie away from the person he was beginning to see as his rival.

Suzie moved Patrick aside to berate him for his lack of friendship: "I know you don't like the club, but you could at least be nice to people I meet through it."

"Be nice?"

"Not so loud," Suzie shushed.

"My God, he'd dance every dance with you if he could. Christianity involves sharing, but that's not what's meant. Saint Andy just has the hots for you."

"We better go outside," Suzie insisted, "to settle a few things." The only thing settled in the parking lot, however, was Sean Foley's fate at LaSalle.

"Suzie, run inside and get somebody quick."

"What are they doing?" She pointed at the four figures skulking together at the far end of the parking lot.

"Nothing good, I'm sure." Patrick instinctively ducked behind a car. "It's Sean and the boys, and that's T.R.'s Chevy."

"God! Be careful, Pat." Suzie kissed Patrick's cheek before scurrying back toward the gym. Emboldened that help would soon follow, Patrick zigzagged around cars toward the enemy.

As he approached the four, Patrick noticed Togneri, Smith, and Jensen carrying out orders from Foley, who barked like a foreman. The car, tires punctured, sat on wheel rims. The three workers dropped paint brushes into a bucket overflowing with oozing, black tar they sloppily spread over the car's broken windows.

"Hey! What are you doing?" Patrick shouted from about twenty-five feet away. Foley whirled to face him.

Jensen dropped his brush and bolted behind a car. Togneri and Smith, brushes still in hands, turned defiantly toward their unexpected witness. As if to demonstrate his control, Foley sauntered toward Patrick. His eyes, however, wild and glazed, betrayed him. Consciously locking his knees, more to stop shaking than to brace himself in anticipation of a punch, Patrick squared off to face Foley.

"Nothing here concerns you, Kiernan. Guess we better come to an understanding since you're the only one who's spotted us." Foley obviously hadn't seen Suzie run for help. Patrick decided to keep him talking so that he wouldn't take off before adult reinforcements arrived. Besides, Patrick needed to demonstrate his courage, to himself, if nobody else.

"So, talk to me. What are you offering, Sean?" Togneri and Smith curled close, waiting for cues from Foley. Jensen sheepishly returned to gather up the bucket and carry it away as if he had planned that all along.

Foley thought fast. "An exclusive about Coach Mack. Some good stuff for *The Star*. I know the facts. That's why I'm here. I'm paying back a debt for the Coach."

Patrick swallowed hard. "No good, Sean. Know all about it. In fact, I was there when it came down. McEntee's out after the season because T.R. taped Donavan's call. Now, everybody's going to know all about this too. This is like the Klan. You've gone too far, Sean. Probably gone. *Au revoir*."

Patrick's French expression set Foley totally off. Instead of punching Patrick, he lowered his head and executed his last tackle as a Lancer, driving his head into Patrick's stomach. In the process, he pushed air out of Patrick as if he were a slashed tire.

Like a tired boxer hanging on by tying up his opponent, Patrick regrouped. He pinned Foley's arms against his body while dragging him to the ground. A crowd, led by Brother Curt, rushed up, effectively freezing Togneri and Smith, otherwise poised to intervene. As Brother Curt reached down to grab Foley by the shirt collar, Patrick gouged Foley's right eye with his thumb. Foley yelled. Looking up at Brother Curt and the gathering crowd, however, Foley didn't offer resistance.

Sitting up to get his breath back, Patrick noticed Brother Curt arranging bodies as if he were a postal worker sorting mail. He isolated the footballers to avoid further repercussions. His temper, however, showed in the way he physically pushed them in the direction of his office to be accompanied by Brother Raymond. Meanwhile, the Dean of Discipline began dispersing onlookers, a number increasing by the minute as word spread inside.

T.R. arrived late. The crowd parted before him as if he were Moses at the Red Sea. When he saw his car, he went wild. "Where is he?" he screamed, and nobody doubted who he meant. A string of high-pitched curses filled the air before Brother Curt moved to calm him. Frustrated, T.R. kicked his car fiercely before stomping toward Patrick. "Man, I shoulda been here. Foley?"

Looking up, Patrick nodded. Patrick spat to his side despite the presence of Suzie, Andy Hill, and Tammy Dickerson, among others, who gathered near him. "Stay cool, man," Patrick advised, as if he were a battle-hardened veteran

T.R. bent over. "You okay?"

"I'll live. Destroyed your car, didn't they?"

"Looks like it."

"Foley's final curtain. He's painted himself right out of the picture."

Indeed, he had.

After midnight, Patrick drove T.R. home after dropping off Suzie and Doris Long. The two talked about what had happened and what they had learned before leaving school. Brother Curt, with the begrudging approval of Brother Charles, expelled Sean Foley. Foley's father came to school and promised to write a check for the car on the spot if civil charges weren't pressed. Brother Charles, almost apologetic to Mr. Foley, held out this crumb as the best he could do, though insisting the youngster had to go. Brother Curt emphasized that future vengeful acts would lead to immediate civil actions.

"I only wish Brother Blood hadn't gotten him outta there so fast. Would've loved a final shot." T.R. spoke methodically, like an executioner. "This check makes me feel better, though." T.R. fingered a check for a thousand dollars, which Mr. Foley had written directly to him. "Punked him. Only paid seven bills for the Chevy, though I loved it."

"Thought you told him nine?"

"Did. Shoulda gone higher."

"Will you look for another car right away?" Patrick pulled in front of T.R.'s house, parked his car, and switched off the lights.

"Yeah. Need wheels. We was used to the bus, but I've been playing chauffeur lately. The family depends on my rides now."

"Want me to come by Monday morning? Drop your mom at work and you at school?"

"Nah, too far. You're righteous, man!" T.R. smiled. "You think this is good?" He held up the check before folding it carefully in two and putting it back in his pocket.

"Foley's old man's supposedly worth a lot."

"Could've seen taking them to court. Would've enjoyed their discomfort."

"Yeah, but what good?" Patrick protested. "A hassle. They might have even grilled you on the stand about Percy and the recruiting thing to blow smoke."

"Nuthin' to do with this," T.R. retorted sharply.

"No, but I think Charles was right this time. Foley gets the boot. Now we forget him."

"The other three will be around. Probation. No football, but still around school."

"They're just followers," Patrick soothed. "We all know whose show this was. They'll bend over backwards to avoid you. We're lucky neither of us has McEntee in class, though. There's the grudge."

"He already passes me in the hallways like I'm not there."

"I'm not sure he's all there." A light flickered in the front window. "You better go in. Your mom's probably upset, though you and Curt talked to her on the phone. What do you think will happen to Foley? Public school or the Marines? We can send him right over to Saudi Arabia where they're staging Operation Desert Shield. He might even like that."

"Who cares?" Ward stole a glance toward his house. "Looked like old man Foley had a toot on when he showed up. I thought he'd punch Sean upside the head himself. And, when Brother Blood told him to write the check on the spot, I thought he'd drop a brick. He hates my Black butt. More than Sean."

"He claimed he didn't know Sean took it, but it was tar from one of his work sites. Wouldn't be surprised if he put him up to it."

T.R. continued: "He did ask me how Percy Forte was doing. He said they've had business dealings but said it kinda funny. Like he was telling me something."

"What'd you say?"

"Nothin'."

"Sean wanted you to know who did it, but nobody would have been able to prove it. That's why they staged that disturbance at the movie they went to earlier. Then, they would've had witnesses they were there, though they snuck out in the middle of the flick. Sean's a lot of things, but not dumb."

"Except you spotted them. Mr. Investigative Reporter doing his thing," T.R. laughed loudly. "Thanks, man, for everything." T.R. clasped Patrick's shoulder with one hand as he jerked the door open with the other.

Patrick chuckled. "Better get out of this neighborhood. I hear small, foreign cars are fair game after midnight."

T.R., who had pried his way out of the little Toyota, looked back in: "At least we don't tar and feather 'em. We be civilized."

17.

LATE OCTOBER
SENIOR YEAR

Patrick worked on the LaSalle basketball press guide during the period set aside for his journalism independent study. Steve Wilson walked in. "Checking up on me?"

"Not really," Wilson began. "Saw your article in *The Star* this morning. Was yours, right?"

"Drafted it, but no byline. Carl thought, considering the subject matter, it should come from the department rather than a high school kid."

"Good judgment, I'd say." The story closed the book on two LaSalle careers:

McEntee and Foley Out at LaSalle

The soap opera saga of LaSalle's football team took a surprising plot turn yesterday.

Alex McEntee, twenty-one years the head coach, resigned effective immediately. He is not only stepping down from his job as football coach but also from his Athletic Directorship and teaching position.

The announcement followed the news that Lancer co-captain Sean Foley, who had just returned from a two-week school suspension for the 20-7 Loyola loss, will transfer from LaSalle effective immediately. Moreover, seniors Franco Togneri and

Ralph Smith and junior Jerry Jensen won't suit up for the team for the remainder of the season.

Assistant Coach Mike Jordan will take the reins for the Lancers. He is in his second year in the program. Jordan assessed, "We will be hard put to compete. Besides the obvious problem we'll have replacing some of our best players, the whole team is in shock."

Coach McEntee refused to comment about his sudden midseason resignation, although sources in the school indicated he had planned to step down at the end of this campaign.

Brother Curt, LaSalle's Vice Principal, refused to comment about what led to all this, citing privacy issues. Brother Charles, LaSalle's longtime Principal, did commend Coach McEntee for his long service coaching and as A.D.: "He helped build a sports program that gives the community pride. As a coach and teacher, he has been dedicated, hard-working, and a credit to the school. We wish Alex the best."

McEntee attended Cal Poly after a Marine stint. Upon graduating, he coached for two years near San Luis Obispo before coming to Sacramento. For four years, he was an assistant before taking charge of varsity football himself. Since, his gridders have compiled a 113–103 record, including this year's 2–4. His charges won league championships four of his first six years but only one since.

Sean Foley, who anchored the Lancers' forward wall on both sides of the ball, was named All-League last year, as well as the team's most inspirational player. Togneri and Smith were also two-year varsity starters. Jensen, a junior, played well in LaSalle's secondary and served as the team's kicker.

"Big-boy story," Wilson offered.

"Hopefully, the last about this mess. The snake has been expelled from the Garden of Eden."

"Listen to you. Biblical allusions. Your Disciple Fellowship attendance?"

"Without realizing it. Suzie and I haven't exactly had a lot of contact lately. Biblical or otherwise.

"Ouch!" Wilson had heard Suzie now saw Andy Hill as much as Patrick. "I'll tell you one thing, though. Just because Foley's not around, don't think evil, like Elvis, has left the building."

"Sounds like a warning my mom would give."

"Great minds think alike."

"In her case, maybe after a gentleman caller left the house. Not many after Dad, but a few."

Wilson gulped. "Did you have McEntee for Civics?"

Patrick talked while arranging copy at a layout table: "Nah, last year for A.P. U.S. The old goat wasn't a bad teacher. Lectured, but pretty good storyteller."

"What'd you get on the test?"

"A five. That, and a four in Bio. If I get my four or five in English, Math, and Civics this year, I might have almost a year of college credits. If I end up at Berkeley while writing for *The Star*, that would help bigtime. I could take less than a full load the first couple of years without falling behind."

"What about Princeton? Your mom says ... "

"Still an option. Mom's in love with the idea, but I'm ... "

"Good to have options," Wilson interrupted.

"McEntee's knowledgeable, but guys in regular U.S. classes hated his narrow-mindedness. Old school and prejudiced as hell, but you could learn if you wanted to. He put in a better effort for A.P. class. Course, you disagreed with him at your peril."

"Did you disagree with Schipper's handling of the story about him?"

"Yeah, hated the vagueness."

Wilson reached down to snip copy. "Don't know what specifics would have accomplished. Even though Foley's over eighteen, still a privacy thing. And liability issues with McEntee. Besides, might discourage eighth-graders from coming here. The general public found out enough. Carl knows what he's doing. He came to me about you after reading this guide last year. I told him you were a Blue Chipper too."

"He says I can still do something more personal but positive. Show the pressure on athletes like T.R. But, I'm not sure. He always preaches that truth is truth, and we're in the business of providing truth."

Steve Wilson straightened up. "Truth is spoken by people. It's important, but you have to be careful with it." He tossed the scissors he held down on the layout table. "It's like a god. It glows so red hot it's good to stand a little way away from it at times to feel its power. It can burn you, though. You can't always print the total truth any more than you can always live it."

The two looked each other in the eyes before quickly glancing down at the blandness of the coldly precise black copy on white paper, some arranged neatly on the layout pages and the rest scattered about on the table.

18.

MID-NOVEMBER
SENIOR YEAR

Before Thanksgiving, the following story appeared in *The Star*:

LaSalle Cage Preview
By: Patrick Kiernan

After a disastrous 2–8 football season, the LaSalle Lancers open pre-season basketball play Wednesday against Davis High School as a preliminary to the U.C. Davis-Alumni contest to christen the Aggies' collegiate season.

Davis, like most prep teams, will gun for the vaunted Lancers knowing upsetting LaSalle would make its season. After finishing second in the region last year, the Lancers return all but two of their first seven players. Stars up from the J.V.'s should more than make up for those losses. The Lancers' alternatively named club team also won the Sacramento City Summer League crown this year, dismantling a fine Carmichael team in the championship game.

Leading the returnees is Blue Chip prospect T.R. Ward. A solid 6'8", 235-pounder, Ward is one of the most highly recruited area hoopsters ever. Echoing other coaches who have attempted to contain Ward, American coach Sal Simi says. "He's an incredible force. I think if he played with only one or two players, he'd give a lot of high school teams a tough test. In fact, if they let him inbound to himself, he might stand off a team alone."

LaSalle coach Jerry Burke, with a career record of 347–185 and a reputation for molding cohesive teams, shrugs off such talk. "It still takes a team to win, and the five starters have to be backed up by able reserves. My senior center's a good one, but he's most valuable because he fits in so unselfishly within the team concept."

Ward, who will announce during Christmas vacation the five colleges he will keep in the running to recruit him, agrees with his coach. "In a different system, I might get bigger numbers, but that's not why I play. Winning is. Playing this type of ball will make me a better player at the next levels."

The rest of the LaSalle starters should include flashy point guard Sammie Spear and shooting guard Larry Nichols. Spear averaged nine points and eight assists last season, while Nichols filled the nets for fifteen points per game, mostly from the outside.

Last year's sixth man, Tom Kuhn, played more minutes than the two departing starters. The other forward should be Terry Crain, last year's J.V. star. Primary backup roles will be filled by Frank Tucci, Lance Hall, and sophomore Rick Pantera. Pantera, raw but extremely talented, will test Coach Burke's legendary reputation, upping the games of young charges over the course of a season.

The popular Lancers will trek all over Northern California before league season starts in January. The biggest test will come in the middle of January during league season when the Lancers will meet traditional SoCal power Mater Dei in a preliminary to a Cal game.

"We look forward to challenges this season," Coach Burke affirmed. "That's the beauty of sports."

"You covering the game for *The Star*?" Brother Curt, offering Patrick some of his popcorn, asked when he ran into

Patrick near the refreshment stand during halftime of the La-Salle/Davis clash.

Patrick sipped a Coke. "No, Carl's got it and the college game too. We decided it'd be cool for me to be a fan for the season opener."

Brother Curt grinned. "A lot to yell about. Heard the U.C. Davis coach telling Jerry he's glad to be playing his alums rather than us. A twenty-one-point lead, even with all the second-quarter subbing. The Davis High kids would need a straight-jacket to stop T.R."

"Can't stop myself from keeping stats, even when I'm not working. He got fifteen."

"And at least ten boards," Brother Curt enthused. "Sammie looks good too. And, nice to see Tucci enjoying a game for a change. He deserves it after football season."

"You see the play toward the end when he got hacked?" Patrick laughed. "Thought he was going to straight-arm the guy."

Others strode by to say hello to either Brother Curt or Patrick or both before the Christian Brother resumed the conversation: "Good crowd."

"Yeah, us in a prelim's a good idea, even for a school with no hope getting a Blue Chipper like T.R.," Patrick opined authoritatively. "Adds crowd revenue, generates interest, provides a good doubleheader, and spotlights a sure D-1 star."

Brother Curt agreed: "Good publicity. And maybe they try to pick up a few of the other players. I could see guys like Sammie, or maybe even Lance, playing in a few years on a good D-II school or maybe even a lower echelon D-1."

"Lance might fool you," Patrick responded. "T.R. says he's coming on in practice. He'll probably play most of the second half at forward, and at center when T.R. sits."

"Jerry better go deeper than that to hold down the score."

"I wish," Patrick sighed, "some of our last football opponents thought that way."

"Yep. Looking for a little revenge during basketball season."

Brother Curt craned his neck to peer through an open door out to the basketball court. "The teams are back warming up. Hope our rooters stick around for the college game. It wouldn't look good if everyone just got up and left after our game."

"Not sure students will, though I'm hoping to stay through the first half. I'm with Suzie and Doris, so we'll at least ..."

"That's good," Brother Curt interrupted. "I'd heard you and Suzie were on and off lately."

"We'll work through it," Patrick retorted before turning the conversation. "We have to wait for T.R. to change. That'll take at least until half, especially if he needs to dodge recruiters who just happen to be there when he comes out of the locker room. Then we're going to get a bite to eat."

"Hey, Bro," Kelly Kerwin cut in, affecting a Black dialect that gave Brother Curt pause. "Thanksgiving dinner coming soon; better watch that popcorn," he smirked, rubbing his tummy. "A little over a week and then pounds of turkey." Although Kerwin could be abrasive, his intelligence and wit charmed Brother Curt, much to the surprise of many who would have thought the two might have clashed.

Kerwin, tall and lanky, wore a striped button-down shirt under an oversized jeans jacket with its collar flipped up. His almost neon blue pants seemed a bit incongruous to Patrick, himself wearing a Lancer T-shirt over his DKNY stylish jeans and his old Converses.

"You're the only turkey I'd like to stuff, Kerwin," Brother Curt bellowed as he took a playful swipe at Kerwin's collar. Kerwin feigned jumping for his life but quickly leaned back into the conversation.

"Whoa. A heavyweight boxer too."

"Thought you'd be headed back to fire up the cheering section, Killer," Patrick needled, using the nickname that annoyed his peer.

"Decided you and Brother Blood here yearned for my scintillating dialogue. Maybe even more than the Davis pompom girls. Them farm girls were probably salivating, hoping us La-Salle men would chat 'em up at half."

"Turkey stuffing, indeed. You're full of something," Brother Curt chided.

"Hey, be nice. On top of everything, I'm a champ-een today." Kerwin drew the word out as if savoring it.

"In what?" Patrick returned. "The Guinness record for nonstop jabbering? Most time spent in a hallway during class?"

"He already claimed that one," Brother Curt announced.

"Video games. Specifically, the one at Merlin's." Kerwin referred to a well-known after-school hangout where Patrick dropped by infrequently. "That new game they got in the corner."

Patrick knew. Classmates more interested than him talked about it, and the one time he had been there lately, about fifteen students had crowded around it. "Yeah, seen it," he replied as Brother Curt, for once, looked out of his element.

"Broke the record today. Sixty-eight thousand points. Beat that, sucker."

"Plunk out a quarter to play?" Patrick asked innocuously.

"Course," Kerwin devoured the bait. "Even my good looks ..."

"When you were done racking up points, did you get your quarter back? Or double or triple it?"

"No, but my name's there ..."

"Well then, who really won?" Patrick enjoyed the banter. "I'd say the machine and the people who own it, no matter whose name it flashed. When we read *Gatsby*, Mr. Wilson always said you gotta follow the money to find America's real winners."

Silenced for a second, Kerwin watched open-mouthed as Patrick dashed away toward the door to return to Suzie and Doris in the stands.

Near an entrance, Patrick walked right into a couple familiar figures, heads down, moving toward the Davis side. "Mr. Foley. Sean," Patrick uttered reflexively before quickly wondering if he should have just walked past.

Sean Foley, however, stopped and spun around, "Kiernan,"

he snapped, attracting his father's immediate attention. "Here to do a hatchet job on someone?"

"No room to talk about hatchet jobs, Sean," Patrick challenged through one of his usually disarming smiles. "Where you going to school now?"

"Grant. We came to see Frank play," he offered, anticipating Patrick's unasked question.

"He's playing well and having fun."

"Course, Dad sort of has an interest too."

"Damned right," Mr. Foley thundered. "I'm still President of the Boosters Club. I pay a lot of these kids," he continued as if all scholarship money came from him personally, "and I wanted to see how they're doing."

"Earning their pay?" Patrick muttered, but Mr. Foley either didn't hear or didn't notice the sarcasm. "Why not sit on our side?"

"You know why," Mr. Foley spat. "Brother Jig might not approve of Sean being near the rooting section. Oldtimers in the Club figure he's got to get taken down a peg or two. Our school before his." A trickle of saliva dribbled from his suddenly worked-up mouth onto his red-veined jaw. He wiped it onto his plaid jacket. "Him and his boys. A few more, we'll look like the Globetrotters, or the N.B.A."

Patrick started to protest the facts, if not the attitude. Though three LaSalle J.V. starters were African American, T.R. and Sammie were the only two in the eight-man rotation of LaSalle's varsity. Patrick caught himself, though, deciding any argument based on facts would be an exercise in futility with Mr. Foley and wouldn't address the real problem.

He sidestepped to walk away, but before he could move around the stockily-built older man, he felt a hand cup his shoulder. "One thing, Kiernan."

"What's that?" Patrick turned to face Mr. Foley, oblivious to people passing in both directions as the buzzer sounded for second-half play to begin.

"Last month, you wrote that article about Coach Mack resigning and Sean getting expelled."

"Transferring."

"Everybody knew it was an expulsion. Still, not a bad article."

Patrick braced himself the same way he had the last time he had faced off with Foley's son. "My name wasn't on it, but yeah, I had a hand in it."

"That's what my sources told me." Mr. Foley dropped his hand to his side as people milled past. "But then two weeks later, the other one came out. The one with behind-the-scenes dirt. The one that made Sean out to be a bigot picking on those Black boys. I'm old school. My beliefs aren't going to change, but Sean here," Patrick peeked to see Sean looking embarrassed, "doesn't mind playing with spades. I know Schipper had his name on the garbage, but who fed him the dirt? You? Ward? Curt?"

Patrick swallowed. "He's a reporter and was around when a lot of this came down. Carl talked to everybody who would talk to him." Patrick shrugged. He agreed the article never should have been published, though he hadn't been able to convince Schipper, whose judgment he otherwise trusted.

Schipper had compiled background on the parking lot incident, including the longstanding feud between basketball and football teams and the prior fight concerning the Disciple Fellowship Club, into a long feature that ran in *The Star*. Though impeccably factual, the piece made Patrick uncomfortable with its focus on high school kids, though the main participants were over eighteen. He knew that a lot of details had come from him though he hadn't been aware Carl would use them. Naked truth could be burdensome.

"Honestly, I agree it didn't need to be that specific."

Not recognizing Patrick's sincerity, Mr. Foley laughed. "And you come across as the big hero. The *Star* reporter doubling as Superman. Smelling out a story in the parking lot and going out ... "

Sean stepped between the two and turned his father around.

"Let's go. It's starting." Only then, the potential ugliness of the scene struck Patrick. He had had his fill of unsavory confrontations. Sean caught Patrick's stare. "Good game, huh? We ripped 'em apart that half." And, the two were gone, leaving Patrick to his thoughts and a second half of basketball that seemed anticlimactic. He did notice that Sean had said "we."

19.

TOWARD LATE DECEMBER
SENIOR YEAR

Only a few red, orange, brown, and golden leaves clung to trees marching along suburban streets such as Patrick's in Carmichael a couple days after Christmas. Like those leaves, the LaSalle Lancers' basketball team hung tenaciously, in its case to perfection, as a *Star* article proclaimed:

Lancers Ranked #1 in NorCal
By: Patrick Kiernan

With league season ten days away, Sacramento's LaSalle Lancers, the number one rated NorCal prep basketball team, escaped the preseason undefeated, if not untested. The Lancers played three games down to the final buzzer but won every time.

"We haven't played consistently, but we've shown potential and guts," shrugged Coach Jerry Burke, who has added twelve wins to his impressive lifetime total. "This is a perfect week for a break." The Lancers will play one more preseason game against what looks like an overmatched Lodi team before opening league season against American after New Year's.

The Lancers have been led, as expected, by senior standout T.R. Ward, who has averaged 23 points and 11 rebounds a game despite limited fourth-quarter duty in three-quarters of the games and special defenses designed to thwart his output. LaSalle romped over its other nine foes but had trouble with the Sacred Heart Cathedral Fighting Irish of San Francisco, the Berkeley High Yellowjackets, and traditional rival Loyola, who they bested in the recent thrilling finale to the Wildcats' own Holiday Festival in suburban Carmichael.

The Lancers bested SHC on the road despite early foul trouble for T.R. Ward. Sammie Spear and Larry Nichols hit key shots down the stretch, and Ward, despite four fouls, finished the 73–70 victory with two big slams. Promising Lance Hall, though he didn't start, collaborated with Ward to eke out a 75–73 win against the Yellowjackets on a feed from the post by the Lancers' Blue Chip prospect.

Loyola threw various zones and double teams at the Lancers. Deliberate on offense, they took shots late in possessions, often from deep. The Wildcats tied the game at 54–54 with twelve seconds left on a Billy Gemma three. Finally, it was LaSalle's time to be deliberate. With three seconds left, T.R. Ward skied through six clutching hands for a Sammie Spear pass and wheeled toward the basket. It seemed three 'Cats fouled him. He would have to march to the line to shoot a one-and-one to prevent overtime.

After Loyola called a timeout to test Ward's nerves, the big man withstood the din of the crowd to calmly drop in the winning point as if it were a summer practice session. Though he missed the second unimportant shot, time expired, and the Lancers had their winning margin.

After T.R. spent the night at Patrick's Carmichael home, the two killed time until Patrick drove T.R. to Sacramento Metro to catch his Friday noon flight to Los Angeles for his weekend visit to U.C.L.A.

Patrick slipped his Toyota into the fog clinging to the ground. "It's thick out here, man. Can't wait for that SoCal sunshine," Ward beamed.

"This time of year?" Patrick joked. "Hear they're predicting snow for the Rose Bowl."

"No concern for Bruin fans. It's basketball season. Hey, man, follow those lights." Ward pointed to a passing bus.

"Too late," Patrick piped up. "It's doing Greyhound speed cutting through the fog."

"Yeah, that doggie's movin'. 'Preciate you doing this so I didn't have to take the bus or leave the new wheels in the lot. Sure different, though, going to sleep with all that quiet."

"Carmichael specializes in quiet. You and Doris coming to the New Year's Eve party at our house?"

"Yeah, if I make it through the airport press announcement."

"Shouldn't be bad," Patrick reassured, "if you can get onto the plane and sit apart from those L.A. reporters following you up, the press announcement should be cake. Besides, you're giving us the exclusive five for our early edition, so that should hold down the number of reporters and photographers at the presser."

"Can you see," Ward laughed, "if I didn't name U.C.L.A with those reporter dudes on the same plane?"

"You did give U.C.L.A. some word, didn't you?"

"But didn't promise nothing."

"You going to phone the night before to make sure we're on the same page? Assume still the same five."

"Probably. Unless someone loses by forty this weekend. The *Trib* listed about every school in America as being my five choices this week."

"Throw enough dirt, some might stick. I'm surprised they haven't had you followed to see if you were wearing college garb to tip your choices. Lance has been coming on lately."

"The string bean's better than people think. Lacked some confidence, but practice makes perfect. Like the way I talk. White people grammar and that stuff ain't natural, but I practice and get better. Know it's important going forward."

"There'll always be interviews."

"Getting more confident. Like Lance on the court. He wants the ball now. I see it in his eyes."

Patrick pondered the fact that T.R. had shared something intimate with him. "Fog's clearing."

"Plane's gonna make it up."

"And down," Patrick rejoined.

"Messing with me? Best hope down, too, man. Where it's supposed to land." T.R. laughed nervously. "Truth. I hold on tighter up and down in a plane than a junkyard dog on a piece of meat. Another thing to improve going forward."

"I saw Forte at the Citrus Heights game," Patrick blurted as the automatic gate to the airport parking lot spit out a receipt.

"It'd take all day getting a spot close. You don't have to come in."

"We'll walk from the outskirts. I like airport bustle."

"Didn't see him 'til after the game. They can't keep him from going to games."

"He said about the same thing, a little more colorfully." T.R. snickered as Patrick continued: "Thought he'd burst when he brought up those recruiters playing the bump game with you while he was shut out."

"Yeah, a shuck. They happen to bump into me, and it's okay according to N.C.A.A. rules. Mom still sees Percy," T.R. confided as Patrick darted into a parking space, rocking T.R.'s head back and forth. "Yeah, I miss the dude. Makes it easier on the family. Money's tight again, and Brother Blood warned me old man Foley might make a play to jerk away my scholarship bank next semester."

Disbelieving, Patrick spun to face T.R. "You're kidding? I thought we were done with Percy and the Foleys."

"My mom's upset." Patrick flipped the handle on his door. "Wait, man. There's something ... I want ... I got to tell you. I'm starting to see Percy's game."

"What?" Patrick said incredulously. "Something illegal?"

"Nothing I did. Things I found out when I told Mom about

Foley's scholarship threat."

"Heard rumblings. Boosters and alums sending money for youth groups and building projects at the Center? Stretches the rules, but lots of folks donate stuff. Not really illegal and for a good cause."

"His Caddy," T.R. scoffed. "That a great cause? And, the sharp threads he wears."

"What?"

"That building—the extension, the new gym—the thing's getting put up by a contractor Forte's silent partners with. Can you imagine the dude being silent 'bout anything? And somehow, Percy's been in bed with old man Foley before. Forte fundraises, which he's damned good at it, and somehow Foley profits too. And Percy gets money under the table on the back end. I guess I'm the poster boy for him asking for donations for the Club."

"Wow. Foley and Forte had done slimy things together, Percy's skimming, and Foley knows about it?"

"Bad blood now."

"Their relationship gone south," Patrick almost laughed. "Getting to Forte through you?"

"Foley probably knows Forte's been slipping Mom money to get by, to improve the house. And Percy dangling my recruitment out there to solicit donations. Maybe overplayed his hand for his own benefit. The fact that I don't really blame Percy bothers me some, but it's the truth in my world."

"No blame for the position it puts you in?"

"I go on recruiting trips and see the money dudes throw around just 'cause I'm a player. Then I come back and see how my family lives. My neighbors. Something's wrong. You see it in movies and on the tube, it's one thing. You see it for real, it's different."

"Wow."

The two walked silently before T.R. continued: "People on River Road don't live far from us, but it might as well be Mars.

Yeah, Percy looks out for himself, but he helps his own. I get screwed by Foley, and my man, in contrast, looks righteous. He knows the world's a big, bad, ugly place sometimes, and he doesn't give in."

Patrick quietly walked T.R. into the terminal. On the way to the boarding area, they got stopped by a ratty-robed young man thrusting pamphlets about the Reverend Sun Myung Moon into the hands of passers-by that solicited donations while promising spiritual happiness for believers. T.R. glared at the pamphlet and then back at the skinny zealot. "No thanks, man; I'll find my own."

20.

NEW YEAR'S EVE
SENIOR YEAR

Patrick's last story of the year, a scoop picked up by national wire services, appeared on New Year's Eve morning:

Blue Chip Prospect Narrows Collegiate Selections
By: Patrick Kiernan

The Sacramento Star has learned exclusively the names of the five collegiate basketball programs still in the running to win the recruiting battle for the services of LaSalle Blue Chip prospect T.R. Ward next year.

Ward, who will make the announcement at Sacramento Metro Airport this afternoon, will name U.C.L.A., Notre Dame, Georgetown, St. John's, and D.C.'s Capital College as his five choices.

By narrowing options to five schools early, on the advice of LaSalle basketball coach Jerry Burke, Ward hopes to minimize the recruiting onslaught engulfing him. Most D-1 high school recruits will sign letters of intent by April 15th. Between now and then, Ward hopes to evaluate his five finalists in depth.

"I want the chance to play right away," Ward noted. "It would be equally rewarding adding to the legacy of a big-time program or pushing a program in the wings to the top. And, of course, my family, advisors, and I will look at what's

offered educationally to fit my needs."

Ward, 6'8" and 235 pounds, should fit right in at the collegiate level as a power forward. Despite playing center for LaSalle (the number-two ranked NorCal basketball team just behind Alameda's St. Josephs Notre Dame with its junior sensation Jason Kidd), Ward projects to be an immediate starter and contributor at the top collegiate level according to numerous recruiters.

His ballhandling skills and shooting range make such a projection realistic. Often double- and triple-teamed and facing defenses designed to deny him the ball or swarm him when he gets it, Ward has demonstrated a knack for spotting open teammates and getting them good looks.

"I could be happy with all five," Ward noted. "They're all near media centers and are either solid or up-and-coming basketball programs." Ward also pointed to the quality of the schools eliminated in narrowing selections: "Despite hassles, I met a lot of nice people and found out about quality schools throughout the land."

Ward, who claims his choice among the five is "wide open," will make the formal announcement this afternoon when his P.S.A. flight touches down. He will be met at the airport by his mother and three brothers, Coach Burke, friends from his South Sac neighborhood, school officials, and other advisors for the scheduled 2:45 p.m. formal announcement at a specially setup area near Landing Gate #23.

Though not formally binding, Ward's limiting his choices to five represents his desire to make this selection process transparent and manageable. "I'm looking forward to focusing on school and basketball during this semester," the LaSalle star concluded.

The Kiernan's New Year's Eve party mixed about twenty teenagers with twice that number of adults. Sheila Kiernan's work friends joined neighbors and a LaSalle contingent to quaff their way into the new year.

Patrick sidled up to his mother while headed toward the enclosed patio, cleared for dancing and socializing. "Mom," he tapped her shoulder.

"Taking those to the patio," Sheila Kiernan pointed to the *hors d'oeuvres* Patrick carried, "or the garage, where it seems you've already spent a lot of time?" The two had begrudgingly reached a compromise that students could keep some beers in the refrigerator in the garage if they drank them there, otherwise mingled, and didn't drink if they'd be driving. Patrick had sworn he'd make sure drinkers didn't drive.

"No, to my room for a snack while I study."

"Mr. Sarcasm. You and Suzie fighting?"

"Not yet." Patrick scooped a stuffed egg in his mouth. "Should I have left this in the kitchen? The party's there."

"No, outside as planned. Maybe appetizers will lure people. It's warm enough with the space heaters, isn't it?"

"Sure. You won't have to worry about anybody connected to Disciple Fellowship drinking unless they start turning water into wine. Just worry about me and Killer, but we both aren't driving. And the basketball players won't be drinking." Patrick threw a glance at Coach Burke and his wife, who had just entered. "I've signed up a few to chauffeur people home," he needled as his friend strutted past to greet the Coach.

The party lurched along at first. Nobody gathered on the patio. After another trip to the garage and back, Patrick tried unsuccessfully to cajole a few classmates to the empty space. He happened upon Mr. Wilson and his wife standing near the sliding glass door. "Not too successful, sport. I told Sheila to set the bar up out there." With Patrick's attention captured, Mr. Wilson characterized his view of party planning: "People stay close to alcohol and food. Put them where you want the party to happen."

"Like Steve here," Mrs. Wilson grunted before moving toward the kitchen.

"Hey, I was out here with you, wasn't I?" Mr. Wilson offered as she walked away.

Though typically awed by his mentor, Patrick thought Mr. Wilson had given himself a head start with alcohol, just as he had.

Suzie had somehow coerced him into inviting Andy Hill. Patrick couldn't believe he had relented. Truly, he knew he didn't want to take a chance that Suzie might not come herself. Despite the iciness he had felt since picking her up, Patrick reassured himself the alternative would have been worse. He couldn't imagine explaining away her absence.

Patrick returned to the kitchen after chugging some beer during a brief garage stop. A large crowd gathered around T.R., who narrated stories Patrick had heard about his U.C.L.A. excursion. Patrick looked around for Suzie but didn't see her. He slid into the conversation, by now about the new basketball rule the last couple of years, offering three points for shots from a distance. It included Carl Schipper, who had told Patrick he and his date would probably only stay for a while before heading off to another party. That they stayed the entire evening was only one of the facts Patrick sorted through during his next morning's hangover.

Almost relieved to miss confronting her unusually wayward son, Sheila Kiernan disappeared that next morning before noon to a New Year's Day brunch. Patrick, sprawled on a couch, guiltily reviewed his own performance the night before while mindlessly watching bowl games unreel on television.

Fittingly with his literary bent, he fashioned what he dreaded remembering into a five-act play.

Act One: Steve Wilson at the piano as the party moved to the living room and revved up. Show tunes. Requests. Wilson worked the gathering crowd like a pro. Singing. Some dancing. Wilson sipping drinks between every song. Laughter. Patrick, arm in arm with Suzie, who Wilson even coaxed to lead a song or two, felt good.

Act Two: Bell rang. Andy Hill, making his entrance, arrived.

Was it Patrick's imagination, or did all eyes turn to watch him open the door and mumble a greeting to the collegian? The room grew silent, even the piano. Patrick watched Andy head straight toward Suzie as if nobody else existed. Not feeling great. Quick walks to the garage when Suzie bounced back and forth from him to Andy.

Act Three: The dance. A highpoint. The ancient Mrs. Glass, LaSalle's demure Registrar, performed "Frankie and Johnny." Like a Broadway star bringing the curtain down before intermission, she vamped her way through the old torch song about jealousy. Her rendition—something seen to be believed—left even Brother Curt speechless. The usually reserved little old lady slinked and strutted as the piano beat intensified. She ended up, after a mimed embrace and final twirl, on the piano bench with Mr. Wilson, her arms seductively around his neck. Midnight. Clink of glasses. Kisses. New Year. A new Patrick?

Act Four: The reversal and falling action. Right before and after midnight. Patrick's attitude, conduct, and evening exploded like fizzled fireworks. Words with Suzie. Words with his mother. Words with Andy Hill. Patrick trying to provoke Andy into a fight, but Andy evading the trap as deftly as Patrick himself often had with others in equally absurd situations. Even T.R. shook his head at Patrick's performance.

Act Five: The *denouement*. A fancy French word for "conclusion." Mr. Wilson had preached in class "to enjoy them in plays and movies," that "life doesn't usually offer them quite as neatly." Patrick lived a sloppy one that night. A punch thrown at a wall. Slinking off to the bathroom while Suzie, very upset, got comforted by a crying Sheila Kiernan before being taken home by the knightly Andy Hill. Throwing up. Being piled into bed by Steve Wilson. Passing out.

Acts Four and Five barely existed in Patrick's memory, but a long conversation with Steve Wilson as Act Three ended somehow remained vivid, even in his alcohol-induced fog:

"This Mom's idea? I saw you talking to her," Patrick challenged.

"Let's just say she didn't think it a bad idea." The truth, tactfully put, disarmed Patrick as Wilson whisked him outside.

Wilson sat on the bottom of three stairs leading to the front porch. He set to readying his pipe without talking. Patrick paced behind him until T.R., Sammie, and Lance Hall strode briskly up the front walk. "Hey, guys, firing up the enthusiasm a bit?" Patrick needled.

Guiltily, all three giggled. "Hey, man, just talkin' hoops," Sammie protested. He turned to Wilson. "What you got in your pipe?"

"Nothing that transforms all who smell it into good grammarians," Wilson quipped. "Wouldn't interest you, Sammie." Wilson's voice became measured, his teacher voice. "You guys better get inside before Coach Burke sends a search party."

"Coach, hell," T.R. interjected. "Doris would send the search party." The three laughed uproariously while moving toward the door. "Hey, man," T.R. nudged Patrick as he passed, "be cool. Mellow out. Suzie's really uncomfortable."

"Her problem," Patrick snapped before collecting himself, a smile returning with his composure. "And some advice for my buddy. Try the Visine on my dresser and a breath mint before getting within fifty feet of Coach."

"The smoke inside, man. That's why we took a walk." T.R. winked and was gone.

Patrick turned to Wilson. "Probably should have gone with them. Might've helped."

"Not your image. Besides, they were just talking, right?"

"My image. Often the problem. Living up to it." Patrick sprawled on the top stair. "Gets tiring sometimes."

"Woe is you," Wilson teased. "We all get sick of ourselves now and then. But it is you. Acting otherwise, you'd feel guilty. Maybe it's being Catholic, but I always thought a little shot of guilt every now and then isn't that harmful."

"Amen."

"Maybe even a little healthy. Not bad slipping out of character at times just so you remember who you are. Better put, maybe tapping into other parts of your persona. That's probably why everybody loved what Ginny did tonight. Completely out of character. Knocked 'em dead."

"Looked like you two had practiced for months."

"As if, not like."

"Give me a grammar break."

"No, no practice, but we had done it before. At a party at Foley's house about a year ago. Then, it surprised me so much I could hardly keep up with her. Everybody needs special attention every now and then. Marriages fail, teachers struggle, and kids get set on wrong paths because people forget that. You're lucky. Even at your age, you get constant attention for good things. Always a price to pay, though, and I guess you're paying it now with Suzie."

Patrick raised his eyebrows. "What price does Mrs. Glass pay? Everybody loved it."

"The price came in summoning the courage to pull it off. You can't tell this to anyone." Riveted, Patrick nodded agreement. "That party, the booster thing at Foley's. After she sang, pretty much tonight's act, nobody could talk about anything else. Even old man Foley had to admit he wasn't that night's star. Anyway, about a half an hour later, I go upstairs to take a leak."

"How el-gantly put by the best English teacher I've ever had," Patrick interrupted.

"And how el-gantly slurred," Wilson mimicked, "by the best student I've ever taught. Guess we're both in the cups a bit. Let me finish."

"Sorry."

"Not as sorry as I was when I found the head occupied. Thought I'd wet my pants. Anyway, I'm waiting in the hallway more patiently than I thought possible when I hear this big thump. I figure someone's getting it on in there and should have gone downstairs to find another bathroom. Course, I was curious."

"Oh, no," Patrick couldn't stop himself, "you're not going

to tell me Mrs. Glass was in there with some guy, are you?"

"Hardly, but it was Mrs. Glass. She lets out a futile cry. You should have heard it. Like a cat fight. Really vulnerable. Just thirty minutes before, she had been belting out that song just like tonight, and then a helpless screech."

"What happened?" Patrick said as he slipped down a step closer.

"Luckily, the door was open. I barged in, and there she was. You've been at Foley's house before, right?"

"Not recently, of course, but, yeah, a few times," Patrick impatiently answered.

"They have pretensions of good taste, though they are the Foleys. Like the Grangerfords and Shepherdsons in *Huck Finn*. Pretensions of class. Anyway, they have an old bathtub, the kind that sits on little legs. She was sprawled on her back in it like a turtle without its shell. At first, I worried she had broken a leg or something, but she wasn't feeling any pain, except to her dignity. That's the price she paid for that inaugural performance."

"What?"

"She had to get herself snockered to do it. Maybe, what you've been doing tonight for whatever's coming. But afterward, relieved and without the adrenalin flowing, she just let it all go. She fell in the tub getting that same garter off she played with again tonight during her performance. I got her out and drove her home without notice. Just Mrs. Foley, who's not a bad woman despite her sketchy taste in furnishings and husbands, and my wife. My darling went off on me for leaving her there alone. I guess the old man cornered her, bragging about his investments. Anyway, if people had known, it would have robbed Ginny's performance of its luster. I was helping her retain her dignity."

"What about tonight?"

"She'll be fine. The first time's the hardest. Just before I came out here, she pulled me aside and reminded me about that incident. She said she'd leave her garter on tonight and laughed.

A fine old lady."

Patrick stood. "Maybe, I'm a bit thick tonight, but I'm not sure I get the point."

"The point is you don't need something dramatic and out of character to get attention. You get it all the time. Precisely because you're so damned nice."

"Mr. Nice Guy would like to go in and punch Andy Hill's lights out."

"For what? To be like Sean? From what I've seen, your rival's just about as nice as you. Maybe that bothers you. Believe me, though, he doesn't have your substance. And Suzie would detest you for it."

"Everything had been so perfect before."

"Nothing's ever perfect. We all muddle through, though you just seem muddled tonight. Still, nobody can expect you to be perfect. Oh, by the way, Becky and Anne, who do think you're perfect, both said to say hello to their favorite babysitter. I think they expected an invite." Wilson wheeled around, stood up, and moved past Patrick. "Sheila, come out to see your two favorite men?"

Patrick meandered off halfway down the path leading to the sidewalk as his mother and Mr. Wilson talked quietly for a minute near the door. They both nodded before Sheila Kiernan looked out toward Patrick. She started to say something but seemed to think better of it before turning back into the house. Patrick wandered back toward the steps as Mr. Wilson bent over to empty his pipe on the dirt under some roses. "Did she tell you her nice little boy's acting like a jerk?"

"Didn't have to. She told me she loves me, but I should be spending time with my wife instead of out here with you." Wilson looked at his pipe as he reloaded and tamped.

"You crack me up. You make a joke, take me off guard, and take the edge off."

"Sounds like a formula for you the rest of the night. Maybe, go in and tell Suzie you've made an important decision. No more romantic triangle, but you're choosing, not her."

"You mean make her jealous? Put the moves on Tammy or someone?"

"Too cliché. Besides, you couldn't pull it off the shape you're in. No, everybody likes being chosen and the attention that comes with it. This recruiting act T.R.'s starring in shows that. Isn't there a new rule that prospects can sign on with a college before the season starts?"

"Yeah, Not signing officially, but declaring. To avoid recruiting overload during a season."

"Well, I didn't hear T.R. even considering it. Jerry would have loved it, but T.R. likes being wooed, even though he got forced to play Jerry's game by cutting choices to five. Nothing like today, the big press conference, if he had committed earlier. Hate to be sexist, but Suzie's probably like most women, enjoying Andy's adulation. You get picked all the time. In class. Activities. Socially. *The Star.* Or, take Ginny again. She made people pick her tonight as the party's star. Left them no choice."

"With a nod to you, the other star."

"I like attention too. We all like to be loved. And, I guess I'm not giving my wife a lot now, but that's my problem, which I'll deal with when midnight rings in. Time to go in. You want to try something different?

"Sure, Professor. What?"

"It'd be like a play. Hope you can pull it off, but I'll enjoy watching in any case, and unless you're totally un-Patrick-like, I can't see much harm since you could always laugh it off."

"What?"

"Tell Suzie you've made the choice. Right after midnight, of course. Spend a lot of time schmoozing Andy. He'll be hanging around Suzie anyway. Pump him up about that Disciple Fellowship thing. Be attentive. He's a nice guy too. He'll go along, or he wouldn't have come to your house tonight. Fawn over him. Ask him about college. His philosophy of life. Everything. People like being asked about things important to them, another form of attention. Then, in front of Suzie, tell him you're really in love with him and that you'll fight Suzie to the death over him. At least, it might cut the tension."

"That could be rish," Patrick slurred. "Maybe she'll see how it makes me feel when she's juggling the two of us."

"Could be rich? Collect yourself. No more drinks for the next hour." In retrospect, Patrick thought Mr. Wilson's suggestion was just his mentor's way of trying to get him to lay off drinking for an hour, assuming he wouldn't follow through with the silly plan.

If so, Mr. Wilson misread Patrick's sincerity when the young man asked, "Will it work?"

"I'm just a director, but I would enjoy watching. Hard to make more of an ass of yourself than you already have."

Steve Wilson was wrong. The script unraveled. Patrick ignored his director's no-alcohol warning after some intense maneuvering to see who would be with Suzie at midnight. Instead of coming across as self-deprecating and whimsical, Patrick came across as obnoxious, seemingly poking fun at Suzie and implying Andy was gay.

Steve Wilson, not doing so well himself with the attention he intended to pay his wife, frowned as he watched the scene play out. Patrick grimaced the next day, recalling the fool he had made of himself. He must have looked more like Mrs. Glass in the bathtub than Mrs. Glass playing the crowd. As a result, he spent all New Year's Day and much of the week or two after in his own shell.

21.

MID-JANUARY
SENIOR YEAR

About two weeks later, Patrick suffered what he considered an indignity when Carl Schipper completely rewrote a game story. This was the copy Patrick had submitted:

Lancers Falter Against Loyola
By: Patrick Kiernan

The mighty have fallen again! For the second time in two weeks, the highly rated LaSalle Lancers dropped a basketball game, this time to suburban rival Loyola, 47–43. Credit the Wildcats, but the Lancers looked distracted, a sudden concern for Coach Jerry Burke's nationally-ranked team.

LaSierra had dropped the previously unbeaten Lancers in LaSalle's final pre-league tune-up right after the new year. Then, the Lancers barely escaped close games with American and River View in stumbling to a 2–0 league mark. With last night's defeat, the seemingly invincible Lancers have dropped a game behind archrival Loyola in league standings.

Once again, the Lancers missed Lance Hall, hobbled for a second week with a pulled muscle. Without him in the lineup, the pesky Wildcats collapsed more than ever on all-everything center T.R. Ward. Ward did score twelve of his eighteen points as a result of offensive follow-ups, suggesting the effectiveness of Coach Ted Carroll's 'Cats in denying LaSalle's big man the ball and room to maneuver.

Carroll effusively praised his spunky team: "We played our game tonight, slowing it down and then finding the big shot." Loyola guard Billy Gemma paced all scorers with twenty-one points. Three of his six hoops came from three-point land, and he added six charity tosses in seven attempts. The Wildcats led all the way through the dull encounter.

"We came out flat and fell behind early 13–4, which set the tone," Burke lamented. "We had to play their game the rest of the way. We missed Hall, who should be back next week. [Terry] Crain and [Tom] Kuhn still aren't giving us the consistent performances we expected, and [Rich] Pantera made mistakes you'd expect from a youngster. Even our guards were off. Sammie [Spear] had more turnovers than assists." Blue Chipper T.R. Ward himself looked distracted at times.

After the story appeared differently in *The Star*, Patrick sought out a sick Carl Schipper, prowling around his office the next morning. "Relax," Schipper soothed, "I get that you're upset with the changes."

"Changes?" Patrick responded. "A total rewrite. What was so wrong?"

Schipper paused to sneeze. "Calm down, kid. Not the end of the world. The bigger apocalyptic concern is with what's happening with Operation Desert Storm in Iraq, where we're dropping tons of bombs, and they're firing scuds at Israel." He paused for effect. "I've almost always run yours pretty much as is, unless cutting for length."

"That's just it, Carl. Why this one? Feels like everything's sideways lately, not just angst about what's going on half a world away. This wasn't for length. You changed the lead and slant. A lot of stats and scorebook stuff, but kinda lifeless."

"Nothing personal. And surely not a reflection of your talent." Schipper fiddled with some copy on his desk, took a sip of his coffee, and blew his nose before continuing with what he hoped would be a calmed-down Patrick: "You know I think you write better than me. Eighteen years old, and you're a whiz kid. Still, I'm good at editing and know my readership."

Mollified a bit, Patrick rocked back and forth on his heels while thinking of a restrained reply. Not entirely honestly, he stammered, "Th-thanks, Carl, but you write well. I'm not suggesting ..."

"That my story was white bread?" Schiffer offered in his flu-affected growl. "No soul. The antithesis of Vanilla Ice belting out 'Play Some Funky Music, White Boy' on Saturday Night Live last week."

Patrick paused, unsuccessfully trying to imagine Schipper getting down on a dance floor, especially with his red nose making him look like Rudolph. "Hell, Carl, you're making this tough. You know what I think of you. It's just that ..."

"You were disappointed, a little defensive, been feeling down lately, your Lancers lost, and I took away a story you worked late to finish on deadline."

"Quite a litany, but, yeah."

"And reading between the lines, I'd guess you wanted to make a point about LaSalle too, and T.R., that something's amiss in paradise, but I negated that. A paper's not for sending subtle messages."

"I get that," Patrick acknowledged. "I try to stay objective. You did tell me, though, to slant the LaSalle basketball stories toward them since it's the biggest ongoing sports story, with Ward's recruitment, in the area."

"My fault. I should have said something to you yesterday, or even this morning, and then let you rewrite it, but I felt sicker than a dog and rewrote it myself to save time. Yeah, I do want the slant toward LaSalle, but not with that game. I changed my mind, Patrick. Bottom line."

"Why?" Patrick persisted. "My story?"

"Partly, but also the game itself. You've done well covering Loyola games, painting them as plucky underdogs. They've raised the bar. Thought they'd be just over .500 this year, but they've exceeded expectations. The underdog bit the big dog. That story, with the Lancers' ongoing soap opera, will keep our readers interested all season. I highlighted the positive. You highlighted the negative and, yes, did so following the marching orders I had given you."

Patrick admitted to himself that Carl was making sense.

"Instead of Sammie's off night, you should have played up Loyola's ball-hawking zone. They deserved it, and people at the game would see ignoring that as bias. I do regret I didn't give you a heads-up about changing the slant when I got the score from you on the phone. And, in the morning, when I might have given it back to you to rewrite, I felt the way you looked at that New Year's party."

"Don't remind me," Patrick blurted. "That bad, huh?"

"Only the strongest things I've been drinking are coffee and a horrid cough syrup." Schipper blew his nose loudly into a rumpled handkerchief. "Don't know where this stuff comes from. Maybe I should throw a Shakespeare reference at Mr. Literature. How about 'Out, out, damned snot!' *MacBeth*, right?"

The two locked eyes for a few seconds before breaking into laughter. "God, Carl, something's rotten in Scotland rather than Denmark with that word play, but love the effort!"

"Pretty bad," Schipper returned, "but I'm just a sportswriter. God, it hurts to laugh. My lips are so chapped they've cracked. Don't stand close. Don't want you getting it." Schipper then proceeded to pull off a teaching performance that would have made Steve Wilson proud. Before moving to Patrick's rejected story, he pulled up his own and painstakingly self-edited it almost word by word. He noted the bland lead and pointed out words that lacked power. He ticked off a few other flaws before concluding with a wry summation: "Yeah, the guy who wrote this must've been on his deathbed, but at least it had the right slant." Patrick nodded almost involuntarily. "Now, let's look at yours."

"Lead on, MacDuff."

"Literary again?"

"From *MacBeth*."

"The lead. Not bad. A little skimpy and, of course, as you now agree, the wrong slant and less than objective. Again, my fault. You're so good, I sometimes think you'll anticipate what I'm thinking. Always take the David versus Goliath thing," he reiterated. "The Joe Namath Jets beating the Colts in the third Super Bowl. The Miracle Mets. The U.S. Hockey team and Al Michaels' 'Miracle on Ice' in the 1980 Olympics. You can never pass up a slant like that. Even when a big underdog comes close. A few weeks ago, when LaSalle tripped up against LaSierra, that was a joke. Obviously, came out flat after vacation, and Ward had this flu. Jerry even called it a fluke. But, against a big rival, they shouldn't have been flat. I was at the State game, but Loyola must have played well to win."

"They had a game plan and worked hard at both ends."

"But," Schipper pounced, "you called it 'dull' here toward the end."

Like a witness caught in a trap by a smart lawyer, Patrick squirmed. "Yeah, I did, didn't I? Editorializing. The cardinal sin. You'd think Coach Burke wrote the article," Patrick tried to recover.

"Nah," Schipper scoffed. "I know Jerry. He never considers it dull when he loses. Tragic, maybe, like one of your Shakespeare plays, but not dull. Sounds like that word came from a typical high school paper, presenting things entirely one-sided," Schipper slipped in softly.

"Like a high school cheerleader," Patrick conceded. "I hate that homer stuff when I read it or hear it, even from game announcers."

"That impressed me when I read your stories in *The Lance*. I spend time reading high school papers. Gives me ideas for stories in them sometimes, but most are hilarious. Seems two out of three sports articles end up saying, 'go out and support the team and watch them win.' Yours were never like that."

"Mr. Wilson's a good teacher," Patrick complemented. "Some school morons don't understand why *The Lance* isn't totally biased. They think that's the way it should be: kudos to everybody who plays."

"Beat writers face the same problem with the big boys. If you take over Pete's job with the baseball teams, you'll see. Some players think local writers should shine things on. Something critical, even if objective, can buy silence or an offer to step outside. At least we don't send reporters on road trips. That's when it gets real sticky. Especially when players flaunt their infidelities or don't hide drinking and drug abuse. Yep, not always a business for people who need to be liked."

Patrick zoned out a bit as Schipper concluded. Mention of the job that he realized he wanted more than ever almost separated him from reality. When he snapped back from his dreams, he considered asking directly about his chances, but checked himself.

"This makes me think," Schipper said, "you need to write a feature for a change of pace. About the pressure the recruiting process brings to high school sports. Focused on T.R. but broader. Readers would devour a piece like that."

"If written well," Patrick smirked.

"You've got a helluva future, kid. Taking criticism with good grace isn't easy either."

"Thanks. And, you're like Mr. Wilson in the classroom, getting people to reflect on what they've done, what they're doing, without being threatened, bullied, or put off. A good teacher."

"Nice complement coming from Mr. School," Schipper deflected, touched but not wanting the conversation to get too maudlin. "It's good when adults talk out problems."

Carl had a last card to play before shooing Patrick out so he could go home to nap. He asked, in the context of the feature he suggested, if Patrick had any updates about T.R., who had been playing lethargically.

Patrick confided that T.R.'s possible scholarship reduction could be decided within the week and even admitted his friend had been unusually withdrawn of late. He did, however, hold other things back. After he left the office, Patrick bemoaned the fact that, at one point, it would have been Suzie with whom he could have talked without ever holding anything back. He headed to the River for solace. It had never let him down.

22.

TOWARD THE END OF JANUARY
SENIOR YEAR

About a week later, Patrick dropped off the following note to
Carl Schipper on his way to school:

Carl,
A HEADS-UP, NOT FOR PRINT:

*Old man Foley and the Booster's Club jerked away some of
T.R.'s scholarship money. The final word on scholarship disburse-
ment is up to the school and Brother Charles, but he usually
goes along with the Club's recommendations. Apparently,
after quite a battle at a closed-door meeting two nights ago,
Brother Curt came out and called Foley and some of his cronies
"racists," but it didn't sway the outcome. The fundraising part
of that group isn't really controlled by the school, I guess.*

*Charles probably feared acting against Foley after the
way the Sean thing came down. That he'd cut off other fund-
ing. It used to cover athletic department frills, but most of
those things (equipment, etc.) have become necessities. Foley
also personally donates building and site improvements through
his contractor business. His Booster's Club's full of bitter
McEntee people. Foley's own fiefdom.*

*They clung to the point they weren't after specific tar-
gets but wanted to spread more money to more kids. That's*

supposedly why they stipulated nobody should get more than a 50% ride from the funds they controlled. They take a grain of truth—yes, it's admirable if more kids get scholarship money, and, yes, the Brothers try to spread scholarship money around as part of their mission—but then stretch it to suit their vendetta while hiding behind supposed good intentions. I get more jaded about the world every day.

Jerry argued it wasn't fair to change rules in the middle of the game, to withdraw money after T.R. and the other basketball players above the plateau (Pantera, and one of the J.V. players, I think) had counted on it.

That's when Charles worked out his typical compromise. Foley figured since T.R. got the whole first-semester scholarship, he should get nothing the second. Charles convinced him the first semester was history. It would be 50% of the second semester's tuition. Still, I wonder if Foley's trying to sandbag T.R., Forte, and his mom. Other scholarship sources might look fishy now.

Brother Curt's irate. T.R. seems to be taking it well. A bitter smile? Or, maybe he's just glad to have it done and focus on basketball. He doesn't seem particularly worried about coming up with the half tuition, but he's not talking about that.

I'll call about weekend assignments,
Patrick

Late that afternoon, Patrick drifted to the River, where he heard classmates would celebrate the start of their last semester. He had noticed River gatherings being muted, the innocence and easy conviviality of times past fading into memory.

Kelly Kerwin dominated the scene as eight seniors huddled in the fading remnants of a crisp winter's day. As Patrick appeared, he heard the last ironic comments about how TV footage from the Gulf War bombing brought to mind Game Boy dot-matrix screens. Then, in detail, Kerwin satirized the test Mr. McEntee's sub had given for his semester Civics final. Patrick remained on the periphery of the crowd as others lampooned people, places, and things about LaSalle, the very people, places, and things that drew all present together.

After a while, without a word to the others, Patrick strolled away toward the cold River.

"Hey, Patrick, okay?" Kerwin inquired about five minutes later. He had parted some overhanging branches awkwardly with his long skinny arms to approach the solitary figure stopped beyond a fallen tree.

Patrick turned. "Sure, Killer. Just thinking about going for a swim."

"In there?" Kerwin's voice rose incredulously. "And they think I do crazy things."

"You do. Let's do it."

"I'd freeze my *pelotas* off. It's cold enough drinking my frosties."

"Yeah, probably right," Patrick wheeled to face Kerwin for the first time, "but it'd sure be fun. How you doing with your video games?"

"Good. Got our own computer at home. An Apple."

"Incredible machines. The future. I word-process with a Bank Street Writers floppy, and it changes everything. So much time saved from a typewriter."

"Well, my Apple's light years better than those Radio Shack things at school. I'm trying to teach myself to program games." Kerwin drew closer, crawling up on top and then over the downed tree. "Getting pretty good. Come over sometime, and I'll show you. Not that impressive, but a start. Learning code."

"I'd like that." Patrick shuffled in place and looked toward the River. "Been pretty busy lately ..."

Kerwin cut in, drawing Patrick's stare. "No time for us peons anymore."

Patrick broke into a grin as he took a few steps to pick up a pebble. He flung it into the swirling water and then looked up again. "Peon, huh? Always thought you had a higher regard for yourself."

"I do. It's just you're out there making it in the real world already. I'm jealous. Maybe when I finish writing a good program, a game, I can join you."

"Take your time," Patrick advised. "That world's not always what it's cracked up to be. When my father still lived with us, he told me to enjoy being young. It just might be the best time of life. Hope not. He left when I was six."

"I think he was wrong."

"Maybe about a lot."

"You seem kinda down. Want to talk, or me to leave you alone?" Kerwin ventured.

"I do want some quiet time," Patrick responded, surprising Kerwin, who wasn't used to people taking him seriously enough to be frank.

"Sure, Patrick." He hopped back up on top of the tree trunk. "If you need anything, yell. I'll be at the clearing with the rest of the rock pile." Jumping down on the other side, he stumbled but caught himself. He looked up sheepishly, but Patrick's eyes stayed affixed on the River.

Patrick turned. "Kelly, you understand, right? You've become a real friend, and I don't want to hurt your feelings."

"We're good. You're one of the few people who act like I have any."

"You know who I saw here a week ago?"

"Who?"

"Sean. Sean Foley."

"God, I hope I never ..."

"No." Patrick stopped him. "We had a good talk. He seemed mellowed out. A real good talk. I think he'd like to change a few things. Sounds like he was always pissed at his dad. He wasn't looking to make excuses, but their relationship does sound toxic. You were talking about McEntee's sub with everybody. Made me think about that conversation. Sean was dedicated to the old goat too, but McEntee hasn't answered any letters since he moved to Calistoga. That really upsets Sean. He used the word 'untethered.' I forgot how smart he was, a real stand-out in frosh English."

"Don't know what to say." Kerwin shook his head before saying, "I probably would've ducked for cover if I'd seen him. Sounds as if you were hearing confession, saving souls, like Suzie. Course, you talked to him, and I didn't. I sometimes have trouble saving myself."

"Miss what I had with Suzie. She was the one I could tell everything. Ain't life a bitch sometimes?"

"Maybe I could earn that friendship. You know, I would have dived in to save you if you went in there," his head jerked in the direction of the River, "if you got in trouble."

"Impressive, Kelly. You'd freeze your *pelotas* off for me, huh?" Patrick hopped the tree confidently. "I'll go back up with you. I need to drop by the *Star* before it gets too late, but if you're good with it, maybe I can drop by your house on the way home so you can show me how your computer creation works."

23.

END OF JANUARY
SENIOR YEAR

Carl Schipper compiled the game story for the Mater Dei–La-Salle contest, which took place in Berkeley before the Oregon/California game the last Saturday afternoon in January. Patrick's sidebar accompanied the game account:

Changes Promise Future Success
By: Patrick Kiernan

"Sometimes you have to face uncomfortable truths," said La-Salle Coach Jerry Burke in explaining his second-half strategy against Santa Ana power Mater Dei at venerable Harmon Gym on the Berkeley Campus yesterday afternoon. The fact that the Lancers eventually lost the rousing contest against their highly regarded opponent from down south, 91–89 in double overtime, didn't detract from the success and promise of the move.

The swift, high-leaping SoCal contingent opened a ten-point lead before halftime while LaSalle's all-everything center T.R. Ward sat after two disputed foul calls. When Ward reentered the game, Mater Dei immediately switched to a collapsing zone, the look most opponents have given LaSalle to thwart the Lancer's Blue Chipper.

"It was fun running with them until near the end of the

first half," exclaimed Sammie Spear, LaSalle's point guard. *"They're really talented, but nobody's played us straight up all year. After they got the double-digit lead, they tried to take T.R. out of the offense. We had to give them the new look."*

The new look is one the Lancers have kept under wraps for a couple weeks. It looks like a keeper for league play.

Starting forwards Terry Crain and Tom Kuhn didn't start the second half. Sweet-shooting Larry Nichols moved to forward, joining Lance Hall, who had been getting increasing minutes before a recent muscle pull slowed him down. "We haven't been getting good shooting from the corners," Coach Burke noted, "and that allowed teams to sag on the big fellow."

Burke lauded the attitude of Crain and Kuhn, "team players who'll still help us big time." Frank Tucci, LaSalle's football quarterback, teamed with Sammie Spear in the backcourt in the new alignment. "We give away rebounding and height on defense with basically a three-guard alignment," said Coach Burke, "but we get better outside shooting, create spacing on the floor, and allow Ward more room to roam."

The Lancers, now 16–3 on the season and 4–1 in league play, saw Ward pump in thirty-seven points, Nichols added nineteen, and Hall chipped in seventeen. The basket that tied the game at the end of the first overtime suggested the strategic ploy might cause future opponents fits. Drawing defenders to him, Ward slipped the ball to Hall, who feathered in the tying basket from the baseline beyond the key. "I wouldn't be surprised if we win out from here," offered exemplary team player Tom Kuhn. Ironically, in a loss, the LaSalle Lancers might have found the formula for success.

"You seem happy with the story you gave Carl," Suzie enthused the night of the afternoon contest in Berkeley. "And great that Carl will drive it back after treating us to dinner so you didn't have to phone it in or rush back."

In virtual silence, the two took a long walk toward the end of Berkeley's Recreational Pier, which jutted like a long arrow into San Francisco Bay.

Picking up the train of thought minutes later, Suzie resumed, "Course, you had an exciting game to work with." Bundling herself against the wind whipping near the edge of the Bay as the two slowed to a stop, she explained, "Even the Cal rooters got excited with the finish, though it held up their game. I'm always amazed, though, how quickly you come up with finished stories right after games."

"That's why I'm terrible to watch a game with," Patrick offered, looking over the railing at the choppy water swirling below. "Plotting strategy and direction, tracking the game, and writing sentences at the same time, many of which get left on the cutting room floor. And then zipping to the locker room to get quotes. I'm sure," he offered whimsically, "you and Doris enjoyed the Cal game waiting for me and T.R."

"Wasn't bad," retorted Suzie. "That Cal forward with the wavy hair was pretty cute. Loved the way he wore his shorts."

"Give me a break," Patrick pleaded. He sat down with Suzie on one of the wooden benches bisecting the pier sporadically like passing lanes on a rural highway. "You're just saying that 'cause you know how good I look in shorts. At least I don't dress like Carl, the stereotypical reporter."

"You're lucky to have mentors. The fact he picked you for the job in the first place and gives you so much responsibility's incredible. I'm not sure you know how lucky you are," Suzie concluded almost icily, her mood darkening like the fog blowing through the Golden Gate straight to the East Bay.

Patrick stared at her blankly like the drunk the two had passed as they first stepped onto the wooden pier. "This morning was fun," Patrick offered as if words could wave away the fog. He leaned toward Suzie while deliberately locking his propped hands around his flexed right knee. "Worth getting up before the roosters to drive down," he added hastily.

"It was," Suzie agreed unconvincingly.

"I hadn't been on that merry-go-round at Tilden Park for years. Not since my father ..."

"You know why it was fun?" Suzie interrupted. "We weren't just sitting and talking. Like this. Like we always end up doing lately. We were doing something. It's as if you've become a sportswriter in life too. Sit down; talk about it; summarize it; analyze it. This morning we were laughing, not lost in ourselves." Suzie's voice cracked as she continued: "Every time we go out, we end up having a serious talk. Or, rather, you push for that. Convince me. Make me change. I just want to have fun. Don't you anymore?"

"Well, I ..." Patrick began, but stopped as he noticed Suzie's eyes mist over.

"Always so serious. You make fun of Disciple Fellowship, but those meetings are like comedy revues compared to our dates lately. It's wearing." Suzie fumbled for the snaps on her coat's hood, which she pulled up to encircle her hair.

Instinctively, Patrick swayed toward Suzie. He checked himself, however, as she dabbed her sleeve at her eyes.

"Make sense?" she implored, raising her voice. "This morning was the way it used to be. Laughing and playing, and running, without thinking. You weren't worried about manipulating the moment, or me. I could've stayed on that merry-go-round forever."

Patrick sought the words to wrap into a rebuttal. "You changed it," he accused, "a few months ago. You found Jesus, while I'm just flesh and blood and mind and feelings."

"So was He. That's what's amazing about our God."

"I'm not amazing and can't compete, but I do love you."

"Stuff it, Pat," Suzie flared. "You know it all, don't you?"

"I don't know anything, Suze. I thought I did, but I don't. All I know is I don't want to lose you. I'd feel untethered." Suzie shot to her feet and walked dramatically to the railing across from her above the choppy water.

Patrick trotted after her before stopping abruptly as Suzie

spun around to face him. "We have to get this settled, Pat. I love you too, but I'm not ready to push ahead, everything else be damned, like you seem to want. Not now," Suzie proclaimed as if she had rehearsed the scene. Patrick brooded, not wanting to say the wrong thing.

Mistakenly, Suzie considered this a sign of petulance. Looking into his eyes, however, she saw fear and concern. She reached out to caress his face. "Say something, Pat. What more can I say?" she blurted before doing so. "I love you. And, yes, I look forward to making love, but not now. I have to stay true to myself, and I don't want to rush to the altar. I promised my father I'd finish college, and being married young wouldn't work with that."

"My mom talks about her mistake marrying so young. Though, of course, I wouldn't be here if she didn't."

"Your mom's the perfect example. Very bright but didn't finish college. Divorced young. And truly Catholic, making another marriage complicated."

"Selfishly, I'm glad she never got married or had a string of boyfriends."

"You were her focus. Maybe, she'll go wild when you're out of the nest." Suzie quickly reconsidered: "She's not the type. I sometimes feel as if she's my older sister." Patrick rocked back with that thought. "Yes, I'm going to keep my promise to my father the easy way, but I don't revel in being the Virgin Queen, you know."

He didn't mean to, but Patrick laughed. He tried to stifle it but couldn't. He reached out and gently took Suzie in his arms. The two swayed together in the windswept whirls of fog. "At least you know," Patrick smirked, "you're not the only eighteen-year-old virgin left in America, although, God knows, it wouldn't be my clear choice."

"Hold me, Pat. I love you," Suzie nuzzled up and kissed Patrick with a great deal of affection, if not passion.

"What do we do?"

"Have fun. See where life takes us next year. It'll be right when it's right. I want you to go on seeing me on these terms. It's hard on me too, you know, and I know it's hard for you."

Patrick resisted pointing out the double entendre, and Suzie continued, "God knows, I'd be crushed if you still didn't want to go out. I think, and pray, everything can work out someday. Patience. My father stressed that."

"Patience," Patrick repeated with resignation, if not conviction. He wondered to himself if Mr. Andrus had been rewarded for his patience before cancer cut him down so unexpectedly, but he realized that was the last thought he should voice.

"And, if it's meant to be like I think, it'll last."

"What about Andy?" Patrick asked, holding Suzie tight but bobbing his head like a fighter in a clinch.

"He's a friend."

"Which you want me to be satisfied being, right?"

"Don't be absurd, Pat. Do I have to draw you a picture? I told you, I love you. He's just a friend."

"I suppose he's going to be a priest or something."

Suzie broke completely away and backhandedly grabbed the railing behind her. "You got it. About him. Yes, he's thinking of being a priest."

"Jesus Christ," Patrick uttered.

"Yeah, that would be his boss, Pat," Suzie rejoined smugly.

"I wouldn't have guessed. Why didn't you say something? You knew I was jealous. You sure he's not just playing you?"

"Give me some credit, Pat. I can see your mind churning. He'd talk about feelings like that as some perverse way to try to get into my pants? C'mon. Yes, we've had intimate talks about his vocation and whether it'd be right, but talks. You haven't been very easy to talk with lately."

"I thought he was horning in. I feel stupid now. Let's walk back. It's getting cold. I feel terrible. Sorry."

Suzie took his hand, and the two stood still for a minute until Suzie spoke up: "We're still going together, right?"

"Of course," Patrick smiled. "Let me get this straight. Or, maybe I'm not supposed to get it straight."

"Repressed virility," Suzie announced with a smile, unburdened after pulling off what Mr. Wilson, quoting Elliot, called "forcing the moment to its crisis." She almost sounded sexy when she asked, "You can keep the burner on medium-low, can't you?"

"Yeah, I guess. A helluva steamy PG romantic triangle: The Blessed Virgin, a horny St. Joseph, and an almost eunuch entering the priesthood."

"Not sure about it being a good movie," Suzie responded as she moved back toward the pier entrance slowly. "Besides, he's not a eunuch. Ought to appeal to your sense of irony. The only one who isn't a virgin is the one who's going to be a priest. He confided that so I could assure him his vocation could still be right."

Patrick stopped dead as if the fog had suddenly solidified in his path. "He, he told you ... that?" Patrick stammered.

"You won't repeat it, will you?" she asked as if really saying, "You better not." She, too, stopped. "I trusted you with this."

"Suzie, did you tell him about us?" Before she could respond, Patrick added, "Intimate details? The triples hitter who stops at third rather than circling the bases?"

"Be reasonable. Your male ego's talking."

"Screw my male ego!" he snapped.

"And besides, you're slipping into sports analogies, just like you say Carl does when he's upset."

"Dammit, Suzie, stop analyzing me." He stomped toward the railing across from them.

Suzie followed. "Pat, I told you about Andy because when things are good, I always tell you everything."

"Me too. Are they good?"

"We've needed to have this conversation, a real one and not the ones you've been hemming and hawing about since before New Year's. To make things good. To have fun together again." Adroitly, Suzie stepped around and in front of Patrick. "I didn't tell him anything about us. He probably thinks I'm a bunny with you. He needed the confession, not me. And, I need you. Just on my terms for a while. You still love me?"

"It's hard," he laughed, "but, of course. Yes."

Patrick reached to kiss her, but she slipped away, smiling. "Then catch me first. Action, not talk." With that, she broke into a run back toward the pier entrance's solid ground.

"Women!" Patrick shrugged toward the hidden sky as, transfixed, he watched Suzie open space up between them. Running himself, he found a release in the furious pursuit past puzzled onlookers on the pier late at night for various and sundry reasons.

Patrick's heart pounded as he caught Suzie just before she exited the pier. The two laughed, a laugh deep from the gut that Patrick hadn't felt, let alone shared, for weeks. As he skidded to a stop to embrace Suzie, the couple nearly piled into the same drunk they had passed on the way out. Tattered and unshaven, he huddled near a maintenance box. Coming out of his own fog, he rasped, "Hey, man. Spare change?"

"Sure." Patrick reached into his pocket, lifted out a couple coins, and slipped them into a half-gloved hand. "I can always spare a change or two. Peace, brother."

Patrick unburdened himself on the ride home. About his meeting with Sean Foley. His hopes for the job covering the A's and Giants while attending Berkeley. The details he knew and imagined about T.R.'s situation. His own angst about the future. Suzie listened, responded, and soothed. "I do feel good again," Patrick announced at Suzie's front door.

"You want to come in for a minute?"

"No, too late. I'll take a rain check. Damn," he snickered, "a sports analogy again. Maybe by tomorrow night I'll be cured. Let's study together then. I'm playing some hoops in the afternoon." Patrick laughed loudly. He kissed her hand gallantly before the two locked into an embrace as fresh as the cleansed air. When Patrick pulled away to leave, he blurted over his shoulder, "Peace, sister. I like the change."

24.

FIRST DAY OF FEBRUARY
SENIOR YEAR

Patrick left a note for his mother before leaving for Mass, dropping by Kelly Kerwin's house for lunch, and going to LaSalle's gym:

Mom,

Going to 10:30 Mass and eventually to play basketball with the guys. Got the message you left that you had talked to Mr. Wilson about his joining us for the pickup game. Left him a message and tried to call, but he was out with the girls. Mrs. Wilson didn't know we had invited him and whether he would be there. She said she and the kids were away all day yesterday and then stayed overnight at her mother's house and hadn't talked with him this morning.

If he phones, tell him we'll be starting after 12:15 Mass at St. John's, which I presume you'll go to since I guess you got in later than me. Brother Curt's also going to play with us along with Mr. W.

Good day yesterday, though we lost the game. Left the paper open on the kitchen table to my story. Good talk with Suzie last night, though I still think all women take weird pills at times. Do you? Just joking.

Carl took Suzie and me to dinner at Zachary's, that deep-dish pizza place you've raved about. Yummy. Nice of him.

Love, Pat

P.S. Hope you had fun yesterday. I'm going to Suzie's to-night to study, but I'll be home before that for dinner.

Mr. Wilson sauntered into LaSalle's gym with most of the other pickup game players already warmed up. Most hooted at their teacher's ensemble, consisting of green athletic shorts, a red tee-shirt, and lowcut, black Converse tennis shoes over grey sox. Kelly Kerwin, as usual, got in the loudest shot: "Your kids dress you? Italian Olympic team?"

The object of the good-natured barbs responded, "I heard who was playing and, outside of Brother Curt, figured this was the Nerd League. Dressed accordingly."

In fact, during the next two hours, Brother Curt and Patrick, who had gotten playing time on the freshman basketball squad, led their teams. Until he tired out, Mr. Wilson held his own, as did Miguel Ayala and Chris Weaver throughout. Kelly Kerwin, Tomas Salazar, and Leroy Horton knew what they were doing, even if they didn't always have the skills to accomplish what they tried. The last chosen, Student Body President Teddy Gervais and Dave Koeppen, guarded each other and generally stayed out of the way.

The game action pleased Patrick, responding to Suzie's challenge to stop watching others do things. Patrick wondered why he always sweated so profusely. He often watched Sammie Hill play a game or dance up a storm and look as if he had just taken a nap in an air-conditioned room. Patrick, on the other hand, oozed sweat the way T.R.'s old Chevy oozed oil.

After a few games to twenty, all the participants except Koeppen hung around, sprawled on wooden benches, or propped against the gym wall. Brother Curt went to the Brothers' House to bring back some Cokes. "Make mine a Bud," Kerwin protested, but Brother Curt simply ignored him, apart from the almost ritualistically rendered grimace and shake of the head.

All but one stayed for about an hour, sparked in part by a locker-room camaraderie usually not part of their lives. At first, the conversation consisted of game recaps embellished through the prism of various points of view. At one point, Brother Curt roared, "If you guys keep talking, I'm gonna leave here convinced us good guys lost that last game we won."

The conversation unexpectedly veered toward seriousness for a minute, surprisingly moved there by Kerwin. He voiced his concern for Koeppen, hoping the school's star chess player hadn't left early out of embarrassment over his lack of physical prowess.

Quickly though, as if too much seriousness might drive everybody to the showers and home, the tone shifted back. Wilson summed up what followed as "a good old-fashioned locker room rag session."

Brother Curt, however, got serious again when he noted that African American Leroy Horton was at the top of his game in these exchanges. He looked at the others. "You hear about Black athletes, especially N.B.A. and N.F.L. guys, being trash talkers. Most white people probably think it's a ghetto thing, but the roots go deeper."

"The Dozens," Mr. Wilson succinctly stated, as if to demonstrate he wasn't unaware of African American culture and history.

"Yeah, the Dozens. Killer, you're often the man with the jokes. You've heard the 'Yo' Mama ones,' right?"

Kerwin judged Brother Curt's tone too serious to offer a flip answer: "Yeah. So?"

Brother Curt directed his gaze at Mr. Wilson to avoid targeting one of the kids. He got in his face: "Yo' mama so fat, the elephant rides her in the parade." The young men, even Horton, didn't know whether to laugh or not. "Putdowns a lot worse than that. You've probably heard a few."

"And, like Brother's getting at, with bigtime historical importance," Mr. Wilson pointed out.

"When our people were slaves, they had to learn not to strike out, no matter what they got called, no matter how overseers trashed them. Cruel taunts about their mothers, other loved ones, or their sexuality. If they spoke out, they might get whipped or even killed. That's why the Dozens came about, the life game that evolved into modern trash-talking. Being man enough to take it. Yeah, it's from the 'hood, but it was always important culturally. The young bucks in the field would have to ignore the Man when he verbally robbed them of dignity and pride to make himself feel superior. Life and death, not just for them, but for families. Today, it toughens people up since the Man's still out there, even if he doesn't always carry a whip."

After an unspoken silence, Kerwin shifted the tone once again: "I'm not famous for 'Yo' mama' jokes, but you all know chicken jokes are my new specialty. You know," he continued as if he held a microphone, "like 'Why did the chicken cross the road?' That genre. That the right word, Steve, uh, Mr. Wilson?"

"Close, Mr. Kerwin," Wilson answered, though failing in his attempt to slip into his classroom voice and demeanor amidst the banter. "Hopefully, evolved from the other genre you specialized in when we read *The Miracle Worker* freshmen year, your mean-spirited Helen Keller jokes."

"Yeah, old news. Anyway, here's a couple good ones. Chicken jokes, that is. Not the reading the waffle iron ones." Kerwin looked to Mr. Wilson for a reaction, but he remained nonplussed. Kerwin, however, played it as if the teacher had gone off. "Now, now, Mr. W." he consoled. "I know it was an inspirational play."

"C'mon, Killer," Patrick ventured. "You're taking us down a ... blind alley. Get on with it." Mr. Wilson winced.

"Yeah, knew you couldn't wait, Scoop. Mr. Newsboy here won't admit it, but he's my best audience for chicken jokes. Anyway, here goes. How did the punk rocker cross the road?"

"Punk rocker? What happened to the chicken jokes?" the earnest Teddy Gervais spat out, not realizing he was becoming Killer's straight man.

"How did he cross the road? Stapled to a chicken, of course."

Gervais slumped visibly, with none of the affected disdain

the others felt compelled to register. "You're really beyond the fringe sometimes," he weakly retorted.

"Okay, an even better one, one even Teddy here might admire after he gets it. Why did the chicken cross the basketball court?" He looked around to draw out the silence. "Anybody?"

"Okay, we give," Patrick capitulated. "Why?"

"Because he heard the guy in the striped shirt blew fouls." Kerwin slapped his knees as the punch line sank in slowly among some. "Fouls. Fowls." He spelled the homonyms. "Get it?"

Mr. Wilson broke into a smile. Others laughed while trying to shake their heads disapprovingly. A few looked to Brother Curt, as if to see if laughing was proper. Gervais finally blurted: "That's gross, Kerwin. Homophobic. This is a Catholic school ..."

"Yes," Brother Curt boomed without rancor, "but it's Kerwin. Maybe one we shouldn't repeat, but I'll give him the clever play on words."

A few minutes later, in the shower room, Patrick, amused, continued shaking his head while the warm torrents of water pounded onto his knotted shoulder blades. After a while, with a month's worth of tension seemingly drained away, he tromped out to dry off and get dressed. Teasing Kerwin on the way, he handed him his bar of soap. "Here, this is for your mouth when Gervais alerts the Disciple Fellowship, and they decide to wash it out."

"You know where you can put it," Kerwin responded.

"Yo' mama," Patrick got in last licks.

25.

MID-FEBRUARY
SENIOR YEAR

Patrick spent the first weeks of February writing stories, feeling relief that the Gulf War was reaching a quick and victorious outcome, prepping for A.P.s, hanging out with different acquaintances, including Sean Foley, who he saw a couple times at the River for surprisingly meaningful encounters, and, most intentionally, doing things with, and to please, Suzie.

Two major highlights of those weeks surprised him as much as his ongoing reconciliation with Foley.

One conflicting moment during Patrick's two weeks of bliss came just before the Riverview game when he wrote a feature about LaSalle sub Tom Kuhn, one of the two seniors Coach Burke had demoted from the starting lineup.

After reading the piece, Mr. Wilson prodded Patrick to acknowledge the LaSalle coach orchestrated the feature, promising and delivering great quotes. In exchange, he got a published story to build up Kuhn as a super sub. In short, Wilson suggested, he had recruited Patrick to write the feature for his own motivational purposes. And, he pointed out, it was a win-win since Patrick got an exclusive article after pitching it successfully to Carl.

"Nothing wrong," Wilson said, "just so you're aware. Jerry once told me good coaches at any level recruit their press as carefully as their players. He probably sees Carl and you as his recruits."

Patrick started to protest before Wilson finished his teaching moment.

"It's not a breach of ethics or a mark against your professionalism," he reassured. "The best journalism often comes through contacts and developed sources. Like Woodward and Bernstein with Watergate. Schipper's an expert at nurturing sources, and the guy from the *Tribune* was clearly in cahoots with old man Foley. The point is, though, all recruited sources can't be trusted. It's the same in critiquing literature. Only, journalism's more immediate, more public, and doesn't always allow for reflection."

Patrick didn't know if Mr. Wilson was warning him about something specific, but he refrained from asking. He feared the warning might be about T.R., a friend and a source, himself relatively shut down around school lately.

In any case, the game story he filed after the Riverview game couldn't be questioned. Possibly overreacting, he even cut out two or three folksy Jerry Burke quotes:

Lancers Roll to Win
By: Patrick Kiernan

The LaSalle Lancers won their second road game of the week last night with a convincing 83–62 triumph over Riverdale in the Lions' gym. "The fact that we won two in a row on the road, going into the Lion's den, so to speak, and coming out alive, gives us momentum heading into next Friday's rematch with league-leading Loyola," veteran coach Jerry Burke observed.

Loyola, meanwhile, won a taut 48–45 contest with American to maintain its undefeated league record [see accompanying story]. The Lancers trail the Wildcats by a game after falling to their rivals earlier.

Burke added, "We've now played our toughest road games and survived. If we get revenge against Loyola, we should be in pretty good shape for our stretch run."

The Lancers will draw a bye next Tuesday before entertaining Loyola on Friday, a Lancer home game moved to Sacramento State to accommodate what's expected to be a big crowd.

The Lancers turned in another well-balanced effort to coast home for season win number 18. T.R. Ward led the Lancers with twenty-one, despite spending much of the contest leading cheers from the bench. Lance Hall (14) and Larry Nichols (13) joined him in double-figure scoring. Sammie Spear, Tom Kuhn, and Frank Tucci all chipped in six apiece, while super-soph Rick Pantera, playing the whole fourth quarter, lit it up for nine points.

"Our young centers [6'7" junior Mark Shaw and 6'8" sophomore Eddie Banchero] got taken to school tonight," Riverview coach Ed Robertson admitted. "That Ward is a handful, and the players around him shot the lights out." Riverview guard Casey Johnston tallied fifteen points for the losing Lions.

Patrick's two highlights during the two-week period sandwiched the Riverview game. That Wednesday after school, Patrick accompanied Suzie and Tammy Dickerson to the Catholic Worker's Kitchen on a sleazy part of J Street.

Suzie spent the better part of the ride there making excuses: First, why other Disciple Fellowship students weren't accompanying them ("Usually, a couple others, but they're doing other projects"); second, why membership had slid ("Seniors are into college admissions this semester, but the twenty-one involved are who we want involved"); and third, why Andy wasn't going to meet them at the site ("Something important came up at the last minute").

In truth, Patrick was happy to have Suzie almost to himself while doing something meaningful for her. He didn't let on he had gloated to Mr. Wilson that Disciple Fellowship was practically going underground at LaSalle like the early Christians in Rome. Most tellingly for the day, he was overjoyed when he found out he wouldn't have to play nice with "Father Andy."

He did, however, take to the four hours plus he spent with the people in what Brother Raymond disdainfully called "that kook Dorothy Day's socialist food giveaway place." For the first time in months, he totally lost himself with others.

The only setback came with the parking ticket he found when returning to the car and hearing Tammy proclaim, "Andy doesn't get tickets because he drops us off and parks where there's no meters." Patrick had fed his meter once but couldn't bring himself to ask anybody in the soup kitchen for change when, immersed in his interactions, he realized the first two-hour period had flown by. The fine was worth the day's good feelings.

Such good feelings predominated the Saturday through Monday after the Riverview game when Patrick accompanied Suzie to Yreka to see cousin Daphne and her family and check out Southern Oregon College across the border in Ashland. Suzie drove, and after a late night getting his game story in, Patrick slept until they were about forty minutes away from the Andrus home in the tiny town that boasted a population of just over 6,000.

"Hey, sleepyhead, almost there," Suzie teased as I-5 stretched out under the shadow of Mount Shasta.

"My God, it's remote," Patrick pronounced as he wiped the sleep from his eyes. The winter sun played hide-and-seek in the overcast. "At least no snow this weekend. My mom and I took about two hours one May sliding down Siskiyou Summit without chains when we hit a freak May snowstorm coming home from the Shakespeare Festival."

"Hope not this Monday when we're leaving Ashland after our play and my college visit."

"Weather reports say we'll be good. Cool having two three-day weekends in a row with Presidents Day next week and playing hooky this Monday."

"Yeah, great that your mom didn't mind you missing school

to come with me. I did want you to get to know Daphne and her family better. And I'm glad you're going on the visit with me to the college Monday morning. I'm excited."

"And, Sunday's play at the Shakespeare Festival. I love Ashland, though it'll be strange seeing *Dracula* at a Shakespeare Festival. I guess for the inside winter schedule, they do mix in other works. Mom was jealous. She always loved our Ashland excursions to see good theater in a great setting. Good restaurants and that wonderful Lithia Park too. I just wish we had more time to sightsee."

"We will if I end up going to school at S.O.C. The recruiter is suggesting I might get a break on out-of-state tuition and that something might get worked out with the Festival to arrange a part-time job there."

"Well, you have great grades from a good school and a strong drama background. Your Dulcinea in *Man of La Mancha* last year was memorable, and you had other good roles over the years, especially in *Mockingbird* and *Our Town*, though that play's not my favorite. College in Ashland sounds like a good fit. Course, I'd rather you were at Berkeley with me if that's where I end up."

"I did tell Daphne we'd go to a local dance at the Elks Club Saturday night. You're going to get the whole Yreka experience."

"Love the name of this little place we're passing: Weed. Kerwin should live here. George and Lennie from Steinbeck's *Of Mice and Men* ended up on the Monterey Peninsula after being chased out of Weed. Most students tittered at the name."

"And about a third the size of Yreka."

"Clearly, that's why Yreka's the county seat. Bigtime," Patrick smirked.

"Be nice. Daphne said Weed's town motto is 'Weed like to Welcome You.' At least somebody's clever there, and any town or person with a sense of humor about itself can't be all bad."

"For sure. Wonder how many people get Yreka mixed up with Eureka."

"Don't know, but you better not dig too deep with trivia, like that Steinbeck reference, if we end up playing Trivial Pursuit with Daphne's family. They might think my boyfriend's a big showoff. The family likes their board games."

"Except they probably call them bored games here. Sure is desolate."

"Now, now. No big-city partiality. The family's the salt of the earth, and the community's cute and close. I'm even thinking of living with them the first semester or two if I go to Southern Oregon College and don't get the financial aid package I'd want. So, get used to it. You might be coming here often."

Patrick liked the fact that Suzie unabashedly included him in her future. He also, it turned out, loved his stay in Yreka. Suzie's uncle, aunt, their three boys, and Daphne easily and effortlessly enveloped Patrick and Suzie in their fun, games, conversations, and generally boisterous family life. For Patrick, the experience with the large family was as unfamiliar and welcome as his experience in the soup kitchen had been.

Though bundled against the cold, Patrick played basketball on the driveway for hours with Daphne's sixth-, seventh-, and ninth-grade brothers. The boys incessantly talked sports with Patrick, whose work writing about that subject practically qualified him as a god.

Daphne's mother's cooking belied the fact that she looked like she could run a marathon. Sally was so congenial and outgoing during family board game time—no Trivial Pursuit, but Clue and Chutes and Ladders—and the games of Hearts in which four teams of two played, switching opponents with every deal, Patrick had first thought she was acting sweet to be liked. He, however, quickly realized she was being herself.

Al Andrus, Suzie's father's younger brother, sold and serviced tractors and other farm equipment, though he seemed as interested in movies and books, which he loved, and politics and politicians, whom he generally loathed, as he was about farming. A bit phlegmatic, he nevertheless radiated caring. Although his wife kidded him about hours spent talking to people on the road, no doubt his genuine affection for and interest in people contributed greatly to his thriving business and to the fact that he had been named President of the Men's Club at St. Joe's Parish.

The Saturday night dance was fun, providing the visitors a chance, as Daphne, looking Sacramento hip in her fashionable loose-cut green jumpsuit, wryly exaggerated, "to meet everybody in town" while dancing everything from polkas to line dances. Classic rock though, Yreka style, ruled the evening. Captivated, Patrick suggested to Daphne that she should write vignettes about her home town, emulating the tender viewpoint Sandra Cisneros employed about her house on Mango Street in a work Patrick and his class had read in the 9th grade.

Patrick saw Daphne in a new light. She wasn't just a Bible-toting, Catholic "born again" who had "stolen" his girlfriend; rather, she was much like what he surmised would be a small-town Suzie.

Daphne, especially after Patrick reverently related his experience at the soup kitchen and wholeheartedly participated in the 5:00 Mass the family attended, understood what Suzie firmly believed, that Patrick was attuned to the main tenets of the Disciple Fellowship, loving God and loving your neighbors, if resisting the formal identification.

Patrick also met Daphne's boyfriend Edwin Yahr, who appeared pleasant. It seemed she would solve any chastity issues she felt by marrying young, with plans to follow her intended to the community college in Weed and maybe to the altar after graduating high school.

Patrick slept soundly on the couch that night while Suzie shared Daphne's room.

The Southern Oregon College Disciple Fellowship Club and the school's Admissions Department, within walking distance of the Oregon Shakespeare Festival, arranged separate room shares in a dorm for Sunday night for Patrick, Suzie, and Daphne, who went with them to Ashland. Patrick later remarked that his first night in a college dorm was tamer than a night at home.

Patrick and Suzie, like coaches breaking down game film, reflected on the weekend after dropping Daphne off on their drive home late Monday afternoon through weather that held off over the 4,300 feet summit and all the way back down the valley.

They debated nuances about *Dracula*, talked about other plays, and marveled at other Festival offerings and programs, as well as agreeing upon the awesomeness of Ashland.

"I enjoyed being with Suzie's family," Patrick admitted as they passed back through Weed. "You're right: the salt of the earth."

"I didn't think the boys would let you leave Sunday."

"Very cool," Patrick said almost wistfully. "I'm used to just Mom and me. Don't mean to get sappy, but it made me miss that kind of family. I'm still not totally over my dad walking out on us."

"I know. It's sad you have a stepbrother and stepsister about the age of the boys, but you've never met them, except for once, almost by accident."

"His choice. He couldn't even stand the Bay Area, let alone Sacramento. He called it a cow town."

"My God, what would he call Weed or Yreka?"

"He wouldn't call at all. Just like he's never called me. Mom thinks it's better that way after all these years. He has his life with that publishing house in New York City and must be happy."

"You always said it wasn't a good breakup."

"And Mom always said it wasn't a good marriage. Young and foolish, not even agreeing where they should live."

"Except that it produced you. He must be smart and good-looking too."

"The big family was enticing. You think ..." his voice trailed off.

"Yes, I do think ..." Suzie let hers trail off too.

"I love you," Patrick reached up and kissed her cheek, though she concentrated on steadying the wheel.

After some quiet reflection passing undeveloped countryside, Patrick turned the conversation to Suzie's impressions of Southern Oregon College. He could tell she had been taken by the visit, but he wanted to give her the spotlight to sing its praises. "You liked just about everything you saw and heard today, right?

"Yeah, I pretty much made up my mind. The people, the connection with the Festival where it sounds like I could be ushering, the drama department in the school with connections to the actors and actresses, the Disciple Fellowship with a presence on campus, what's not to like?"

"And though she wasn't slick, that Admissions person was a good recruiter too. Knowledgeable and passionate about what she was selling."

"And even gave you the little Red Raider pennant."

"I'll treasure it," Patrick teased.

"Well, it's not Ivy League or even a U.C., but the counseling department always says finding the right college is like finding a marriage partner, what's right for you and the match-up rather than the reputation."

"Sounds then like Berkeley would be my best fit, and I'd put lots of mileage on the little Toyota."

"Well, don't forget. I can drive too."

26.

MID-FEBRUARY
SENIOR YEAR (A COUPLE DAYS LATER)

Patrick got caught up in LaSalle's "basketball madness" in anticipation of Friday's Loyola game, and with the unhappiness of football season washed away like debris down a river. On Wednesday, Patrick gave Brother Curt this note to leave in Mr. Wilson's faculty mailbox:

Mr. W.:

Was going to talk to you after A.P. class, but figured I'd see you during independent study last period. Guess you got a sub or something. I'd wait, but I'm dashing to practice right after the bell. Coach said I could watch, though he usually closes it off.

Been busy working on game programs besides my Star assignments. I have a good idea for a feature for The Lance. It would involve some legwork Friday before and during half-time of the game, but though Carl's writing the game story, I'll be busy readying a sidebar.

Maybe Horton or somebody can follow up with my feature idea about LaSalle fans and alums. Recent grads and older guys before the school went coed, together a real supportive group. Friday's crowd would be a great opportunity for Horton to interview people and get their stories about why they feel such loyalty.

Had something about fan loyalty at the end of my last game story, but Carl, rightfully in retrospect, cut it. The story might also be a good vehicle to suck up to administrators who will love the outreach by the student publication to potential donors. You can tell Leroy, or whoever you give the assignment, you had to pull me OFF OF it! Just tell him not to interview old man Foley.

P.K.

Grunts and groans punctuated the Lancer practice. Jerry Burke challenged his troops: "Work hard, men. Loyola's playing tonight, but this is your prep game."

Patrick forgot the notes he meant to take, mesmerized by every detail of the battle-like practice until Matt Mullan got banged to the floor by Tom Kuhn, twisting his ankle as he went down.

"Dammit!" Burke growled, seemingly more upset by the disruption of plans than over Mullan's fate. "Of all days," he muttered before commanding his players to break into groups and shoot free throws so he could attend to his fallen sub. Frank Lavin, the young team manager, and Patrick walked over to the bleachers to help. "The J.V.'s and Frosh are playing on the road today, and I needed all the bodies for our last drill," Burke lamented while fingering Mullan's ankle. He scanned the gym before measuring Lavin and Patrick. "Kiernan," he implored, "give us a hand, will you?"

"Sure, Coach, you want me to run over and get a Brother to drive ..."

"No, Lavin can do that. I want you to play. I needed everybody for our final drill. You played as a freshman, and you're wearing sneakers. Put your pen and paper down, borrow Matt's practice jersey, and help us play some defense."

"Yeah, sure. Don't think I'd be much good guarding T.R., and ..."

"I'll arrange you with everybody else. Get loose while I finish up with Matt here." Mullan, though biting his lip in pain, peeled off his practice jersey and handed it to Patrick. Patrick immediately began stretching while his mind raced with fantasies of a great practice followed by a summons to join the team in time for Friday's game before Burke's whistle jarred him back to reality. He trotted over to the Coach, who had gathered his players at center court. They gave a cheer for Mullan, the last man off the bench when he got any game time at all, limping out of the gym.

"What you doing here, man?" T.R. wondered as Patrick blended into the huddle. He had been so focused on his free throws he hadn't noticed what transpired in the first row of the bleachers.

Patrick began to stammer an answer, but Coach Burke, not wanting to lose more time, saved him the effort: "He's taking Matt's place. We need bodies for this last half-hour, half-court drill. Now, everybody, pay attention so we can work hard, go home, and meet at the Loyola game outside their gym at 6:30.

"I'll be on time. Tell the new guy here." T.R. nodded toward Patrick.

"If he's covering the game, he usually gets there before you," the Coach snapped. "Starters, turn your jerseys to the white side. Everybody else in green plays 'D.' At the same time. In a zone. I'll position you in a second. Play 'em tough. Deny 'em easy passes inside. Make 'em work. I'll play too, so it'll be eight against five. We'll play half-court and only stop when a basket's made, the defense rebounds or steals the ball, or I yell 'stop.' Got it?"

Listening to his tone, nobody dared speak up.

Burke turned to his white-shirted first-stringers gravitating together. "No wild shots. Work the ball good and get it inside. If it takes five minutes, get a good look. No heaves from the outside. We need to beat their zone to win Friday. Everything, even open threes, comes from inside out."

Burke set his defense, Patrick on top of the key on a wing. He felt like a fifth or sixth defensive back on an obvious N.F.L. passing down. Burke deployed the defense with three on top and four underneath near the bucket, allowing himself the freedom to challenge the ball or front T.R.

Burke once again exhorted his offense: "Playing against eight should make the Loyola defense look like Swiss cheese Friday. Like baseball batters swinging a lead bat in the on-deck circle to make real swings easier." He barely noticed when Brother Curt popped in to yell that Mullan was in adult hands. "Work hard now, boys. You know Matt would do anything to win. No wild heaves if you get frustrated. Work for good shots." He fired the ball to Sammie at half-court and blew his whistle.

The offense operated tentatively at first. Any rat-tat-tat of the ball bouncing on the hardwood produced screams from Burke about the value of quick passes against a zone rather than dribbling around it. Almost to punctuate Burke's point, Sammie Spear and Lance Hall got tied up the next two possessions when they put the ball on the floor. "It'll seem like Loyola has eight men in their zone too. The last time you played them, you made it look like thirty and as if they all were waving brooms. Tony, don't go to sleep in the post. Demand the ball and position yourself to get it. Offense, constant motion. Screen for each other. And, defense, make 'em work. Even if you don't get in Friday, your hard work here'll make it your win too."

Though he hadn't touched the ball except for one intercepted pass and a rebound that caromed to him, Patrick felt good. Anticipating moves or screens, he blocked a few cuts to the basket and clogged passing lanes as if defending holy ground.

Crisp passes and jarring picks finally enabled the offense to get better shots sooner, as the starters dug deep to execute the fundamentals drilled into them so often. T.R.'s physical presence asserted itself as the other starters found ways to get him the ball. A devastating wheel to the basket and dunk followed an exchange in which T.R. shoved Terry Crain to the floor while establishing position.

Elbows and shoulders found flesh as the half-court seemed to shrink under the intensity of trench warfare.

Kuhn and Crain took brief shifts on offense, but the players had returned to their original sides when Burke blew his whistle. "Take a minute. Then, fifteen more quality minutes, and we're done. Think of each sequence as the last play of a close game. That's always about who wants it more." Patrick drew in air like a dying man. Brushing past T.R. as they crossed back onto the court, he started to compliment the big man on his play, possibly to elicit some reciprocal praise. T.R.'s huge chest heaved as he walked, but the scowl written across his game face indicated he was so into the moment that he probably hadn't noticed Patrick's presence as other than an opponent.

Fatigue resulting from the intense scrimmage manifested itself after some minutes as defensive parries became reach-ins, attempted steals became hacks, and uncalled fouls elicited whines. Sammie Spear, not used to an octopus of defenders' arms rather than the one or two he usually controlled, charged down the key in one sequence and ran right over Coach Burke. The players froze when Burke toppled awkwardly to the floor. When he bounced to his feet, Burke barked, "That's a charge, Sammie. Play under control no matter the pressure." He released Sammie from his stare and took in the rest of the players: "And, why stop? I didn't tell you to, and I didn't see the ball go through the hoop."

A few minutes later, after a few baskets, the defense stiffened despite pinpoint passing and probing. Larry Nichols backed up and tossed up a three, which swished through the net. The players looked to Burke, settling into a slow burn: "I don't care how pretty it looked. Still not a good percentage shot. Inside and then back out for an uncontested three would be okay, but we win if we get it to the big man and play through him." The criticism worked. Lance Hall concluded the next play with a rim-rattling dunk.

On the other side of the key, however, as bodies crashed for a potential rebound, Tom Kuhn inadvertently hooked T.R. with an elbow. Out of self-defense rather than animosity, T.R.

cleared him with a shoulder shiver that sent Kuhn sliding across the hardwood. Rick Pantera, himself only cognizant of jersey color, stepped in to prevent any escalation and got sent spinning by the big man.

"Okay, gentlemen, it looks as if you're ready for battle now," Burke shrieked, stopping play for the afternoon. "For Friday, keep your fight within the rules, but, yes, take no prisoners under the glass. You okay, Tom?"

Kuhn remained slumped on the court, though listening attentively. "Yeah, I'm okay."

"Help him up, Tony. Didn't your mama teach you to pick up what you knocked down?"

T.R. grinned as he extended his hand to his fallen teammate. "Sorry, man. Forgot for a second. Pictured someone else blocking me out."

On the way off the court, Pantera walked with Patrick, who had the good feeling of stepping off an invigorating roller coaster ride. "See the big fellow throw me like a rag doll?" the sophomore beamed. "He's going to kill those guys Friday. That's the first time I've seen him completely focused on the court in a month. He's got the Moses Malone look in his eyes again."

"Kiernan," Burke interrupted. "Thanks. Looked pretty good out there."

"Sure, Coach, if you need me tomorrow since Matt's probably not going to be able ..."

"Nah, J.V.s are back." He paused as Patrick stopped and Pantera headed toward the locker room. "If Coach Mack was still A.D., he'd have my ass for letting you out there without a clearance, and I plan to lighten up tomorrow anyway. We're chomping at the bit, ready to play now."

Patrick didn't succeed in getting quotes from T.R. as he thought he might. In fact, LaSalle's Blue Chipper had been uncommunicative for weeks. Patrick attributed that to the pressure T.R. and the team constantly faced, a pressure he felt a bit firsthand in being on the court with the Lancers, even in a limited role.

27.

ALMOST PRESIDENTS' DAY WEEKEND
SENIOR YEAR (THE NEXT DAY)

Patrick stopped by *The Star* after school Thursday to deliver his preview story that appeared the morning of the big game:

League Leaders Clash at Sac State
By: Patrick Kiernan

Even though this weekend's holiday honors Lincoln and Washington and all U.S. Presidents, it falls closer to the traditional celebration honoring founding father George Washington, a man known for devotion to truth. Fittingly, the truth about this year's S.S.V.L. hoops race should come into focus tonight at Sacramento State's Hornet Gym when the LaSalle Lancers meet the upstart, league-leading Loyola Wildcats.

The Wildcats, who triumphed over their archrival in league play, enjoy a one-game lead for the regular season crown, which awards the victor a "point" in the playoffs (they would have to be beaten twice). Since the Lancers won a pre-league tournament game, this will mark a rubber match. The Wildcats are 9–0 in league play and 17–5 for the season. The pre-season favored Lancers sit at 8–1 in league and 20–3 overall, with one loss coming in a thrilling overtime contest against SoCal power, Mater Dei.

Jerry Burke's Lancers hold the number one ranking in the area, despite trailing Loyola in league standings. LaSalle center T.J. Ward is arguably the best prep basketballer in the area since Billy Cartwright starred at Elk Grove High School in the early '70s. Ward's list of potential collegiate destinations reads like a short list of big-time programs.

Ted Carroll's Wildcats rank number three in the area. They're led by sharpshooting guard Billy Gemma, the team's magician in pulling out close games, and a stifling zone defense that has given the Lancers fits in previous match-ups. Arguing the merits of the two rivals is akin to arguing whether Lincoln or Washington was the better President.

The Lancers seem bolstered in recent outings by a personnel adjustment (a shorter, faster lineup) that should make this rematch riveting. Although a few tickets remain, they're expected to be gobbled up before game time so that a full house should be on hand to see whose cherry tree gets chopped down tonight.

"Pretty clever line about cherry trees," Sean Foley complemented after reading the draft of the article Patrick showed him when the two met at the River an hour before dusk. "Charles will go nuts, but students will love it." Foley referred to the LaSalle administration's campaign to eradicate LaSalle's history calling Loyola students "cherries" to mock their preppy, elite, snobbishly intellectual image LaSalle students thought Jesuits cultivated. "And truth told, I thought you should have been a cherry yourself freshman year."

"Not a bad allusion, huh?" Patrick smiled as he squished his way along a rain-soaked path to the River. He turned back to the following Foley, dressed in fatigue pants and a USMC tee-shirt topped by an unbuttoned, untucked flannel jacket. "Like writers behind the Iron Curtain. The truth coded or disguised so readers know what writers are talking about but the authorities don't or aren't sure. With this, students and alums will know, the administration won't be able to prove anything, and the general audience won't have a clue. Love it, right?"

"It's good, Kiernan, but you ain't no Eastern European freedom fighter." The reference reiterated how recent get-togethers with Foley had reminded him about the intelligence of his not-too-long-ago adversary. "Kiernan, we're going to have to stop meeting like this. Somebody might get the wrong idea." Foley guffawed loudly as if the thought of anyone questioning his masculinity was laughable. "Want to share a hit or two?"

"Go ahead. I'm back at school tonight for the rally. Too bad you can't come with me."

Surprised, Foley looked up. He put the joint back into his pocket and instead fished out a tin of Kodiak.

"Maybe if you went with me ..."

"The Kiernan Good Housekeeping Seal of Approval, huh?" Foley meticulously dropped a pinch of tobacco under his lip.

"Just a thought."

Foley took a few steps to the River to spit. "Actually, I appreciate your sentiment. I miss LaSalle. My old man's bitter, but that's nothing new. I just wish I was back. No spirit where I'm at."

"What about the game tomorrow? You haven't seen a league game yet, have you?"

"Nah, I'd have to go with the old man, and watching games with him these days is pretty uncomfortable. And, awkward for Paul and my former buddies who've been told to act like I don't exist." Foley spat at a tree branch streaming by. "With the big gym, though, maybe I could hide in the crowd. We're going to get Loyola back big time."

"Can I quote you on that?"

"Right. Tell the story in *The Star*, which Dad wouldn't let in the house to wipe his behind, about what a nice guy I really am. Play up that the loyal LaSalle crowd includes one-time jerks like me who need to be 'born again.' My father molded my jerk attitude. Maybe, you should quote him instead."

"Sean, you don't make a good martyr, and you're not the

only one screwed over by a father." Patrick and Sean had previously compared feelings about their less-than-stellar father experiences. "There's going to be an article in *The Lance* about loyal supporters who still root for the school. I'll give your quote to Horton, who's going to write it."

"And, unlike my father, I wouldn't mind that he's Black."

"It would be good for the school to hear from you in a positive light, and it would actually make me feel better to let others know what I've found out recently in our River meetings."

Foley thought about that for a minute as he pressed his jaw to mix more saliva with his tobacco. He reached out and bearhugged Patrick playfully. "You're all right, Kiernan." He smiled. "Patrick."

"Give me a break, Sean," Patrick said as he jerked away. "And don't dribble that stuff on me."

"Snuff, not stuff. Get your facts right. Seriously, I don't know how to say this well, but I do appreciate talking to you about things. It wasn't like that with Paul and Ralph and Jerry. We'd horse around, but they aren't that bright. Besides, they don't have any ..." Foley cupped his right hand near his crotch, letting the gesture finish the sentence for him. He spat right past that hand before adding, "None of them stuck with me after I got my ticket out. I'm sure their parents warned them away from the 'bad apple,' but they didn't even try on the sly. Still can't believe Coach Mack didn't try to contact me when I reached out. That hurt. He used to be like a father ever since I met him at elementary school football camps."

"Yeah, fathers and father figures of all sorts can crap on us, my friend. You've said that the Marine recruiter who talked you into the deferred admittance sort of stepped in, though, right?"

"You peaceniks who protested when we stepped in to save Kuwait and get revenge on the Iraqis for taking our hostages back in the day wouldn't believe it, but he actually talks me through things, like not being afraid to be vulnerable and stuff. To be true to myself and my ideals. He says that to act like a man, you first have to feel things like a man, to not be afraid of feelings."

"You're right. Doesn't fit my stereotype."

"Life can surprise. Can you believe, though I still think Sammie's a wiseass, I always respected Ward? He's a helluva basketball player and a pretty good guy."

"And would have been a good football teammate, too, huh?" Both chuckled.

"I've been mulling over whether I should, but I can't stay afraid of my father. I want to give you information that might help Ward. God," he interrupted himself, "if it keeps raining this winter and snowing in the Sierra, this River's going to be awesome in the spring. Look at it move."

"And you're helping by spitting another bucket into it," Patrick teased.

"I'm not usually a fink, but I gotta give you this. Maybe a little atonement, though I don't know what you can do with it."

"What?"

"Heard my old man talking with Donovan from the *Trib*. Think Donovan has something pretty solid on Ward. My father might have even helped him get it. Something tied to Capital, the college trying to go big-time in D.C. I think they have proof money's changed hands against N.C.A.A. rules and maybe even against the law. They're holding it until they can do the most damage. Maybe, you can warn Ward. You talk to him about this recruiting stuff, right?"

"Not much lately," Patrick blurted. "Focused on Suzie, and T.R.'s been distant at school. All the pressure and stuff, I figured. You should have seen him at practice yesterday, though. Tossing bodies around like a Kung Fu movie. Can't wait to see him play tomorrow night. Come early and sneak upstairs with me. You can sit with me in the press box. I'll get you a pass."

28.

FRIDAY OF
PRESIDENTS' DAY WEEKEND
SENIOR YEAR

Sean Foley sat to one side of Patrick in the Sac State press box, while a couple chairs down on the other side Carl Schipper unloaded sandwiches and chips with his portable typewriter, notes, programs, and pressbooks sprawled in front of him. Schipper didn't seem to recognize the ex-LaSalle football stalwart, but Ed Donovan did from the far side of the booth. He almost stumbled over some cables coming up from the Loyola cheering section below when he spotted Sean with Patrick. Patrick jotted game notes for the first half for his anticipated feature to accompany Carl's game story:

Starters:
C[ats]:   *L[ancers]:*
Gem-Billy Gemma   *G*   *S-Sammie*
Will-Jim Willis   *G*   *F-Frank*
El-Todd Eliot   *C*   *T.R.*
Mac-Bob McCarver   *F*   *N-Nichols*
Sol-Solomon Ford   *F*   *H-Hall*
1Q

5:14 Great ball movement like practice. Inside out, S to T.R.
to N for 3. (6–1)

3:32 Box-and-one D on Gem, with S shadowing him—ask J.B. about it. (9–3)

2:40 T.R. monster jam. (11–5)

1:12 Kuhn follow-up off miss; tenacious D. (13–5)

0:00 3-point play by T.R. caps almost perfect quarter. (16–5)

2Q

7:40 Both rooting sections outrageously loud. (16–7)

6:09 Cs miss two bunnies—intimidated by T.R.'s presence. (20–7)

5:40 2nd foul on S; F running the point. (22–8)

3:55 Offenses heat up; T.R. dominating boards; 2 threes for Gem. (31–14)

2:40 S back; all passes, no dribbling on breaks after T.R. outlets. (36–16)

1:05 Cs look confused—zone being exploited; silly 3rd foul on S. (38–18)

0:00 WOW! (40–18) Only thing J.B. will have to yell about will be S's foul trouble.

At halftime, Patrick bounded out of the press box to find Suzie amidst the throng in the lobby. Sean Foley remained behind. Patrick stood with Suzie and Doris, almost his height, while gleeful LaSalle rooters intermingled with dour Loyola fans. "Can you believe it?" Kelly Kerwin enthused after wedging through the crowd. "Thought it would be another close one."

"Not over yet; Sammie has three fouls," Patrick cautioned, but like everybody, he knew it was.

"T.R. could probably handle them himself. Right, Doris?" Kerwin shrieked above the din. "Gotta run." He turned away. "Some foxes probably looking for me." He winked and disappeared back into the crowd.

"Pat, Doris was surprised when I told her Sean Foley came

to the game with us. Where is he?" Suzie asked.

"Upstairs. He wants to avoid his old man, who's over there," Patrick nodded, "holding court. And, get this, Sean doesn't want to embarrass his old football buddies, who treat him like he has a contagious virus."

"Probably their parents' call," Suzie ventured.

"Suzie, to avoid problems, he's going to meet us after the game at the car rather than milling around in here. It'll be a few minutes until I come out of the locker room."

"I'll wait for you with Doris near the bench."

"Unless you can get us in there as reporters," Doris joked before turning serious. "Surprised you'd let Mr. Destruction near your car with his history. What's my man think about you playing nice with him?"

"Don't know," Patrick confessed. "Haven't talked to T.R. much lately. Something bothering him? He mad at me?"

Doris shook her head from side to side. Patrick interpreted it as a "don't know" rather than a "no."

"If I don't get the chance in the locker room, tell T.R. I want to have a good talk with him next week. Hey, Brother," Patrick spun around to face Brother Curt. "Great half, huh? Told you we were ready."

"After football and the loss earlier, vengeance is sweet. Supposed to be God's, but I appreciate Him sharing it a bit. How many did T.R. get?"

"Fourteen. And Lance and Larry got eight, and Sammie six."

"Hear Sean's with you."

Patrick did a double take. "Your spy network again?"

"Ve haf our vays," Brother Curt pronounced in an over-the-top Nazi accent. "No, Kelly said he saw you guys above the Loyola rooting section outside the press box. How is he?"

"Still and always a LaSalle fan. Gotten to know him better recently. We sort of drifted together." Suzie raised her eyebrows at the oblique reference to the River. "Really, a pretty decent guy. I think he had been badly influenced by his dad and Coach Mack."

"There was a former President at St. Mary's College who, in his eighties, tottered around campus repeating 'They're all good boys' before the school went coed. The longer I'm in education, the more I realize it wasn't wishful thinking. Sometimes, it takes looking damned hard, but the good is there. Tell Sean I'd like it if he dropped by to see me this week after school."

"Sure," Patrick said while Doris and Suzie looked puzzled.

A smile played across Brother Curt's lips. "I'm off. Have to make sure the boys don't get too rambunctious reminding the other side what the score is." He turned to glare at Patrick as if too much happy talk might spoil his image. "And to make sure nobody's throwing cherries at some nice Loyola boys. Hard to believe, but I had to confiscate a couple baskets at the gate from some of our misguided sophomores. Seems they got the idea from some newspaper article or something. Can you imagine that?" As he turned to leave, he asked, "We playing a Nerd League game this Sunday?"

"Monday," Patrick yelled. "I'll leave you a message about what time." After Doris and Suzie headed back to their rooting section, Patrick looked around to see if Mr. Wilson was there, but he didn't see him, though he usually loved to attend games, sometimes with his daughters and sometimes with his faculty drinking buddies. Patrick did see Leroy Horton and convinced him he was serious about him using the Foley quote he gave him, along with all the other great lines Horton said he was getting from LaSalle adherents.

On his way toward the stairs up to the press box, Patrick passed Mr. Foley. "Hey, Kiernan," Mr. Foley yelled, "you driving Sean, or am I?" The boosters he stood with silenced themselves immediately.

"I am. No problem, Mr. Foley," Patrick yelled back over his shoulder from the stairs, which he took two at a time.

Patrick found Sean locked in an intense conversation with Ed Donovan. It broke off quickly, however, when Patrick approached. Donovan brushed past Carl Schipper without a word on his way back to his spot. Oblivious, Schipper ate a hot dog while tabulating columns of game stats. "What did Donovan want?" Patrick asked Sean.

"Nothing important," Sean tossed off as if disinterested. "I'll tell you after the game. Bedlam down there?"

"Yeah, some mighty happy people wearing green. By the way, Brother Curt said hello, that you should see him at school some late afternoon this week."

"Yeah? What about?"

"Didn't say, but sounded pretty serious. Have to scoot past you and talk with Carl." Patrick climbed over a chair that had become an annex for Schipper's spillover material. The *Star*'s sports editor agreed with Patrick that the sidebar they had anticipated Patrick writing would be perfect if the score held. It did. The Lancers ended up blasting Loyola, 74–48.

Despite the thrashing and thoroughly dominating the game before sitting out much of the fourth quarter, T.R. didn't have a lot to offer Patrick and other reporters amidst the otherwise jubilant locker room. "Aren't you happy?" Patrick asked.

"Felt good, but ain't won nothin' yet." T.R. offered stoically.

Patrick shook his head as he left the locker room to meet Suzie and then Sean. He had plenty for his story that evening, which he would compose back at the *Star* after dropping Suzie and Sean off near school to get their cars, but the larger story of the season still confused him as much as the new LaSalle strategy had confused the Loyola defense.

29.

SATURDAY OF
PRESIDENTS' DAY WEEKEND
SENIOR YEAR

Patrick showed his mother his printed game sidebar around noon the next day:

LaSalle Reaches Higher Zone
By: Patrick Kiernan

LaSalle's convincing 74–48 win over Loyola left no doubt the Lancers' inability to combat a tightly packed zone may be history. The Lancers attacked the heretofore troublesome Wildcats' zone to jump out to what point guard Sammie Spear called "a perfect first half."

"Before," explained junior forward Lance Hall, who tallied seventeen points, "we would try to get the lead right away to get a team out of their zone." A team that's trailing must play the ball when warned to do so by a referee or risk incurring a technical foul. "Teams have trouble matching up against us one-on-one," Hall continued, "especially with T.R." Hall referred to T.R. Ward, LaSalle's Blue Chip center who powered his way through the Loyola zone for twenty- three points, though playing just a minute of the fourth quarter.

"We practiced hard to beat a zone," dependable Larry Nichols, who added twelve points, emphasized. "Coach [Jerry

Burke] wanted us prepared for good zones, and, likely, we'll see Loyola's again in the playoffs. This will give them something to remember. Instead of playing to pull a team out of a zone, Coach wanted us to keep attacking."

Since starting Lance Hall and Frank Tucci, after finding success with that lineup in a thrilling loss to a tough Mater Dei team from Orange County, the Lancers have hit their stride against zone defenses. Since, LaSalle has won five in a row, but none as convincingly as last night's triumph over the 'Cats, previously undefeated in league play.

Loyola's Coach Ted Carroll was more impressed by La-Salle's execution than strategic changes: "They're always an explosion waiting to happen. Tonight, we fanned the flames and got burned." Another bit of strategy, however, helped limit the Loyola offense. Coach Burke employed a zone of his own, a box-and-one defense that had Sammie Spear shadowing Loyola sharpshooter Billy Gemma, with T.R. Ward lurking under the basket anchoring a four-player zone.

Spear, who held Gemma four points below his season average and dished out eight assists, had the last word: "In practice, Coach Burke had the offense try to penetrate a zone that had eight defenders. As good as Loyola is, with only five men, they looked like Swiss cheese with holes we could find." Last night, in a higher zone of their own, it wasn't troublesome at all for the Lancers to steal the cheese from the 'Cats.

"Some game," Sheila Kiernan said after reading her son's article. "Guys from work not affiliated with either team went."

"Good basketball's good basketball," Patrick replied. "We looked like an N.B.A. team. Sean, with me in the press box, had a hard time not cheering."

"Sean Foley?"

"Yeah. Told you I've run into him here and there. A pretty decent guy now that I've had a chance to get to know him."

Across the table, Patrick and his mom ate different meals,

Patrick breakfast and his mom lunch, after Patrick's late night at *The Star*. "Has he changed?"

Patrick gobbled his buttered English muffin. "Maybe hasn't changed so much as things around him have. I never really knew him that well."

"Ironic, you becoming friends after the incident," Sheila Kiernan picked at her cottage cheese and sliced avocado with a fork.

"You don't always choose your friends."

Sheila Kiernan looked up before putting down her fork. Standing up and crossing to the sink, she refilled her water glass. A minute or so passed, time for Patrick to devour his muffin and take aim at the ham and hardboiled eggs he had readied after crawling out of bed hours after Sheila Kiernan. Finally, Mrs. Kiernan returned to her seat. "You and Suzie going out tonight?"

"Uh-huh. To the movies. Doubling with Sean and Tammy. You up to anything?"

"A get-together down the block. I think Shirley from work will go up the lake with me tomorrow if the road looks clear through Monday."

"Blackjack action?" Patrick surmised.

"Any action would be nice. The rain and fog's getting to me. Back East, I expected bad weather."

"Maybe we've sinned too much in California, and God's punishing us. Better than a big quake, though."

"Hey, speak for yourself in the sinning department. Something on your mind?"

Patrick flared, "Back at you. Something bothering you? Been on edge a bit lately."

"Don't get full of yourself, Pat," Sheila Kiernan snapped. "You're thriving in your adult job, but remember you're still in high school."

"Not for long, and it's you who's pushing me to go to school a long way from here. Pretty hypocritical to call me a high school kid one moment and encourage me to go three thousand miles away the next."

"You're twisting things."

"Aren't you the one pushing Princeton? It shouldn't matter that you met my father there. He's forgotten us, and you cashed out early to marry him. It's almost like you want a second chance through me."

"That hurt. I want what's best for you. Don't want you selling yourself short for some newspaper job." Sheila Kiernan measured her words carefully. "You've worked hard to do as well as you have, but I've worked hard for you too. Hasn't always been easy on my own."

"I respect that, Mom, but my idea of best might not match yours. Bet a lot of people would think Suze can do better than Southern Oregon, but she won't let anybody push her from her choice if she's happy. I've submitted my application to Princeton and intend to keep an open mind, but I'm leaning toward Berkeley. And who knows, I might not get into Princeton."

"With your grades, scores, and legacy?"

"Of sorts. Unless he'd renounce that."

"Truth? I'd love to keep you close. Fairly close. I assumed you'd like to get away, to look for a bigger stage. I let you choose LaSalle when people thought you should go to Loyola. And I'll support you with this. I've talked to people to guard against being the overprotective mom with her only son. I've tried."

Patrick stood up and circled the table. "I love you, Mom. Don't always understand you, though. God, I think all women are ..."

"Troublesome?" Sheila Kiernan offered. "Like a zone defense?"

Patrick chuckled at the reference to his story as he gave his mother a peck on her cheek.

"That reminds me of a basketball joke I heard," Sheila Kiernan said, attempting to hang onto the sudden warm moment.

Patrick moved toward the sink to begin garbage-disposing a fatty piece of ham left on his plate. "Here, I'll get that with mine," he added, taking his mom's plate to rinse.

Sheila Kiernan stood and hovered behind her son. "A little off-color, but it's about basketball. Why did the chicken cross the basketball court?" Patrick turned to face her while jerking off the water. As their blue eyes met, Sheila Kiernan sensed something was wrong, but defensively, she continued, "Because he heard the referee ..."

"Heard it," Patrick interrupted, spinning back toward the sink. Confused, his mom didn't finish. In trying to make an intimate moment linger, she wondered if she had overstepped the taboo of talking about anything, even couched in a silly joke, of a sexual nature with an almost adult son.

Uncomfortable, though not sure why it affected him so much, Patrick vaguely felt betrayed. That joke had existed in his exclusively male world. Freed from the locker room, it became foul, an embarrassment, told by his mother.

He tried imagining an architect recounting that joke in his mom's office, but he had trouble wrapping his mind around the image. Then again, he had always had trouble thinking of his mom as a sexual being, especially since she had always seemed to exist just for him. And truth be told, since he didn't want her thinking about his sexuality, he was probably more vulnerable than he should have been.

Almost silent, mother and son drifted to the garden over the next few minutes to attend to the mindless pruning and clearing they had agreed to do together if Saturday dawned without rain or fog. Maybe trying to rekindle the mood before the problematic joke or to assuage any guilt she felt telling it, Sheila Kiernan informed Patrick she had secured the use of the funky cabin her boss owned above Placerville on the American River for Patrick and his friends for the Memorial Day weekend. Patrick had asked her to do so, thinking it would be a great last high school adventure with the boys. Though thanking her, he did consider that maybe all women, even his mom and Suzie sometimes, were, to some extent, troublesome.

30.

EARLY MARCH
SENIOR YEAR

March arrived with T.R. seemingly distant. This bothered Patrick, though he and Suzie were getting along well and he was spending more and more time with Sean Foley at the River and socially. The basketball team rolled on, though seemingly without joy for T.R., as a story in *The Star* suggested:

Lancers Positioned to Nab Title
By: Patrick Kiernan

The LaSalle Lancers captured their seventh victory in a row last night, posting an 80–58 thumping over a game but overmatched University High team.

The win upheld the Lancers' one-game S.S.V.L. lead over Loyola, which beat Sacramento Christian last night after dropping their second game in a row Wednesday night when this same University team upset them, 57–50.

The Lancers are now in the driver's seat to win the regular season championship and gain the playoff point, which would allow the luxury of one loss in the Mid-March league playoffs.

"It's in our hands now," Coach Jerry Burke enthused after watching star center T.R. Ward score thirty-four points and grab twelve rebounds. LaSalle will try to wrap up at

least a share of the league crown when they face Roseville at the Lancers' gym. A win in that game and Friday against Watt High will ensure the regular season championship for LaSalle, no matter what Loyola does.

After the contest, T.R. Ward didn't seem satisfied: "Coach has us playing up. We want to win NorCals and maybe face Mater Dei again for the state championship. On the way, we'd be in tough against teams like San Joaquin Memorial or that Jason Kidd team (St. Joseph Notre Dame) from the Bay Area, but going down that road would be welcomed. A league championship would just be a step toward that."

Patrick hesitated after pulling his little Toyota in behind T.R.'s three-year-old red Thunderbird outside Ward's South Sacramento home. He thought about the terrible situation and unrest he heard about on the news after the Rodney King police beating in L.A. King, stopped for a traffic violation on what Brother Curt called "neutral territory, the 210," was filmed getting roughed up horrifically by four policemen after a traffic stop. Black neighborhoods all over the state, like the one he had just ridden into, though South Sac was no South Central, were justifiably outraged and inevitably volatile. Brother Curt noted that news reports said King had been born in Sacramento.

More pragmatically, Patrick worried T.R. wouldn't remember the early Saturday morning meeting his friend had begrudgingly agreed upon, even after talking about an early afternoon team meeting and the work he needed to handle.

"Wha's happenin'?" T.R. growled as he imposingly filled the door wearing only his boxers after about fifteen rings and knocks. Rubbing half-closed eyes, T.R. inquired, "Ten already?"

"A few minutes after." The easy intimacy the two had enjoyed seemed strained beyond the fact that Patrick was obviously cutting into T.R.'s sleep time.

Awakening, T.R. waved Patrick in. "Told Otis to take the twerps down the courts this morning, that if they woke me, he'd be in trouble. Good for him that he did it." His voice suddenly rumbled loudly: "Hey, Mom." No response came. He laughed at his waking self. "Course, she would've answered the door if she was here. Sit down; I'm gonna splash some water on my face and get dressed."

Patrick spotted an old oak case in the center of the room he remembered had held a fan. He saw it now housed a veritable shrine to T.R.'s basketball exploits, brimming with trophies and mementos. He was still looking through them when T.R., wearing sweats and looking wider awake, reentered the living room.

"Not bad, huh? Room for some big ones starting next week. Team meeting at noon, and I'm working at one thirty," he announced. "Want some toast?"

"Why don't I take you to breakfast? We can talk there, and then you can head right to your meeting."

After a short look of uncertainty, T.R. agreed: "Why not? I'm hungry. I'll leave and follow you, then motor to school from where we're at. Hang on a minute. It's cold in here, isn't it?" T.R. shuddered. "We got air conditioning, cheaper to install during winter, but I swear the damned thing kicks on by itself. Colder than a motha' in here. Where you want to go?"

"How 'bout Merlin's near school. That'll get you close enough we won't need to rush."

"Sure, but I need to stop by the courts to make sure Otis has a key. Then, I'll follow you."

As Patrick was pulling away, he stopped, thinking T.R.'s car might not have started. Watching in the rearview mirror, though, from half a block away, he saw T.R. jump out of his car awkwardly to greet a big white Cadillac that deposited his mother, still dressed to the nines, on the curb. T.R. leaned in the window for a minute.

Feeling like a spy, Patrick drove off to the playground. There, some among the twenty or thirty African American kids, who claimed the neighborhood courts before being usurped by the older guys later in the day, stared at the white guy standing outside his parked car across the street until T.R.'s brother Otis ran over to high-five him. The Ward imprimatur was more than enough; games resumed immediately.

A few minutes later, T.R. pulled his T-bird behind Patrick's car. This time the games stopped and didn't restart right away as the youngsters flocked around their neighborhood hero. T.R. yelled to Otis, "Mom's home, but she's splitting after she changes. Got a key?" Patrick jumped back in his car, wondering if he should have met T.R. at Merlin's. He drove off as T.R. walked across to huddle with his brother and acknowledge his younger siblings.

T.R. joined Patrick at Merlin's, jamming himself into the other side of a booth. While scanning the chalkboard menus posted throughout, Patrick noticed the video games in the corner stood unused. After ordering from a kindly-looking old waitress who reminded Patrick of Mrs. Glass, T.R. lurched into a rambling dialogue: "What's this about you hanging with Foley? You crazy?"

"True," Patrick smiled. "Not that I'm crazy, but about Foley. I ran into him at the River weeks back. No wild drink-ups. Just the two of us, man to man." Patrick rambled on, narrating highlights of some of his meetings and conversations with their erstwhile antagonist until Mrs. Glass's look-a-like served the food. "My God," Patrick stated when she left, "this whole table's covered with plates."

"Hungry," T.R. bit off as he proceeded to attack his food. "You know, Brother Blood called me in the other day to tell me he talked to Sean too. He wants to let him back in. I didn't believe it at first. Got a little hot and told him what I thought. He said he talked to you about Sean at your Nerd League hoops game Monday but didn't tell you he was going to give him another chance at LaSalle."

"He saw him? No, he didn't tell me he'd let him back into school. Did you agree?"

"What could I say. Don't have veto power. Hey, veto power. I learned something in Civics. I can ignore him for three months. Curt said about the same thing as you, that Sean ain't such a bad dude but just got set wrong by Coach Mack and his father, that ..."

T.R. stopped himself as the waitress returned to the table. "Everything okay, boys?" she asked while filling T.R.'s coffee cup.

"Wonderful, ma'am," Patrick chirped.

"Love the taters," T.R. complimented.

"Good. Holler if you need anything."

"You know," Patrick began when she was out of earshot, "Sean told me his old man and Donovan are sitting on something pretty solid they have on you with this recruiting thing. You know what he's talking about? I mean, Sean said he doesn't know what and doesn't have anything to do with it."

T.R. put down his fork, picked up his napkin, and wiped his mouth. "You talking as a reporter or friend? I mean, if the price of breakfast is ..."

"A friend," Patrick hastily cut in. "Is that it? You've been distant with me lately. A friend first and foremost. You should know that? Do they have anything?"

"Ask them."

"Let me rephrase it. Could they have something?"

T.R. leaned in. "Told you weeks ago some things were coming down I couldn't control. It hasn't stopped."

"Your car? Your job? To pay the tuition they jerked away?"

"Piddly stuff. Nah, nothing's too bad with those things. My mom's working for a friend of Forte's now and seeing Percy too. Did you know that? It complicates everything but also provides an out for stuff."

"That's all?"

"Well, I think money's being funneled to different places. Maybe to Mom, though I don't know for sure. Maybe she's just the highest-paid ex-postal worker in the state."

"Sounds like you're innocent."

"Something's going down, but I haven't asked for anything. And, God knows, when I see Otis and the boys getting a few more things to live a little better, it doesn't bother me a bit. But, what's the word? More Civics language. Circumstantial."

"Why not go to Burke or the N.C.A.A.?"

"Can't do that, man. There's Percy, my mother, my family, my 'hood."

"Have an idea which college?"

"Capital, I think. They're on the make for the big time. Even offering a scholarship to Doris, I hear."

"Really?"

"But apparently, got burned last year. Same deal, but the girlfriend took hers, but the player didn't. Now, they'll wait until I commit, if hearsay's right. Gets scary, like being owned or something, but their Wall Street alums did bigtime me when I was back East."

"And, will probably get worse."

"If Donovan has something, why hasn't he used it? You know he hates my guts after the tape stuff."

"I wondered. Thought maybe a bluff, and they staged Sean overhearing, but Sean did suggest reasons that make sense." Patrick pushed his one plate aside and sprawled back, wrapping his hands behind his head on the padded seatback. "Donovan's in old man Foley's pocket. He'll do anything. Maybe, Foley still has feelings for LaSalle and wants to wait until after the season to blow the whistle."

"Bull. The guy loves himself, not LaSalle. With the Boosters, he thinks of himself like some professional G.M. Besides, Brother Curt burned his son. He's a racist. Why would he wait?"

"Better reason: They go public now, the college might take the rap, but you might get off the hook. Innocent, like you've been saying. But Foley and Donovan wait until after you sign your letter of intent next month, then maybe you go down with Capital's ship."

"Lose eligibility and have to transfer too late?"

"At least. Maybe more. Depending on Capital's reaction. And, you know they'd sacrifice you for their program, especially if they claim it's alums and boosters and not the school. Other schools might not touch you."

"Damn!" T.R. threw the crust of his toast on the plate. "The bastards!"

"Don't know what I can do, but I want to help. At least Sean let us know something's up. You think you should talk it over with Jerry?"

"No way. He's so straight he'd probably bench me until everything sorted out. The season would be over then. Can't do that. I'll keep Curt clued in. He's my main man. And like I say, I ain't done nothin' really wrong myself. You can't be blamed for what your mother does, can you?"

31.

TOWARD MID-MARCH
SENIOR YEAR

The LaSalle campus, senioritis abounding, whirred all week, marked by good spring weather, an anticipated league championship, Desert Storm being called a victory, and a few surprises. A shock to many occurred on Tuesday when, after another long talk with Brother Curt, Sean Foley rejoined the student body. At various points, Foley's dad and mom, T.R. Ward, Patrick, and Brother Charles participated in the two-hour meeting to make it happen.

Though he low-keyed his presence around campus the rest of the week, Foley, in silence, elicited more buzz than an outrageous stunt might have for the well-known "born-again" Lancer. He even sat, relatively restrained, with Suzie and Tammy Dickerson at the Wednesday night game, cheering for his team but not circulating in the lobby at halftime or before or after the game.

The fact that Sean accompanied Patrick, Suzie, and Tammy to the Catholic Worker Kitchen, where they met Andy Hill on Thursday, drew comments from Sean's football buddies, who otherwise reacted to his presence on campus as if he were Hamlet's ghost.

On Friday morning, T.R. was named a top-twenty Blue Chipper by *Sports Illustrated*, and Patrick found out he had been accepted by Princeton, U.C. Berkeley, and other universities, in addition to state colleges. Patrick's Friday game story appeared in Saturday's *Star:*

Lancers Win S.S.V.L League Title
By: Patrick Kiernan

"Sometimes doing what's expected is difficult," summarized *LaSalle Coach Jerry Burke after his Lancers, pre-season favorites, won the Sacramento Superior Valley League crown by posting a routine 76–54 victory over Watt High.*

The victory gives LaSalle a 13–1 league mark and the all-important point for next week's playoffs. For good measure, Loyola, the second-place league finisher, dropped its game last night [see accompanying story], falling to 11–3.

Thus, the playoff lineup is set for Thursday night's double-header at Sacramento State. Loyola will take on third-place finisher American (9–5) at 6:30. Immediately following, at around eight-thirty, LaSalle will play University (7–7).

T.R. Ward, recently listed by Sports Illustrated among the top twenty prep prospects in America, had twenty-one points and fifteen rebounds, providing fuel for LaSalle's high-powered attack. A U.C.L.A. recruiter marveled that "he swept the boards clean," before adding, "He's as solid a big man as you'll see. We'd love him to choose us." Ward's collegiate choice will be announced at the end of the season, which looks as if it will go on for a while, the way the Lancers are playing.

Larry Nichols and Lance Hall each netted fourteen points, while Tom Kuhn contributed ten off the bench. Sal Curcio, who dropped in thirteen, led the Steamers.

"We're looking forward to the playoffs," Coach Burke said. "But we'll enjoy this accomplishment first."

On that Saturday morning, Patrick started another expedition into the woods when Carl Schipper, headed in another direction, said, "You do the preview for Thursday's games, and

I'll do the game stories. Then, we'll see if there's a good feature. You can have the game next Saturday. Assume it will be LaSalle/Loyola. I'm going to the Bay Area to cover for Pete, who's off to spring training for a few days."

"Great," Patrick swallowed, glad to take the focus from his plight. "Unless I'm still out here on the seventeenth or eighteenth fairway next week looking for tee shots." The verdant Ancil Hoffman Golf Course had taken the measure of Carl and Patrick, again searching for errant shots, this time off the sixteenth fairway. The two old geezers playing with them seemingly hit every ball relatively short but straight down the middle while the two reporters hit long but, in Carl's words, "played botanist," seeing "every plant and tree on the property."

The conversation they had when they hit the clubhouse for lunch evolved into something just as hazardous as their treks amongst the trees on the course. "Congrats about Princeton," Carl lauded.

"Thanks. Contingent on no second-semester Ds or Fs."

"No problem, I'm sure."

"Same with Berkeley, my other top choice. In, but no Ds or Fs. In a few other schools too, including my safety schools, Sac State, and S.F. State."

"Tigers or Golden Bears, huh?" Carl prided himself on knowing most college sports team nicknames.

"We haven't spoken about that baseball job in a while. Any word from Pete? Still a chance I'll get that job covering the Giants and A's home games, even part-time or working with him at first?"

"Well, Pete's been on *The Star* forever. Things are on his terms. Still, lots to work through." Patrick sat back, disappointed, but Schipper took the conversation in a different direction: "I might be leaving. For another job."

"Where? When?" Patrick's eyes flashed. He imagined his shot at the Bay Area *Star* beat going down the hole, unlike most of his putts.

"I'm trusting you to keep this quiet. Don't want my boss knowing yet. Just a possibility. Good one, though. *Denver News.*"

"Sports?"

"No, writing obituaries. Of course, sports. You think I could do anything else? Or want to?"

"When do you find out?"

"Not for a while. Have an interview scheduled back there next month. Had a prelim with their recruiter, who met me here last week. Got the impression I have a good shot."

"Congratulations," Patrick haltingly offered.

"Still premature," Carl responded, waving for the waitress. "Want another Coke?" He ordered another beer before continuing: "The guy liked your stories too. I made a point of showing him your work and development. They have a pretty young staff, and he was impressed."

"Really."

"I can't promise anything," Schipper, leaning forward, whispered, "but I can certainly recommend Pete taking over as Editor and you taking his current gig, with help at first. It just might work."

"Don't want to wish you away, but that would be great." A few minutes later, Patrick wondered if good news always came with strings attached. "With my A.P. class credits, I could arrange my U.C. schedule around *Star* assignments."

"You've been everything I could've hoped for when I took the chance in hiring you, selling it to management as a good paying internship. Obviously, it's become more than that, though technically, you're still an independent contractor."

The conversation turned to Colorado's sporting scene, how Sacramento sports coverage had changed since the Kings moved to town, whether Dick Motta was the best fit for coaching the Kings, who would win the NBA championship, whether U.N.L.V. would win the N.C.A.A. Tournament for a second year in a row, and whether the Giants or A's would win more games in 1991.

"It's little over a month before Ward announces," Schipper redirected the conversation. "I still want that story badly, where he's going, especially now with this in the hopper. Don't want some big-city paper scooping us in our backyard," Carl affirmed.

"Just don't know," Patrick hesitated. "I would have guessed U.C.L.A., but ..." Patrick trailed off, not sure what to reveal if anything.

Carl prodded: "It's important to me, and to you. The recommendation that you can handle that job down there would carry more weight up top if you landed this story. Some people will think you're too young to unearth scoops."

Thinking of Donovan and the *Trib* stealing *The Star*'s year-long story with shattering revelations about T.R. that might make his college selection a moot point, Patrick fidgeted. His conversation with T.R. the week before, conversations with Sean Foley, and frequent conversations in his own mind echoed.

Patrick imagined the responsibilities of his job jousting with the confidences of his friendship. "Dammit, Carl, no solid facts. All hearsay."

"Well, hearsay's to be heard? What school?"

"Capital."

"They buying him?"

"Think so." Patrick chewed on a small remnant of ice which melted like his innocence. "That is, buying his entourage. Forte. His mother. Hell, I don't know. And, even this is in real confidence. Like what you told me."

Unnerved, Patrick told Carl a lot of what he had heard, couching everything with the caveat that T.R. himself seemed uncertain. Golfers came and went as the animated conversation played out, and Carl grilled Patrick.

Patrick finally pleaded, "Carl, this story's not as important as T.R. He's my friend."

Patrick interpreted his mentor's silence as disagreement. At length, Carl verbalized a response: "If Donovan has it, it'll come out anyway. He's Foley's puppet. When Foley pulls the string, it'll appear. Probably waiting until after signing day,

April fifteenth, and then drop down like an I.R.S. audit."

"I can't be the one with this byline."

"Regardless, they'll ruin Ward, Patrick. Maybe if we did it, handled it right rather than letting Donovan get his claws in, it would be better. Donovan will paint him like a ghetto prostitute. With what you're saying, we can spin it differently. Paint him as the victim of some high-powered booster scam at Capital rather than a kid on the make. Then, maybe he could go to another school and be done with it. Like he got sucked into the whole thing unknowingly, and maybe even save his mother too, if possible.

Patrick hung onto that scenario as tightly as he gripped his empty glass. Schipper's conjecture enabled him to squish his conscience, seeing himself as acting in T.R.'s best interest as well as his own. "Just one thing, Carl. You write the story. Your name, your story."

"Sure, I'll keep you clear, check what you said, and only print what I verify. I have excellent sources, you know." Patrick winced. After all, he was one of them. "Even at the *Trib*." Carl winked, but that statement gave Patrick a deniability he thought he could cling to if things went south. "Someday, especially if you get the major league job, you're going to have to put your name on controversial stories. It's not like literature, where writers can hide behind pseudonyms or fiction. Journalism's the real world, with real people and real moral choices."

"I know," Patrick sighed.

32.

MARCH 15TH
SENIOR YEAR

While Schipper spent the week digging, resolutely and quietly, for facts about T.R.'s recruitment, Patrick attempted to ignore what he had set in motion. Concentrating on school and games, he composed the following preview for Thursday night's playoff games:

S.S.V.L. Playoffs Tonight
By: Patrick Kiernan

Beware the Ides of March! Tonight, at Sacramento State, two S.S.V.L. teams will realize they should have done so. If form prevails, those teams will be American and University, who, by virtue of finishing third and fourth place, respectively, must battle league leaders Loyola and LaSalle.

Loyola, which notched eleven league wins, will duel American, starting at 6:30. LaSalle, the number one ranked metro team with a 13–1 league record, will then face off with University twenty minutes after the conclusion of the first game.

The Ides of March, of course, signifies the mighty falling. Historically, S.S.V.L. playoffs have established that precedent. Although last year's LaSalle championship team wrapped up the crown in two games, the league winner had at least one playoff loss in the previous four years. In two of those years, upstarts ultimately prevailed, Loyola after finishing

third during the regular season three years ago and River-
view after finishing fourth the year after that.

The first game pits Loyola's sticky defense and patient
ball-control offense against a bigger but slower Eagles team.
Ted Carroll's 'Cats are led by guard Billy Gemma, and the
Eagles by forward Justin Love. The nightcap will feature
the area's number-one Blue Chip prospect, T.R. Ward, the
Lancers' star center, dueling with Britt Conroy, a 6'7" junior
transfer from West Germany, where his dad was stationed
in the Air Force before transferring to McClellan.

The championship game will be Saturday night at 8:30.
Should the Lancers get upset tonight or Saturday, another
game will be played Tuesday night.

"What should I do?" Patrick blurted to Mr. Wilson at last
period after baring his soul Thursday. The two had left the newspaper office to sit on a bench in LaSalle's sundrenched plaza.

Mr. Wilson packed tobacco into his pipe with each of his
fingers on his right hand, though he couldn't light it there.
Wilson wanted to move the conversation again, this time to
his office where he could light up, though he wasn't supposed
to do so. He realized, though, that Patrick's angst-ridden conversation concerning T.R.'s plight was only Act I and that with
this switch to a discussion of Suzie and Andy Hill, it would not
be a good time to move again. "Like I said about the recruiting
thing, sometimes it's best not to do anything. Even if offered
the chance, you should decline."

"I knew he'd do it," Patrick huffed. "Talk about being a priest.
The tortured soul bothered because he isn't a virgin," Patrick
tossed off sarcastically. "And taking Suzie in his confidence. I
knew he'd make a move on her."

"And fail."

"Yeah, and fail. I hoped so."

"And then trot off to the seminary."

"You sound like you sympathize with him," Patrick snapped.

"Probably mixed up like the rest of us when making a life
decision. Don't judge him too harshly. In fact, don't judge him

at all. Stay away. And, don't judge Suzie. Telling her you told her so would be the worst thing she could hear. She knows it. Didn't know why, but she looked down during class this morning. The fact she confided this with you, despite your warning before, confirms how much she cares for you."

"Such a rat, though. Desperate need to talk. Had to meet Suzie at some secluded spot, like a retreat." Patrick shook his head disdainfully.

"So, he has feet of clay. Ever hear that expression?"

"Means he's not all he's cracked up to be. Like a fatal flaw."

"We all have them. I read a reprinted story about Muhammed Ali when I was young. From when he was still called Cassius Clay. Titled 'Feat of Clay.' With an 'a.' Clever wordplay!" Wilson drew the last words out for emphasis. "His fast feet made him as a boxer, his feats were becoming legendary, and still, he had a look of vulnerability about him despite his brashness. That story title wrapped everything together. Marvelous."

"Your point?" Patrick almost scolded.

"Remember Ali's style? Clay's? 'Float like a butterfly, and sting like a bee.' Well, now you should be floating like a butterfly. A beautiful, proud butterfly above the insect world. Put that stinger away. It'll only get you into trouble. Suzie will appreciate your reaction over time if she doesn't now. No foolish wounded pride. This shouldn't hurt you a bit. She passed a test. Will you? She's hurt. Don't do anything except be there and comfort her when, and that's the key, when she wants it."

"And never go to Father Andy for confession," Patrick spat sarcastically.

Wilson jumped up and put his filled pipe in his pocket. "Priests have flaws too. Even favorite English teachers do." He smiled. "Look at your buddy, Sean. Never thought I'd use him as a good example. When he came back, everybody expected something. Fireworks. Obstinance. Conflict. A show. But he did nothing, is keeping a low profile, and it's the best approach. I suggest you do the same with both problems. The cards are dealt. Just hold them and play them when the time comes."

33.

MID-MARCH
SENIOR YEAR (THE NEXT COUPLE DAYS)

"Maybe I should steal your name," Mr. Wilson informed Patrick at school. "A Patty Kiernan might get free drinks at Harrington's in San Francisco on St. Patrick's Day easier than Steve Wilson."

"So, that's why you're skipping the championship game, huh?"

"We lose, we get 'em again Tuesday," Wilson said. "And even though they upset Loyola, they won't beat us once, let alone twice."

"Double overtime, last shot win, maybe a Cinderella team."

"Well, Cinderella's going to get her shoe put somewhere else. And, even if we lose in these playoffs, we'd still go to the regionals. T.R. makes us a big draw. That's why they're bumping us to D-1 despite our enrollment. Money talks, even with prep basketball."

"Well, if you're looking for free drinks, maybe it talks for you too. My Mom's going to the city for the night too."

"Is she? Quite a blowout every year. They close the street in front of Harrington's in the Financial District and draw big crowds. Meeting college buddies. A tradition celebrating the green that night. My wife used to go, but she's not big on crowds anymore."

"Maybe you'll see Mom."

"Big city. Doubt it. Write a good game story. I'll read about our annihilation of American in *The Star* Sunday morning, probably through bleary eyes."

Patrick's game story, however, did not highlight a LaSalle blowout:

Luck of the Irish?
Lancers Escape American to Advance to Regionals
By: Patrick Kiernan

LaSalle needed the "luck of the Irish" on St. Patrick's Day to escape with a 60–59 victory over upstart American, win the S.S.V.L. crown, and nail down a number one seed in the big-school regional playoffs.

"I knew we'd have it tough," victorious Coach Jerry Burke said of his green-clad Lancers. "The kids expected to get Loyola and didn't take the Eagles seriously." American Coach Sal Simi thought his team got robbed on a charge call that set Sammie Spear up for the winning free throws with six seconds left.

"I'm glad we don't have to play them again Tuesday," Spear sighed after the game. On the last play, he drove the lane and got fouled by Don Burl.

"A bailout," Simi charged after the game. "He was out of control. Donny was there, and we had Ward bottled up." T.R. Ward, in foul trouble much of the game with calls he objected to, tallied sixteen, well below his average, to lead the Lancers.

Veteran referee John Perez had the last call after the game: "The kid was planted. Would've been a charge, but at the last moment, he anticipated contact and moved. Calls should be the same all game. A defensive foul without a doubt."

Coach Burke wasn't above calling out his star: "The Eagles were tough, no doubt. But, for whatever reason, T.R. wasn't into the game. His mind seemed elsewhere. His second and fourth fouls came from needless reach-ins. He's better than that." Ward did hit two key baskets coming down the stretch.

LaSalle will face a yet-undetermined wild card team in the first round of the regionals, while the other matchup will be between City League champion Sacramento High and number three seed St. Mary's of Stockton.

Coach Burke, Irish himself, had the last word on St. Patrick's Day: "Sometimes it's better to be lucky than good."

Mr. Wilson read the game story Sunday late afternoon when he got home. As he told his wife, "No way I could drive in that condition; I spent the night at my classmate's place."

That same afternoon Suzie and Patrick hiked a trail near the less accessible side of Folsom Lake. "I'm lucky you're you. I was shattered when Andy did what he did, but you acted perfectly when I told you. Comforting, and yet not cloying. You were right; I was wrong. He's mixed up and sounds contrite, but that's no excuse. It was horrible—like he lost all reason. I feel guilt, though God knows I never led him on. I'm so glad I could tell you without you going all Neanderthal, know-it-all, or I-told-you-so."

"I was pissed but didn't want to overreact. Let's enjoy ourselves today. Only lately we've seen sunny days like this," Patrick soothed, wiping his brow.

Suzie smiled broadly. "You really are special." She reached up and held him tight. "Let's wind back around to the swimming area. Think it's warm enough we can put on our suits and take a dip. It'd feel like baptizing away guilt, even though I know I shouldn't feel any."

"Sure," Patrick said, himself enjoying his own luck of the Irish and the benefit of good advice.

34.

TOWARD THE END OF MARCH
SENIOR YEAR

"Tying things together about Ward's recruitment debacle," Schipper announced the morning of the regional semifinals. "Maybe ready to publish next week."

"You sure it'd be a good idea to rush ..."

"Just remember, Donovan has the story too. I'm sure of that from my, uh, chats with my *Trib* source."

"How did you land him?"

"Her. Think she has a future here." Schipper laughed at his machinations. "Doing puff pieces there. Bowling. Dart tourneys. Crap like that. Don't think Donovan knows how to work with a female. If he wasn't such a chauvinist and learned to type faster, I doubt she'd have any clue about this Ward story."

"What about T.R. and Coach? When do we approach them to give them a chance to respond on the record?"

"After the story's drafted and checked. Just remember, Donovan wouldn't do that, or won't if he beats us. Meanwhile, drop a few hints to Ward to maintain trust. Might soften things a bit when the time comes. And I will make clear, Donovan's the real villain, if not old man Foley. I'll be the heavy with my name on the story. Get the feeling the N.C.A.A.'s sniffing around, too, though they're so understaffed they won't gear up until summer. I'll offer, if possible, to help Ward set things straight so he comes across as a victim rather than an instigator. And, outlaws to blame, the renegades from Capital."

"Wish the big scoop was where he was going to play," Patrick murmured.

"No more. This is the story. By the way, you want the La-Salle game tonight instead of just a sidebar?"

"Sure. I didn't think I'd get a playoff game story."

"I have a meeting at five. You take the early game. I'll do the Sacramento/St. Mary's late one for inside. And get this: My interview in Denver's set for April fifth. You should get LaSalle's first game in Oakland trying to win the State Championships."

"If they make it. Sacramento's pretty good, and even Sutter has ..."

"They'll be there. As an at-large if they lose. After all the attention we've given them, they wouldn't disappoint us."

LaSalle didn't disappoint that night, as Patrick's game story attested:

LaSalle Whips Sutter: To Meet
Chieftains for Regional Title
By: Patrick Kiernan

After a narrow win in last week's S.S.V.L. championship game, the LaSalle Lancers righted themselves, hanging a convincing regional semifinal defeat on the Sutter Pioneers, 98–73, last night in the first game at Sacramento State University.

The Lancers will meet the Sacramento Chieftains Tuesday to determine the automatic regional representative to the NorCal big school finals, a prelude to a state championship showdown. Sacramento outlasted Stockton's St. Mary's Rams, 78–73, in the nightcap.

"If I could've, I might have thrown a white towel," moaned Sutter Coach Steve Bennett. "Jerry's [Coach Burke of the Lancers] teams are talented and well-coached, but this is the best I've seen. I told the kids it would be like our high school baseball team playing the current A's. Ward is their Mark

McGwire and Jose Canseco rolled into one."

T.R. Ward, the Lancers' basketball superstar, poured in thirty-two points after being held to sixteen in his previous foul-plagued outing. He also grabbed nineteen rebounds. His dominance, even with Pioneers swarming him, enabled four other Lancers to light it up. Sammie Spear (16), Lance Hall (15), Larry Nichols (11), and Terry Crain (10) all scored in double figures.

The defense also shined. Even after pumping in twenty-one points, Eric Wagner, N.C.L. player of the year, gave credit to a Lancer who only scored one point: "[Frank] Tucci hounded me all over the court. I hope he's not waiting when I leave the locker room."

Sacramento, ranked number two in the region, will try to stop the Lancers Tuesday night at ARCO Arena. If they don't, the Lancers will move on toward their date with state championship contention destiny.

The following Monday, Patrick ran into T.R. at the start of upper-division lunch. "You got a minute?" Patrick asked. "Hardly see you lately."

"Have to see Brother Blood. Been in his office so much, I should rent space."

"Wouldn't work. Curt wouldn't let you play your music."

"Ain't that right. No 'Hammer Time' in there. You'd think he'd love it."

"Protecting his image. Older and wiser. Though I do love some of his old blues and jazz stuff."

T.R. switched off his music device. "We all worry about our image. Funny that with sports, it's you writers and commentators who can make or break a player's image."

"You didn't like my game story?" Patrick asked defensively.

"Not talkin' specifics. In general. I liked your story, the baseball comparison. But I think you missed something in the American story."

Patrick's curiosity was aroused as he tried to remember a week or so back: "What?"

"You wrote about how I stunk the joint out ..."

"Whoa! Didn't say that," Patrick protested.

"Not in so many words, but, anyways, you was right. For the first three quarters. I did have stuff on my mind, but I came through in the fourth quarter, big-time, and you didn't say that."

Patrick thought back. "Think I said something about clutch baskets and good defense at the end."

"Maybe. I was prouder of the last six minutes of that game than any other stretch all season, except Mater Dei. It was a bigger deal than the Sutter game, and you called me a combination of Mark McGwire and Jose Canseco in that one."

"The Sutter coach did. Just quoted him."

"Whatever. Your story; you choose quotes. Like Coach said, I wasn't into that game. I had had a big go-round with my mom and Percy that afternoon, hotter than good rib sauce." Patrick's mind jumped back and forth between defensiveness and curiosity. "Weren't no fun, and then I'm sitting on the bench because of some pissy foul calls with nuthin' to do but think. But I went back in, scored a couple big buckets, played D, and we won. Even though those guys were all over me like stink on ..."

"Why didn't you say something about that in the locker room? I would have loved to have quoted you. You looked like you had died when I went into the locker room, which was rocking out otherwise."

"Used to like talking to reporters. You, Carl, others. Out-of-town guys. Even Donovan, jiving with him."

"What changed? The recruiting? On guard and wary—especially with the press?"

"Gotta go now. Curt's waiting. Guess I should get back to enjoying reporters. What do they say? Any publicity's good publicity."

"Maybe not." Patrick considered his next words as T.R. stopped short. Confronted by the presence of his own interests,

Patrick danced around the truth like a point guard slipping through a porous defense. "I hear Donovan's got something solid," he clipped off rapidly. "And Carl too. Donovan had it first, and Carl got it in part through a source he has there. The source says that Donovan's going to use it soon if *The Star* doesn't run it first."

Stunned, T.R. stared straight ahead. "Carl?"

"Carl thinks Donovan would crucify you. He says if we come out first, he'd write it to nail the school and its money-men instead of you. And maybe you could go someplace else, someplace first-class, instead of Capital."

"What do you have?"

"Told you. Nothing. I haven't told Carl what you told me except for generalities," Patrick lied. "I acted surprised when he started matching details you told me from his sources, but it's clearly his baby. And he thinks he'd be your best friend getting this out there."

T.R. didn't respond verbally, but his posture and expression said enough. He slouched so much his eyes would have met Patrick's if his classmate hadn't looked away.

"I was hoping to do a feature on you for tomorrow night, playing old neighborhood friends in a big game like this. It would make ..."

"Do what you want, man."

"Maybe interview you after you meet Curt. I kept a bunch of quotes from you and your homies from Summer League, but I'd love to get some updated ..."

"Don't matter. Do what you want," T.R. directed.

"I could show you an outline, but I'd still love new quotes ..."

With his voice booming, T.R. wheeled on Patrick, stopping the *Star* reporter in midsentence: "Said it don't matter. Make up quotes. Print what you will, regardless of people involved. Isn't that what the press does?"

35.

END OF MARCH
SENIOR YEAR (THE NEXT DAY)

Patrick didn't make up quotes. He used ones he had gotten during summer league games and from previous talks with T.R. He also unearthed current ones when he drove over to a Monday afternoon Sacramento High School practice. T.R.'s homies, with their coach's blessing, loved the idea of a feature story before the big game about their playground games with T.R. and Sammie:

Lifelong Friends Vie for Regional Championship
By: Patrick Kiernan

"We've played hoops together since we were young," T.R. Ward, LaSalle's star center, reminisced. Tomorrow, his team will meet Sacramento High and its trio of stalwarts—Isaac Sims, Mel Shaw, and Cedric Hardy—for the Sacramento Regional prep basketball championship at ARCO Arena. Lancer teammate Sammie Spear also participated in games that molded the five into hoopsters with big futures.

"Some people don't know what playground games are all about," Ward insisted. "That hardtop at the South Sac Rec Center and those steel-netted baskets were our paradise, even while promising a ticket out to the bigger world."

Ward and his three Sacramento High buddies are sure to

get collegiate offers, while Sammie Spear is also prepped to play at the next level. The competition nationally to recruit Blue Chipper Ward has been an ongoing saga throughout this high school season.

"Those games were about pride. Accomplishment. Manhood. Belonging," Sims noted, as he, too, remembered good times all twelve months of the years. He, Shaw, and Hardy came to the courts at the age of eight or nine "for the best basketball in the city." He remembered, "My older brother played there, and I saw it as the best playing the best in every age group. Mel and Cedric came with me when I talked it up. And talked up the big fella, Ward, who eventually teamed up with us and Sammie. We'd play all day, often on the main court, taking on older guys."

T.R. Ward is still a hero to many in his neighborhood. Ward noted, "I've worked hard to learn how to speak formally, especially with help from the Brothers [the Christian Brothers at LaSalle], but I could always express myself with a basketball on that playground."

Mel Shaw recounted, "You play until you lose in ongoing pickup games. We got so good guys started coming up from the Bay to challenge us."

Ward stressed it was the perfect place to practice moves and get schooled by experienced players: "I've learned a lot from Coach Burke [at LaSalle], but the Rec's courts are where my basketball education got refined. People think pickup games in the 'hood are about showing off and jacking up impossible shots, but that's ignorant. It can get wild sometimes, but day after day, it's a basketball clinic."

Cedric Hardy puts tomorrow's game into context: "Half the players on the court for tomorrow's big game come from the same basketball crib. We'll feel like we're back home, and all of us will want to be on the winning side for bragging rights, just like when we were kids."

The Chieftains rank second in the region; the Lancers

first. The stage is set for 8:00 tonight, though it will be played at ARCO rather than the hardtop outside the South Sac Rec Center. As Sacramento Coach Oscar Williams said, "We're looking forward to this, and I'm sure they are too. It'll be back to the roots for those kids, fun. I can't wait for the show."

"Quite a preview," Schipper indicated when he saw Patrick in the Sac State press box before game time. "Even when I cut some out, it was still long, and I'm sure you like I got it front-paged."

"Surprised me. Slow news day?"

"No, big story and great slant, more personal than typical high school game previews. Great insight into the playground hoops culture most people don't hear about. My editors loved that."

"Super. Course, you realize when T.R. talks about 'some people,' he means 'white people?'"

"Guess that's what I meant too. The timing's great, too, setting up what's coming down. You made him sound like the Yoda of the hardtop. I'm aiming for Friday for the big story."

"This Friday? Before the games in Oakland?"

"Before Donovan. This Friday," Carl repeated firmly. "Going downstairs during warmups. Prefer high school gyms where I'm next to the scorer's table. Set up my scorebook for me while I'm away."

Carl, however, came right back and burst into the enclosure, looking frantic. He gestured to Patrick to step outside with him. "What's going on?" he snorted before composing himself. "Jerry's fit to be tied. Was Ward in school today?"

Almost dumbly, Patrick shook his head from side to side and then up and down. "No," he hesitated. "Yes. That is, he was out all day but came last period. You have to be at school to play, but he got there by sixth. Administrators don't like it but let athletes play if they're in school for part of the day or have a school-sanctioned excuse. Maybe, he was getting psyched for the game. Maybe on the hardtop."

"Is that his usual practice?"

"Not at all. But, as you read, this one's meaningful personally."

"Jerry actually drove out looking for him at lunch. Couldn't get ahold of him all day. He must have breezed in and out again 'cause Jerry didn't see him at the end of the day. Didn't you get any of this at school?"

"Nope."

"My God. My star reporter misses a big story under his nose."

"Went out with Suzie right after school. I had missed her yesterday when I interviewed the three Chieftain players."

"Does he know about the story coming down?"

"I, uh, guess he might have a clue."

"Sammie told Jerry he should ask me when I asked him where Ward was. Seems he said something to Sammie last night about *The Star* being on his case, but Sammie didn't think anything of it until Ward didn't show for school today. The blame game's starting early."

"Already?"

"There he is," Carl shouted. Patrick peered toward the court until he spotted the unmistakable strutting figure of T.R. Ward cutting across the floor to the dressing room as if he didn't have a care in the world. "What timing. I'm going down to see what's up."

Donovan and a few others entered the press box during the next twenty minutes, but Patrick hardly noticed. The wait for Carl seemed interminable. Finally, he returned. Ward had come out dressed only a few minutes after the rest of the team and had huddled with Coach Burke before charging onto the floor with his teammates. He saluted his opponents at the opposite end of the court. "Well?" Patrick inquired impatiently.

"Told Jerry everything's fine. Just wanted time to get his head right for the big one."

Joined with T.R. in an unspoken bond of silent complicity, Patrick hoped his friend would have a great game. He didn't realize it would be his last for LaSalle.

36.

END OF MARCH
SENIOR YEAR (THE SAME NIGHT)

Patrick empathized so totally with LaSalle's Blue Chip recruit he felt physical pain and fatigue when the fast-paced contest ended.

Patrick didn't write the game story, but his locker room feature captured the essence of T.R.'s joyful performance, which Ward and his teammates celebrated amidst the chaos of the Oakland-bound Lancers' locker room.

"Guess I was wrong, kid," Schipper whispered to Patrick when he pulled him aside to escape the din that reverberated off the locker room's low ceiling. "Ward says he didn't know what Spear was talking about. Funny, I often said the same about Sammie myself. Ward seems overjoyed. Guess the psych job worked. He dominated."

Patrick's feature emphasized T.R.'s domination:

Lancers Secure NorCal Playoff Berth
By: Patrick Kiernan

LaSalle center T.R. Ward's triumph was complete. His Lancers' 93–84 victory over City League champion Sacramento High last night at ARCO assured LaSalle being the region's representative to the big-school NorCal finals in Oakland. The triumph gave the heavily recruited star, playing against three of his best childhood running mates, a personal victory.

"We won the regional final against a great team, and nobody can take that from us," Ward beamed in the jubilant LaSalle locker room.

"He dominated," LaSalle Coach Jerry Burke emphasized after witnessing a twenty-eight-point, nineteen-rebound performance, "a game he really wanted." Ward added five blocks, four steals, and four assists to a stat line sure to leave recruiters drooling.

"That's the best defense we've seen all year," Isaac Sims of the Chieftains exclaimed. "They're all active, but T.R.'s the key, sitting back there like a goalie. We tried to tire him out going up and down, but Sammie [Spear] and the other guards denied us outlets, and the big man ran and ran and ran."

"We knew this one was special for T.R.," junior forward Lance Hall, who pumped in twenty for the Lancers, added. "There was talk about the loser being invited to Oakland anyway, but we wanted to go as champions. And I know T.R. wanted to go with a win over his friends."

One play late with the contest still in doubt best demonstrated Ward's mastery. Going high to grab a rebound, he threw a perfect outlet to Sammie Spear, who pounded the ball downcourt until cut off at the free throw line. The point guard's pass went to the trailing Ward, who filled the lane like a giant gazelle. T.R.'s resounding slam brought the house down, almost brought the backboard down, and surely contributed to bringing the Chieftains down.

"Some people think those plays are showboating," Ward allowed, "but that's shortsighted. You learn in the schoolyard that a jam intimidates opponents and psyches up teammates and fans. Some baskets are worth more than just the two they give you." And some players prove to be stars wherever they play, whether on a South Sacramento hardtop, in school gyms and college arenas, or even at ARCO or the Oakland-Alameda County Coliseum Arena, the next stop for the Lancers.

An hour after the game and before Patrick had written that story, everybody else had left the locker room. T.R. had shooed Sammie out to "stalk the Sacramento cheerleaders."

"You were awesome," Patrick gushed. "You must feel good, despite what I told you yesterday."

"I do feel good. About everything. Mostly about myself. For the first time in months. I don't care what happens. I decided today when I was walking around my safe place that I'd play every game like it's my last. Don't matter what they print, what comes down. I feel good about this game, about playing basketball."

Patrick hung onto T.R.'s "they" as he slipped out of the locker room. If he were the enemy, he at least blurred into the whole system that had its claws into basketball away from the courts. T.R., on the other hand, knew that his kingdom was the court itself, no matter its composition or location.

37.

FIRST DAY OF APRIL
SENIOR YEAR

Carl Schipper's Friday newspaper scoop enunciated detailed allegations about Capital College's shady recruitment practices of LaSalle Blue Chipper, T.R. Ward. It noted the N.C.A.A. was aware of and investigating the substance of the report. The story took dead aim at Capital's boosters as the main culprits. It did not, however, spare T.R.'s family or unnamed intermediaries but, as Schipper had promised Patrick, painted T.R. himself as a victim rather than a perpetrator.

Patrick was grateful he didn't have to attend a marathon meeting at LaSalle the night before the article's publication. At various times, it included Carl Schipper, Brother Charles, Brother Curt, T.R.'s mom June, Percy Forte, T.R., Coach Burke, and, according to Mrs. Glass, even Mr. Foley. Patrick was also happy he was slated to write the follow-up, next-day article.

Patrick later found out T.R. agreed to go along with sitting out state championship bracket games rather than insisting on his "right to play" despite protestations by his mom and Forte. Moreover, Sammie later told Patrick that T.R. felt compelled to accept the role of victim, though he hated looking weak, to try to maintain his basketball-playing status when all was said and done.

The student body, which had worked itself into a frenzy about the upcoming Oakland tournament, turned inward—

puzzled, shocked, and angry. Luckily for Patrick, the anger seemed directed at Carl Schipper and Capital College rather than at him. In writing his Saturday article, Patrick avoided calendar references he had used, like his Presidents' Day and St. Patrick's Day allusions, in previous features. He couldn't bring himself to riff off the fact that this story was published on April Fool's Day:

LaSalle Star to Miss NorCal Playoffs
By:Patrick Kiernan

As a result of revelations revealed exclusively in yesterday's Star, LaSalle's T.R. Ward will sit out basketball games until his collegiate recruiting situation gets resolved. Since that might not come until summer, let alone next week, Ward will miss LaSalle's next game, Tuesday night, in Oakland against San Joaquin Memorial of Fresno. It's the first game in a single elimination eight-team tournament to crown a NorCal champion.

The alleged recruiting violations, which the N.C.A.A. will investigate, involve Capital College of Washington, D.C. "There's no evidence Ward himself took money from the college or its representatives, either for personal use or to pay his LaSalle tuition," Sacramento Star Sports Editor Carl Schipper, who broke the story yesterday, emphasized.

"I've no doubt, however," the veteran reporter continued, "that money was exchanged." Schipper's story in yesterday's Star unveiled possible collusion between alums or boosters from Capital and family, friends, or mentors of what may be an unsuspecting student-athlete. As Schipper notes, "Middlemen often crop up as players when details get revealed about things like this."

Schipper pointed out, "Ward is one of the most decent young men and best players I've ever covered at the prep level. I didn't intend to hurt him, particularly if he's as innocent as I think, but a newspaper exists to tell the truth, and that is what The Star is all about. I do think that people who prey on kids and sports should be held accountable."

The LaSalle administration reluctantly agreed to sit Ward in upcoming games even though he only faces allegations. Vice Principal Brother Curt, F.S.C., said, "We certainly don't want to take things away from students merely on suspicions. Mr. Ward's guilt would be out of character for the student-athlete we know. Still, we operate at LaSalle under principles that make his participation problematic with questions swirling. Therefore, all, including T.R., have agreed that he will sit out while putting his attention to resolving this matter."

It will certainly affect the coach and the team, readying for a first-round NorCal clash, ironically with another Christian Brothers' team, San Joaquin Memorial of Fresno. Coach Jerry Burke issued a statement: "As far as we're concerned, T.R.'s the best basketball player in the state, but we'll show up regardless. The Panthers will know they were in a game."

T.R. Ward and his family withheld comment. Ward, sought by over a hundred and fifty colleges, had narrowed his choice to five on New Year's Eve. Besides Capital, he also named U.C.L.A., St. John's, Notre Dame, and Georgetown as finalists in his recruitment sweepstakes.

"Mr. Wilson's going to join us," Patrick informed his mother. "Suzie's coming too,"

"Good to talk things out with trustworthy people," Sheila Kiernan soothed.

"I haven't really cried in ages," Patrick volunteered, "but I feel like a traitor today. Maybe, I should quit my job."

"Talk it over with Steve. He usually has a good perspective."

Suzie arrived first, followed shortly by Steve Wilson. "I need to talk with people I trust with my life," Patrick began when everybody gathered at the kitchen table. Sheila poured iced tea and put out a few snacks. "I feel like I'm losing control."

Patrick launched into a long confession about his "self-serving distortion of the truth." He reconstructed a myriad of details about the long journey to this first day in April regarding "the story," even though the other three were familiar with the narrative. It was, after all, his confession.

When Patrick finished, Mr. Wilson jumped in to "provide perspective." He emphasized Patrick had been doing his job, he had never wanted to hurt T.R., and revelations would have emerged regardless.

Suzie, however, interjected: "Lies are lies, even if it looks as if you won't have to own up to them since Carl had his *Trib* source."

"Right," Steve Wilson agreed, "but Patrick's clearly paying for his lies. I'm just saying he doesn't need to play hero and tell T.R. or anybody that he fed initial facts to Carl."

"Steve's right," Sheila jumped in. "That wouldn't do any good."

Wilson turned to Suzie: "You know, sometimes a little compassion for human frailty is the most Christian thing. That's why Catholics emphasize confession. Like Jesus, we know people are imperfect sinners." He suddenly became embarrassed by his self-realized tendency to preach. "If I open a window, does anybody mind if I smoke my pipe?" When nobody objected and Sheila Kiernan nodded yes, he moved to the window over the kitchen sink, which he opened before crossing to the cupboard where Sheila Kiernan kept the only ashtray in the house. Returning to the table, he loaded and tamped his pipe, though distracted enough not to light it.

"If Pat lied," Sheila lamented, "it was because T.R. told him too much. I'm sure he was motivated to protect his friend, getting Schipper to write the story rather than Donovan, who would have smeared him."

"And protecting myself and my interests," Patrick added.

"Interests? Including doing right for everybody taking you into their confidence?" Wilson jumped back in. "You're a high school student, not a Supreme Court Judge. And to have a shot at a job you'd really like to get? Everybody should remember

Carl's good at getting what he wants. Probably the job he's after too. He became the story in today's piece. Not a bad selling point for his Denver paper."

"Remember," Patrick cautioned, "nobody's supposed to know about that."

"They won't," Sheila Kiernan promised, as if speaking for the three.

"The point before is well taken," Wilson indicated. "Everybody's confiding things to Patrick. Sean and T.R. and Carl about the job, and ..." Mr. Wilson threw a quick glance Suzie's way, "maybe other people, for all I know. That says something positive about him, but you can only fill a cup so full before it overflows." Again, he glanced at Suzie. "Even a gold chalice."

"Sure," Suzie concurred. "It's tough when different confidences conflict." Suzie reached out and clasped Patrick's wrist, reacting personally, unaware Patrick had talked to Mr. Wilson about her Andy Hill revelations.

"And again, Carl gets what he wants. People get fooled by his dress and manner, but when he's after something, he charges ahead like a captain of industry." Patrick winced as Wilson drove home his next statement: "The way he recruited you at the beginning of the school year to make sure he had an edge with the Ward story shows that, even though I'm sure the way you worked out as a writer pleasantly surprised him. I bet he thought you'd just be a good stringer and source."

"Recruited?" The word jolted Patrick out of the comfort Mr. Wilson's spirited defense provided. The notion, however, did more than surprise; it appealed to his sense of irony that often led him to discovery. "Yeah, maybe I was," he said wistfully.

"Nothing to be ashamed about. Life is about recruiting," Steve Wilson ran with the thought. "People need other people. So, we recruit. Friends. Spouses. Workers. It's the style and intent we do it with that matters. Makes it tolerable, maybe even right, when recruiting friends or lovers. And, if nothing else, people recruit for their own versions of the truth." He paused for a second to lock eyes with everybody else at the table. "In a sense, you've been busy recruiting yourself to land that Bay Area *Star* assignment just as surely as he recruited you. Lastly, a little guilt's fine. You probably should feel it. We've discussed that, but you shouldn't wallow in it."

"Bet T.R.'s feeling guilty too, even if he's a victim," Sheila Kiernan said. "Guilt comes with living."

"Yeah," Suzie agreed, "no details, but I feel guilty about something that wasn't my fault." Patrick reached over and grasped her wrist.

Taking back the initiative, Wilson continued, "T.R.s got to feel guilt. There's no way he and others at Thursday night's meeting agreed to him sitting out without knowing the article told truths about shady dealings. Especially with Curt there. I'm sure Curt's also seeing this as a personal defeat. T.R. could have stopped everything, claiming he was totally innocent and demanding nothing happen until his so-called day in court. The fact he didn't want to fight the school's decision, without even knowing what the N.C.A.A. plans, tells you something."

"I hope they hang Forte," Patrick blurted.

"They won't, in all probability," Wilson countered assuredly. "T.R.'ll go down. Maybe people associated with the college. But, guys like Forte often skate."

"Doesn't T.R. have a chance?" Suzie wondered.

"He's dead," Wilson pronounced. "Though he hasn't admitted it, he clearly knew something was up. I'm surprised there wasn't talk of LaSalle forfeiting last week's game. The public high schools, which think Catholic schools steal athletic talent, probably decided this means he got shady money to attend LaSalle too. Not true, but that's what they'll believe. Remember, I said we fight for our own versions of truth, sometimes without facts."

"I heard yesterday," Patrick said, fearful of mentioning his source, Mrs. Glass, "that Jerry went along with the consensus to make sure the team got one game at least in Oakland.

If Ward tried to play with all this swirling, the C.I.F. might have stepped in to forfeit games and championships already played. His not playing should take the pressure off of them to do something. Lawsuits. Threats."

"Lawsuits over high school basketball? What are we coming to?" Sheila Kiernan shook her head incredulously.

"Don't be naïve, Sheila. You know what the world's like." Wilson finally lit the pipe he had been playing with through the conversation. "Lawsuits. People fighting over their own versions of the truth. Here, for greed or power." Turning toward Patrick, Wilson persisted, "Carl's quote in your article made me laugh. He said the business of a newspaper is to reveal the truth. The truth," he chuckled sarcastically. "Remember, Patrick, especially if you pursue journalism, the business of a newspaper, like all businesses, is to make money for someone. And money and power are married in this culture. And sports are big money and power at every level."

"God, Mr. Wilson, you paint a bleak picture," Suzie protested.

"Didn't paint it," he replied. "Just observe it. I also observe, Patrick, that despite everything, the world spins on. Especially for you with your future. You said you trusted the three of us. Others don't have the luxury of three people to trust, people who know our faults and doubts and still love and care for us. Remember, I mentioned that headline before, 'Feats of Clay'? Everybody fears being found out, often for not living up to who we want to be. But what a blessing to trust that the people around you will love you no matter what. Bet T.R.'s struggling with thoughts like that today with what he's found about himself."

"Good advice, Steve," Sheila Kiernan applauded.

At almost the same time, Suzie wondered, "Shouldn't Patrick try squaring things with T.R.?"

"Sure," Wilson climbed to his pulpit again, "but maybe in good time. I bet Patrick finds things aren't as bad for him as he thinks. And timing's good; school's out for Easter vacation on Wednesday. Soul-searching time for many. No spotlight on you, Patrick. I've given you the same advice before. Kipling called it 'the art of judicious leaving alone.' I looked it up. Our whole society's about instant reaction. Instant resolution, like on TV or in a game. Instant coffee. Instant tea. Instant everything. Sometimes, it's better, as Joan Didion says, to 'play it as it lays.'"

As the conversation played out, Patrick felt momentarily better. Still, he dreaded the short week ahead at school and covering the game Wednesday night.

38.

FIRST WEEK OF APRIL
SENIOR YEAR

Patrick's three-day school week seemed endless. He had always wondered what days must be like for students who hated getting up every morning to face school. That week, he got a sense.

T.R.,'s absence from school all three days left Patrick relieved he didn't have to confront the person who had confided in him, though he played out scenarios in his mind as to what T.R. was doing. Still, Patrick's guilt ratcheted up as rumors about T.R.'s fall and exile swept through the student body, rocked by scandal once again.

Patrick happily avoided Coach Burke. Before his flight to Denver for his Wednesday interview, Carl handled the tourney preview after conversations with Jerry, who was said to have remained amicable with the reporter though Carl earned the wrath of most students.

"Easter vacation's going to save my ass this year," Patrick confided to Mr. Wilson.

"Suzie might say it's supposed to save something else," Mr. Wilson chided playfully, trying to cut through Patrick's angst. "You're staying in the Bay Area for the weekend after the game, right?"

"Yeah, with Pete Eaton, though I've never met him. Bunking at the Emeryville apartment *The Star* leases. Suzie's going to Yreka with her mom and sister. After coming home for Easter Sunday, I'll go back down for the A's season opener. Friday and Saturday, I'm going with Pete to the last of the exhibition Bay Bridge series between the Giants and A's in home ballparks. The *Star*'s going to use wire service stuff for Sunday, though, so we can be home Easter."

"I've told you my favorite quote by an educational theorist, Paulo Freire. To paraphrase, he says that every day in the classroom has the potential of Easter Sunday. Maybe, this year, a day soon will be about your resurrection."

Surprisingly, it was the Lancers who almost rose from the dead Wednesday night, as Patrick chronicled in his game story, sent on the apartment's new fax machine after midnight:

Valiant Lancers Nipped in Overtime
By:Patrick Kiernan

The LaSalle Lancers, playing without superstar center T.R. Ward, gave San Joaquin Memorial (24–5) everything the Panthers could handle last night before falling in overtime, 63–62.

The Fresno school will meet St. Joseph Notre Dame, which defeated Balboa of San Francisco, 81–78, in the other match-up. The NorCal team that emerges will then face the SoCal winner for the state title.

The Lancers, who held off the Panthers at the end of regulation, had a chance to win with a few seconds left in overtime. Junior Lance Hall, moved from forward to center in place of Ward, missed an open ten-footer at the buzzer. Hall, who played all but one minute, led the Lancers with eighteen points. He was backed most notably by sophomore Rick Pantera, who went for fifteen points in his first-ever varsity start.

Hall bemoaned his miss after the game that cost the Lancers their fourth defeat of the season, but Lancer Coach Jerry Burke and Hall's teammates all pointed to his big effort throughout. "He had clearly left it all on the floor," Burke expressed. "He didn't have anything left."

Sammie Spear, playing his last game as a Lancer, tallied eight points but dished nine assists. "Lance did it all," he echoed his coach, "but if we have the best player in the state playing, we win handily."

Memorial Coach Jeff Hensley wasn't ready to acknowledge that, but he did call the Lancers' effort "valiant." Marcus Long led the Panthers with twenty-one points. The athletic forward missed playing against Ward, who he might see at the collegiate level, but did admire the pluck of the LaSalle team playing without him.

In losing, the Lancers proved themselves champions. Facing long odds, the Sacramento regional winners refused to quit. "I'm prouder of this team than any I've coached," Coach Burke observed. "A great team and great bunch of kids. And I'm talking about everybody who put on a uniform for us this season."

Out of the darkness beyond which sat the outdoor stadium adjacent to the Oakland-Alameda County Coliseum Arena and its other parking lot, two black-clad figures emerged as Patrick headed to his car after the game and before he wrote and filed his story. "Patrick? That you?" Brother Curt's familiar voice disarmed the briefcase and satchel-packing young reporter who noticed the nondescript Brother Kevin accompanying LaSalle's more imposing Dean.

"They hire you for security?" Patrick asked.

"Making sure the kids get out safely," Brother Kevin stated, as if he, too, wanted to hit the road.

"They might not be as at home in these neighborhoods as me," Brother Curt offered. "We saw the rooter buses off, and we're making sure there's no stragglers." Changing the subject, Brother Curt exclaimed, "The team played great tonight."

Patrick responded, "Thought we had 'em." He too quickly changed subjects: "Talk to T.R.?"

"In contact all week. Suzie or Sean here with you?"

"Suzie's headed to Yreka for Easter weekend with her mother and sister. Sean left today for some Marine Corps thing until Saturday, something with his deferred enlistment option.

Maybe an officer candidate recruiting thing."

"I knew when it was you interacting with him, it would work."

"Huh?"

"Recruiting you to get a sense of what he'd be like coming back. He's been a delight. Seems that Marine captain's a healthy influence after his father. Some guys from the old neighborhood benefited from time in the Corps. Made some but broke others. Sean might have a future there. Staying down here for the weekend, right?"

"Yeah. Looking forward to seeing major league games from press boxes."

"We'll walk you to your car so we can keep talking," Brother Curt said as much for Brother Kevin as for Patrick. "Tony's having it pretty tough. Feels terrible. Couldn't bring himself to come tonight."

"Noticed. The college recruiters didn't have as much to watch without him here, though now maybe Lance will get some play next year."

"Recruiters have done enough."

"You mean Capital's?"

"All. Vultures. Just a matter of who the kids want to fly with. Phone Tony over vacation. He needs to talk to somebody besides me. He's feeling isolated. Sammie and others are there for him, but they're not that good at nurturing somebody or talking things out."

"Don't forget where I work. I might not be at the top of T.R.'s nurturing list these days."

"Nonsense," Brother Curt snapped as he picked up his pace, leaving Brother Kevin straggling behind. "He told me yesterday you're about the only student he could talk to about all this."

Staring at Brother Curt at the same time, the two of them, before Brother Kevin, cut the roundness off a big curve along the walkway by veering downhill through a sparsely greened patch of dirt, and Patrick nearly tripped. "Yesterday?"

"Or the day before. Been phoning so much this week the

days blend together. I told him to take a few days off until after vacation. Always love the fact Catholic schools take the week after Easter instead of before. Tony knows it was Carl's show. Carl emphasized that and told us about his source at the *Trib* at last Thursday's meeting. Tony doesn't resent you at all."

"I'm sure Carl wrote up the story better for Tony than Donovan would have."

Brother Curt stopped in his tracks, bringing Patrick to a halt. He turned to Brother Kevin when he caught up, whispered to him briefly, and watched the other Christian Brother saunter off. "Probably true about Donovan," he said while shaking his head wistfully and turning back to face Patrick. "But that's the irony. Donovan wasn't going to use the story."

Patrick stood transfixed. "Not use it? Donovan? Foley's puppet? You kidding?" Patrick almost pleaded. "We figured ... that is, Carl told me he was probably just waiting until letter-of-intent day. Nail him after signing to limit his options. And Foley getting revenge on T.R. and the school."

"That's the key. Old man Foley was behind it. His real grudge was against Forte. Dealings they had that soured. Tony became the pawn in that. The two men had been in bed together for years with construction stuff all over the city. Foley got relief from critics who said he didn't hire minority workers or subcontractors. Forte always stuck up for him, and in turn, Foley used Percy's minority contacts on all the jobs Foley Construction had in South Sac. Forte basically used Foley to build his projects in South Sac and with redevelopment work that he glommed onto and orchestrated downtown. Things unraveled last summer over what Percy called 'accounting practices.'"

"You're kidding?" Sean blurted incredulously. "By accounting practices, I assume you mean funneling money."

"The real world. Percy threw some money at others in the community. Jobs. Direct handouts. Sort of the Godfather of South Sac, but mostly aboveboard in the big picture. Probably what he was doing with the Capital money: some skimmed off for the Rec Center, some for Tony's mother and family, and some for himself for 'future projects.' A bit shady, but with room to wriggle out publicly."

"Like his Caddy."

"Now, now. Business leaders, labor leaders, and politicians skim all the time. Payouts, shell corporations, money laundering. Money funneled to personal coffers or things they care about. When a Black man does something similar, he gets pillaged. Say what you will, but Percy was, and is, good for the neighborhood and the people who live there."

"A lot to chew on. I thought you were going to tell me old man Foley didn't want Donovan to print the story because of his love for LaSalle."

"Hardly. The quicker he's out of our hair, and maybe Sean's too, the better. No, it's easier to understand than that. He bribed me, and I took it. That's why Sean got back in school after you sorta vetted him for me."

"My God! You mean for letting Sean back into LaSalle, Foley was going to make sure Donovan didn't use that stuff? Maybe ever? Did Sean know?"

"Nobody knows but Sean's dad, Donovan, and me. And now you," Brother Curt told the numbed Patrick Kiernan. "I wasn't proud making a bargain with the devil. And, of course, Charles loved it without hearing the details. Sean's been a revelation, almost 'born again,' to use your pet phrase, without pressure from his father to perform or follow his agenda."

Patrick started walking forward a few steps to avoid looking Brother Curt in the eyes. "Jesus."

"Course, the story Schipper laid out was pretty much spot-on. Tony didn't have control, but he knew. Not all the details, but enough to be troubled, though he understands the inequities in how these things play out. I've been talking to June too, and Percy, to see if we could have gotten Tony off the hook from Capital. We hoped we could have played things out to get him directed to another college before any story appeared."

"And gotten him through the tournament. Our revered principal would have loved that."

"Tony would have loved it. Not playing crushes him. I feared that if it came out later, it would look like we just wanted to get him through the state championship at any cost rather than having Tony's best interests at heart. I wanted to do right by him, and, God knows, that's what I was trying to do, taking old man Foley's offer." Brother Kevin strolled back over to the two, acting nonchalant.

"I'm sure you did," Patrick said to Curt, ignoring Kevin. "Here I am," he announced to both, though his car was closer to where Kevin had been standing. "Gotta finish my game story. We have one of those new machines where I'm staying. I can fax it in, like taking a picture of it and sending it, but still need to get it done soon for the first edition."

"Let's go, Kevin. And Patrick, tell the story of the game like it was. We might have lost, but we're champions."

With this latest revelation jarring his soul, Patrick felt like anything but a champion. He jumped in his car and zipped to the other side of the empty parking lot, where he turned off the ignition and cried his eyes out. Surely, he wasn't the only spectator who had cried in that parking lot after a loss, though few had cried over a loss of innocence.

He intended to write his last LaSalle game story of the year from his heart. Instead, he wrote it from instinct, all he had left that evening.

39.

EASTER VACATION
SENIOR YEAR

Though first-class postage was a quarter, Patrick sprang for more than double that to mail a letter, to arrive by Saturday, to Suzie at Daphne's house. He didn't want to ask Pete Eaton, whom he had picked up at the Oakland Airport Thursday morning, if he could ring up charges on the phone in the Emeryville apartment since he hardly knew him and didn't know if Pete paid for the line or the *Star* did. In either case, feeling as if he might be auditioning for a job, he refrained from asking.

He also ruled out phoning collect or dialing Daphne's house with a pocket full of change from a phone booth. Aware that anyone from Suzie's sister to Daphne's family might be intrigued by Suzie getting mail at her cousin's house and pester her to read it aloud, Patrick toned down the mushiness:

Holy Thursday

Suzie,

Miss you. Strange not seeing you Easter weekend, though I'm sure you're enjoying Daphne's family. Also, hope the time in Ashland and at S.O.C. and the Festival with your mom and sister will have been wonderful. Neat that you'll help direct Cristin in her eighth-grade play next week. It says a lot that Mrs. Broadbear from your elementary school chose you to help direct little sis and her classmates.

I wish you had been the lead in Bye Bye Birdie at school. Though I only saw that one performance and might not have been too responsive with everything happening, I think you pretty much stole the show.

I'll phone on Sunday afternoon, hopefully before you sit down for Easter dinner. Mom and I are going to The Firehouse in Old Sacramento. Eating out that day's our tradition, as you'll remember from last year when you guys joined us.

It will be good to hear your voice. A lot more to talk about. I'm resisting the temptation to write on and on and on and on and on, but I look forward to seeing you.

Going to the 'Stick tomorrow night with Pete. Giants home game. Then, the Coliseum Saturday. Pete's sleeping now. Fairly tiny apartment in Emeryville—perfect freeway connection, unless stuck in traffic, going to both stadiums. In our brief conversation during this morning's ride from the airport, I got the feeling Pete likes being down here more than Carl might have thought. Don't think he's a player or anything, but he seems to look forward to time out of his house, though he and his wife are empty nesters in Sacto.

Plan to explore Berkeley after I mail this. Telegraph Avenue's always trippy, and I'm going to walk around campus again.

We nearly won last night, falling 63–62 in overtime. It would have been David bringing down Goliath, us playing without T.R. That, however, wasn't the big news.

Crushed me, but Brother Curt told me after the game that Donovan might not have printed that story about T.R. that Carl did. The one I fed him. The one that brought T.R. down. Seems Curt had taken Sean back in to school as a quid pro quid with Mr. Foley to make sure Donovan didn't use what he had.

You can imagine how that makes me feel, even when I tell myself stuff would have hit the fan eventually anyway.

Curt also gave me lots to think about concerning Forte. Listening to Curt, maybe I've been looking for villains in the wrong places. Or, maybe, not looking at myself and the real world closely enough.

That's why I desperately want to talk with you. I always count on you for truth. You were the only one who didn't think Carl having another source at the Trib took me off the hook. Made me face the fact that falling back on that was an excuse to ignore … lies.

Also found out from Pete that Carl got the Denver job. Thought that greased the way for the dream scenario I was looking toward. I am, however, now concerned that Carl was blowing a little smoke in his assurances. I know he figured I might have to continue as an independent contractor because of my age, but I thought that would be workable. But if Pete wants to keep the gig down here …

Mom said to say hello before I left Wednesday. She might even have gone away for these few days with me down here (get the feeling she might be seeing somebody), but, as I said, we'll meet for Easter dinner. Tell Aunt Sally I'll dream of her Easter dinner, though I do look forward to eating at The Firehouse.

Love, Pat

Patrick relished talking on the phone with Suzie Easter Sunday, though he strained to focus on her ventures in Yreka and Ashland with her mother and Cristin before enumerating things troubling and pleasing him. He had a longer, more soul-searching discussion with Suzie the following Wednesday when she took a lunch break from helping direct her sister's play. Two conversations, however, the Monday and Tuesday after Easter, provided telling details, musings, and considerations during the welcomed respite from classes.

Patrick met T.R. and Sean at the River Monday morning. Their discomfort at his pulling them together, though both knew that to be his plan, was lessened, though not alleviated, during the conversation. He used details of his planned

Memorial Day weekend trip as the best excuse to get them to interact together with him.

"T.R., can't picture you or me in a Marine buzz cut like Sean's," Patrick teased.

"Must not have listened to that Samson stuff. You know, Samson and, what was her name?" T.R. chimed in. "In the Bible. Cutting hair to take the warrior's strength."

"Delilah," Sean finished. "And, the way I heard the story, it was Samson's dreadlocks she sheared, but he still collapsed the temple."

"So," Patrick tried retrieving the conversation, "the cabin in Kyburz is about thirty miles east of Placerville on 50, before you go up and over the summit to South Shore. Mr. Walters, my mother's boss, owns it, but his family doesn't use it much anymore."

"Bet they traded time there for some hot spot closer to Tahoe," Sean spoke as if privy to decisions made like that. "Probably not good enough anymore."

"Well, it's pretty funky. Right in the El Dorado Forest and next to the American River, which rushes through the rocks right by. Was only there once, but Mom brought home pictures to remind me about it and show me where we need to turn on water and stuff."

"A last boys' weekend fling, huh?" Sean seemed more interested than T.R.

"Exactly. Memorial Day's early this year. We finish our last senior tests and have grad practice later that week, and graduation's the next Saturday. Sun, cards, music, fishing if you like, food we bring or grill. And, of course, the River, this one," Patrick nodded beyond them, "though it'll look much different in the mountains."

"Running fast everywhere," T.R. said.

Sean added, "Especially with our warm spring."

"A VCR so we can bring movies, though regular TV reception's out. Granite rocks right next to the place to sunbathe."

"You sure there's no real TV?" T.R. asked.

"No, but we can have beer since we won't need to drive anywhere. Won't even need your expertise buying up, Sean. Supposedly, Mom will arrange a pony keg through her boss if we promise not to drive. They have some service that supplies the cabin on those rare occasions they use it now."

"What if I have business just beyond the Lake? At my favorite ranch?" Sean joked impishly.

"We'd need to clear that with Tammy," Patrick needled. "And cut you off from alcohol. Don't want some vixen playing Delilah with my new buddy before he heads off to boot camp."

"Sounds like he's more interested in booty camp," T.R. teased, sensing Sean was just offering a blast from the past. "At least, when not going all Disciple Fellowship on us with Tammy."

Patrick appreciated that T.R. felt connected enough to banter with Sean. Before Foley arrived, he had spoken with T.R. about two things, how much he hoped for a rapprochement between "an important old and new friend" and how he still felt bad for his part in Carl's recruiting story. He gave up the fact that Carl had pumped him for details and that he had had a difficult time resisting, despite promises made, though again he left out some details. T.R. seemed resigned to his fate, offering forgiveness, though saying it wasn't necessary considering his own reckless determination to run away from everything falling in on him rather than heading things off.

T.R. and Patrick agreed they both dreaded the last month and a half of school. They phrased it differently, though. Patrick compared his anticipated weeks ahead at school to "Odysseus visiting the underworld." T.R. thought it would feel like "doing time."

T.R. did, however, say having access to Brother Curt every day was a major consolation. He and Curt, he said, planned to sit down a number of times during the coming week to figure out the best way to approach N.C.A.A. investigators and T.R.'s future. T.R. told Patrick his mom was petitioning to get her old job back at the post office and that, though they had agreed not to be dependent on each other or even see each other, Percy Forte was going to grease the skids to pull that off.

The upshot of the morning was that Sean and T.R. both said they'd attend Patrick's "Kyburz blow-out," though T.R. thought he might not make the whole weekend because of family commitments. Sean, sounding in other conversations with Patrick as if he was totally estranged from his father though not his mother, had spoken no such concerns.

It was Patrick who ended Tuesday with more concerns. Carl drove Patrick to the A's home opener that morning. Behind the wheel, Carl acted circumspectly, not responding to any of the openings Patrick floated to move the conversation to the possible job opportunity covering baseball and other sports by the Bay. Patrick even brought up the fact that he had already enrolled at S.F. State so he could take a class there during the summer while waiting to start his first semester at Cal. S.F. State counted journalism classes for the mandatory four years of English so that Patrick already had enough units to gain official acceptance at the city's Lake Merced campus.

He would later go into detail about the class with Mr. Wilson. It promised once-a-week meetings and papers about New Journalism, which blurred the distinction between fiction and nonfiction. He gladly anticipated readings by Tom Wolfe, Truman Capote, Hunter S. Thompson, and Sacramento's Joan Didion, and loved the genre's focus on four main stylistic demands as enunciated by Wolfe: 1) dialogue in full; 2) detail in full; 3) scene-by-scene construction; and 4) third person narration even while getting into the mind of the protagonist. With Carl, he instead focused on the class meeting time, Thursday nights: "That should be perfect since most Bay Area MLB Thursday games typically get scheduled in the afternoon, if at all."

Carl, seemingly preoccupied with everything Colorado, didn't respond. He hoped that within five years, Denver might gain both a major league baseball team and an N.H.L. franchise to join the Nuggets and Broncos as potential sports beats.

The really telling conversation took place in the Oakland Coliseum's press room. With Pete gone to chase a locker room story, Carl and Patrick dawdled over the pregame spread, put out for reporters by the team's understaffed but incredibly efficient and welcoming personnel.

"Pretty cool being in the press box for a season opener, no?"

Schipper's tone gave Patrick the impression the day might be his consolation prize, that he had been led astray by Carl's suggestions that he was a good bet to land the beat Pete still so obviously enjoyed. Carefully, though, he tempered his response: "Since Sacramento readers don't take high school baseball as seriously as basketball and football, it's ironic baseball's still my favorite sport to watch."

"Who knows, maybe in five years I'll still be sports editor of the *Denver News* and hire you to cover the major league baseball team they hope to get," Carl said.

"When do you start?"

"June fifteenth. I'll also have a three-times-a-week column besides features whenever I want. A good deal. We have our Kings' guy at *The Star*, but they have two regular beat guys for the Broncos and Nuggets and a full-time guy for collegiate sports. And, three or four other dedicated sports reporters, on staff or contracted."

"Sounds like a step up. Pay too?"

"Indeed," Carl beamed. "Unfortunately," and Patrick sensed it, "the news isn't as good with you and *The Star*."

"When you didn't talk about it on the way down, I was afraid of that."

"Still details to work out. Not a strikeout. Got to chat with Pete again, and this is going to go down from up top, but I think Pete is going to keep this beat. He's good. Maybe helps he's not with the players on road trips, so they don't get sick of him."

"And," Patrick added, trying to be a good soldier, "helps that he's a nice guy. So, what's my prospects?" Patrick added impatiently.

"The people up top have been doing preliminary interviews. I gave 'em a heads-up. I think they have a young hotshot in mind for Editor, a guy from down here. Merle will stay Assistant Editor, a perfect position for him. But, Pete, especially during baseball's offseason, will spend more time in Sacramento, sort of mentoring the new guy about Sactown ways while working with a few of the other reporters."

"And me?" Patrick cut right to it. "You want me to go to Sac State so I can keep writing high school sports?"

Carl grimaced. "No, Pete's onboard with this, and I think upper echelon management is too. You'd be an independent contractor with a guaranteed monthly stipend of, say, five hundred bucks, but as a stringer of sorts, you'd pick up any stories we need down here, even sometimes subbing for Pete. And pay per additional story once you exceed the minimum number for a month, probably five to seven. But the base sum would be guaranteed, to keep you in coffee or books or," and Carl chuckled, "weed, or whatever staples Cal students need these days. Something fair to both parties. Management recognizes your talent, even if they think you're too young for a full-time contract. And with college, I assume that wouldn't work anyway. You need to get your degree."

"Sound like Mom."

"Common sense. I regret never finishing. Thank God, I can't see newspapers ever going away. Course, this assumes you'd be going to school down here to write stories important for our market, like Cal stories when they're decent. Lots of alums our way. Don't think Princeton would work."

"Neither do I. Berkeley, it should be. And I told you about that class at State. I thought I'd be starting down here this summer."

"A summer start should work well. I'll talk to the higher-ups about working up a contract for all this and getting you started right after you graduate. And, pay attention today because if everything goes down the way I'm thinking, Pete might need some coverage help this coming summer."

Patrick resisted asking Carl, now that job prospects had clarified, whether he had recruited him to get an exclusive source close to T.R. and LaSalle basketball. He wasn't sure he wanted the answer. Instead, he enjoyed opening day.

40.

EARLY MAY
SENIOR YEAR

"Okay," Mr. Wilson addressed his fidgety A.P. students, "probably the last time we're all together until after A.P. tests." Cheers erupted from the seniors. "Yeah, thrills me too."

"Does that mean we don't have to take the final the last week of school after all?" Tammy Dickerson asked eagerly.

"No, no, no, and no," Mr. Wilson hastily responded. "I said the last time together," he raised his voice for emphasis, "until after A.P.s. Then, another couple of weeks until Memorial Day. And everybody, including juniors, takes the final during the week after that when we finish with extended periods for senior testing."

"Even if we take the actual A.P.?" Leroy Horton asked.

"Everybody. Told you repeatedly: everyone passes the final to pass the course. I'm a man of my word."

"So," Patrick piped up, "us seniors have two weeks off before Memorial Day?"

"Sound like my style, Mr. Kiernan? Remember last year? The juniors and I will work on poetry while seniors in groups read fun, contemporary nonfiction. Like readings from that New Journalism list you showed me."

"You mean all our readings haven't been fun?" Patrick, who loved most of them, feigned being another senioritis-infected student. "Besides, it's about a hundred and ten outside;

maybe, we can meet and chill at the River before our final."

The rest of the seniors voiced agreement before Mr. Wilson cut them off with one more reminder: "No test; no pass. That simple. If you're on your deathbed, plan to take it when you recover. Your responsibility."

The students were a bit surprised when Mr. Wilson, who treated wasting time from learning about literature and writing as an affront to mankind, announced he would entertain a wide-ranging, free-flowing fifteen-minute discussion about current events.

Topics, surfaced and done with quickly, ran the gamut. They ranged from the April Good Guys! electronics store Sacramento hostage crisis in which three Vietnamese hostage-takers and three hostages ended up dead to the sure-to-be subdued upcoming senior prom, election politics, emerging details about the Rodney King beating, the successfully concluded school play, the Kings, and the weather. At Suzie's tongue-in-cheek urging, students even debated whether Michael J. Fox was a sex symbol in *Back to the Future*.

Keeping his charges off guard, Mr. Wilson halted the discussion to shift to another activity: "You write every week, either a take-home or in-class response from an A.P. prompt. None today with the test later this week, but a writing assignment nonetheless. And, yes, I will read them. Listen carefully to the directions. You'll have ten minutes."

"Ten minutes?" Kelly Kerwin shouted. "I spend longer than that on the toilet."

Mr. Wilson plowed right through the class's groans to finish his directions: "I want you to do a free-write. Ten minutes. Write about something, anything, interesting to you. Have an audience in mind, but write from your heart and mind. No more explanations from me. Take out paper and a pen. You start in exactly one minute."

Patrick's free-write, which he thought about for a minute before committing pen to paper, did come from his heart:

Patrick Kiernan   Advanced English IV – AP test week

Feels good to write freely for a change. I disliked journaling in Brother Kevin's class, usually with a specific prompt, but this is liberating after formal school essays and articles for The Star. So, what's on my mind? You.

Yes, to use our favorite expression, I want to get my heartfelt thanks to you OFF OF my plate before another day goes by.

You've always been there for me, no matter what, with great advice and care. If this were a literary assignment, I'd say that as a father figure, you're 100% Atticus Finch and the antithesis of Pap Finn. Yes, you've been a father figure to me as well as a mentor. Maybe, in that sense, you'd be more like a Jean Valjean from Les Misérables, acting like a father to Cosette.

I hope when I get older, I'm like you. During this trying year, you've been everything to me. I thought for a while that Carl was another mentor and father figure, but recent revelations leave me questioning that. Luckily, with you, there are no questions. I see a similar relationship between T.R. and Brother Curt, who's there for him no matter what.

Since I never really did know my own father well (though people say I look like him and have his intelligence), I've often been told I needed a father figure. Mom was such a good parent that I didn't think that was true. But it is, and you are. Thank you.

You're probably the reason I ended up at LaSalle. Many people—the nuns in elementary school, neighbors, Mom's friends and coworkers—assumed I'd go to Loyola. The LaSalle Open Houses I attended while in seventh and eighth grades made me think twice. Still, it was that special after-school literature seminar for chosen eighth-graders you taught that convinced me beyond doubt.

And my intuition was right. I've loved having you as my English teacher in ninth grade and with the mixed AP class junior and senior years. And that doesn't even count journalism classes or activities. Or "Nerd League" basketball. Or times just hanging out. Or times at your house or ours. Or getting to know your girls.

I remember after "Back-to-School Night" my freshman year, my mom came home glowing after meeting you. She talked about how sensitive you were and how you'd make a perfect role model. She already, four weeks in, knew how much I loved your class but was overjoyed you seemed to take a personal interest in me, recruiting me early to write for The Lance.

I cannot thank you enough. I hope I will live into the person you have guided me to become. A caring and giving person like yourself.

Unlike what Huck Finn did in that famous scene we agree is so important in American literature, this is one "letter" I trust I would never tear up.

You're the best,
Patrick

"I'll enjoy reading these," Mr. Wilson said as he collected student papers. "A bit like an inkblot test where what you wrote will reveal something."

"How will you grade them?" Dave Koeppen wondered, probably the question many A.P. students would ask first.

"Dartboard," Mr. Wilson offered. "Actually, a perfect learning exercise just before taking your actual A.P. Two main points. Anybody figure what I had in mind during the last twenty-five minutes?"

"Take our minds off the test?" Teddy Gervais ventured.

"A bit, but two other teaching points for your test Thursday." Mr. Wilson launched ahead, "I'll be curious how many of you wrote about topics we just discussed. The hostage story. Michael J. Fox. The rest. How many?" Half the class raised hands. "Good lesson, whether taking the test Thursday or next year. On A.P. responses, there's a tendency to bend a prompt to something you just read. It's on your mind, and you remember it best. It's often better to go deep into the vault, something you might have read as a junior, or even as an underclassman, that might be the better entrée to make an important point about literature that responds best to the prompt."

"You tricked us," Kelly Kerwin said. "I had the Kings on my mind after we talked about them."

"Good thing," Mr. Wilson returned as if scripted, "we didn't talk about sex. At best, I might have ended up with ten minutes of you writing about *Lolita* or D. H. Lawrence. Now wait a minute, Kelly, don't jot those names down."

"Funny," Kerwin protested.

"And, speaking of works of literature, I wonder how many of you wrote about literature because you thought that's what I wanted."

Several students, particularly the juniors, looked as if they had just been caught plagiarizing.

"Don't write to please an imagined reader. Another point will also be important if you're taking the test this week. Did you feel free writing? Not stopping every two seconds to correct grammar or redo something or circle back to make a point clear? You want to avoid that during the test. Take a few minutes to think through your answer, and then write it confidently from your mind and heart.

Feeling good, Patrick reflected that he had done just that.

41.

START OF
MEMORIAL DAY WEEKEND
SENIOR YEAR

Mr. Walters' cabin sat amidst two dozen others clustered near Highway 50 about a mile before Kyburz. Designated the Thirty Mile Tract to mark its location from Placerville, the group of rustic cabins dotted the American River. They looked nothing like modern developments springing up around Lake Tahoe, another thirty-five miles and beyond Echo Summit.

In fact, the land under the cabin Sheila Kiernan had borrowed from her firm's partner was owned by the U.S. Forest Service, though leased for ninety-nine years.

The two-story cabin sat just to the mountain side of a bridge across the River. There, you could hear and see the majesty and power of the rampaging water, swollen with runoff from winter's excess. Four bedrooms and a bathroom made up the second story of the homey cabin. The bottom floor consisted of a huge kitchen and family room, dominated by a central fireplace.

Before he had left right after school on Friday, joined on the trek by Sean Foley and Miguel Ayala in Sean's truck and with Leroy Horton, Dave Koeppen, and Kelly Kerwin in his Toyota, Patrick had picked up stuff from home and left this note for his mom:

Friday Afternoon

Mom,

Wanted to thank you for everything this year and, truth be told, my whole life. Typically for this year, I haven't shown you the appreciation I should have for you getting the cabin for me and the boys this weekend. Now that the time's here, I'm really jazzed, even if I haven't acted that way about much lately.

I do appreciate the trust you've always shown in me, like letting this weekend be unsupervised by an adult and yet knowing I won't let you down. I do hope when you treat me like a grownup, you know I'll act like one. Maybe, apart from last New Year's Eve.

I know these eighteen years haven't always been easy for you. You've been both a mom and a dad for me. Though things have been strained a bit this year, I know you always have my back and best interests at heart. I hope I've made you proud and will continue doing so.

Even with what's come down with the Bay Area Star assignment, I am happy with my choice to go to U.C. We won't be that far away, another bonus. In the meantime, I'm looking forward to the Thursday night classes at S.F. State this summer and am happy I'll be able to crash at the Emeryville apartment those nights and others this summer when I'm covering events down there. I guess everything worked out as well as I should have expected, though not perfectly.

And, bonus for us, I hope you'll agree: I'll be staying at home most of this summer before heading off to my dorm in the fall.

Not sure how I'm going to get along with the new hotshot The Star hired to take Carl's place, but I'll work through that. Pete's been pretty good, and he's the one I'll have the most direct contact with.

Hard to believe I'm graduating from high school. I'm overjoyed that I chose LaSalle with Suzie and other people like Mr. Wilson and Brother Curt I love. I'm so glad you let me make that choice pretty much by myself.

*Hoping you'll enjoy yourself this weekend while I'm rough-
ing it with the boys. I'm not even worried about my last
finals and will wait until Monday night to start studying.
The last few should be cake.*

Love you, Pat

After fighting traffic headed to the Lake, the boys scoped
out the cabin and its surroundings. They explored the banks
of the American River, which, in its overflow, trickled up to the
storage area under the house's piers. Patrick and Sean made
sure water and propane got connected.

After joking that Sean should sleep outside in a tent to
keep a Marine guard over their base camp, Patrick announced
that he and his one-time foe would share the biggest bedroom.
That thrilled Kerwin and Horton, who ended up with bedrooms, though quite small, of their own. Kerwin, wearing a
"What, Me Worry?" retro *Mad Magazine* T-shirt, replete with
Alfred E. Neuman caricature, gleefully announced that the decision
had saved his weekend since "my earplugs only keep snoring
out a room away." Others suggested a different reason getting
his own room took away worries.

The boys unpacked and set about organizing the pizzas
to-go they had brought for the evening with the salad and
garlic bread they would also prepare. With Horton helping
Patrick with dinner prep, Koeppen and Ayala iced and tapped
the pony keg while Foley and Kerwin laid out snacks and put
away the rest of the food. Patrick noticed that Sean and Kelly
had slipped into an ongoing friendly banter that only skirted
the boundaries of good taste. Kerwin spent the next day or
two feigning that the most incredible thing in the world would
be if Sean drove him toward Virginia City to the Ranch, where
they could both "impress the ladies."

Besides intimating that "my girl Heather wouldn't be too
impressed with the Killer," Sean kept repeating he had become
a new person. Only after several beers did he clarify more seriously how he could respect and be with a girl like Tammy

Dickerson and yet still yearn for experiences like he had at the Ranch.

"So, you weren't willing to die a virgin or even go into the Marines and admit you were one," Kerwin prodded late in the evening before losing his train of thought and needing to pee off the deck.

Somebody might as well have shouted, "Let the games begin," after finishing dinner and the cake they brought for dessert. Kerwin had packed some intricate electronic games, one of his own creation, which others dabbled in until they got bored, but the most competitive game before the cards came out was an old-fashioned game of charades.

A game of hearts, played by pairs, reminded Patrick of his time with Daphne's family in Yreka, though the beer made this one more boisterous. Eventually, the group settled into a game of poker that, thankfully from Patrick's point of view, had set betting limits so "Sean doesn't buy every pot."

When Patrick woke up the next morning, Sean's snoring rocked the whole room. Sean and Kelly, who during the night had taken a few walks outside to enjoy the night sky enhanced by some weed that Killer had with him, had been the last ones up when he straggled to bed.

The morning was peaceful. Patrick, comfortable in the kitchen, nursed a small hangover as he fixed bacon and eggs in two or three shifts as his friends found their way downstairs at various times. Miguel and Leroy were up and out early. While others had talked about fishing off the rocks near the cabin, they had been serious enough to bring gear and fishing licenses and had headed to Ice House Reservoir to fish for trout. Sean had left the keys to his truck out for them.

T.R. showed up before eleven, just before Miguel and Leroy came back with a string of trout. After a pass at sandwiches from a fridge full of cold cuts, the group, seven strong, drove the mile or two up the highway to the Kyburz stop and its all-purpose mini-store, quasi-bar, and garage. During winter, the property served as a chain-stop before the road sloped up to its final grade toward Stateline. It proved a great alternative game-playing venue.

A pool table, table shuffleboard, pinball machine, foosball game, and old video game offered the magnificent seven a delightful afternoon. Kerwin ordered a beer but got laughed off by the crusty old-timer, who, over the three hours, turned out to be invigorated by his non-stop, junk-food-buying young clientele. Instead of responding to Killer's request, he plunked a Coke down in front of him and charged him a dollar.

Horton dominated the pool competition while Kerwin lectured anyone who tried the video game as if he were a visiting archeologist showing off his latest find. Foosball games proved most compelling. Eventually, when T.R. and Sean found themselves partnered, the matchup proved invincible, the best clash coming against Patrick and Ayala. The battle raged for a long time, the little blue- and red-clad, skewered soccer players spinning and moving furiously as their puppeteers fought for any advantage.

When the Foley/Ward team won the last game against Patrick's team 7–5, on a long shot by one of Foley's backliners, Ward and Foley embraced and high-fived each other as if they had just won a varsity game for the Lancers.

With dinner, featuring barbecued steak, baked potatoes, corn on the cob, and now trout, set for 8:00 or so, Sean and Dave grabbed an hour and a half nap when everybody returned to the cabin. Miguel, Leroy, and Kelly drank beer and pitched horseshoes outside the cabin near the road.

Patrick and T.R. meandered down to the bridge, which spanned the forty-foot-wide River so that cars could pass to the fourteen cabins spread along its far side.

"Incredible," T.R. murmured as the two looked over the bridge. "So powerful. Sounds like a factory, and yet beautiful. Hard to believe it's the same River that flows near us at Paradise Beach."

"This River's important in American history."

"Well, it ain't the Mississippi."

"True, but it's all about the gold rush. The Forty-Niners. Changed American life. The economy. People coming from Europe. The push west and populating the land between. Driving out Native Americans. Even influenced the balance of free and slave states before the Civil War. Karl Marx almost blew off his theories with American River gold making the whole world more prosperous and capital conscious."

"Our River? Bigtime?"

"And you're sort of honoring the Forty-Niners, dressed in those denim overalls, though yours over that white Tee are much more fashionable than the Levi's the miners wore when panning for gold." Patrick sensed the need to revert from his history professor showoff persona. "Or, what you might have worn last summer working the Mullan ranch. Why don't you stay 'til tomorrow? Everybody's doing their own thing, but Sean, Killer, and I are getting up to go tubing at dawn."

"In that water?" T.R. shrieked. "Those rocks gonna cut you up."

"No way. Here would be suicidal. There's a flume, like a big concrete extended lap pool, that runs over the hill on the mountainside. No rocks, and the flow's more even. It runs about ten, fifteen miles southwest. I rode it about halfway down last time I was here, and it was way cool. The tubes are under the house. The flume's about five feet wide and not that dangerous, unless you act stupid, until the end, where it drops off if you go too far."

"Dangerous for me."

"Nah, not bad. Even Mr. Walters and some of the older guys were good with it the last time ..."

"I can't swim." T.R. turned to glare at Patrick. "Thought you knew."

"No, thought everybody ..."

"Because," T.R. seemed to be winding himself up. "My people fear alligators," he thundered before breaking into a hearty laugh.

"No, never learned. Not a lot of swimming pools in South Sac. Why dawn? You guys probably gonna still be hurtin' from tonight."

"It's a utility flume. P.G.& E. or Sacramento Utility, or something. They don't want people using it, but at dawn, nobody should be checking until after we get out. And, the water runs best then. It's frowned upon, but apparently, a lot of people in these houses ride it."

"I got to get back. Otis is singing in church early. Promised Mom I'd be back tonight, even if late. She's into this church thing. The socials. Everything. Been tough at home, and I don't want to mess with her. I won't drink anything and leave after dinner."

Patrick put his hand on T.R.'s arm. "How are you doing?"

"Fine, man. Otis thinks I'm going to get drafted hardship by the N.B.A., but that's far-fetched. I'm not exactly Moses Malone …yet. Those guys would eat me for lunch."

"You don't think any of the big schools will touch you?"

"No quality programs. Not now. They've kinda let me know they're interested, but they want the thing done first."

"When will that be?"

"Probably midsummer. Can't blame them. They don't want to waste no free tickets. Brother Blood's been working with me. A few schools would probably chance it and take me now, but I don't want no second-rate trap. It'll work out. Maybe, after a year."

"I hope," Patrick offered.

"That donation scam I told you 'bout, the one where Percy got the funds toward the center and some got skimmed, came out from the investigators, though they're not public yet. Schools are backing off. I expect I'll end up at Sac City for a year. At least, that's how it looks."

"City. What a waste."

T.R. shrugged. "Still be balling. Life's like that big River. Just pounds down and carries everything along. We're nuthin', man. I'm like that branch there," he pointed quickly, "that got carried away, split off where it shoulda been, and taken for a ride. I've even thought about what if I never play at the level I expected. But at least losing out on a road to a money payoff doesn't bother me. It's never been about money for me. I just want to play—ride it out and see where I end up."

"I feel bad."

"Appreciate that."

"No, I mean somewhat responsible. *The Star* and everything."

"Donovan would have used it. I don't even blame Schipper. I was in too deep. I didn't like it either. In too deep, and I knew I couldn't swim." T.R.'s soft laughter spoke volumes. "I just didn't have control. Of my own life."

"It'll work out," Patrick comforted optimistically, though more hopeful than sure. "Eventually," he added as he picked up a rock to skip through the foam that beckoned below. The bridge, however, was too high above the water, the angle of the throw too sharp, so that the rock simply plunged straight into a large breaking plume of water and disappeared. "Let's head back to enjoy the rest of the afternoon with the boys."

T.R. stopped him for a minute. "The truth is, I didn't tell you the whole thing."

Patrick stopped dead, waiting for some significant revelation.

"Kinda embarrassing, but I'm singing too. In Church. Me and Otis together. That's why I gotta be back tonight. Early services in the morning."

"Embarrassed? Why? That's fabulous. Maybe, you can recruit James and Rupert and be like Michael Jackson's group with his siblings." Patrick sauntered toward the end of the bridge before realizing he was walking alone. T.R. stood, still transfixed by the rushing River.

"Yeah," T.R. yelled. He strode toward Patrick. "You and Curt have kept me going. I don't know where I'd be without the two of you."

Flustered and more than a little guilty, Patrick began babbling something historically accurate but incongruous about how the bridge had been erected by the W.P.A. in the 1930s as the two headed up the road to the cabin. His own bridge with T.R. seemed secure, even if Patrick knew part of the foundation, the part he was holding up, wasn't as solid as it seemed. When their friendship later crumbled away after high school, only to be reborn much later, it would be from distance rather than acrimony as they followed different paths to the future.

42.

MEMORIAL DAY WEEKEND
SENIOR YEAR (SATURDAY NIGHT)

The cabin rocked with music and laughter when T.R. and Patrick returned. Talk centered on the evening's menu and games to be played. Before dinner, Patrick and Sean drove toward Placerville to park Patrick's car off Highway 50 so that the two of them and Kerwin would have wheels to get them back to the cabin the next morning when they exited the flume. Before the two departed, Patrick, ever the host, penned and posted a tongue-in-cheek evening schedule:

6:45   *Dinner Prep*

7:15   *Cocktail Hour, Appetizers, and Entertainment*

Suggested Entertainment:
A) Leroy [Breakdancing & Hip Hopping]
B) Killer [Standup Monologue: Favorite Chicken Jokes]
C) Dave [Lecture: Great Chess Strategies to Impress the Ladies]
D) Sean [Singing: The "Marines' Hymn"]
E) Miguel [Run D.M.C.-like Rap: Biggie Miggy]
F) T.R. [Singing: Thriller, Front Singer of the Ward Four]
G) Patrick [Lecture: How to Prep & Grill the Perfect Steak]

8:15   *Dinner*

9:00   *Clean-up*

9:15   *Chill Time*

10:00 *Farewell to T.R. / Let the Card Games Begin!*

Patrick climbed into Sean's pick-up next to the path winding its way to the flume over ten miles south of the cabin. "Close enough we can walk to see it?" Sean inquired.

"Not far, but there's a substation off this road, and somebody might be there. Don't want a security person seeing us nosing around. Technically, we're not supposed to do this, but if somebody sees you, they supposedly just ask you to leave."

"Better to ask forgiveness than permission if somebody's there tomorrow," Sean said, leaving Patrick the impression he might have learned that lesson from his father.

"And better they don't see us today and again tomorrow. You'll see it then if your eyes focus after the late-night, one-on-one poker game with the Killer comes off you two have been talking about. We should get back anyway. Need to get the corn and potatoes ready and whip up some appetizers." Sean started his truck to pull out to the highway.

"Mr. Domestic. No wonder Suzie considers you a catch."

"I enjoy cooking. But mentioning Suzie reminds me we're missing Mass."

"I'll hear your confession."

"Yours would probably be more interesting. I must say, however, I'm glad after the play and everything, Suzie's dialed back Disciple Fellowship a bit. Still important to her, but she's not ... proselytizing all the time. More in balance now, with everything else."

"Tammy too. A good act of contrition will take us off the hook for missing Mass. God knows, I've said a number in my lifetime, and He's still looking after me."

"Keep it under the speed limit, or He might not be. Expensive tickets, I hear, and aircraft radar connected with C.H.P. cars on the ground. If you keep razzing Killer about going to the Ranch with him tonight, he might need a couple acts of contrition for his impure thoughts. Glad he has his own room."

"I always thought he was a jerk. It's actually fun to joke around with him. And I am looking forward to our winner-take-all, two-man poker game after most people hit the rack. It'll be trash-talking every hand until I clean him out. And, don't worry, we'll each start with a gazillion chips, but the game will only be for a twenty-five-dollar winner-take-all. About winning, not money."

"If you guys play and drink late, and I crash early, I should still wake you in the dark to go tomorrow, right?"

"*Semper Fi*, man. Knocking them back late and getting up early is keeping the faith. Wake me, though. I sleep through any alarm clock. Course, I can't vouch for pretty boy. Killer doesn't seem the type to drink and smoke late and hit the water as the sun's coming out. Bet he's peeing himself thinking about riding the flume. The thought might scare him as much as a trip to the Ranch, no matter what he says. Have to go that early?"

"Yeah, we want to be getting out just a bit after seven to be pretty sure nobody hassles us. You seemed to get along with T.R. today, especially after your foosball victory."

"We both like to compete and win," Sean explained. "Not bad being on the same team with him for a change."

"If it happened sooner, we all might have been better off," Patrick noted.

"Not you," Sean responded, giving Patrick pause. "You made your reputation at *The Star* writing about the controversies."

"There's the turnoff to Ice House where Leroy and Miggy fished," Patrick said, hoping to change the subject as 50 became one lane in each direction.

But Sean plowed on: "What's the story with your job? Happy the way things worked out?"

Patrick gathered himself. "Yes and no. Thought I'd get the Bay Area thing, the major league assignment I told you about, by myself, but I'm only getting it as a stringer of sorts when they need me. They're guaranteeing me several stories a month, though. A great part-time job. I guess it was unrealistic to expect better at my age, but I got pumped up. In retrospect, I'm not sure how much Carl led me on or how much I led myself on."

"My dad pumped me up my whole life. When push came

to shove, though, he made it impossible meeting expectations. His. Maybe things came too easy for a while for you, like they did for me. Seems when they do, a fall's around the corner. Or, maybe it's just my dad's been around the corner waiting for me."

"Well, I won't be making big bucks through college with a full-time job," Patrick laughed as they started looking for the milestone marker and turnoff.

"The Marine Corps doesn't exactly pay well, even compared to my allowance," Sean laughed, "But, it's away from my old man, and hopefully working with people like the officers and enlisted men I've met so far. Good role models. Dad loves the idea of the Marines but can't stand the fact I enlisted."

"When do you go?"

"Signed up for their deferred enlistment option. Not due until February. I took the max. A year from when I signed up."

"Why not right after graduation if you wanted to get away?"

"Have it planned. That'll give me a football season at a junior college. Probably A.R.C. Their coach told me I'll probably start as a freshman. Then I go in the Corps and finally get away from the old man."

"Sounds like you do have it planned."

"Not bad for a guy everybody thought was just pissing in the wind. I figure I'll come out of the Corps buffed up to play big-time football, maybe Pac-10. That's my goal. I figure a real solid linebacker. You gonna recognize the turn-off?"

"You don't want to drive to Kyburz to play foosball, me against the Pac-10 linebacker?" Patrick chuckled. "No, right around the next bend."

Sean maneuvered his truck around a sharp turn and down the road to the cabin. The two were ready for a boys' night, with manhood put on hold for just a bit.

43.

MEMORIAL DAY WEEKEND
SENIOR YEAR (SUNDAY MORNING)

When he rolled out of bed, a sleepy-eyed Foley told Patrick that at 2:30 in the morning Kerwin, indeed, had begged off the dawn excursion. According to Sean, his parting words proclaimed anybody waking him might find his "Killer" moniker legit. Patrick left the following note for Kerwin, Dave, Miguel, and Leroy before coaxing Sean out of the cabin as darkness receded:

First Light Sunday

Guys,

Sean and I off tubing. Tubes and a pump below the house if you want to float in that little eddy below us, but don't think of taking them onto the River itself. Dangerous!

Speaking of dangerous, we left you the Killer. Apparently, he'll still be in bed, probably dreaming of a Ranch visit or tabulating his losses from his poker game with Sean.

Eggs and bacon in the fridge; coffee on the counter. We took snacks and bottled water but might stop for breakfast in Pollock Pines when we get out. If you're going fishing or something, no need to wait. Until dinner tonight, you're pretty much on your own. Enjoy.

You could always walk to the Kyburz store if you need something.

Patrick

The trek across 50 up the path to the flume played out like a situation comedy, with Sean dropping his mesh pack a couple of times while manipulating his inflated tube and stumbling more than once.

"Hope we're not late, and you gulped enough coffee," Patrick scolded his companion when past a watershed and sprawled on the dirt next to the flume. Sean collapsed into his filled tube.

"My God," blurted the red-faced Foley, "if I felt like this last night, I might have lost to Kerwin."

"The water should brace you. First, stuff your shoes, keys, and clothes into the Ziploc bags I gave you to put in the mesh sack with the water and snacks. Your flip flops, too, without the Ziplocs. You're wearing your bathing suit under your clothes, I trust. We're not going commando."

Sean struggled to his knees to look down at the running water. Cupping some in his hands, he splashed his face. "Christ!" he bellowed. "It's freezing. You sure we don't want to wear clothes?"

"The sun's coming up. Wet clothes would be colder."

Sean edged close to the flume with his tube. He looked both ways. "Not the River, but this runs pretty good."

"Flows fairly gently in spots, but, for the most part, it's a good ride. Probably running faster than the last time I rode it with the snowmelt from two months of sun. Ready?"

"To the shores of Tripoli," Sean yelled as he doffed his clothes and sandals and stuffed them into his bag, which Patrick showed him how to tie to his tube.

Patrick handed Sean one of the short paddles he had carried. "So, here's the deal. Listen carefully."

"Yes, sir," Sean gave a half-baked salute.

"The paddle's more for balance than momentum. Let the flow take you. You use this to steady yourself if you start bouncing from one side of the concrete to the other. And, it'll help if you spin around and start floating backwards and don't like that, though it's fun every now and then."

"What was this downhill lap pool for?"

"Floating timber, I think. But now, it's just an efficient way to move the melt-off from this side of the mountain to merge back with the South Fork to flow into Folsom Lake."

"A raft and we're Huck Finn and Tom Sawyer."

"Hardly. You'd have to be a world-class surfer to do this standing. Listen. About every two miles, usually where the water slows with a bit of an upslope for a small stretch, the flume has what looks like catch basins off of the right side. Can't miss 'em. Look like small balconies jutting from the land right up to the lip above the concrete wall."

"We stop at all of them?"

"No, but there's two of them that we'll stop at before the last segment. We'll get out at the second one to talk about the last stop. You can't miss 'em. And this is the key: both have a big cluster of trees right next to the side with branches hanging down you can grab onto. Still, like I said, you'll still see those jutting balcony-looking things. With the branches, it'll be like floating through a little forest, and, if it's the same as last time, the flow does slow in those spots."

"Unless I'm ass-over-teakettle." Waking up a bit, Sean joked as if there was no chance of that. "You remember all this from one run?"

"Pretty much, but I checked in with Mr. Walters' son. He tubed about a month ago and agreed nothing's really changed. Your reconnaissance is accurate, sir." Patrick's salute was a bit sharper than Sean's had been. "Whoever's at those two stops first should wait for the other."

"Just hang onto the side?"

"If you get there first. It's hard to stay together, but when we're both there, we can help each other up and over if we want a few minutes to stretch and grab water or trail mix. Don't try to get out yourself. Too easy to let your tube slip away without you."

"Looks like the concrete enclosure's only four or five feet deep. Can't you just drag your feet to stop?"

"No way. Moving too fast for that, even near the catch-basins. Besides, the fun's riding with your butt in the tube. We'll put our feet through when we're helping each other in and out. And, like I said, grab the hanging branches to hold onto while waiting and when we're helping each other out."

"Let's hit it."

"Yeah, let's go. At our second stop, I'll clue you in about the last stop. It's the one real danger spot, with a drop, but only if, for some reason, you go past our stop."

Wide awake and invigorated as soon as the frosty water started carrying him beyond the next ridge, Patrick let out a yelp. Even though workers had constructed the concrete flume, it nestled amongst such a splendid serenity that it belied the appearance of man. At first, Patrick had to yell to Sean to use his paddle when he started drifting from one side of the concrete to the other, but he eventually got the hang of letting the balance of his weight center him.

Sean seemed completely revived after a few miles when the two made their first stop. "Need to get out for a few minutes?" Patrick asked as they hung onto an overhead branch with one hand and the protruding lip of the flume with their other after propping their paddles over the edge.

"No way, man. This is incredible. Why bring water? Can't we just drink this?"

Sean used one hand to cup water into his mouth.

"Guess so, though the Walters made a big deal about making sure when they used the flume that they didn't abuse it. We can drink out of the plastic bottles at our next stop when we crawl out. Quite a rush, though, isn't it?"

"No lie. I've been on rafting trips with groups lower down on the River, but solo on these big inflated doughnuts at this altitude is like the difference between the Army and the Marines."

It seemed to Patrick that Sean laughed and cheered continuously during the next four-mile stretch. At one point, when the two were still close together, Patrick even yelled, "Tone it down; you're going to wake up the bears." Sean followed Patrick's orders like a good Marine. He had sailed right past a couple other "flume balconies" that didn't have branches reaching over them. Still within hailing distance of Foley, Patrick watched Sean reach up and grab a branch at the appointed spot, bringing himself to a jarring halt against one edge of the flume.

Patrick quickly jerked to a stop there too, and both sidled over the lip onto solid ground after first pushing their paddles and bags over and then wriggling feet down through the tube's opening for stability. From above, it probably would have looked like they were sliding along monkey bars while wearing large rubber donuts for dresses. The two roared with good cheer when they sprawled on the ground.

They talked as they drank water and chomped on snacks, conscious of the fact that they wanted to push off for the last segment quickly to finish as early as possible.

"We read it when we were freshmen in Mr. W's class. Remember in *The Odyssey* when Odysseus gets caught between the proverbial rock and a hard place?" Patrick asked.

Sean's quick response surprised Patrick, who worried he might have nerded out too much with the comment: "Yeah, the monster with all the arms and the whirlpool."

"Impressive. The last two stops have been like that for us. The Big O had to grab onto branches to avoid getting sucked into the whirlpool."

"Well, if you see a pod of octopi in the flume," Sean retorted, completely flabbergasting Patrick, "I might choose the whirlpool, though I don't think Odysseus rode a tube."

"Good memory about Odysseus' other alternative, even after just a few hours of sleep. Don't worry about creatures of the sea, but we do need to stick the landing, as they say in the Olympics."

"Lay it out so we can get back in. This is cool. Maybe, we do it again tomorrow morning before leaving. And make Killer come?"

"Still might not be up to it. So, here's the deal with our dismount."

"Sounds like we should be horsing around."

"My God, you're almost as bad as Killer and me with the wordplay."

"That's why you've grown to love your old enemy. Something that should make the Disciple Fellowship folks proud."

"There's a bridge of sorts over the flume right before we get out. You keep going right past that, and immediately there's the last of our catch basins with the balcony looking the same as these two stops. It also has branches hanging over, so you can stop yourself easily. Gotta stop there. Not the bridge. After our last stop, the flume widens and drops off down a steep concrete embankment. Down there, I think it settles and gets funneled more leisurely, eventually to some sort of energy generators on the way to Folsom Reservoir."

"Got it. Can we ride more from there?"

"No. There's a sort of security shack there with a presence usually, though I think they come on around eight. We need to be in our car and looking for breakfast then."

"Gotcha. Let's race." Sean bellied over the concrete into his tube, which he pushed out in front of him.

Surprised, Patrick reacted less quickly. He trailed Sean by about thirty yards by the time the current started carrying him. Patrick paddled as fast as he could until he nearly caught Sean. Just then, he saw Sean adroitly wriggle his body so that he lay prone on the tube with his paddle maneuvered in both hands in front of his face.

Despite some furious paddling, Patrick noticed Sean gradually lengthening his lead as his draped feet kicked like fins. Like admiring a swimming prospect from afar, Patrick noticed the fluidity of Sean's rippling muscles, which made him cut machine-like through the water. Indeed, he thought, out of the Marines, Sean really might have a promising football future.

Within half a mile of the bridge, Patrick stopped stroking, put aside thoughts of catching Sean, and enjoyed letting the water carry him. He got carried somewhere else, however, when he rounded a bend and immediately saw Sean scrambling to stand on his tube as he approached the bridge, apparently deciding he was going to end his ride with a bit of derring-do.

Patrick almost saw things unfold before they did, though nearly half a football field behind. Sean had apparently opted to reach up and grab the understructure of the bridge, higher than the balconies they had flopped onto, at the same time that he rose from the prone position to a squat. In trying to keep one hand on the attached mesh bag to keep the tube from floating away, he lost his balance.

He slipped.

His tube, propelled by his feet seeking balance, shot straight ahead without him.

His hands clanked off a support of the bridge.

He landed on his back in the water, flailing about.

Looking like an upstream salmon, he tried jumping to the bridge, but way too late.

Patrick screamed but could do nothing. Consistent with other events of the year, he would take on the role of spectator to report on the event later. Though he paddled swiftly, he knew he couldn't do anything. "Swim to your right," he yelled futilely. "To the branches."

Sean tried to square himself to swim but kept spinning around. As strong as he was, even against the current, he made some progress toward the balcony and edge of the widening flume where the branches provided a canopy. The current, though, proved stronger than Sean. Patrick, quickly approaching the bridge himself, remained composed enough to follow the original plan. He could do nothing but steal quick glances as Sean managed to get a hand near the side of the flume, but the current rebuffed his desperate grasps to hook his fingers over the lip.

The effort, however, slowed him some, but he still drifted inexorably to the drop. He was able to flip back to a swimming position to go over the edge like a diver rather than butt-first.

Patrick, past the bridge and now at the planned exit, scrambled out so fast his tube also got away toward the drop. He watched helplessly as Sean flew out into the air as if untethered from a water slide.

Not seeing the landing, Patrick figured his friend was dead. Still, he steadied himself, ran to the drop-off, and threw himself into a long series of half-slides, half-jumps down the dirt hill that ran along the concrete above what looked like a giant swimming pool.

Spotting Sean in the calmer water near where he ended up, Patrick plunged in immediately and tugged him to land. Lifting his stronger friend up and out proved difficult, but Patrick pushed Sean, breathing through his shock, to safety. His swan dive had prevented him from banging his head on the concrete on the way down. He had, though, obviously mashed his bleeding, disjointed legs, but he was alive, though dazed.

A half an hour later, with help from a guard and a quick response from an ambulance, Patrick delivered Sean to a young emergency room doctor in Placerville. Feeling fortunate he had kept his car key in his swimsuit pocket rather than his mesh bag, which he hadn't bothered to find, Patrick followed the ambulance, thinking he might eventually be driving Sean home. In the emergency room, Patrick whispered, "I'll phone your home," as he first held Sean's clenched fist.

Satisfied that Sean was eighteen and had avoided a concussion, the doctor had given Sean meds after stopping his wounds before striding away to set up X-rays. They, however, had yet to take hold. "No," Sean shouted through clamped teeth. "Don't. I don't care what happened; I don't want my old man here."

Patrick stammered, "But, I, uh, have to find out ..."

"What time is it?"

Patrick glanced through the door to the hallway clock. "Seven thirty-six."

"Drive home. Mom always goes to nine o'clock Mass at Holy Spirit after jogging on Sunday mornings and changing at the

Club. By herself. Drive down, get her, and bring her back alone," he exclaimed definitively. "I don't want the old bastard here."

"Nobody'll be with you," Patrick protested, still numbed himself.

"The doctor will. You'll be back by eleven. Nothing much will happen before. I'm sure anything that's necessary, with insurance and stuff, will happen when my mom gets me to Sutter Hospital in Sacramento."

Patrick disappeared to talk to the doctor, who had overheard. After glaring at the admission form, which Patrick had helped fill out, to make sure he had a home phone number in case of complications, and after pumping Patrick for details to verify that the thing between Sean and his father wasn't a temporary spat, the doctor reluctantly agreed. "We have to take X-rays and finish cleaning his wounds anyway. Then read the X-rays before we send him on, probably in an ambulance. You might want to drive his mom back so she can ride down with him. The last thing we need is him getting more upset," he sighed.

"Thanks, Doc," Patrick voiced.

"He's a year younger, I wouldn't do this, but with their facilities, it's probably better to send him to Sutter. There's no way anybody's going to set those bones now anyway. Have his mother phone me to verify as soon as you see her and get her to a phone. If I don't hear by ten, or if there are any complications, I'm phoning his home regardless of what he wants. Can't believe he's not screaming with the damage done," he marveled.

"He's a football player," Patrick said, as if that explained it.

"Was," the doctor responded, maybe a bit unprofessionally. "I just hope he can walk normally again."

Patrick returned to Sean's bedside, shaking his head and hoping Sean hadn't heard. "You sure, now?"

"She's always there. I can even tell you what pew. Front right. And, she can use a phone in the priests' house before you head back."

"I'm on my way then."

Sean, who to Patrick seemed entirely too much in control, reached out to grab Patrick's wrist. "You saved my life, man. I was pretty dazed under the water."

"Be back soon," Patrick said, fighting to control his emotions.

"Drive careful. Silly into Charybdis."

"What?"

"The silly fool, me, floated right into the whirlpool. At our first stop, it sounded as if you couldn't remember the name of the whirlpool in *The Odyssey*. Scylla was the many-armed monster, and Charybdis the whirlpool. And this whirlpool sure got me."

Patrick broke away quickly, ran to the parking lot, climbed into his car, and headed west on 50. He hadn't fully comprehended, having not gone back for his mesh bag, that he was still in his bathing suit with just a surgical gown given to him in the waiting room draped over him and hospital slippers on his feet. Still, as if wearing blinders, he saw only pavement and white lines as he drove, concentrating on not exceeding the speed limit.

His mind, almost blank, started churning again when the foothills ran out and the highway flattened toward California's capital city. Patrick consciously tried to compose himself, knowing it would be awkward getting Mrs. Foley out of the church without causing a fuss or blurting everything to her at once in front of the whole congregation.

The scene played out in his mind as a disaster. If his appearance didn't alarm Mrs. Foley, nothing would. He decided it would only cost a couple minutes to veer off to his house in Carmichael, throw clothes on, and ask his mother to come with him to help. He could then proceed to Land Park and Holy Spirit, nearer the Sacramento River.

Calmed by the rationality of this decision, Patrick spun the radio dial to find out the time. Some religious station announcer declared it 8:33 at the same time Patrick pulled off the Sunrise exit. He was right on schedule to get to the church before 9:15.

Patrick burst through his front door before his car stopped sputtering in the driveway. "Sean's hurt and needs help," he yelled as he bounded down the hall. "Mom, I need help!" Patrick veered through his mother's open bedroom door but pulled up like a basketball player taking a thirty-foot jump shot at the buzzer. Patrick's mother and Steve Wilson looked up at him from Sheila Kiernan's bed as if they were opponents who watched that shot go through the net to defeat them.

It's difficult to say who was startled and upset most that morning. Suffice it to say, it wasn't Mrs. Foley, even though a bleary-eyed young man wearing a bathing suit and surgical gown slid into the pew next to her at Holy Spirit just as the priest on the altar implored the congregation to pray for the forgiveness of sins.

44.

LATE MAY
SENIOR YEAR

Patrick Kiernan stared at the test left on his desk in the otherwise empty classroom. Though he never feared a test, and classmates had taken the same test during senior finals, this one made him quiver.

Standing, Patrick read the three essay questions the way some read horror stories tucked late into an evening. The ugly irony the questions evoked in Patrick's mind built the moment into a climax, like a classic ghost story pulling its reader toward final revelations:

Advanced English IV(AP)　　　　　　　*Spring Semester*
Mr. Wilson—2ⁿᵈ Period

As the syllabus indicated, everyone must pass this test to gain credit, no matter your A.P. score. You have two hours to complete three essay questions. Answers should demonstrate knowledge of significant works of literature.

1) Point of view brings narrative alive. Choosing a literary work in which a character, narrator, or author hides behind a satirical "mask," explain the purpose and effect of point of view in relation to that work as a whole.

2) A common literary theme highlights the clash between generations. Choose one work that accentuates this and detail the way the author addresses it.

3) Choosing a climactic scene in a literary work in which the protagonist makes an important decision or self-discovery, detail the novel's moral evolution that makes that scene dramatic.

The classroom door opened. "Pat, Mr. Wilson sent ... My, God, I'm worried about you." Suzie Andrus moved behind Patrick. "Okay?"

Patrick dropped the test on his desk. The irony the questions evoked gave way to the irony of Suzie acting as Mr. Wilson's messenger. "Fine." Patrick imperceptibly swayed his weight to his back foot. He didn't want Suzie reaching out to him through his ironies. "Wilson send you?"

"Yeah. He says take the test and leave it when you're done." Suzie waved absently at the teacher's desk.

"Wouldn't come himself. Figures." Patrick's voice was strained taut, like his body.

"Been worried about you. Missing grad practices, everything. This test. A lot of us have been."

"Doesn't matter," Patrick bit off.

"You're going to graduation Saturday, aren't you?" Suzie blurted. The couple's senior prom experience, with graduation one of the two main capstone events of senior year, had been dour enough, even before the past weekend's events and revelations.

"Don't know." Patrick maneuvered himself into his desk, shifting it with the weight of his body to maintain his distance. "Probably not. I'm spent. And it all doesn't matter much. Like this." He picked up the test questions only to flop the paper back on the desk. It, however, fell to the floor.

Suzie reached for it but straightened up immediately. She could still read Patrick. For the moment, he wanted it on the floor. "We're getting the final edition of *The Lance* counted for distribution to the class. That's where I was when Mr. Wilson sent me. He looks as troubled as you. Kept glancing at his watch. I thought he had a lower-division class, but he's done like us."

"I was supposed to meet him at ten to make this up," Patrick stated more to himself than to Suzie, "and here I am." He scooped up the paper before ripping it cleanly in two. "Here, give him this."

"Pat, don't do that. Write something."

"What for?" he responded abruptly. He crumpled the paper into a ball and tossed it from hand to hand.

Suzie liked to control situations, especially ones she dreaded. She wanted to reach down and hug Patrick, comfort him the way he had comforted her so many times. Something stopped her. "Do you know what you're doing? Tammy reminded me he emphasized everybody had to take the test or flag the course. Just answer anything. You probably got a five on the A.P.," Suzie rambled, trying to catch words to make everything right. Patrick had a knack for that. He even had the right words the night he stood with her beside her father's casket. She chose wrong: "I've been praying for you."

"Just what I need," Patrick spat sarcastically.

"Why not talk to Mr. Wilson?" she pleaded. "Tell him ... tell him everything this year's gotten to you. He'll arrange something. You were always close."

"Close is a word I don't want to hear about him."

"If you take an F, it'll ruin plans for Berkeley. Or Princeton. Write something. You'll at least get a C for the course. Don't be stubborn ... again." Suzie's last word caught his attention. Patrick's blue eyes measured her, but Suzie charged on verbally: "He says he has to ensure everybody honors the process by passing this test after his warning. A matter of honor. Don't put him in a place to fail you out of principle. You'd destroy both of you."

"Honor? Him? He hasn't already destroyed us both?" Suzie waited out the ensuing silence as tears trickled down her high cheeks. She tossed her long hair as if to toss aside the problem at hand. "Tell him to take this and ..." Patrick caught himself.

"Write something. A note. Anything." Suzie hoped Patrick would find the right words, as he always had.

Patrick ran his fingers through his rumpled hair. "Sure," he announced with a wry smile. "Go compose yourself and come back in five. I'll be finished." Suzie began to protest but then did what he said.

Patrick ironed the test out with his hand on the desk, piecing the two parts carefully together. Excitedly, he wrote the following on the back of the test:

#1 "Julius Caesar." (Paraphrase): Mr. Wilson said to be true. And Mr. Wilson is an honorable man. Mr. Wilson said to be loyal. And Mr. Wilson is an honorable man. Mr. Wilson said a lot, but he isn't an honorable or loyal man.

#2 "Hamlet" (Paraphrase): "To see or not to see. That was the question." I have seen!

#3 Huck Finn (Paraphrase): "All right then, YOU go to hell! (note that this paper is ripped) I'll go to State!

These are all based OFF OF the original sources and my experience with you! PK

Suzie appeared at the door as if on cue. Patrick smiled. "Here, give him this. My senior thesis. Everything he taught me."

"Pat, talk to somebody. T.R. Brother Curt. Your mother. Mr. Wilson himself. Somebody." He breezed past her toward the corridor. "Where you going?" Suzie wanted to follow. To hold him. To talk. Anything. His purposeful strides, however, froze her.

"To the River," he called over his shoulder. "Going swimming." And he was gone to float back through the memories of the past year.

45.

LATE JULY
AFTER SENIOR YEAR

Patrick composed a letter to Steve Wilson during the summer:

SW:

I can't believe you did what you did. To your wife; to Becky and Anne; to me; and to the moral high ground you claimed that I thought made you who you were. To say you crushed me would be an understatement. I blame Mom too, but she wasn't married and must have been charmed and recruited in her loneliness. I can empathize a bit with that since, obviously, you charmed and recruited me too.

I told you I wanted to grow up to be like you, that you were my mentor and father figure. Now, I FEAR I might grow up to be like you. My mentor had "feet of clay"; this father figure didn't work out any better than my real one. Maybe worse, considering I'm more aware of the world now than when he left. I always wished he hadn't chosen to leave. I wish you had left.

Mom told me you claimed that Memorial Day Weekend was the last fling, that the two of you agreed to end what had gone on for over a year. You told her you were going to move back home to SoCal for a new start with your wife and daughters. You made it clear to Mom that, though you said you loved her and wanted to be with her, you didn't want to break up your family or, at least, leave Becky and

Anne without a family. And you didn't think you were strong enough to live near Mom and not backslide. Ironic that you're the one who's going to get left alone now, moving south without your wife and girls. And my mom.

Mom begged me to save your reputation, to keep things relatively quiet, but that wasn't going to happen. I honestly am glad you suffered. Her, too, truth be told. And I'm glad you're moving away. I'll have to deal with holding feelings like that. Suzie doesn't think it's very Christian, but so be it.

Everything came down so strangely that weekend, the whole year; I would have had to have been an actor for people not to know my world had caved in. And you couldn't even face me for that make-up test you insisted I take to pass the stupid class.

I couldn't bear to see you at graduation, probably pretending nothing had happened. I loved LaSalle, but I was done with you and didn't mind not graduating from the stage, if at all. It wasn't until later I found out you gave me my A anyway and I had the right credits to get into Berkeley.

I'm loving my class at State, though, and think I'm going to stay enrolled there. Stubborn? Spiteful? Self-destructive? Maybe you'll recognize those traits. I wonder how often you were talking to yourself when giving me advice. Generally, I think I listened better.

I'm wondering if you gave me the A (and by the way, I did get my five on the English A.P.) because you realized your word was worthless or because Brother Curt pressured you. Before he apparently agreed it would be best if you found another place to teach next year. Yes, I've had conversations about this with others besides Mom.

God knows, it was a scandal-ridden year! They say deaths come in threes. Things died for me with all three scandals. If nothing else, any innocence I ever had got buried forever.

Things have gotten rough with Suzie. The counselor I'm seeing thinks my feelings about relationships have been rocked to the core. Small wonder. And, thank God, it looks as if old man Foley, who was raising hell about suing everybody, *has backed off. Sean stood up and told him doing so would be the last straw on his way out the door. He takes more responsibility than you. So, ultimately, did T.R. Maybe it's just the two of us who are a bit wanting in that department.*

Mom's a wreck. She's always been such a rock for me. Hard to fathom that on so many occasions, St. Patty's Day or over Easter, for example, that the two of you were together. What were you thinking? Were you thinking? About anybody but yourself?

I'm left to question every word of wisdom I thought I learned from you, every bit of appreciation for the things I love that you taught me. And that hurts, too, because I can't conceive of living my life without literature, writing, or thinking. Though, believe me, even in the ninety-mile drives to and from the Bay Area this last month, I've done everything I could to stop thinking at all. But, even at the River where I always found peace, I couldn't.

As an example, I couldn't help thinking about our class discussions about Death of a Salesman. How Biff walks in on his father and "his buyer" in bed. That's the damned thing about literature. It so speaks to life. Like Willy, you're now a very "low man" in my world.

You'd probably tell me not going to Berkeley because of my resentment toward you would be like Biff burning his University of Virginia sneakers. Signifying throwing away his life when he'd been recruited to play football there. I swear, though, even if it takes a while to pick up the pieces, I will not throw away my life because of you. I will live it, as I hope Sean and T.R. will in their worlds, on my own terms, come what may.

PK

A letter came to Patrick from Mr. Wilson in SoCal right after the fourth of July. He held it unopened for weeks. A few weeks later, at the River, after thinking about it for a long time, he tore it up along with the one he had written. He burned both.

46.

EPILOGUE
TODAY

I write this after learning Steve Wilson died recently. Ironic that, to a certain extent, I did follow in his footsteps. I have now taught English at LaSalle for twenty-five years. And love doing so. I had not written or spoken to Mr. Wilson in the forty-plus years since the events related in this story, but at Suzie's urging, I decided it would be appropriate to write a note to Becky and Anne:

Dear Becky and Anne:

With the passing of your dad, I want to tell you I'm sorry for you. I do hope that what I heard from Suzie, who had communicated with your dad a few times over the years, was true: You two did have a meaningful reconciliation with him years later.

Obviously, I chose never to do the same. I do, however, feel forgiveness in my heart. I hope you can forgive me for not taking the next step and communicating that to him during his life. I understand only on reflection that it might have meant more to him than I realized.

In so many ways, your dad was the ideal teacher, mentor, advisor, and model for me. I hope I provided even a portion of that when I taught both of you, though I was inexperienced when you were at LaSalle. I'm sure he taught, guided, inspired, and mentored numerous students in the decades he taught in San Gabriel and Pasadena after moving south.

At one point, I told him I wanted to be him when I grew up. The truth is, in many ways, I've spent my life doing just that.

He was a great storyteller and almost a perfect English teacher. He obviously wasn't perfect as a person, but, as has been emphasized to me then and in all my living since, neither was I. He often paraphrased the educational theorist Paulo Freire when he said that the great thing about teaching is that every day in the classroom has the potential of Easter Sunday. So true!

I trust that in providing an opportunity for so many kids to learn about living through literature and himself (teachers always teach themselves along with their subjects), he himself also felt such a redemption.

If nothing else, I'm sure that, even from afar, and even as he started another family, he was overjoyed that the two of you turned out so well. Speaking of that, say hello from me to your husbands and kids. And, when you talk to her next, give my good wishes to your mom. I'm sure your dad's passing brings back a host of memories, good and bad, for her.

Do you remember a girl at LaSalle named Yvonne Scott-Perez? She was a class below Anne. On back-to-school night when Yvonne was a freshman, her mom asked if all literature we were going to read would be as sad as the summer readings and the readings the first few weeks of school. She said Yvonne cried through many of the readings.

It took me until Yvonne was a senior to formulate a proper answer to mother and daughter. I told them the sadness and hurt often experienced and felt by characters in literature provided a gift to readers. Not to make us feel good because our setbacks weren't as bad as theirs, but to show us that resiliency is the only option when facing catastrophes, whether random, imposed, or of our own making.

I am glad your dad always had literature to nurture his own resiliency. Your dad, I'm sure, enjoyed the gift that literature provided throughout his life. I hope it gave him comfort in his final battles with the cancer that led to his passing.

I am so glad I opted for a lifetime teaching literature rather than becoming the journalist I flirted with being on leaving high school. And that's not just because newspapers have gone into the toilet with the internet. No, it's living out my destiny, my happiness. A destiny and a happiness your dad helped nurture.

Let's get together the next time you're both in Sacramento. May your dad rest in peace!

With affection from your former babysitter and teacher,
Pat Kiernan

Yes, I wrote and sent the email to Steve Wilson's grown children at Suzie's urging. She is my wife, but that story's more interesting than you might imagine. My recent wife. We reconnected online. Her first husband died young. I had married and divorced after running wild while getting my undergraduate degree in literature at San Francisco State. Between us, we have three grown kids. And, because I hadn't been married in the church, we had our wedding in the chapel at LaSalle, a Catholic ceremony that really pleased the new Mrs. Susan Kiernan.

My daughter, Ciara, still lives in Sacramento where I raised her myself during her high school years when her mom moved back to the Bay Area. The relationship between Suzie and me that had been rocked to its core by the events of senior year has rekindled in all its glory. I am a lucky man.

I know, I know, mention of meeting again online suggests how different things would have been if we had cell phones back in the day, and I could have phoned Sean's mom directly from the emergency room in Placerville. When I teach *Romeo and Juliet*, I typically use the example of how things would have been different if Juliet could have used her smartphone to text Romeo in Mantua to share her plans rather than sending a message by donkey.

So much, minor and major, has changed. School starts well

before Labor Day now. Newspapers are almost totally digital, when still in existence. Laptops, and other tech, make a reporter's work totally different. Journalism jargon now calls "leads," the main facts at the start of an inverted pyramid story, "ledes," but I can't bring myself to do so.

In general, tech dramatically and sometimes instantaneously changes, for good and bad, culture and politics, among so many other touchstones of life. Back in the day, T.R. took pride in using the words "veto" and "circumstantial" he learned in Civics class. While they remain relevant in modern life, another key Civics term, "compromise," has seemingly gone the way of the once idealized student-athlete.

There are now two English A.P. exams. C.I.F. state basketball championships now have an "open division," and the playoffs begin earlier. After a most recent sixteen-year playoff drought, the Kings became relevant again. LaSalle moved to a President/Principal model. Brother Curt, Principal of LaSalle when he recruited me to teach there in the mid-nineties, is back now as President. This time he wants to recruit me as principal.

People change too, or, certainly, their circumstances do, even if they remain fundamentally the same. My mom went back to college part-time and eventually earned her degree. When she started selling real estate, she met a good man whom she married.

Sean's father dropped dead of a heart attack just after Sean got his degree at St. Mary's College in Moraga after starting a bit late while dealing with medical issues. He joined his mother in running the construction business they inherited and is now one of the most influential builders in our area. He is also a big donor to Sutter Memorial, which this year named a wing after him. He says he's paying off debts for the incredible work they did to help him walk almost normally after many procedures.

Sean also has a great working relationship with T.R., an incredible community organizer, though, with basketball earnings, he lives in a great house in the "Fab Forties," one of the most exclusive areas in the city. T.R. ended up having a very good, if not great, college career and played two years in the N.B.A. but made most of his money playing for ten years on some of the best European teams.

Kelly Kerwin did end up creating computer games, even some you might have played.

Some things, however, don't change. Sacramento used to be marked on a map socioeconomically with an X, with two quadrants mostly white and two minority. Even with whites now a minority themselves in the city that has won commendations for its diversity, the effects of redlining and urban renewal still leave scarred neighborhoods decades later. Fundamental racism still exists.

The recruitment of basketball Blue Chippers, of athletes in general, remains unsavory, even as payoffs with the coming of NIL become transparent.

The country still seems tragically conflicted. Money and power still rule behavior. People still scorn those with whom they disagree. People today, maybe more than ever, recruit for their versions of the truth.

True enough, this narrative is my version, Patrick Kiernan's version, of the truth.

ABOUT ATMOSPHERE PRESS

Founded in 2015, Atmosphere Press was built on the principles of Honesty, Transparency, Professionalism, Kindness, and Making Your Book Awesome. As an ethical and author-friendly hybrid press, we stay true to that founding mission today.

If you're a reader, enter our giveaway for a free book here:

SCAN TO ENTER
BOOK GIVEAWAY

If you're a writer, submit your manuscript for consideration here:

SCAN TO SUBMIT
MANUSCRIPT

And always feel free to visit Atmosphere Press and our authors online at atmospherepress.com. See you there soon!

Left: Author with Rosslyn Beard after 2008 state title game win at the state capital

While Principal of Sacred Heart Cathedral Prep in San Francisco over a seven-year span, Dr Ken Hogarty participated in trophy ceremonies for the Fighting Irish's five NorCal championships and four California state championships won by boys' and girls' basketball teams. Hogarty's *alma mater* also won three NorCal volleyball championships during those years. SHCP's 2008 team, ranked as the number one girls' high school team in the nation by *USA Today*, was listed among the top 25 all-time girls' basketball teams in a 2020 national story by Kevin Askeland. He summarized its accomplishments: "The Fighting Irish defeated teams from six different states along with some of the top teams in California, including Archbishop Mitty, Sacred Heart Prep (Atherton) and St. Mary's (Stockton), on the way to a state championship and a 33-0 record."

ABOUT THE AUTHOR

DR. KEN HOGARTY lives in San Francisco's East Bay with his wife, Sally. He retired after a 46-year career as a high school teacher and principal, while also teaching collegiately.

Since, he has had over fifty stories, essays, memoirs, and comedy pieces published in the likes of *Sport Literate*, *Sequoia Speaks*, *Woman's Way*, *The Satirist*, and *Good Old Days*. He was a semi-finalist for *Cobalt's* 2021 Earl Weaver Baseball Writing Prize.

Hogarty taught students who went on to became doctors, lawyers, judges, mayors, professors, scientists, writers, actors, teachers, coaches, and professional athletes. Former students included three Olympians, an Emmy winner, and Oscar winner.

In the context of this story's plot, students Hogarty taught currently hold unique positions. Ron Nocetti is California's C.I.F. Executive Director, overseeing the state's high school sports, and Philippe Doherty is the program director of Napa's Prolific Prep, a first of its kind basketball academy founded in 2014 that has sent countless Blue Chip hoopsters to D-1 colleges and the N.B.A.

Milton Keynes UK
Ingram Content Group UK Ltd.
UKHW010631101123
432322UK00006B/384